The Bridal Chair

A NOVEL

Gloria Goldreich

sourcebooks
landmark

For my most important readers (eventually):
Gila Rose, Samuel Nathan, and Lily Esther Sheldon
Ruthy Gal, Saul Eitan, and Ilan Yehuda Amkraut
Koby Matan and Alon Yoav Horowitz

Published by Sourcebooks Landmark, an imprint of Sourcebooks, Inc.
P.O. Box 4410, Naperville, Illinois 60567-4410
(630) 961-3900
Fax: (630) 961-2168
www.sourcebooks.com

Library of Congress Cataloging-in-Publication Data

Goldreich, Gloria.
  The bridal chair : a novel / Gloria Goldreich.
    pages ; cm
  (softcover : acid-free paper)   1. Fathers and daughters—France—Fiction.
2. Artists—France—Fiction. 3. Self-realization in women—Fiction. 4. Self-actualization (Psychology) in women—Fiction. 5. Paris (France)—History—1870-1940—Fiction. I. Title.
  PS3557.O3845B75 2015
  813'.54—dc23
                                    2014044578

Printed and bound in the United States of America.
VP 10 9 8 7 6 5 4 3

Author's Note

*T*he *Bridal Chair* is a work of biofiction, based on the life of Ida Chagall, the only daughter of the artist Marc Chagall. While I have adhered faithfully to the chronology of her life and the historical events that informed it, I have taken the novelist's license and created scenes and conversations that are entirely based on my own imaginings. I have, in all such instances, attempted to remain faithful to the personalities of the protagonists and details of the incidents, relying on insights gleaned from my extensive reading of biographies, letters, and accounts that relate to such invented situations and exchanges. I relied on many sources, but I want to make special mention of Jackie Wullschlager's magnificent *Chagall: A Biography* (New York: Knopf, 2008) and *My Life with Chagall* by Virginia Haggard (New York: Donald I. Fine, 1986).

Chapter One

She is gripped by a terror she cannot name, but she is certain that she is in danger, grave danger. Her breath comes in labored gasps. She is running, racing. The taps on the heels of her patent leather shoes clatter against the cobblestones, and her heart beats wildly as though struggling to match her frantic pace. Her parents grip her hands—her mother's sharp nails dig into her right palm, and her father's grasp on her left is painfully tight.

"Faster, Idotchka. Faster." They speak in unison. She trembles at the fear in their voices.

Their pursuers draw closer, booted feet beating in tympanic hate, horses' hooves pounding ominously.

She cannot go any faster. She feels her energy draining, her legs faltering. Tears streak her cheeks. How angry they will be with her if she should fall. She does not want them to be angry, her *mamochka*, her *papochka*.

And then, suddenly, their race is over, and they are lifted to the heavens. They are soaring, the three of them, hands linked, hearts lightened, flying skyward. Her parents' arms have become wings that scissor their way through a sky no longer draped in velvet darkness but wondrously studded with rainbow-colored flowers. A vagrant wind plays with her auburn curls, and she laughs as the thick tendrils tickle her cheeks. Her pinafore billows out into a great puff of whiteness that will surely keep her afloat.

She glances at her mother, who glides so easily through the air, a blackbird of a woman, her hair a cap of polished ebony, the velvet dress that hugs her slender body the color of night. She turns her head to the left and she sees that her father's beret has fallen and his fine silken hair frames his elfin face; stray strands briefly veil his bright blue eyes. He smiles; his daughter's hand is so light and trusting in his own. He is at home in this flower-strewn heaven. He will paint these skies, she knows, when they are safe and out of harm's way. But for now, their flight continues.

They float, the three of them, like zephyrs borne on soft breezes, cushioned by gentle clouds, high above the burning villages and the dark columns of soldiers tramping the country they had once called their own. Mother Russia has cast them out. They are orphaned refugees, rootless and rejected, but they are winging their way to a safe haven. They do not speak, because language is lost to them. The quiet settles over them in a soothing coverlet embroidered with hope and promise. Wordless, soundless.

Still half asleep, safe in her bed, she stretched languidly and opened her eyes to the golden light of early morning streaming through the wide window of her bedroom. A bird sang with plaintive sweetness and she hurried to the window. The solitary warbler teetered on a fragile branch of the lemon tree and then soared off into the cloudless summer sky.

"*Au revoir,*" she called softly and looked down at the garden where her parents sat opposite each other in their wicker chairs, talking softly as they sipped their morning coffee. Their voices drifted through the open window as their spoons clinked musically against their china cups.

She watched them for a moment and then turned, stripped off her white nightgown, and stood naked before her full-length mirror. She studied the curves of her body, the fine-boned contour of her face. She lifted her mass of bright hair and allowed it to fall again to her shoulders.

Her reflection reassured her. She passed her hands across the tender fullness of her breasts and felt the power of her nascent womanhood. She was no longer the frightened small girl of her nightmare. The dream was banished. The painful past was behind her. She had no need of a celestial haven. She willed herself to triumph over the sadness that too often lingered in the aftermath of her haunted sleep.

She turned her head, glanced at herself in profile, practiced a smile, practiced a frown.

Am I pretty? she wondered. *Am I beautiful? Will Michel find me much changed?*

There was an impatient knock at her bedroom door; her name was called once and then again. "Mademoiselle Ida! Mademoiselle Ida!"

The harsh voice of Katya, the Polish maid, irritable and accusatory, pierced her reverie.

"It is very late. Your parents are waiting for you."

"Tell them I'll be down in just a few minutes."

A grunt and then heavy footfalls retreated in reproach.

Ida shrugged. She knew that Katya did not like her, did not like being a maid in a Jewish home. But that was of no importance. Katya, as her mother frequently pointed out, was lucky to be working for the Chagalls. They were kind employers, Katya's wages were paid on time, she ate the same food as the family, and transport to church on Sundays and festivals was provided.

She dismissed Katya from her thoughts, splashed her face with cold water, and dressed quickly, choosing a pale blue, pearl-buttoned dress of a gossamer fabric that slipped off easily and would let her swiftly disrobe. Her father had told her that he wanted her to pose for him before she left for the alpine encampment so that he might complete the series of nude studies he had begun months earlier, alternating at whim between watercolor and gouache, charcoal and oil.

Her father had used his brush over the years to create a visual journal of her life, chronicling the days of her playful childhood, her moody adolescence, and now her emergent young womanhood. The title of each effort was scrawled in his looping script across the back of the work, a claim of ownership and provenance. There was *Ida on the Swing*, a portrait in motion, painted swiftly as she thrust herself skyward, her chubby legs vigorously pumping, the wind burnishing her cheeks. He had taken more time in painting *Ida at the Window*, capturing her as she stared dreamily through the shimmering glass while the sun sank over their Montchauvet home, setting the waters of the Seine on fire.

"What are you thinking about, Idotchka?" her father had asked that day as his brush flew across the canvas, his eyes narrowed in concentration.

She had thought then to share her recurring dream of frantic flight with him so that he might paint that nocturnal fantasy into a tactile reality, but she had remained silent. The dream was her own, not to be co-opted by his brush and palette. She took a perverse pleasure in keeping it secret. She had, after all, so few secrets from her parents. They had laid claim to every aspect of her life, keeping her close from the day of her birth. Sometimes she thought that they monitored the very breaths she took and seized upon her moods, saddened by her sadness, joyful in her joy. She choked on their vigilance; she resented their obsessive insistence that they possess every aspect of her being and then felt a disloyalty that shamed her. She was fortunate to be their daughter, the beloved legatee of their fame and fortune and unconditional love. And she loved them deeply in return.

She understood that their concern for her was born of the uncertainty and the suffering they had endured. Of course they were frightened. She accepted their fear, submitted to it. She allowed them to believe that they were the conservators of her life. But her dreams, her beautiful and terrifying nocturnal odysseys, those were her own, as was the secret she had held so close within her heart throughout the year. It thrilled her that she had managed to refrain from telling her parents about Michel. He belonged only to her.

Michel. Her Michel. She loved the very sound of his name. She had thought of his fine-featured face, of his soft and thoughtful voice, as the long months of their separation drifted slowly by. Her anticipation of their next meeting had intensified during these last sultry days of summer as she posed for her father, hour after hour, never stirring when he left his easel to more closely examine the dark areolae of her nipples, the tangled rise of the russet curls between her legs. The intensity of that gaze never unnerved her. He was Marc Chagall, and he looked at her neither as man nor father but as an artist in the throes of creation.

It was Michel who saw her with a lover's eye, Michel whom she would see in only a few days' time after the long year of separation.

She smiled at the thought, threaded a blue ribbon through her hair, and glided, barefoot, through the sunlit house to join her parents at breakfast in the walled garden. The French doors slid open and they turned to her at once, their faces bright with pleasure.

"Ah, our Ida."

Her father rose and kissed her on both cheeks. She knelt before her mother, felt Bella's soft hands gentle upon her head. This was, as always, their morning greeting, a coming together after a single night as though they had been long parted. It was as though they saw each day of their togetherness as a gift, her presence in their lives, and perhaps their lives themselves, as a miracle. She wondered if they ever dreamed of desperately fleeing danger and despair and flying into freedom. Perhaps their dreams, like her own, were embroidered with dark-threaded memories of the lost land of their birth, the village of their youth. Did the faces of family and friends, long vanished from their lives, drift above them in the darkness of the night, like the celestial flowers of her own dream?

But of course, they would not share such thoughts with her. She was their pampered virginal daughter, to be vigilantly protected against the harshness of life. They had never even sent her to school because they so feared any threat and danger. Other children were cruel. Crowded classrooms bred disease. Broad avenues and narrow streets were haunted by unknown strangers, speeding vehicles. They could not risk exposing their Ida to danger. She was the repository of their past, their hope for the future, the source of their joyous present, her mother's student, her father's model, an enchanting and exuberant daughter. And she in turn worked hard to please them, to amuse them, to evoke the admiration of their friends.

"Such a bright child."

"Such a creative girl."

"So charming."

Always they had beamed and collected her accolades as though they themselves had earned them. Her effervescence delighted them; her laughter trilled through their home. Their wonderful Ida, so happy, so beautiful, and yes, perhaps even talented. The drawings of her adolescence were clever, and her paintings showed promise.

They allowed her to begin classes at a small neighborhood art school, although Bella stood at the window, awaiting her return home.

Always she saw the lines of tension on their faces ease when she entered, her voice lilting as she invited their amusement, telling them of the absurd tramp she had seen, wearing one red shoe, one blue shoe; the ridiculous boy in her class whose beret fell over his eyes; or the maître who patrolled the studio singing "Sur le Pont d'Avignon." She had an ear, she had an eye, their Ida, they agreed.

She played her role even as she slowly and determinedly forged her way free of the cocoon of their anxiety and laid claim to her life as she wished to live it. She had campaigned for their permission to join in a program geared to the young adult children of Russian Jewish émigrés, held in a French alpine encampment. It would be their gift to her on her seventeenth birthday.

"It will make me so happy, *Mamochka*, *Papochka*. Don't you want your Ida to be happy?"

She had danced toward them, her arms outstretched, and they had smiled, charmed by her charm. Of course they wanted her to be happy. They were pledged to her happiness. They made inquiries. The encampment was well chaperoned, and the young participants were immersed in Russian language and culture and imbued with love for the life and literature of Mother Russia. Such exposure would bring their Ida even closer to them. She would have a new understanding of their past. And most important of all, she would be happy. They agreed and paid her tuition, purchased her train ticket.

Excitedly, during that first journey on her own, she had peered through the windows of her first-class carriage as it sped through the mountains. Shyly, she formed her first tentative friendships with other young Russian Jews. Joyously, she had locked eyes with tall and slender Michel Rapaport who spoke all the languages of her heart. She soared on the wings of her new freedom, wandered barefoot with Michel through the waving alpine grass, sat beside him at the blazing bonfires as they sang Russian folk songs and lilting chansons.

He was a reluctant law student, a devoted son who helped his parents in their small Paris shop, determined to ease their lives by becoming a successful *avocat*. He and Ida were mutually constrained by familial obligations. They acknowledged that it would be impossible to meet during the ensuing months. But they were not discouraged. They would see each other at the next retreat. They were young. Oceans of time stretched out before them. In the intervening months, he sent her books of poetry and she sent him her drawings. Their intimate, innocent exchanges, packets of hope and love wrapped in brown paper, arrived by post and were easily explained away.

"A gift from a friend," Ida told her mother.

The months had passed, and Ida counted the days. Soon, she would count the hours and then she would board the train and travel southeast to the alpine hamlet where Michel would await her, his face bright with love.

Seated with her parents in the garden on this sunlit morning when the branches of the fruit trees were heavy with golden pears and carmine cherries and the air was thick with the scent of rosemary that clung to the stone walls, she was suffused with contentment.

She smiled at her parents, smiled even at sulky Katya who poured her coffee. Her father plucked up a piece of toast, crunched it noisily, and wandered into the garden, stretching out beneath the shade of an ancient olive tree.

"Did you sleep well?" her mother asked as she spread Ida's croissant with the raspberry jam she made herself, following the instructions of the cook who had reigned over her parents' kitchen in faraway Vitebsk, the village that had been home to both Marc and Bella.

"Very well, *Mamochka*. And you?"

"We were up early. Your father didn't want to miss the first light. He is still working on the wedding studies."

"Are they almost finished?" Ida asked. "You look tired but oh so beautiful."

Bella wore a wide-sleeved, many-layered dress of sheer white organdy; white lilies crowned her dark hair, and pale blue circlets of kohl shadowed her eyes. The dress was familiar to Ida. Bella wore it often enough, posing as a bride beneath a wedding canopy and then as a corpse in a satin-lined casket. Marc never tired of painting her. Bella and Ida both, he claimed, were ideal models, born to his brush. They laughed at his claim, but there was pride in their melodic laughter. They were willing accomplices to the tyranny of his art, a tyranny that was occasionally arbitrary.

Ida remembered complaining to her father that he never asked her to pose in bridal finery, nor in the winding linen of a shroud, her mother's frequent roles. Bella had looked at her warningly and Marc's blue eyes glinted in anger.

"Foolish girl," he had said. "Foolish Idotchka. I will not paint you like that because I don't want to lose you. Not to death. Not to marriage. Not yet. Perhaps not ever."

"But why do you paint *Mamochka* like that?" she had persisted mischievously.

"Ah, your *mamochka*, my Bella. I will never lose her. She is mine forever, in life and in death."

Bella had turned pale then, as though frightened by the fierceness of his words.

Ida took note of that familiar pallor beneath her mother's carefully rouged cheeks. It was, she knew, a mark of her fatigue, a precursor of the terrible headaches that too often assaulted her.

"I thought Papa planned to paint me this morning," she said. "That would have given you a chance to rest."

"He will paint you now," Bella assured her. "He is full of ideas today."

She smiled with subdued pride at the precocity of the elfin-faced artist with whom she had fallen in love when she was a teenager, no older than Ida.

Ida poured herself another cup of coffee as Marc sprang to his feet, strode across the garden, cut two sunflowers free of their long stalks, and placed a canvas on his easel. His renewed energy did not surprise her. Her father was a man who was refreshed by the briefest of naps, endlessly propelled by an explosion of fantastic visions. He had no time to lose, no time to waste. Reality and illusion collided, and the brilliance of his imagination impelled him to action.

"Are you ready, Ida?" he asked.

"Of course."

Swiftly she glided into the garden, stood beneath the lemon tree, slipped out of her dress, and tossed it onto the grass. He held the sunflowers out to her.

"Stretch out beneath the tree. Just so. The flowers between your breasts. *Comme ça.* One leg over the other. Yes. Like that. Just like that."

His hands were deft as he arranged and rearranged her limbs, removed the ribbon from her hair, and draped her long, copper-colored hair over her shoulders. She remained silent as he squeezed the tubes of oil onto his palette, mingling blues and greens, vermilion and acid yellow, and then lifted his fine-haired sable brush and began to paint.

Bella draped Ida's dress carefully over a chair as Katya beckoned to her. She hurried into the house but turned to look at her husband and her daughter, as though to memorize this sunlit moment of their togetherness.

Ida lay still as her father worked steadily, his avian features relaxed, a smile playing at his lips. It was safe to talk to him now, to ask him questions, to coax forth his laughter, and to tease out tales of his youth.

"What will you work on when I am away?" she asked.

"I think I will return to painting scenes of my village. My Vitebsk. Do you remember Vitebsk, Ida?"

She laughed. "*Papochka*, be serious. I was only four years old when we left Vitebsk. How could I remember?"

In her mind, Vitebsk was the fairy landscape of his paintings where he and her mother, poor boy and rich girl, had met, walked across the bridge that spanned the Western Dvina River, and fallen in love staring down at their own reflections. Vitebsk was a mystical hamlet where everyone, even the animals, spoke a Yiddish threaded with humor and sweetness.

It was Russia, she remembered in all its actuality, the Russia they had fled when she was six years old, a country of frightening enormity, grim and cold. That was the haunting dreamscape of her troubled sleep in which her parents' hands gripped her own.

She would not tell her father that she had vague and not so vague memories of their harrowing journey from Vitebsk to Moscow, where they slept on the hard, cold floor of the Moscow Jewish Theater. There he had created the sets for a production of the stories of Sholem Aleichem as her mother sewed the costumes and he painted the heavy fabrics as though they were canvases. She would not share her memory of their respite in the Jewish orphanage at Malakhovka where Marc taught art and Bella wept and she herself feared that she might one day share the fate of the pale, parentless children with whom she shared toys crafted of twigs and stones.

How cold she had been and how hungry. She shivered at the recollection, knowing she had not imagined that cold, that hunger, nor had she imagined the heat of her mother's tears when she pressed her face to Ida's as they lay together in the narrow bed allotted to the three of them. She could still taste the Comice pears plucked from a wild tree that briefly sated her and then caused her to vomit.

She had locked those frightening memories away, but they escaped as she slept and became that recurrent dream, of triumphant escape, an airborne journey into the golden warmth that drifted across her naked body as her father's brush sailed so effortlessly across the canvas.

"Soon no one will remember Vitebsk," he said sadly. "That is why I must paint it. My village. My home."

Ida closed her eyes and thought of her father's paintings of his vanished world. She listened as he spoke wistfully of the hamlet of his childhood, of his family, of his brother David, killed in the Crimea, of his beautiful sisters whose fates were unknown, of the sheltered graveyard where his parents were buried.

"Vitebsk."

He intoned the name of the village, whispered it as in prayer.

She thought it strange that although he sketched the small synagogue where he had celebrated his bar mitzvah and painted bearded rabbis wrapped in prayer shawls and wearing phylacteries, he never went to synagogue, not even on the anniversaries of his parents' deaths. She knew that he considered Jewish holidays to be an annoyance, although he reluctantly accompanied Bella and Ida to Passover seders at the home of Yaakov Rosenfeld, Bella's brother, their only family in Paris. Although her father spoke affectionately of his sisters, he made no effort to discover their whereabouts. Such inconsistency puzzled her, but she dared not speak of it. Vitebsk and his childhood were the sacred territory of his past, the landscape of his imagination.

But there was no tenderness in his graphic re-creation of that landscape. Ida perceived violence and chaos in his phantasmagoric canvases on which barn animals leapt over rooftops, a green violinist perched precariously on a parapet, a graceful church spire towered over the tiny crouched homes of the Jews. His depiction of a milkmaid who pressed the udder of a cow improbably positioned in the head of a large-eyed goat frightened her although she knew that such canvases were coveted by the sophisticated collectors who haunted Parisian art galleries, that art critics analyzed them in turgid essays tracing their symbolism. She much preferred his paintings of her mother, especially the one he had painted when he and Bella were newly engaged, a whimsical rendering of himself as a lover, flying toward his beloved across a room, his arms laden with a gift of flowers. Thinking of that painting now, she smiled and imagined Michel flying toward her, a bouquet of edelweiss in his hands.

She sighed. The sun was hot and she longed to shift position. She did not want to hear about Vitebsk or listen yet again to stories of the grandparents she would never know, the aunts, uncles, and cousins she would never meet. She moved ever so slightly and one of the sunflowers slipped from the valley between her breasts onto the grass. She stretched her arm out to retrieve it. Marc shook his head warningly and waved his brush as though it was a baton and he a conductor summoning the crescendo that would conclude his visual symphony. Until then, all movement was forbidden to her.

He paused at last. "Good, my Ida. It is finished. Come look at what we have accomplished."

She stood, stretched, and slipped into her dress. Still buttoning those tiny pearl buttons that she imagined Michel unfastening oh so slowly in a few days' time, she approached the easel and smiled appreciatively. He had captured the soft golden tones of her sun-burnished skin, almost matching them to the hue of the fallen wide-petaled flower. He had painted her face in repose, her eyes closed, copper-colored lashes brushing her cheeks.

"But I wasn't sleeping," she protested.

"No. But you were dreaming."

She did not ask how he had known that but watched as he removed the canvas from the easel, holding it carefully so that the fresh, glistening oil paint would not smear. Without looking back, his mind already racing toward his next project, he carried it into the shed that served as studio and storage area. She knew that within its dimness, he would prepare a fresh canvas while he listened to the news on his small radio. He had in recent months become obsessed with broadcasts from Germany, the rantings of Adolf Hitler.

"A dangerous man," he muttered, although all their friends asserted that the mustachioed maniac would surely be thrust from power within weeks.

"Maniacs have great endurance," he insisted. "Particularly evil homicidal maniacs."

He gave voice, Ida knew, to his instinctive pessimism. Always he anticipated encroaching darkness. Threatening clouds hovered over even his brightest landscapes.

She sighed, relieved that she was free to study the leather-bound copy of *Eugene Onegin* that Michel had sent her. He had urged her to memorize at least four of Pushkin's quatrains. So far she had managed only one, but she was sure that Michel would forgive her. She would smile and he would forgive her anything. As would her father. As would her mother. Ida had great confidence in the power of her smile.

She lifted her arms skyward and felt a surge of happiness. It was glorious to be her parents' daughter, glorious to be in the country as summer swept its way across field and meadow, gilding lavender and sunflowers, silvering the leaves of olive trees and the fronds of stately palms. It was glorious to know that as the days grew shorter, she and Michel would walk again through mountain glades hand in hand, at a distance from their too vigilant parents.

They had spoken of their dearly beloved and overly concerned mothers and fathers, haunted émigrés, enmeshed in their memories of the land they had fled, forever polishing their battered samovars, speaking Russian softly, studying sepia-tinted photos of relatives they would never see again. They were history's orphans, her parents and Michel's.

"My poor mother, my poor father," Michel had murmured, lifting her hand to his lips as they lay sprawled across the grass, her head resting on his chest.

"And my poor mother. My poor father." She echoed his words, matching sorrow for sorrow, thinking of her mother who wept as she filled copy book after copy book with graceful Yiddish script that recounted the vanished days of her pampered childhood, the byways of her beloved village. And of course there was her father, his brush as heavy with paint as his heart was heavy with sorrow. He raced after the past in dizzying strokes and wild bursts of color. She trembled as she thought of his stark etching of his father's grave, the grave that he would never see.

Tears had streaked her cheeks and moistened Michel's shirt. He had kissed her fingers one by one. They were children of exile both, offering each other the comfort of tenderness.

Suffused with those memories, she glanced toward the wild garden and saw her mother kneeling beside a bed of lavender, a basket of cherries on the grass beside her. Bella had changed into the loose cotton robe that Marc had bought for her in the Arab marketplace of Jerusalem. He had chosen it for the subtlety of its color, a melding of pale blues and greens achieved by skillful dying. Ida remembered how he had asked the Arab vendor for the secrets of his formula and the toothless merchant had shaken his head. He would no more share the secrets of his craft than Marc would share the mystery of his palette.

Bella stood and waved to Ida. The robe exposed her slender body, her small firm breasts, her narrow hips. Her mother's fragility of form always startled Ida. When she was younger, she had often pondered the mystery of delicate Bella giving birth to a daughter as lusty and chubby as Ida, a naïveté that caused her to smile.

"Do you want help, *Maman*?" she called, setting aside the volume of Pushkin. She wandered through the tall grass toward her mother, who was adding clumps of the star-shaped azure flowers to her basket of cherries. "You've picked so much lavender," she said reprovingly.

"Not that much. I need it for the fresh sachets I am making for your trunk. The scent will remind you of us." Bella added yet another floral cluster, tucking it beneath the long-stemmed, ruby-colored fruit.

"Do you think I could so easily forget you?" Ida asked playfully, lifting the basket and inhaling the fragrance of the blossoms. She popped a cherry into her mouth and spat the pit onto the grass.

"When you unpack, scatter the sachets in your drawers and I'll tie strings around some of them so that you can hang them in your wardrobe. And of course, I'll make salts for your bath. Just toss them in when the water grows warm," Bella advised.

"*Mamochka*, I'm not a child," Ida protested, struggling to overcome her irritation. She would indulge her mother. She would soon be on her own, remote from her parents' suffocating anxiety, their protective instructions. "I'm eighteen years old," she continued. "I know how to unpack and guess what—I even know how to prepare my bath."

"All right. You're eighteen. Not a great age, Idotchka."

"When you were eighteen, you were already engaged to *Papochka*," Ida retorted.

Bella nodded.

"Yes. But I understood the world. I had studied drama in Moscow. I knew how to take care of myself, how to live among strangers, how to prepare my own food and manage my own money. Your life has been very different."

"Because you made it different," Ida countered. The lightness of her tone masked her latent bitterness.

She remembered the days she had stood alone at the window of their Paris apartment and watched girls her age walking home from school in their uniforms, their arms linked, their heads bent close as they exchanged secrets and laughter. She had no school mates. She was taught by her mother or by the sad-eyed tutors who sat beside her at the dining room table.

"We tried to do what was best." Bella's voice was lightly tinged with regret. "You are so precious to us. Ah, Ida, we had seen so much danger, so much suffering. We wanted to protect you. That is what we still want."

"I understand that. But now you must let me grow into my own life." She spoke soothingly, but her cheeks were flushed.

"I know." Bella smiled thinly. "After all, you are eighteen years old."

Together they walked back to the veranda where Katya had placed tall glasses of freshly squeezed lemonade on the wrought iron table. They sat opposite each other, Bella taking tiny sips, Ida draining her glass and tilting it so that the last granules of sugar slid across her tongue.

"You're so like your father. Sweets and more sweets. The first time he came to my parents' home, he ate every cake on the table and sucked three lumps of sugar." Bella laughed at the memory, but almost at once, her expression changed. "Of course that was because there were never any sweets in his own house. They were so poor, his family, always struggling. There was barely enough food on the table. Oh yes, herring. Always herring because your grandfather Chagall worked for the herring merchant." She wrinkled her nose, as though the remembered stink of the herring soured the air of their beautiful garden. She reached for another cherry and lifted the sunflower the maid had placed on the table. "Do you know what I noticed today, Idotchka?" she asked as she plucked one petal after another. "I saw that sunflowers turn their faces away from the sun when they reach full bloom. Isn't that curious? I would have thought they would derive their strength from the sun and seek out its warmth."

Ida smiled. "But I am not turning my face away from you, *Mamochka*," she said softly. "I am just trying to grow up, to become my own person."

"You will. And all too soon. Life will see to that," Bella replied. "Come. Let us see how Katya is managing with the lunch."

As they left the garden, Marc Chagall emerged from his studio and stared after his wife and daughter, their colorful skirts swinging about their legs. He saw them as graceful sylphs, gliding through rays of sunlight toward the wide-windowed house.

Chapter Two

arc and Bella awakened early on the day of Ida's departure for the encampment. The sun was a pale orb, barely visible in the steel-gray sky. Bella wandered into the garden and stared up at the ominous dark clouds. It was just as well, she thought, that Ida was still asleep. The weather might unnerve her. She herself was an uneasy traveler, haunted by paralyzing migraines, and she ascribed the same frailty to her daughter.

She shivered and went into the kitchen where Marc sat over his coffee, his chin cupped in his hands, his forehead wreathed in lines of worry. He had set aside his charcoal drawing sticks and the pad of coarse butcher's paper on which he had made preliminary sketches. His attention was focused on the radio newscast, the announcer's somber voice drifting through the dimly lit room.

"It may rain," Bella said worriedly as Katya filled her cup. "Perhaps Ida ought to travel later in the week when the weather is better."

He waved her into silence. He was listening with pursed lips to a broadcast of an Agence France-Presse report from Berlin summarizing a vicious speech by Adolf Hitler, announcing new boycotts against the German Jewish community.

"It is Hitler we should be worrying about, not a rainstorm," he said bitterly, switching off the radio. "Trains do not stop running because of bad weather. Of course Ida must leave today. Let her laugh and sing and be with friends. Who knows for how long it will be possible for her to do that? He is mad, this Hitler. Dangerous and mad."

"Don't be so foolish, Marc," Bella retorted harshly. "Hitler is across the border in Germany. We are in France. We are safe. Our Ida is safe."

She spoke with a certainty she did not feel. They had so often in the past felt themselves to be secure and then been deceived. She had not forgotten their optimism after the Communist revolution and their suffering when the ideological dream morphed into a nightmare. One day Marc was celebrated as Commissar of the Arts in their native Vitebsk and then, without warning, they were refugees, seeking elusive safety in one urban enclave after another, always barely escaping the mobs that had traded hatred for the czar for hatred of the Jews. Always holding Ida close, always atremble with fear, they had boarded trains, crossed borders, traded languages, told lies until they had at last reached Germany.

In Berlin, they had yet again thought themselves safe. Marc's paintings hung in distinguished galleries and they were welcome guests at fashionable salons. There was money and recognition. Their émigré status gave them an esoteric cast; their beauty and style were much admired. They had dressed for their roles. Slender Bella, her jet-black hair framing her delicate face, wore loose-fitting silk dresses in vivid shades. Marc sported dashing hats and the high-collared, belted shirts of the Russian peasant. Ida was an adorable child in her ruffled white dresses, her bright hair crowned with the mob caps and bonnets that Bella fashioned to amuse herself. Their lives in Germany were pleasant, laced with prosperity.

But they were vigilant. Conditioned to danger, they recognized that a haze of anti-Semitism hovered in the air, its stink growing stronger each day. Their friend Paul Cassirer was denounced by Hitler as a corrupt Jewish millionaire. The writer Ilya Ehrenburg arrived at their home pale with terror. He had passed several homes on which the words "Death to the Jews" had been painted.

"The handwriting is on the wall," he told Marc.

"And on the doorposts," Marc agreed wryly.

He and Bella had stared at each other in mute agreement. The safety of Berlin had been illusory. They moved to Paris.

France was different, Bella had assured herself then, and now again. It was the land of *liberté, égalité, fraternité*; Paris was the City of

Light. They would make France their home. And she had not been wrong. Paris welcomed them, celebrated them. Marc's work was appreciated. Writers and poets, intellectuals and diplomats visited their home. They sat beside Picasso and Matisse in the Café de Flore where waiters greeted them by name, kissed Ida on both her cheeks. Surely they were safe. They had to be safe. She was too exhausted to take flight again, and the ominous clouds passed. They did not always signal the onset of tempestuous storms.

Though her husband's pessimism on this grim morning angered her, she too felt apprehensive. She had awakened in the night, her heart pounding, and rushed into Ida's room. Staring down at her sleeping daughter, she tried to recall the traveler's prayer her orthodox father had recited when she journeyed from their Vitebsk home to the university in Moscow. Still, she would not share her nocturnal fears with Marc. She would not feed the fire of his anxiety, even as she herself felt its heat. They were survivors. They would be fine. Ida would be fine.

"We will be safe," she repeated defiantly.

Marc refilled his coffee cup, ran his fingers through his thick thatch of irrepressible curls. Bella noticed for the first time that his hair was tinged with streaks of gray, and that new recognition saddened her. They were growing older, the two of them.

He took a long sip of his coffee and added sugar.

"Jews are never safe, Bella," he said. "We are the children of Isaac, always in danger of the sacrificial knife."

She saw then that the sketches he had been working on were studies of the biblical patriarch Isaac, bound for sacrifice on Mount Moriah. He had been working on illustrations for the Bible intermittently since their journey to Palestine, an odyssey undertaken three years earlier in celebration of Ida's fifteenth birthday. The landscape of the holy land had inspired him. He had wept in Jerusalem and then apologized for his tears, as always ambivalent about his Judaism.

It occurred to Bella that his biblical drawings were his answer to Hitler, his graphic assertion that the Jewish people would survive even as Isaac had survived. She touched the drawing, then lifted her finger, smudged by the charcoal, to Marc's face, stroking it gently.

"But we will keep Ida safe," she repeated.

"Of course we will keep our Ida safe," he assured her.

"You have no need to worry. I will keep myself safe!" Ida's voice lilted with gaiety as she burst into the room and dashed up to her parents, her face radiant, her hair brushed into a fiery blaze. She was already dressed for the journey in a white linen dress, a green traveling cape draping her shoulders. She hugged them both, planted kisses on their cheeks, as though determined to infuse them with her own joyous excitement, and snatched a croissant from the table.

"Katya, fresh coffee," she called, taking a seat between them.

She crammed strawberries into her mouth and chattered excitedly about her plans for the weeks ahead. She wanted to hike a mountain trail. There was a wonderful café in the town near the encampment. She hoped that the friends she had made the previous year would be back. Oh, the mountain nights were so beautiful. Star-studded heavens. She had her watercolors with her and she might even try to work in oils. It must be exciting to paint at night.

Her exuberance ambushed them, briefly banishing their fears.

Katya brought her a cup of coffee to which she added one teaspoon of sugar after another in imitation of her father's cravings. She nodded absently as Bella advised her to take a seat on the train near the window, to keep her portmanteau always on her lap, to make sure the purse that held her money was buried at the bottom of her bag.

"Don't worry. I'll be careful. Don't you trust me?"

"Oh, we trust you, Idotchka. It is the rest of the world we don't trust," Marc replied wryly.

Bella said nothing but placed a neatly wrapped packet of food in Ida's portmanteau.

"Pirogen. The potato ones that you like. Don't let yourself get hungry."

Ida smiled and pressed her mother's hand to her lips. "You must not worry about me," she said. "I know how to take care of myself."

The sky grew lighter as they drove to the station. Bella's heart sank at the sight of the train impatiently belching forth black clouds of smoke, its whistle screeching angrily as it lurched to a stop. The conductor stood imperiously at the carriage door, waiting for the passengers to board. An insistent premonition caused Bella's hands to shake, her throat to grow dry. The pain at her temple intensified. She felt that she must do something, anything, to keep Ida with them. Perhaps she could grip her arm and plead with her not to leave. But of course she would say nothing, do nothing. Her irrationality shamed her. Her heart beat faster; she rested her head on Marc's shoulder. The train whistle shrieked again. Ida's arms encircled them in one last embrace, and she scampered up the iron steps behind the porter who carried her small trunk. She waved to them from the window of her carriage as the whistle emitted another long, angry blast and the train sped away, staining the air with its coal-dark fumes.

Bella remembered an old woman in Vitebsk who had claimed that she could read the future in trails of smoke. She was an ugly hunchbacked woman with warts on her hands and sour breath, but her predictions had almost always come true. The infertile wife, whose happy future she had read in the smoke of her Sabbath candles, conceived. The sick child, whose death she had predicted, died. Bella sighed and studied the wisps of gray that streaked the sky as the train sped away. She wondered sadly what those vagrant strands might reveal about Ida's future and their own.

Chapter Three

*S*ettled in a window seat in her first-class compartment, Ida removed her cape and undid the top buttons of her white linen dress. She looked at herself approvingly in the window of the speeding train, removed a silver compact from her bag, and lightly rouged her cheeks and her lips. She replaced the compact, fumbled until she found a small vial of perfume, and dabbed a droplet behind each ear. The aroma of lilac wafted through the air, and the plump older woman who sat opposite her smiled benignly.

"They say that lilac is the scent of lovers, mademoiselle," she said.

"Do they?" Ida asked and opened her copy of *Eugene Onegin*. She did not want to dilute these precious moments of solitude with casual conversation.

When the train stopped at Lyon, she handed the packet of food her mother had prepared to a tramp who lingered on the platform and bought herself a baguette and a café au lait at the station buffet. The simple transaction delighted her. She counted out the coins carefully, reveling in her independence. She sipped the coffee and ate half the baguette on the train, carefully rewrapping it because she was certain that Michel would be hungry when they met.

As they had planned, he was waiting for her on the platform in Embrun, the tiny hamlet nestled in the shadow of the Hautes-Alpes. Her heart skipped a beat at the sight of him, so tall and handsome in his high astrakhan hat and the loose dark leather cloak favored by Sorbonne students. He did not see her at first, and his eyes, dark with disappointment, scoured the platform.

"Michel!" she called.

He rushed toward her, his arms opened wide. "Ida!"

She rushed into his embrace, and he held her close. The baguette she clutched in her hand was crushed, and they laughed as crumbs snowed down onto the gritty platform.

"And I was really hungry," he said ruefully.

"Never mind. I will buy you another. A truckload of baguettes, if you like," she promised as he thrust her small trunk into the cab he had engaged to drive them to the encampment. She leaned against him. They were reunited, their yearnings of the past year realized. The cab skittered dangerously on a mountain pass and he held her close. Smiling, she relaxed into the protection of his embrace.

———

"What do you think your parents are doing right now, at this very moment?" Michel asked her the next day as they walked together down a mountain path into a glade where edelweiss glinted whitely against the rough, dark alpine grass. The easy rhythm of the previous summer had been effortlessly resumed.

"My father is painting and my mother is posing for him, dreaming all the while of her childhood, dreaming a poem, dreaming a story," Ida replied without hesitation.

She remembered that she had once asked her mother why she so often closed her eyes when she posed.

"But you must close your eyes if you are to dream," Bella had replied.

Ida had understood. She knew her mother's dreams were translated into stories and fragments of poetry, which appeared in Yiddish script in the copy books she kept in the drawer of her escritoire. Bella's every reverie became a short narrative, the warming flame of memory captured forever in the graceful strokes of her pen.

"And what are your mother and father doing?" she asked Michel teasingly in turn.

She had never met the Rapaports, although she knew that her parents had occasionally spoken with them at the gatherings of Jewish

Russian émigrés at the Temple of Montmartre that they attended with feigned reluctance. Marc and Bella went to such soirees, Ida knew, because they yearned to speak their native langue, to scavenge news of friends and relatives in their abandoned homeland. Marc, always intent on weighing the achievements of others against his own, returned happily from such evenings, satisfied that his own accomplishments, his fame, exceeded those of all the other attendees. He, the son of a man who had hauled herrings and a woman who ran a tiny grocery store, could afford a life in Paris that could not be attained by the now dispossessed sons of Russia's most privileged classes, the bankers, attorneys, and doctors, those who would have scorned him during his student days in Moscow and St. Petersburg. Ida had asked him, oh so casually, if he had ever met the Rapaports.

"Bourgeois Muscovites. They once had a town house in the capital, a dacha in Zaloshe, but now they have a small shop in Le Marais and live in a flat in its rear. Shopkeepers. That's all they are. Shopkeepers," he had replied derisively.

"It's no crime to be a shopkeeper. Your own mother was a shop-keeper," Bella had protested mildly. His prejudices amused her.

Ida was not amused, but she said nothing. She did not want her parents to question her interest in *la famille* Rapaport. She waited patiently for Michel's reply.

He glanced at his watch.

"Let me see. It is ten thirty in the morning. My mother is proba-bly bargaining with a customer who wants to buy a length of fabric for half the price she is demanding. My father is reading *Le Monde*, checking the prices on the Bourse, looking for ways to invest money that he doesn't have," he said ruefully.

Ida laughed. They were, both of them, the wise and protective children of foolish parents who remained uneasy with their new lives in France. Michel's parents relied on him to study law diligently so that he might restore the family to their lost prosperity and prestige. The Chagalls depended on Ida to energize them, to fill their lives with joy and beauty, to replace the families that had been lost to them.

"Ten thirty," Ida said musingly. "The hour when father interrupts his work to listen to the BBC broadcast. If you want to know what Adolf Hitler had for dinner last night in Berlin, ask Marc Chagall the next morning."

"He takes the ugly little Austrian seriously then?" Michel asked.

"I think we should all take him seriously," Ida replied soberly.

Michel leaned against a juniper tree. He did not want to discuss Hitler. They were on holiday from sadness. "Perhaps we should go back. The lecture on literature will begin soon. A professor of Russian from the Sorbonne is speaking," he said.

"I don't want to hear another word about Turgenev or Tolstoy. And I don't want to listen to those boring girls who only talk about dances and parties and their dreams of becoming pharmacists or teachers. I don't want to be a pharmacist. I don't want to be a teacher. There is no one here who interests me."

She made a face, a charming moue such as she had often practiced before her mirror and that Matisse himself had applauded when she trained it on him in a café. The girls in her dormitory, the ordinary, conventional daughters of Russian émigrés, wedded to respectability, had probably never heard of Matisse. Their whispered intimacies at bedtime irritated her. Uneasy with their bodies, they undressed beneath the bedclothes, while Ida, who had posed nude for her father, walked about the dormitory room unclothed. She listened to them speak of Ivan and Boris, Natalya wondering if she should allow Ivan to touch her breasts, Anna confiding with great solemnity that Boris had kissed her. "On the lips," she reported in a rapturous whisper.

"Silly geese," Ida had muttered to Elsa, the doctor who served as a resident adviser in the girls' dormitory.

"Not silly. Just young," Elsa had replied.

"No one in the entire encampment interests you?" Michel asked teasingly.

"Perhaps Elsa."

"And no one besides Elsa," he persisted mischievously.

"All right. You interest me. I don't know why, but you do." She laughed and tossed her head so vigorously that her bright hair whipped her face. Her beret fluttered off and was caught up in a sudden wind.

They sprinted after it together. Pouncing upon it, they fell to the ground, his body heavy upon her own, her fingers gripping the beret and then releasing it so that her hand was free to touch his cheek and trace the curve of his mouth, the arch of his eyebrow.

"Ida," he murmured.

"Michel."

Their names were pledges that fell from their lips, lips that met softly at first in tender friendship, and then with a rousing urgency. There, in the alpine meadow, for the very first time, they shed their clothes. There beneath the juniper tree, he spread wide his leather cloak and they came together in joy, her cry of pain subdued by the sudden explosion of pleasure that caused her to cry out in rapture. Their hearts beat against each other in wild rhythm. Exhausted, they stared up at the cloudless sky. She thought of her foolish classmates who giggled as they spoke of stolen kisses, tentative touches.

She was not such a girl. She was a woman, the woman she had told her mother she would become. She was her parents' daughter, proud of her body, delighting in the caress of wind and sun upon her bare skin, delighting in the freedom and power of her feelings for Michel, of his feelings for her.

He took her hand in his own, kissed her fingers one by one.

"You're not sorry, are you, *ma chérie*?" he asked softly.

"Sorry? Why would I be sorry?" she replied and placed her head on his shoulder, pressed his palm to her cheek.

They dressed swiftly then and walked back to the encampment, where the discussion of Turgenev had ended and lunch was being set out on long wooden tables.

During the remaining weeks of the holiday camp, they were inseparable. They sat side by side at the few lectures they attended. They spoke the requisite amount of Russian, learned the songs of the Volga boatmen and the folk dances of Ukrainian peasants. They sat in the front of the room on the day an impassioned poet discussed the work of Sholem Aleichem. He read selections aloud, not in the author's lyrical Yiddish but in an awkward Russian translation favored by pretentious intellectuals. *A stupid conceit*, Ida thought.

"Do any of you know the work of Sholem Aleichem?" he asked the young people, who did not bother to hide their boredom.

"I do. My father painted the sets for the Jewish Theater when his plays were performed in Moscow," Ida volunteered laconically.

The poet looked at her with interest.

"Your father? Are you Marc Chagall's daughter? His Idotchka. I remember seeing you when you were a little girl. Perhaps in Berlin. Yes, surely in Berlin. You, of course, do not remember me, but please give my regards to your dear parents."

He peered at her over the podium, perhaps seeing in his mind's eye the impish auburn-haired child who had been the pampered pet of their small community.

"Idotchka." Her nickname was whispered derisively through the room. Her classmates pointed at her and nudged each other.

Ida ignored them and shrugged indifferently.

"I will do that, monsieur le professeur," she assured him.

She knew that in all probability her parents would not even recognize his name. He was not famous enough to be included either in their circle of intimates or in their roster of acquaintances whose names and phone numbers they inscribed in a black leather address book. One never knew who might one day prove useful. Their peripatetic life had taught them as much.

The elderly professor beamed at her.

"Ah, little Ida," he murmured and turned back to his notes.

"Ah, if only he knew how grown up his little Ida is," Michel whispered into her ear.

"Perhaps I will tell him how grown up I am. Perhaps I will tell everyone," Ida teased, suppressing her laughter.

But of course she would tell no one, nor would Michel. They delighted in the secrecy of their sweet intimacy.

Each afternoon, they escaped the activities of the encampment and dashed across the meadow to an abandoned shepherd's shack. And each day their lovemaking was slower, more deliberate.

"We must be careful," Michel had cautioned, and she had nodded in agreement and laughed. She was the daughter of enlightened parents. Bella had explained the monthly cycle to her the day her menses began, blushing only slightly but determined to be a modern woman, a modern mother. No shtetl ignorance of her body for her Ida, *la fille Parisienne*.

"I know what I'm doing, Michel," she had assured him. "My body is my friend. We understand each other."

They undressed each other, Michel always fumbling with the buttons of her dresses as she had known he would. She knelt to remove his boots and to stroke his long, pale feet. They examined each other with knowing eyes and tender touch. Naked, they raced across the earthen floor, their games of tag ending in tumultuous and merry surrender. They played house, offered each other pretend meals of alpine grass and acorns. They built themselves a bower, a canopy of tangled vines, and Michel fashioned a soft bed out of the branches of conifers over which he spread his long leather cloak. Bright green pine needles glinted in her copper-colored curls, and she plucked them out carefully one by one as they walked very slowly back to the encampment.

Her sleep was untroubled, her dreams pleasant but unremembered. She awakened smiling and serene.

She went to the communal shower house late one evening and was toweling her hair dry when Elsa sat down beside her. Ida smiled at her. She liked grave-eyed Elsa, who was so unlike the other girls. Orphaned in Moscow, Elsa had made her way to Paris with the help of Jewish relief organizations and had stoically taken control of her own life. She had studied medicine while working at odd jobs and managing scholarship grants that provided her with modest stipends. Somehow she had found time to fall in love with André, a young surgeon. She had shown Ida his photograph. He was rotund, prematurely bald, his nose prominent, his eyes narrow.

"He is not handsome, I know," she had said frankly. "But then I am not beautiful. We love each other for who we are, not for how we look. He is faithful and diligent, brilliant in his work. And he cares for me. It has been a long time since someone has cared for me."

"And you? Do you care for him?" Ida had asked.

"I love him," she had replied without hesitation.

André and Elsa were engaged to be married. Their future was their own. Ida admired Elsa and envied her independence. Elsa had no parents to answer to, no famous family name to uphold. She was free to live her own life. It occurred to Ida, with a shudder of guilt, that she envied Elsa her orphanhood.

"Are you enjoying the encampment, Ida?" Elsa asked, passing her a comb.

"Very much," Ida replied cautiously.

"You and Michel have grown very close, I've noticed," Elsa continued.

"We met here last summer and wrote to each other throughout the year. We are very good friends."

"I think that you are more than friends," Elsa said knowingly.

"Yes. You are right. We are more than friends." Her cheeks burned with a crimson brightness that would be foreign to her father's brush. She wanted to share her secret with Elsa, who stared at her gravely. Elsa would understand. She might even approve.

"We are *amoureux*, lovers," she added, her heart beating rapidly, her body suffused with warmth. It was a relief to have spoken the words aloud.

"I am not surprised. I thought as much," Elsa said. She smiled. "I assume you are being careful."

"Careful?" Ida was briefly puzzled.

"Surely you know what I mean." Elsa looked at her in surprise.

"Yes, of course I do," she said too swiftly.

Careful. Michel had used that very word and she had laughed his concern away. She understood the rhythms of her body, the days of fertility and infertility.

There was no need for him to worry, Ida had assured Michel. She was not worried. Why would she worry? She carefully recorded the dates of her menstrual cycle and understood its vagaries. Nothing could go wrong. She was fortune's favorite, always cherished, always protected, her parents' magical daughter imbued with zest and energy. And now she was Michel's *belle amante*, his beautiful beloved. She had ruffled his hair, mocked his concern.

Impulsively, she turned to Elsa and hugged her. "It is good of you to be concerned about us, but we are fine."

"Yes. Of course you are. Everyone is fine until they are not so fine," Elsa replied wryly.

On the last day of the encampment, Elsa handed Ida a slip of paper. "My address in Paris," she said. "Should you ever need me."

"*Merci*. But may I come to see you even if I don't need you?" Ida asked mischievously.

"Of course. We are friends, after all. I am on duty on the wards at night, but I am at home in the afternoon. And my door is never locked."

"I plan to come to your room and kidnap you. Michel and I will take you and your André to a wonderful café on the Rive Gauche."

Ida was aglow with excitement. Friendship with another young woman was a new experience for her. It would be wonderful to sit at a table on the terrace with her lover and her friends and watch the lights of Paris dance across the waters of the Seine.

She tucked Elsa's address into a corner of her case, next to the sachets of lavender that she had never placed in her drawers.

She and Michel traveled to Paris together. He carried a bouquet of the late-blooming alpine roses for his mother. It pained him that his mother who so loved flowers and gardens had been imprisoned in their small shop throughout the summer, fearing the loss of even a few francs. His parents' poverty saddened him. The sacrifices they made on his behalf filled him with guilt.

Ida carried no floral offerings. Marc and Bella had left Montchauvet and were settling into their Paris home near the Bois de Boulogne. She knew that Bella went to the flower market each day and returned home, her arms laden with the russet blooms of autumn. Always house proud, Bella obsessively arranged and rearranged furniture and paintings, filled bowls and vases with flowers. Her home was her insular fortress, her safe haven in the face of an ugly and uncertain world.

She had written to Ida, describing the way she had redecorated her bedroom. Sheer white draperies were at the windows, a rug of oriental design on the floor, a silk canopy of deep purple above the bed. The new comforter was pink and she had scattered plump pillows across it. Ida's books were on the shelves, the carved wooden animals she had collected since childhood on the bureau.

"How happy you will be there, *ma fille*," Bella had written.

Ida had smiled when she read the letter, smiled when she passed it to Michel.

"My mother has furnished a child's room. Toys and picture books and fluffy pillows. She doesn't recognize that I have grown up. I am not her *petite fille*. I am a *jeune personne*."

"She wants to please you. Don't be angry with her," Michel cautioned.

Soft-spoken and gentle, Michel always chose the path of peace. His parents had cautioned him to remain unnoticed and avoid confrontation. In silence, they, like the Chagalls, though without their resources, had navigated their way from Russia to Berlin and then finally reached France.

"We must not call attention to ourselves," his father had reminded him again and again. It was important that Jews cloak themselves in silence and anonymity.

His father's advice had impacted on Michel. Ida's exuberance, her vigorous assertiveness, was alien to him. Her passionate energy both intrigued and exhausted him. Her father's fame intimidated him. But none of that mattered. She bewitched him. Her self-confidence and her beauty, her vitality, the tenderness of her touch fascinated him. He loved her. Of that much he was certain. He fell asleep thinking about her and awakened to thoughts of her laughter, the exciting explosions of her joy.

"Of course I won't be angry with her," Ida assured him. "We are never *enragé* with each other, my parents and I."

The Chagalls dared not indulge in the luxury of anger. They were too dependent on each other, too conscious of their visibility, always in costume for the tableau they presented to the world. They knew that they were perceived to be an enchanted trio—lively, elfin-faced Marc; fragile, dark-haired Bella; and Ida, their precocious, vivacious daughter whose hair was the color of firelight.

As their train pulled into the Gare de Lyon, Ida and Michel, as they had agreed, went into separate compartments. They did not want their parents to see them disembark together. They had decided that they would explain their closeness, their "friendship," in due course. For the present, Michel would return to his legal studies and Ida would enroll in studio classes at La Palette in Montparnasse, close enough to the Sorbonne for them to meet with relative ease. Her parents had already agreed that La Palette offered more sophisticated training than the academy where she had previously studied.

The coming months stretched out before her in an enchanted highway of time. She and Michel would snatch the hours between his classes and hers for hasty lunches in the cafés of the Left Bank. They would walk hand in hand along the Seine and, at the twilight hour, *l'heure bleue*, they would stand together on the Pont Neuf and watch the reflection of the first stars of evening dance across the dark waters.

Smiling, Ida listened to the screech of the train's brakes and then watched Michel alight and stride across the platform to greet the short, silver-haired woman in the dark suit who stood on tiptoe to kiss her tall son and smile as she accepted the bouquet of roses he offered her. She waited, and then she too descended and rushed toward her parents.

"*Mamochka. Papochka.* How happy I am to see you. I had the most wonderful time, but I missed you. I missed you every single moment."

A dynamo of exuberance, she fell into her mother's arms and

smiled happily at her father. Marc placed his hand on her head and lifted a cluster of her silken curls to his cheek. He studied his daughter's flushed face and wondered why it was she looked so different to him.

"Welcome home, Idotchka," he said softly. *"Soyez la bienvenue."*

Arm in arm, they left the station, and as they waited at the exit for their driver, Ida saw Michel and his mother disappear into the Métro station. Michel's arm rested protectively on his mother's narrow shoulders and she clutched the bloodred roses to her heart.

Chapter Four

*I*da had slept peacefully at the encampment, but the terrifying recurrent dream assaulted her when she returned to Paris. Once again, there was the desperate race down dark and unfamiliar roads, the harsh shouts and the thudding hoofbeats of mounted pursuers whose eyes glinted with hatred, and then the mysterious celestial escape. Then suddenly the dreamscape was dangerously altered. As she floated through the flower-studded sky, dizziness overwhelmed her. She rocketed away from her parents' protective grasp and plunged into a sea of fetid darkness, struggling against a wave of nausea that thrust her, gasping for breath, onto the shore of wakefulness. Sleep was abandoned. She sat up, her eyes open and burning, her throat raw. Sour vomit filled her mouth.

Startled and frightened, she struggled out of bed and stumbled through the milky predawn light to the bathroom, where she retched, clutching her abdomen. The room whirled about her; she gripped the wall and lowered herself onto the cold tile floor. At last the dizziness abated, the nausea passed. She washed her face with cold water, brushed her teeth, and, moving very slowly, returned to her bedroom.

I'm sick, she thought as she tossed uneasily, tangling herself in the sweat-dampened bedclothes.

She remembered then that Yvette, the student who worked at an adjacent easel in the La Palette studio, had complained of stomach pains. Perhaps she had infected Ida, who, like her mother, was vulnerable to viruses. Ida was familiar with Bella's toxic headaches, her bouts of intestinal discomfort, and inexplicable muscle aches. Oddly shaped jars of patent medicines and homeopathic mixtures stood beside gem-colored vials of perfume and tubes of kohl on Bella's cluttered dressing table.

Only toward morning did she fall into a fitful sleep, and when she awakened, the nausea had passed. She smiled wanly at her mother, who stood in the doorway of her room holding a croissant and a cup of café au lait.

"I'm not really hungry," she said apologetically.

"But you must eat," Bella protested.

"I'll eat something at the studio. I don't want to be late this morning. A nude model will be posing."

Bella looked at her daughter searchingly.

"Are you feeling well, Idotchka?" she asked. "You look pale."

"I'm fine. I felt a bit ill earlier, but I'm perfectly all right now."

"Perhaps it's your time of the month?"

"No," Ida replied curtly.

Her mother's question irritated her. She resented its invasiveness. She was capable of calculating her own menstrual cycles.

"I thought that perhaps it was," Bella persisted. "Katya mentioned that she had not found any of the cloths you use for your monthly in the laundry."

"Katya should mind her own business. Perhaps it should have occurred to her that I prefer to do such intimate laundering myself. In fact, she should be grateful that I relieved her of such an unpleasant chore."

Ida kept her tone even, but she did not look at her mother. She concentrated on buckling her shoes, her head bent low. She ignored the dizziness that took her by surprise when she rose to brush her hair and countered it by drawing the brush vigorously through her tangled copper-colored curls.

Bella glanced at her watch and left the room.

Ida rummaged through her desk drawer and found the calendar on which she carefully recorded the dates of her menstrual cycle. She realized that it had been some weeks since she had made an entry. No, not weeks, she noted with a sinking heart. Almost two months had passed.

She willed herself to calm; she reminded herself that she was often irregular. She tried to remember if she had ever been this late. But of course, she had never before had reason to be concerned.

She counted the days since her last menses, then counted them again and recalled her nocturnal nausea, the light-headedness that had overcome her that very morning.

"No," she said aloud. "It can't be."

She turned to her long mirror and studied her reflection, concentrating on the narrowness of her waist, the flatness of her abdomen. There was no intimation that her body had been invaded by nascent life. She touched her breasts, so full and firm beneath the high-collared green bodice that matched her eyes. She never imprisoned them in either a brassiere or the laced tightness of a restraining chemise. She slipped her fingers between the buttons of her bodice and felt their tenderness. Were they perhaps unusually tender, she wondered, and, if so, did that signify anything?

Her hands trembling, she went to her drawer and fumbled through her handkerchiefs and found the scrap of paper on which Elsa had scrawled her address. She tucked it into her bag, tossed the croissant out the window, poured the coffee down the toilet, and hurried downstairs.

"Good-bye, *Mamochka*," she said, handing Bella the empty cup. "Thank you for breakfast. I'm sorry I was so irritable. Oh, I forgot to tell you. I won't be home for dinner. I'm meeting a friend."

She kissed her mother on both cheeks and rushed out, closing the door against Bella's protest, her inevitable questions.

"What friend? Where are you meeting? Will you call?"

Bella's strained voice, her unanswered questions, echoed through the empty room, startling Marc, who entered soundlessly. It was his habit to work in stockinged feet, always fearful that droplets of paint might stain his shoes. He had not forgotten his impoverished boyhood when he and his brother, David, had shared a single pair of shoes and attended school on alternate days.

Bella sighed in reluctant recognition of how their painful past haunted their present.

"To whom were you speaking, Bella?" he asked as he poured himself a cup of coffee.

"I thought I was speaking to Ida, but she left so quickly, she never heard me. She said she wouldn't be home for dinner because she was meeting a friend, but she didn't say whom she was meeting or where," she replied plaintively.

"Perhaps it's that law student, Michel Rapaport," Marc speculated. "She said that they became good friends at the encampment. I expect that she'll tire of him soon enough."

"Yes, probably," Bella said wearily. "I worry about her. She's so young, so naive."

"No younger than you were when we first met," he said, smiling.

"I know that. But we lived in different times, a different place. We understood boundaries. We knew what was permissible and what was forbidden."

"Did we have any choice?" he asked bitterly. "There was no escape from the prying eyes of the gossips of Vitebsk. We could not play deaf to the voices of the rabbis, the warnings of our parents. They were so frightened that we might do something that would bring shame upon them."

"Were they so wrong to worry?" she asked.

"Perhaps not. They worried us into marriage. They worried us into happiness." He smiled.

They knew that their hard-earned happiness relied on the firm foundation of communal acceptance. They still adhered to conventional Vitebsk, its embrace of respectability.

He stirred his coffee, added more sugar.

"But there is no need to be concerned about our Ida," he added. "She's a child still, a wisp of a girl."

"Not quite a wisp," Bella said, smiling for the first time that morning. "Our Ida is a beautiful young woman. Your artist friends see that. Surely you've noticed how young men stare at her whenever we're with her in a café, how they turn to look after her when we walk down the street?"

She did not tell him that their daughter's loveliness filled her with an odd commingling of pride and fear.

"Bella, Bella, you are creating worries where none exist. There are problems enough in the world. So our Ida is beautiful and men are aware of it. There is no need to be concerned."

"And what concerns you, Marc?" she asked caustically.

"What concerns me? Adolf Hitler concerns me. What's happening in Germany concerns me," he replied.

"Germany is across the border. We live in France," she said flatly. It was the mantra she intoned whenever he discussed the ominous headlines in *Le Monde* or the monitory newscasts.

"The Great War ended only sixteen years ago," she continued. "Do you think the German people actually want another war? The very idea is ridiculous. Of course there is anti-Semitism in Germany—we knew that when we left Berlin—but anti-Semitism does not mean war. You worry too much, Marc."

He shrugged. "Perhaps. Let's agree: you'll stop worrying about Ida, and I'll stop worrying about Hitler."

"A fair exchange," she said, and they laughed.

They smiled at each other and she moved toward him, rested her head on his shoulder. He gently stroked the silken cap of her dark hair.

"We have an invitation to a performance at the Théâtre de l'Athénée this evening. Shall we go?" he asked.

It was, she knew, a gesture of conciliation.

She nodded, grateful for the diversion, which would free her from worrying about Ida, about where she was spending the evening and when she would return.

"It will be a pleasant evening," he said. "All the artists of Paris will be there. Even the Spaniard."

"He's so arrogant, that Picasso," she said.

She did not add that when she and Ida had stopped for coffee at Les Deux Magots, Picasso had quickly sketched Ida in profile and flashed his pad at them as he left. A charcoal drawing, deft and minimal, but he had captured their daughter's latent sensuality.

Marc shrugged and left the kitchen, anxious to return to his studio. Bella went to her study and reread the prose poem she had written the previous day, a memoir of her childhood in a family and a community that no longer existed.

—

Ida spent the morning at her easel, becoming increasingly frustrated. She had always been fascinated by the way her father worked, his swift and certain brushstrokes, his instinctive selection of daring colors. Her own efforts were labored. She stared at the nude model standing motionless and bored on the platform, her greasy ash blond hair tied into a scraggly knot. Ida struggled, without success, to paint the woman's sagging breasts, her heavy legs, but she knew her efforts were unsuccessful. The maître, who patrolled the cavernous studio critiquing his students' work, paused and studied her canvas.

"It would be helpful, perhaps, if you outlined your subject before you start to paint," he said.

"My father never does that," Ida protested.

"But you are not your father, Mademoiselle Chagall," he replied, smiling maliciously.

She was relieved when the afternoon recess was declared. The model slipped into a faded blue dressing gown and accepted a cigarette and a glass of water from the studio assistant.

"She's so ugly," Ida muttered, and Yvette, who once again had painted beside her, frowned.

"Is it because she is so ugly that you find it difficult to paint her?" she asked sardonically. "You should have more sympathy for her. How can a woman who is ugly and poor support herself? Do you think she actually wants to pose naked in this freezing studio? What choices do women like her have?"

Ida did not reply. Yvette's words shamed her.

Despondently, she discarded her smock, smoothed her hair, and left the studio. The sweetness of the autumn air, the gentleness of the breeze soothed her, and she walked briskly to the café where she and Michel had agreed to meet.

He sat, as she had known he would, at a small table in the rear. It was their habit to rendezvous in the darkened corners of unfashionable cafés. They were reluctant to encounter either their parents' friends or their own fellow students. That self-ordained secrecy added romantic mystery to their stolen shared hours. Michel leaned forward, took her hand, and pressed it to his lips. Half a baguette lay on his plate, and his coffee cup was nearly empty.

"I'm sorry, *chérie*, but I have very little time today. I have books on reserve at the law library, and I promised my parents that I would help in the shop. Do you forgive me?"

She swallowed her disappointment. "But will we see each other this evening?" she asked.

"It's not possible. I have a study session with the students in my class on the laws of property. We have an important examination next week. Please don't be angry."

He feared Ida's anger as he feared her sudden moods, her irritation if he rejected her plans for an afternoon outing or her choice of a café. She had, from childhood on, always had her own way, while he had always prioritized the needs of his parents, unwilling to add to their heavy burden of sadness and pain. Still, her explosions were brief, his forgiveness inevitable and immediate.

"No. I'm not angry."

Relieved, he kissed her cheek. She watched him hurry out, bowed by the weight of his book bag. It occurred to her that he looked very ordinary in his shabby brown cloth student jacket. The disloyalty of the thought surprised her. She ordered a coffee and a croque monsieur. She had thought to tell Michel about her predawn illness and its implications, but she did not regret her silence. It would have been foolish to speak to him before she was absolutely certain of her condition. She fished Elsa's address out of her bag. She knew how to establish that certainty.

She ate very slowly, turning the oil-stained pages of the café's copy of *Le Monde* as she sipped her coffee. There was more bad news from Germany, more warnings from Winston Churchill about the likelihood of war. She sighed. Many of her parents' friends were already planning to leave Europe. She would urge them yet again to file visa applications at the United States embassy, although she knew they would be resistant. They had spent so much of their lives in flight. Her mother was exhausted, and her father, for all his apprehensions about Hitler, assumed that his fame would protect him. She replaced the newspaper on its wooden rack, paid her bill, and left the café.

But she did not return to the studio. The thought of the sad model's coarse features, of Yvette's unkindness and the maître's criticism, impelled her to walk in the opposite direction. Exhilarated by her new leisure, she wandered into a fashionable shop in the Faubourg Saint-Germain. She fingered several garments and then tried on various cloaks before selecting a sky-blue cape of the softest cashmere. The eager saleswoman offered her a matching beret, which she also bought, setting it at a jaunty angle and arranging her hair so the coppery tendrils fringed her forehead.

Pleased with her reflection in the shop's mirror, she felt a surge of confidence. The cape rested lightly on her shoulders. She smiled as she remembered how often her mother bought new outfits to fend off encroaching melancholy. Bella was right. New and fashionable clothing was empowering. She felt newly confident; the fear that had haunted her since the break of dawn dissipated. She was reinvigorated. No matter what, she would cope. She was Ida Chagall, the claimant of her parents' devotion, Michel's love, and her own optimistic expectation of a future laced with brightness.

Chapter Five

She hurried across the city and made her way to Elsa's address on the Right Bank. She was elated to find Elsa at home, newly arrived from the hospital. They embraced and Ida stood at the window as Elsa changed from her white hospital coat into a shapeless gray wool dress. She knew that Elsa was a woman whose work would always take precedence over her appearance. Her mother would never approve. Bella insisted that beauty and style were key in the treacherous game of social survival. Her family's Vitebsk values had leeched into her perception of the world.

Elsa bubbled with news of her new rotation at the women's hospital financed by the Rothschild family.

"I have decided to specialize in gynecology," she told Ida. "I'll complete my residency in two years if I work double shifts. André has been promised a position at Beth Israel Hospital in New York. I will join him there when I have my visa."

"Why would you want to work that hard?" Ida asked. "Surely, André can wait until you qualify and then you can emigrate together."

"We are in a race against Hitler. Don't you read the papers, Ida? The Austrian madman has expelled all Polish Jews without proper papers from Germany. My sister and brother and their families are living in a barracks in that no-man's-land between the borders of Poland and Germany, scrambling for food. It will be our turn next. We'd be fools to believe that the Jews of France will be spared if Hitler invades, and it is almost certain that he will. So yes—we are moving as fast as we can."

Ida sighed. "My father is worried also, but he thinks his name and his fame will protect us."

"If Hitler does invade France, no Jew will have any protection. Not even the great Marc Chagall," Elsa said caustically. "But surely you didn't come here to discuss world affairs. Tell me what you've been doing, Ida. Are you enjoying the work at La Palette? And how is Michel?"

"The painting is difficult. I have an easier time in the drawing classes. Michel is working very hard and he seems well."

"And you, Ida. Are you well?"

Ida averted her eyes. Her hands trembled and her voice dropped to a whisper.

"No. Actually, I'm not. I think—I think I may be pregnant."

Her cheeks burned, but she felt a sense of relief at having finally uttered the word she had thought throughout the day.

"And what makes you think that?" Elsa asked, her tone cool and professional.

Ida sank into a chair and spoke in a monotone. "I've had a nocturnal bout of nausea. Vomiting. And then in the morning, I was dizzy and light-headed. I checked my calendar. I seem to have missed one or perhaps two periods. I know what that combination might mean."

"Yes. It might indicate a pregnancy, but we can't be sure. You should be examined. Surely your mother sees a gynecologist whom you could consult."

"But I don't want my parents to know. At least not until I myself am certain. Could you examine me, Elsa?" She turned away, fearful of Elsa's reply to a request she knew she had no right to make. Theirs was not a friendship of equals.

Elsa hesitated. She removed her thick spectacles, wiped them on the hem of her dress, and replaced them.

"Ida, I am not very experienced," she said at last. "It's true that I've had some training, but I'm not yet qualified. You should go to a clinic."

"Elsa, please. I don't want to speak with a stranger. And I would have to fill out a form at a clinic, provide them with a *carte d'identité*. The Chagall name is not unknown in Paris. There would surely be gossip. Can't you help me?"

Elsa stared at her in thoughtful silence. "All right," she said at last and sighed heavily.

Her agreement was reluctant, but her actions were swift. She took her black medical bag from the armoire and heated a pot of water on the charcoal brazier. She poured the warm water into a basin and washed her hands using a cake of noxious yellow soap.

"Please, Ida, lie on my bed. Remove your undergarments and lift your skirt up high. You understand that you will have to open your legs as wide as possible."

Obediently, Ida did as she was told. She spread her new sky-blue cape across Elsa's flimsy blanket. She rested her head on the thin pillow and realized that she still wore her beret. She imagined how ridiculous she must look, with her skirts hiked high, her naked thighs spread wide and exposed, the beret still perched jauntily atop her tangled curls.

Gently, Elsa examined her, probing the soft membranes of the vaginal wall with a shining steel instrument. Despite her care, Ida gasped with pain although she did not cry out.

"I'm sorry," Elsa said. "I'm very sorry. I'm trying not to hurt you."

She withdrew her hand, and Ida sighed with relief.

"I can't be sure," Elsa said hesitantly. "But I did feel something. The cells of the placenta form only days after conception. That might have been what I felt. We can only be certain when we have the results of a urine test. But I would venture to guess that you are, in fact, in a very early stage of pregnancy, just weeks into the first tri-mester. I worried that this might happen. I should have been more direct when I spoke to you at the encampment."

"It's not your fault, Elsa. You did warn me."

Ida sat up. She dressed quickly and rushed to the bathroom, clutching the towel Elsa held out to her. She did not look at her friend when she emerged but washed her hands vigorously, using the heated water and the carbolic soap.

"What will you do?" Elsa asked softly.

Ida shrugged but did not reply.

"Does Michel know?'

"No." She adjusted her cape, fingered the soft fabric. "Do you think this color becomes me?" she asked mischievously.

"Ida, you must be serious, you know," Elsa said reprovingly.

"I know. Of course I know."

"If you are indeed pregnant, it is very early, which means you have a choice. There is a procedure, a way to terminate the pregnancy. It can be done. After all, we are in Paris, not in eastern Europe."

"*Avortement.* That is what you are suggesting."

The word was not unfamiliar to her. *Avortement.* Abortion. She knew that her mother had arranged an abortion for Katya, their maid. Ida had overhead Bella discussing Katya with her friend Raïssa Maritain as she bent over her drawing pad in a corner of the garden. It was true that her parents had been supportive of their Polish maid, but how would they react to their own daughter who was in the same position?

The answer came to her at once. Of course they would be supportive. She was their Idotchka, their precious princess. Her father would open his arms to her and comfort her, as would her mother, as they always had. She could do no wrong in their eyes. But what was her will now? And she would not be alone in this decision. What would be Michel's will?

"Would your parents be against an abortion?" Elsa asked.

"More to the point, would I be against it?" Ida smiled grimly. Her question floated through the quiet room, its silence broken only by the shrill siren of a tugboat laboring its way up the Seine.

"That is what you must decide," Elsa said sadly. "Please keep in touch with me, Ida. Perhaps André and I can be of assistance to you."

"Of course. We'll speak soon. Thank you, Elsa." She buttoned her cape, and Elsa put her hand out and stroked the soft wool.

"It is a beautiful color, Ida," she said and they smiled at each other. For that brief moment, they were simply two carefree young women whose major concern was the color and texture of a garment, their lives unaffected by the ranting of a German dictator or an unplanned pregnancy.

Ida was relieved that her parents were out when she arrived home.

"They went to the theater. But they left a meal for you, mademoiselle. Shall I set it out?" Katya asked.

"No." The very thought of food repelled her. "But thank you," she added and looked hard at Katya, noting for the first time that the maid seemed pale and her face, always surly, was newly expressionless. But that was to be expected, Ida supposed. Katya had been expelled from innocence.

Slowly, Ida mounted the stairs to her own room. She studied her face in the mirror and saw, with relief, that her skin retained its glow, her eyes their emerald brightness.

"Everything will be all right," she assured herself.

She closed her eyes and fell into a deep and dreamless sleep.

Chapter Six

*I*da awakened late the next morning and stared out at the mist that clouded the windowpanes. Impulsively, she thrust the window open and leaned out, allowing the cool moisture to bathe her face. The door to her room was slightly ajar, and she could hear her mother discussing the chores of the day with Katya. There was laundry to be done and silver to be polished, the carpets needed airing, and the dining room floor had to be waxed. Ida listened, soothed by the cadence of Bella's voice and by the unaltered pattern of the day's routine. Her world might have changed, but it had not, after all, come to an end.

She dressed quickly, selecting a white woolen dress that both her parents particularly liked. She acknowledged, as she twisted her hair into a coppery coil, that she was dressing to please them, and she knew exactly why she was making such an effort. Bella and Marc, consummate actors on so many stages in so many countries, had taught her the importance of costume, the impact of appearances. She glanced at herself in the mirror, brushed a stray tendril away from her forehead, and left her room.

Bella was seated at her escritoire, pen in hand, studying the entries she had made in her copy book the previous day. Ida knew that it was her mother's habit to reread her work each morning, often discarding much of it in her endless pursuit of perfection. Ida carried her coffee and croissant into the salon.

"*Bon matin, Maman*," she said, placing her hand on Bella's shoulder.

Bella smiled and looked up at her. "It's late. Aren't you going to La Palette today?"

"No. I had a difficult time at the studio yesterday. My work there, at least the painting, is not going well."

"Painting does not come easily. Nor does writing," Bella said ruefully and glanced down at her notebook.

"It comes easily enough to *Papochka*." Ida dipped her croissant into the milky coffee, relieved that she was able to eat without experiencing the nausea of the previous morning.

"But your father is a genius," Bella responded reprovingly.

"Where is he this morning?" Ida asked.

"He went to an exhibition of Matisse's work. He's interested in Henri's use of mirrors."

"And I suppose he's interested in mastering the technique himself," Ida said, and she and Bella exchanged smiles in shared recognition of Marc's incessant pursuit of the secrets of other artists, his unbridled determination to emulate and exceed. Like a greedy precocious child, he gobbled up new skills. He would be a ceramist, and a painter; he would work on stained glass and create intricate etchings. He would design stage sets and illustrate fables and biblical tales. His boundless energy and his capacity for work and for the acquisition of new skills aroused both their admiration and amusement.

"Actually, he thought of asking you to go with him," Bella continued, "because Henri was always so fond of you. But I told him you would probably be too tired. Katya said you came in rather late last evening."

"Yes. I went shopping and then I visited a friend."

"Someone we know?" Bella asked cautiously.

"No. A friend I met at the encampment. A doctor. Elsa Liebowitz."

"Liebowitz?" Bella's brow was furrowed. "A Polish girl?"

"It didn't occur to me to ask," Ida replied coldly.

Her parents' snobbery irritated her. Marc and Bella cultivated friendships with the intellectual and artistic elite of Paris. The Jewish refugees from Poland and Lithuania, who lived in the tenements of Le Marais, were an embarrassment to them. Marc even scorned Bella's beloved brother, Yaakov Rosenfeld, wryly imitating his pronounced Yiddish accent.

"What didn't it occur to you to ask?" Marc asked, and they turned as he tossed his beret onto the hat rack and clapped in celebration of his own perfect aim.

He had entered the house soundlessly, as he often did, and stood in the portico, an impish smile playing on his lips, his hair wind tousled. He had won his oft-repeated boyish game of stealing into his own dining room and surprising them with his presence. And he did look like a boy, Ida thought. An aging, graying boy.

"Oh, I was just curious about Ida's friend," Bella said, and she hurried to pour him a cup of coffee. "Was Henri's new work interesting?"

"Very impressive," Marc replied. "A real effort to integrate cubism and impressionism. I envy him his good fortune. He has the luxury to thrust himself into the future. He is not held hostage to a vanished world."

His tone was casual, but his words were laced with bitterness. His own art reflected his past; his imagination was ignited by the Jewish experience. Like his friend, Chaim Soutine, he painted houses without foundations, rootless trees, wandering animals, and floating lovers, the landscape of a stateless people. The Judaism he rejected hobbled and encumbered him. The village of his childhood demanded his brush. Matisse, a son of France, was not impeded by lingering imagery, nor was he haunted by sad memories. His landscapes were sylvan vistas of peace, his models strangers to sorrow.

"Everyone at La Palette admires your work, Papa," Ida said quickly. "They marvel at your themes, at your use of color. 'Where does your father get such ideas?' they ask me."

"Where indeed?" Marc parried. "I myself do not know. I lift my brush and lovers and cows, clowns and violinists, dance across my canvas." He laughed. Ida's words had banished his despondency. He was delighted anew by the mystery of his own talent.

"But why are you not at La Palette this morning?" he asked.

"I was tired and I wanted to talk to you. To you and *Maman*."

"I have no time to talk. I want to get to the studio. We will speak at dinner."

"No, Papa," she said. "We will speak now. What I have to say is very important."

Ida's spoon rattled against her cup and she set it down, unable to control her trembling fingers, but her voice was steady, her expression grave.

"All right then."

He did not bother to mask his irritation as he pulled out a chair and sat beside Bella, who covered his hand with her own. Irritably, he brushed it aside. He resented this diversion from his daily routine. "Then speak," he commanded. All playfulness had faded from his tone.

"I must tell you that I believe, that I am almost certain, that I am enceinte. Pregnant." Ida spoke calmly, but her hands were tightly clasped and her eyes were fixed on her parents' shocked faces.

"Enceinte?"

They stared at their daughter and spoke the word in unison, their voices rising in disbelief, as though their very doubt would nullify what she had said. Marc stared at Bella and she looked pleadingly at Ida, her face blanched of all color.

Bella gasped. "You must be mistaken. It cannot be."

Ida did not flinch. "I'm not mistaken. All signs point to it," she said, her voice dangerously calm.

They did not ask what the signs were. They sat opposite her, mute and immobile. A single tear pearled Bella's pale cheek and fell unheeded into the corner of her mouth. Marc's blue eyes glinted icily. His narrow face contorted into a mask that commingled sorrow and fury. He stared at his daughter, dressed this morning in the white he had always favored. How often he had painted her in ivory-colored dresses, frocks of snow-white silk, crowns of white lilies on her bright hair. When she was a small girl, they had dressed her in a ruffled white dress, lace fringed white socks, and white patent leather pumps. She had posed in that costume for a studio photograph they had packaged carefully and sent to their families in Russia, never knowing if it would reach them. That very daguerreotype held pride of place on the mantelpiece of their salon. He glanced at it and turned away.

He had always thought of his Ida as a vibrant and virginal child, her beauty and precocity a hard-earned legacy, a validation of the lives he and Bella had lived. She was their pride and their comfort. They had given her everything, protected her from all danger and darkness. And now that love, that indulgence, that devotion, had been betrayed. How could she so willfully, so carelessly, make a mockery of their dreams, their hopes? Their Ida, pregnant and unmarried! How could she have shamed them? He stared at her, seeking out the daughter he had coddled, the playful child, the vibrant young girl whom he had painted year after year, and then turned away, ablaze with anger.

He subdued a wild desire to tear the soft white woolen dress from her body and paint it as he had painted the costumes of the actors of the Moscow Jewish Theater. He would choose the scarlet of spilled blood, the acid yellow of disappointment and disgust. He remembered those long-ago days in Moscow, shivering in the freezing theater as he frantically moved his brush against coarse fabric scavenged by the wardrobe mistress. As he worked, Ida, then so small and innocent, had played at his feet, his Idotchka, now grown into the defiant young woman who sat opposite him, her head held high, her eyes that matched his own, staring at him unflinchingly. And unapologetically. Had she no remorse? Didn't she understand what she had done to him, to her mother? He looked at her as though she had suddenly become a stranger, an unwelcome alien at his table. But oh, how beautiful she was! Rage and love tore at his heart.

"I'm sorry," she said at last.

"Sorry. Of course you are sorry." Bella's voice broke.

Marc rose, paced the room. "And who is the father?" he asked harshly.

The question startled Ida. She had not thought of herself as a mother, much less had she thought of Michel as a father.

"Michel," she said softly. "Michel Rapaport."

"The law student?"

She nodded.

"You're certain that it was he?"

Her heart sank at the iciness of his tone, at the punishing impli-cation of his question. Had she been transformed, during these last painful moments, from his adored daughter into a promiscuous whore with multiple lovers?

"Of course I'm certain," she said. "How could you think otherwise?"

"Perhaps because I don't know what to think. Perhaps because I no longer know who you are."

"How many monthlies have you missed?" Bella asked quietly.

"One. Perhaps two."

"Then perhaps you are only late."

"No. There are other symptoms. My friend Elsa Liebowitz, the doctor whom I visited last night, examined me. She is in training to become a gynecologist. She understands a woman's body."

"It is a pity she did not share her knowledge with you earlier," Marc said bitterly.

Bella and Ida ignored him.

"Have you told Michel, Michel Rapaport?" Bella asked.

"No."

"He must be told," she said firmly.

"I know. I will tell him this afternoon. We are meeting at a café." She shook her hair loose, toyed with the pins that had held the coil in place. "As we often do," she added. She was done with deception.

"Change your dress before you see him." Marc's voice was harsh. He did not want Ida to wear white today, not today, perhaps never again. He turned on his heel. "I am going to my studio," he said. "I have work to do." He slammed the door.

Ida's eyes burned, and her hands trembled. The optimism of early morning had faded, and she felt herself sinking into the quicksand of despair. She gasped for breath, her heart so heavy she thought that it might break. She had counted on her parents' support, their sympathy, but she had misread their love, misunderstood their devo-tion. It was not unconditional after all. She had been foolish not to anticipate her father's fierce anger, her mother's grief. Their shared disappointment hovered over the room that grew darker as the morning mist morphed into an encroaching storm. She felt herself abandoned, alone.

A bolt of thunder shattered the silence. Bella drew the drapes against the sudden dimness and moved to sit beside her. She took Ida's hand, her fingers ice-cold and rigid, into her own.

"How are you, my daughter?" she asked softly. She spoke in Yiddish, the tender language of her heart.

Ida answered her, her voice barely audible.

"*Ikh volt oysgeyn. Je voudrais mourir*," she said, first in Yiddish, then in French. "I want to die."

She swayed as though in prayerful sorrow. Bella cradled her in her arms until at last she was soothed into stillness, her head resting on her mother's breast.

"You will not die. Everything will be all right. Rest for a while. The storm will pass. Storms always do. Then go and meet your Michel."

"All right, *Maman*."

Ida rose and walked stiffly, almost robotically, to her room. She, who rushed through life imbued with electric energy, felt herself in the grip of an unfamiliar inertia. She sat at her dressing table and studied her reflection in the mirror as though prepared to confront a stranger. She was surprised to see that her color was high, her green eyes strangely calm. She brushed her hair, twisted it into a bun, then into a chignon, and at last allowed it to fall to her shoulders. She smiled at herself, took note of her beauty: her rose-gold skin, high cheekbones, and generous mouth. She was still, after all, Ida Chagall.

Oddly reassured, she went to the window. A strong wind whipped the branches of the cypress tree, but the rain had ceased. After some minutes, the wind itself abated. Her mother was right. Storms passed.

She did not change her dress. She tossed her new blue cloak over her shoulders and adjusted the matching beret so that her long, loose hair framed her face in radiance. She wanted to look beautiful when she spoke with Michel. She relied on her beauty to subdue his fear and bewilderment. She left the house, closing the heavy front door very softly behind her. She did not turn back and so she did not see Bella's face pressed to the front window, her eyes following Ida's progress until she disappeared into the Bois de Boulogne.

Michel, as always, was on time. He waited for her at the student café, as considerate a lover as he was a son.

Still, he glanced at his watch as she slipped into the seat opposite him, a silent reprimand, meant to remind her that her lateness interfered with the demands of his schedule, his afternoon seminar, his determination to help his parents at their small shop so that they could manage a swift dinner.

"I'm sorry, Michel. The Métro was slow."

She uttered the lie effortlessly. She could not tell him that she was late because she was slowed by the heaviness of her heart. She would not tell him that she had crossed broad avenues slowly as though daring the speeding cars to run her down.

Je voudrais mourir. *I want to die*, she had repeated to herself as angry drivers blared their horns and shouted epithets at her. But she had not been run down. She had arrived safely at this small café where Michel awaited her, love in his eyes, tenderness on his lips.

"It's all right. You look beautiful, wonderful. That blue becomes you."

He fingered her cape, lifted the beret from her head, and kissed her cheek.

"I don't feel wonderful."

"What's wrong?"

The waiter approached.

"What will you have?" he asked.

"A pot of English tea," Ida said. "A brie platter and one baguette."

She ordered swiftly, authoritatively, as she usually did, rarely bothering to ask Michel what he might prefer. He felt a brief stirring of annoyance and then realized that Ida, as always, had known exactly what he wanted. Tea, cheese, a bit of bread was all he needed, Smiling, surrendering to her self-proclaimed authority, he lifted her hand to his lips and kissed her fingers one by one, always his affectionate tactile celebration of their new togetherness. But today she withdrew her hand.

"You asked me what was wrong," she reminded him.

"Yes. I did. Was there difficulty at the studio?"

"I didn't go to the studio today."

"Oh."

He waited.

She bowed her head. He leaned forward because she spoke so faintly he could barely hear her.

"I'm pregnant, Michel. Pregnant with your child. Enceinte."

He stared at her as though she had plucked a word from an unfamiliar lexicon.

"Pregnant?" he repeated, his voice aquiver with fear.

She nodded.

Wearily, for the second time that day, she explained the reason for her certainty, adding that she would take the test Elsa had told her would be definitive.

"But I have no doubts," she added.

The waiter arrived with their food, and Michel marveled that Ida could so expertly cut the brie, that she could slice the baguette in half with such accuracy, and then he marveled that he himself could eat it, that he could even relish the crusty dough still warm from the oven.

"Have you told your mother and father?"

"Yes."

"What did they say? What do they want you to do?"

"What they said, what they may want, is of no importance. The decision must be ours. It is we who must decide what we are going to do."

"What will you do?" he asked. "My God, what will you do?"

"What will we do?" she corrected him, her voice steady.

"Yes. Of course. What will we do?"

Swiftly, he recognized the enormity of his responsibility. His head spun. He would have to leave the university and find employment if he and Ida were to marry and raise a child. He thought of his parents, his mother who laboriously counted out hard-earned franc notes for his tuition, his father who pasted strips of cardboard beneath the soles of his own shoes in order to pay for Michel's boots, his textbooks, his clothing. Their hopes were fixed on him. How could he betray them? But then how could he betray Ida, his beautiful radiant love? There were choices to be made, but he was so stunned he could neither fathom nor articulate them.

He pondered their options. He did not remind her that she was eighteen, that he was twenty, that they were both students, dependent on their parents. It occurred to him that Ida, ever the romantic, might see their very youth and the onset of poverty as a dramatic challenge. His foolish, brave, wonderful Ida. He looked at her tenderly.

"Whatever decision we come to, we will come to together," he murmured.

"Together," she repeated. *"Ensemble."* The very utterance of the word comforted her. She placed her arm on his, and he stroked the soft wool of her sleeve.

"I love the way you look in white," he said. "And I love the color of your new cape, your beret."

She smiled. She did not love the way he looked in his shabby brown jacket, his shirt collar frayed, his dark cotton trousers worn thin. She would buy him a new jacket, as elegant as the leather cloak he held in reserve for special occasions. She would fashion a shirt for him of the heavy broadcloth her father favored. How reliable he was, how caring a son, how tender a lover. She lifted his hand and kissed his fingers one by one.

"We will manage," she said softly. "Somehow we will manage. Together. *Ensemble.*"

They drank their tea in silence and left too large a tip for their surly, ungrateful waiter.

It was Elsa who arranged for the definitive test and reported, some days later, that the results were conclusive. Ida was pregnant.

"What will you do?" Elsa asked.

"I don't know." Ida spoke in a monotone.

She was pale, her eyes dull, her hair carelessly twisted into a lank knot. She did not drink the tea Elsa had prepared. All food and drink nauseated her, she said.

"You must speak to your parents," Elsa said firmly.

"Tonight," Ida promised. "Tonight."

Dinner that evening was a tense meal eaten in silence. Marc criticized the dessert. Bella spilled a glass of red wine. Ida waited until Katya had cleared the table and closed the kitchen door behind her, and then she turned to her parents.

"The laboratory tests confirm my condition," she said, staring down at the crimson wine stain that was slowly spreading across the white tablecloth.

Marc pushed his chair back so forcefully that it fell to the floor. He did not pause to pick it up but left the room without looking at her.

Bella pierced a strawberry tart with her fork and watched it bleed onto her plate. "I have a headache," she said plaintively. "A very bad headache. I must lie down." She lifted her hands to her temples, her eyes bright with tears, and hurried away.

Alone in the dining room, Ida set the fallen chair in place. She paced the floor, pausing to stare hard at the photograph on the mantel, a beloved portrait of her parents sitting side by side on a divan. Suddenly, she saw them as strangers. The mother and father she had known and relied upon with such certainty, such hopeful expectation, no longer existed for her. She looked around the room, at the walls hung with her father's paintings, the crystal chandelier, the windows draped in the green velvet. The fortress of beauty and permanence that her refugee parents had defiantly furnished in celebration of their new prosperity, their new security, was no longer her safe haven. She felt herself an unwelcome stranger in a home that was no longer her own.

She and Michel met the next afternoon in the Tuileries Garden. "There is no doubt. I am pregnant. I told my parents last night," she said, her voice quivering. Tears streaked her cheeks.

He drew her close, stroked her hair. "What did they say?" he asked.

"They said nothing. I think that they were too angry, too disappointed to speak. It was almost as though I had betrayed them, as though I was no longer their daughter."

"It will be all right, Ida," he said. He held out a handkerchief and dried her eyes, buried his face in her hair.

They sat in silence on a bench and watched a group of schoolchildren at play. A bright green ball skittered away, and a small boy and girl danced past them to retrieve it.

"Do you want to have this child, Ida?" he asked quietly.

"I want to want it. I want to be brave enough to have it. But the truth is I do not want a child, not now, and I am not brave enough. This was not how I saw my life, Michel."

She spoke very softly, each word a pellet of pain. She did not tell him how she had awakened in the night, her body damp with sweat, her stomach heaving. She rode nightmares of terror, her dreamscape altered. She ran, as she had always run, but her restless sleep was haunted by the amalgam of cells growing deep within her body, crazily morphed into a malignant imp. Faceless and infinitesimal, it pursued her, an internal invader that chased through her organs and caused her to writhe in pain. Twice she had awakened and shouted, "*Je voudrais mourir.*" Bella had hurried into her room and stood sorrowfully by her bedside, her hand on Ida's forehead, until the terror passed. She had shaken away her mother's hand and turned her face to the wall.

"What I want is to be free of this pregnancy," she said at last, her voice sad but firm.

"I know."

She heard the relief in his voice and was comforted.

"You can be free of it. This is Paris, not Vitebsk," he said. "There are skilled doctors who know how to terminate a pregnancy."

He spoke with certitude. He had spoken to a fellow student whose fiancée had opted for a termination. "*Très facile*, very easy," his friend had assured him.

"We must speak to your parents together. Tonight."

"Yes. Tonight," she agreed.

"Ida, my Ida, I hope that you do not want to be free of me." He smiled at her, inviting a new complicity.

"Ah, Michel." She smiled, placed her hand on his cheek, pressed her lips to his, and then hurried away.

He did not realize until she was gone from his sight that she had not, in fact, answered his question. He did not return to the Sorbonne for his afternoon seminar. He went instead to his father's shop. He too had to speak with his parents.

Chapter Seven

*I*da called her mother from the Métro station and told her that she and Michel would join them for dinner.

"Yes, of course," Bella said. "We will be expecting you."

She replaced the receiver and turned to Marc.

"They are coming for dinner. Ida and her Michel. What must we say to them?"

"We know what we must say to them," he replied impatiently. "Ida cannot have this child. She's eighteen, a child herself. A foolish irresponsible child."

"Our child. She is our child, foolish as she may be," Bella said. "But I agree with you. Of course she's too young. Too young. Still, I worry that an *avortement* is a dangerous procedure."

"Dangerous?" he asked, his voice cold, his eyes shards of blue ice. "I will tell you what is dangerous. It is dangerous to bring a Jewish child into the world at a time like this. Hitler is bellowing threats against Jews in Germany. Dizengoff wrote me from Tel Aviv, describing how the Arabs are rioting against Jews, killing them in the Galilee, killing them in Hebron. In Russia, they are burning synagogues. Why should a Jewish child be born into a world filled with such hatred and danger?"

Bella stared at him angrily. She closed the door that led to the kitchen. She did not want Katya to hear them. She wheeled around and looked hard at Marc.

"It has always been dangerous to bring Jewish children into the world," she said coldly. "Weren't you yourself born the night a fire was set by anti-Semitic hoodlums in Vitebsk? Didn't I give birth to Ida during the Great War when Jewish boys were being conscripted into the Russian army? Has there ever been a time when it was safe for a Jewish child to be born? Should we stop loving each other, stop having children, because there are those who want us dead? The danger I worry about is not the danger that might confront a Jewish child. I worry about whether having an abortion involves a risk to *our* child, to Ida. Is such a procedure dangerous? It is a simple enough question. I did not ask you for a lesson in current events."

He flinched, startled by her retort, her unfamiliar, barely contained fury. Always, he anticipated her acquiescence, her acceptance of his pronouncements. But of course, she was fiercely protective of Ida. As he was. He went to the samovar, filled a glass with tea, and placed two sugar cubes beneath his tongue, willing their sweetness to counter the bitterness that caused his heart to burn.

"All right then. I should have told you that I spoke to Dr. Hollander this morning. You recall him, that wealthy gynecologist who bought some etchings last year? I told him I was asking about it on behalf of a model. He assured me that the procedure is routine, far less dangerous than childbirth."

"And of course, you have always been terrified of childbirth," she said wryly.

"I never denied that."

He had told her of how he had been frozen with fear, watching his mother give birth to his sister Lisa. He had stood too close to her bed and when the spongy, bloody mass of the afterbirth catapulted from her body, droplets of blood spattered onto his face. He had been certain that the blood signified that she was being drained of life. He had recorded that memory in the series of works he called "Birth."

Bella realized that just as she worried about the dangers of abortion, he was terrified that Ida's life might be endangered by childbirth. His fury masked his fear that his family was like the acrobats he so often painted, uneasily balanced on the trembling high wire of life that might, at any moment, snap and betray them.

He turned to her and spoke very softly, very slowly.

"You are right. It frightens me to think of Ida having a child. She is so young, so unprepared. But as I told you, Dr. Hollander assured me that this early in a pregnancy, there is little to fear from a termination. Women come to Paris for the procedure because the physicians here are so skilled and well trained. There is an excellent clinic at Neuilly. Ida will be safe."

"I suppose you're right," she agreed sadly. "According to Raïssa Maritain, abortion is a mortal sin."

"Raïssa is now a Catholic," he said harshly. "We are still Jews. We do not believe in mortal sin."

"And what do we, as Jews, believe about abortion?" she asked.

"I don't know and it is of no interest to me," he replied impatiently. "Judaism does not dictate the way I live my life."

"No. It only supplies you with subjects for your paintings. Your bearded rabbis, your klezmer musicians, your floating synagogues," she retorted. "What kind of a Jew are you, Marc?"

He stared at her in surprise. She had never before questioned his artistic integrity, the sincerity of his themes, the contradiction between his life and his art. He could not answer her question. He himself did not know what kind of a Jew he was.

"I'm going to my studio," he said. "I'm completing a painting of a Jewish wedding." He smiled to show that he had not taken offense. "And you, what will you do today?"

"I am going to visit my brother Yaakov. And then, of course, I will help Katya prepare dinner for Ida and her Michel."

"Her Michel," he repeated, tainting the words with his contempt.

He watched from the window as she walked toward the avenue, moved as always by her grace and her fragility. He had not asked why she had decided to visit her Orthodox brother. He did not want to know.

Yaakov Rosenfeld welcomed his sister into his shabby apartment on the rue des Rosiers. It was redolent with the remembered odors of her childhood, onions and potatoes frying in rendered chicken fat, meat simmering in a pot of boiling borscht, pirogen browning in her sister-in-law's small oven. Marc would have been repelled by the aroma, but Bella found it comforting. It transported her back to her childhood in Vitebsk, to the memory of her girlhood as the pampered daughter of a wealthy jeweler whose meals were prepared by the family's cook.

Yaakov's wife, Hinde, bustled in with a pot of tea and the almond horns she had baked using her mother-in-law's recipe and then left brother and sister alone.

Bella and Yaakov sat in companionable silence, the taste of their mother's pastry sweet upon their tongues. Bella glanced about the room, her eyes resting on the bookshelves filled with Yaakov's Talmudic and medical texts. He had filled the crates with his library, leaving behind in Russia the sterling silver tea service and place settings. Pious Hinde had not objected. Her husband's books were more important than her silver.

Yaakov filled their glasses with tea and tucked a sugar cube beneath his tongue. He took a sip and turned to his sister. Her visit was unusual. The Chagalls ventured into Le Marais only for the Passover seder and the kindling of the Hanukkah candles.

"What is it, Bella?" he asked gently.

He had noticed at once the pallor of her skin, the trembling of her hands. It had been Bella's way, from earliest childhood, to retreat into illness at the onset of any disappointment, any difficulty.

"It is Ida," she said.

"Ida." He sucked on the sugar cube and waited.

"She's pregnant."

Tears streaked her cheeks, and he took his frayed white handkerchief, wiped her eyes, and waited yet again.

"Who is the father?" he asked at last.

"His name is Michel Rapaport. He's a law student. Jewish. His parents are Russian. He is twenty years old."

Yaakov sighed. "They are young. Very young," he said sadly. "I understand how upset you are. Still, they are not the first young couple to find themselves in such a predicament. Arrangements can be made. There are choices."

"Marc says there is no choice. He says that Ida must have an abortion."

Bella fingered her necklace, rose from her chair, and wandered over to the window. School had just let out, and the rue des Rosiers was crowded with children. Two young mothers pushing prams, baguettes tucked beneath their arms, chatted with each other. *Were they older than Ida, younger than Ida?* Bella wondered. The irrelevance of the question shamed her. She shrugged and turned to her brother.

"Ida's choice is more important than Marc's. What does Ida want?" he asked softly.

"She says—oh, Yaakov—she says she wants to die. Last night she had a nightmare, and the night before as well. She dreams of death. She does not sleep. She barely eats."

"Then she must not have this baby," he said gravely. "The Talmud forbids it."

"The Talmud?" she asked incredulously.

She sank back into her chair as Yaakov surveyed his bookshelves, plucked out an oversized volume, and flipped the pages until he found a particular text.

"Here is the ruling," he said. "The rabbis discuss a pursuer, which in Hebrew is called a *rodef.* If a pursuer, a *rodef,* threatens someone's life, then it is permissible to kill the threatener. Such an act would not be called murder but would be considered to be an act of self-defense. By extension, if a pregnant woman's health is threatened, either her mental health or her physical health, then the fetus is construed to be a *rodef* and may be aborted to save the pregnant woman's life. You say that Ida is making herself ill, not eating and not sleeping, that she speaks of wanting to die. Her life is indeed in danger. The child she carries is therefore a *rodef.* It must be done away with, aborted."

Bella stared down at the text that she could not read. Her heart beat rapidly, and her cheeks were flushed.

"You have heard of such a situation before, Yaakov?" she asked.

He nodded. "Do you remember Malka Feinstein from Vitebsk?"

"Yes. The fishmonger's daughter."

"You were too young to know the entire story. But the poor girl was unmarried and she became pregnant. Some said the father was a Russian peasant who raped her; others said it was a yeshiva student who took meals at her parents' home. No matter. She was pregnant and ill with shame and grief. She wept, spoke of taking her own life. She wandered the streets barefoot and half dressed. She plunged into the Dvina River and was rescued by a passing schoolboy. Clearly, she was descending into madness. Her parents went to a rabbinic court and it was ruled that the child she was carrying was a *rodef*. She had an abortion." He tapped his spoon against his glass and sighed.

"What happened to this Malka?" Bella asked. She remembered her vaguely, a slight girl with watery blue eyes and lank hair the color of straw; the piscine odor of her father's shop seemed to cling to her tattered dresses.

"She married. I believe her husband was the same yeshiva student rumored to be the father. They went to America. If, in fact, he was the father of that child, the rabbis may have considered them to be already married. Some rabbis rule that sexual intimacy, the very act of intercourse, is the equivalent of marriage."

He looked at his sister, her chiseled, delicate features a mask of sadness, tendrils of her gleaming dark hair escaping her black velvet cloche, and he was overcome with pity. He knew that it was not easy to be the wife of the great Marc Chagall, nor was it easy to be the artist's daughter. He thought of his niece Ida, so beautiful, so vibrant, so naive, and grieved for her.

When Bella rose to leave, Yaakov took her hand and pressed it to his lips. "You will do what is right," he said. "Of that I am sure."

"Thank you, Yaakov," she said, her voice so faint that he had to strain to hear her.

She left then, closing the heavy front door quietly behind her. The autumn day was warm, and she lifted her face to the gentle cooling breeze. Her decision was made. She paused at a very expensive patisserie and bought a selection of gâteaux, choosing the napoleons that Marc particularly liked. She knew his weakness. She would cajole him with sweetness.

Chapter Eight

ella set the dinner table with great care, using the white linen cloth and the heavy silver cutlery, reminiscent of that of her childhood home, purchased with the proceeds from Marc's gouache illustrations of La Fontaine's *Fables*. She set a crystal vase filled with the last white roses of the season on the table and then swiftly removed the pristine flowers and replaced them with a bouquet of purple irises. This was not a night for white roses.

Marc dressed carefully, selecting a burgundy velvet jacket and cream-colored trousers, looping a white satin ascot about his neck. Bella, in her simple black dress of the softest wool, watched as he studied himself in the mirror, as he brushed his thick, silver-tinged, curling hair and pinched his cheeks sharply to add color.

In his youth, Marc had rouged his cheeks and lips. Always his preening, his fascination with his own reflection, had amused her, although it had distressed her parents. They had not understood that he saw everything—his clothing, the decor of his surroundings—with the artist's eye, that demanded color and drama.

He followed her into the dining room, surveyed the beautifully set table, and removed a drooping iris from the vase.

"All this to impress the son of a shopkeeper?" he asked sarcastically.

She arranged her paisley shawl into graceful folds and ignored the question, setting four small glasses on a tray and filling them with vodka. Marc lifted one to his lips.

"*L'chaim*. To life," he said, then downed the drink just as the door opened and Ida and Michel came into the room.

"Are you drinking to life then, *Papochka*?" Ida asked dryly and kissed him on both cheeks.

The irony of her question caused him to flush, and it was Bella who replied, even as she held her hands out to Michel.

"But of course we are drinking to life. It is the toast of our people. Welcome, Michel."

He smiled nervously, and she liked him for his unease.

"I am pleased to be here. I thank you for your invitation, Madame Chagall, Monsieur Chagall," he said politely and held out the bottle of *vin ordinaire* his parents had insisted that he bring. Marc accepted it, stared at the label, and frowned.

Bella set it on the sideboard. "We have already decanted wine for this evening," she said apologetically, and he understood that his gift was rejected.

Ida moved closer to Michel. She knew how he had feared meeting her parents. He had told her, as they walked toward the Bois de Boulogne, that he would offer no excuses but would accept all responsibility. She admired his courage and thought that he looked very handsome in the dark suit and white shirt his mother had pressed with great care. Her amber-skinned lover of summer days and starry nights was restored to her. She handed him a glass of vodka, held out another to her mother, and lifted her own drink. Marc refilled his glass.

"*L'chaim*," Ida echoed her father, her voice firm. "To life."

They nodded and drank without pleasure.

They sat at the table, their conversation stilted and awkward. Michel admired the flowers. Marc asked what newspapers Michel read. Bella refilled the bread basket. Their spoons clinked against the soup bowls. The salt was politely passed. Ida said nothing and ate nothing, moving the food about on her plate.

Katya drifted in and out of the room with serving dishes. They spoke Russian as she circled the table. They were complicit in their reticence, at one in the mutuality of their unease. They ate the excellent coq au vin without comment, speared the asparagus, and toyed with the salad. It was only after Katya placed the platter of gâteaux on the table and left the room that Bella turned to Michel and spoke to him in a soothing maternal tone. There would be no blame, no anger.

"Michel, of course you know that Ida has told us of her condition."

He nodded.

Marc plucked a napoleon from the platter, licked a trace of cream from his finger, and frowned. "We assume that neither of you wants this pregnancy to progress," he said before Bella could say anything else.

His voice was cold, matter-of-fact. Ida stared at him in surprise. She had anticipated his anger, even his fury. She had not imagined this distancing, nor the frigidity that turned her father's eyes into slivers of blue ice.

"That is correct. Ida and I are in agreement about that," Michel replied. "We care for each other, but we recognize that we are young, that having a child at this point in our lives would be a mistake."

Bella breathed a sigh of relief. "Then we know what must be done," she said. She reached for Ida's hand and stroked it gently.

Ida pulled away. Her mother's comforting touch had come too late. "Yes. We too know what must be done, *Maman*," she said.

"Very well. We must find a competent doctor. A good clinic," Marc said. "It must be in a convenient location. There is such a well-reputed place in Neuilly."

Ida stared at him, startled by his dispassion. He spoke of finding a competent doctor, a convenient location, as he might speak of finding a skilled framer or a convenient art supply shop. He had not met her eyes, had not reached out to comfort her, not with a touch, not with a caress. Was this the father who had so adored her, who had chronicled her life in painting and drawing? Did she fill him with a shame so deep that he could not bear to look at her? She turned away.

"We know of that clinic," she said curtly, her voice suddenly strong, invigorated by her hurt and anger. "My friend Elsa, who is a doctor herself, will make the arrangements. Neuilly is very conveniently located," she added sarcastically. "I will not be registered as Ida Chagall so our sacred name will be protected. Elsa will obtain a false *carte d'identité* for me. She will see to everything. My so-called condition, as you and *Maman* refer to it, will be resolved within the week, and no one will be the wiser, if that is what you fear."

Marc nodded. Bella sighed.

"Of course, these arrangements will be expensive," Ida added with malicious pleasure.

"It is my responsibility. It is I who should pay," Michel interposed, his voice heavy with misery.

Ida stared at him, surprised and pleased. How good he was, how responsible.

Michel leaned back in his chair. The impact of his words dizzied him. The amount needed was overwhelming. He and his parents had discussed it. His mother had made tentative suggestions. There was a wealthy uncle, a family friend who frequented the Bourse with great success, a Jewish loan society.

"No, Michel," Bella said. "Ida is our daughter. We will assume the responsibility."

Marc clenched and unclenched his fists, but he did not disagree. When he spoke, his tone was calm but cold. "I see that you are a young man of integrity, Michel, but we would not want to burden your family with such an expense. Still, your offer tells us that you will be a good and responsible husband to our Ida. You can be married within a month. Ida will be fully recovered, and it will still be warm in Yvelines. It would be preferable not to have the wedding in Paris. Perhaps it will still be warm enough to have the ceremony in the garden."

Ida stared at her father, her eyes flashing with anger, her face flushed with disbelief.

"Married? Wedding? What are you talking about? If the pregnancy is terminated, surely there is no need for us to marry. We love each other, yes, but we want to wait. At least until Michel's studies are completed, I am older, and we both know how we want to live our lives."

She gripped her mother's hand. Surely Bella would protect her from such unreasonableness. Surely she would acknowledge the absurdity of the suggestion.

But Bella only nodded her assent. "Of course you must marry," she said quietly. "You and Michel have been together. You have shared intimacy as man and wife. My brother Yaakov says that according to some rabbinic laws, you are already married. The community will demand it."

"*Maman*, have you gone mad? Rabbinic law? What do you care about rabbinic law? This is Paris in the twentieth century. What community? We have no community. We do not even go to synagogue. Has a rabbi ever been a guest in our home? How can this nonexistent community demand anything at all of us? And if it did exist, what would give them the right to tell us how we must live?" she shouted. "Michel, can you believe what they are saying?"

Michel shook his head helplessly. His parents had also spoken of marriage. The Chagalls' words had echoed those of his father. Michel and Ida had known each other in the biblical sense; their bodies had merged, and his seed had been poured into her womb. In the tradition of Abraham and Sarah, of Isaac and Rebecca, in adherence to the conventional values of their Russian Jewish community, it was incumbent upon them to marry.

"But who will know if we do not?" Michel had asked.

"You will know," his mother had replied in a broken voice. "And we will know. And this is a small community. People whisper. Rumors travel. Already there is talk. Those who were with you and Ida Chagall at the encampment have spoken of it."

He had not argued with them, recognizing the sacrifices they had made for him, the nuggets of truth in their argument. He and Ida were young. They had their whole lives before them. It was only right that they assuage their refugee parents' desperate hunger for respectability. Obedience was demanded of them. And they did, after all, love each other. They would surely marry in a few years' time. So why not now when it would bring solace to their parents, his as well as hers? When they could be together, live together, openly and honestly?

He placed his hand on Ida's quivering shoulders, buried his face in her bright hair, indifferent to her parents' presence. "I love you, *ma chérie*. I love you with all my heart."

His words were an acknowledgment of his quiescence and, she thought angrily, of his weakness. But she would not be so easily swayed. She broke free of his embrace and glared at Marc and Bella. She was not defeated.

"And if I refuse to marry? If I tell you that I want to wait until Michel finishes his studies, until I myself have decided how I want to live my life, what then?" she asked defiantly. "Will you disown me or will I disown you?"

Michel pressed his hand to her cheek, but she ignored him and did not avert her gaze from her father, who was pale with anger. When he spoke, his tone matched her own, anger for anger, threat for threat.

"If you refuse to marry, I will not pay for the *avortement*. If you refuse to marry, you will no longer be a daughter of this house. You will have to support yourself. This will no longer be your home."

Their eyes locked. They were pitted against each other in a battle they both would lose. Ida choked back the words she could not say. She wanted to tell him that she did not need his help, his money, that she would support herself. That she would find herself another home. But even in her anger, she recognized the absurdity of such words. What would she do? Could she become a waitress, a sales clerk, an artist's model? She remembered Yvette's dismissive words about the slovenly woman who posed in the nude for their class. "What choices did she have?" Yvette had asked. And what choices did she, Ida Chagall, have? She was no different from the model. She had no education, no skills. Nothing had prepared her for an independent life.

"You must decide, Ida," Marc said. He rose suddenly, his face very pale, and left the room, slamming the door behind him.

Bella turned to Michel. "Speak to *your* Ida. Reason with her," she pleaded, her own claim to her daughter relinquished.

She retreated into the kitchen. Minutes later, they heard her speaking harshly to Katya. A dish had been broken, a pot burned. These small domestic disturbances mitigated the focus of her grief. She had no power over Marc, no power over Ida, but in her kitchen, she had absolute domain.

Ida and Michel sat in silence at the table. Ida lifted a flower from the vase and ripped the blossom apart, scattering the purple petals across the white cloth.

"What can we do? What can we do, Michel?" she asked plaintively.

"We have very little choice. No choice. We will marry. It is the right thing to do. We love each other. We love our parents. We don't want to hurt them," he replied gravely.

"Yes," she parroted back. "We love each other. We love our parents."

The anger, the disappointment in her voice, terrified him. He trembled and wondered how he might comfort her. Gently, tentatively, he drew her close.

"Ida, my Ida," he said softly.

Defeated, she rested her head on his shoulder. Drained of anger, drained of certitude, the passion of her protest spent, she allowed him to gently, rhythmically stroke her hair, then bury his face on the soft pillow of her too tender breasts.

Chapter Nine

The days passed slowly, the weeks too swiftly. Ida returned from the Neuilly clinic to convalesce in her parents' home. She drifted sadly and reluctantly back into health, a lethargic bride-to-be barely participating in the frenetic prewedding activities of the household. There were arrangements to be made, a wedding dress to be fitted, caterers to be contacted. There was the journey to Montchauvet laden with suitcases and parcels, the readying of the house and garden for the hastily arranged marriage that would nevertheless be tastefully celebrated. The bride, after all, was the only daughter of Marc and Bella Chagall.

Ida woke on the morning of her wedding day and was perversely pleased that although there had been a glorious autumn, a storm threatened. Gray clouds drifted through the darkening sky. Sudden winds rattled the branches of the trees, and brittle leaves danced across the sere earth of the garden. She turned away from the window and tried, without success, to will herself back to sleep.

Despite the weather, an ambience of subdued excitement prevailed in the salon where the reception would be held. Bella rushed in and out of the room. She adjusted the white cloth that covered the buffet table on which rows of crystal champagne flutes sparkled and then aligned the platters of artfully arranged artisan cheeses, fresh fruit, and elegant pastries.

"Katya, we need more spoons, more cake plates," she called and glanced nervously at her watch. The flowers had not yet been delivered, and the musicians were late.

She sighed with relief as the florist and his assistant arrived, their arms laden with roses. They filled every vase and bowl with the full-petaled blossoms whose fragrance permeated the house. She herself arranged ferns and pale yellow buds in the copper bowl at the entry and stepped back to study the effect. It was perfect, she decided. Marc would be pleased.

"We have the bride's bouquet, madame. Where shall we put it?" the young assistant asked.

She took the spray of white roses from him. Marc himself had designed the bouquet, sketching it for the florist who had faithfully adhered to it. Buds and full-blown blooms alternated with greenery and baby's breath, all held together with a narrow white satin ribbon. Bella held the bouquet to her face, felt the moist brush of the soft petals, inhaled its fragrance, and set it down.

There was a timid knock at the door. Katya rushed to open it, and the klezmer musicians, a pale violinist and an elderly flautist, entered shyly. They doffed their caps, gratefully drank the coffee Katya offered them, set up their music stands, and immediately launched into a rehearsal of their repertoire. They played the poignant wedding tunes of eastern Europe, the melodies now mournful, now joyous, pausing to correct false notes, to substitute one piece for another, speaking softly in Yiddish.

Bella wandered onto the veranda, leaned against the lemon tree, bereft of its golden fruit, and listened, transported back to the distant day of her own marriage in her parents' garden. She remembered the brightness of the summer sky, the gaiety of the guests, the joyous dancing to the music played by a full band of klezmer musicians. How festive that day had been, how full of excitement and optimism. She had thought herself a fairy princess in her long white gown, her gossamer veil trailing after her as she moved, escorted by a coterie of her laughing friends, to her seat of honor on the bridal throne, which had been carried from the synagogue to a place of pride in her parents' garden. A red velvet cushion covered its seat, and its dark wooden arms had been worn thin by the touch of so many Vitebsk brides, all of whom had surely felt like fairy princesses on their wedding days. Ida's own bridal throne was makeshift, a chair plucked from their dining room suite and covered with a white sheet. It was bereft of history and tradition.

Bella sighed and fingered the intricately tatted white lace cuff of her green velvet dress. It saddened her that on this, her wedding day, her Ida would not feel like a fairy princess. She stared up at her daughter's room, oddly grateful that Ida, in all probability, was still asleep. Katya had carried up her breakfast tray and left it outside the door when her knock was ignored.

"I would not wake her," the maid had said primly. "A bride needs her sleep."

"Of course," Bella agreed. "A bride surely needs her sleep."

But Ida had slept very little. Lying abed, she waited for Katya to leave and then opened the door and carried the tray into her room. She stood at the open window in her dressing gown, sipped the coffee, and stared down at the garden. She watched her mother bend to pluck up a single wizened lemon. Bella sniffed at the fruit and then, with girlish grace, lifted her arm high and tossed it into the distant foliage.

Ida smiled. The graceful gesture was familiar, reminiscent of the games of her childhood, when she and Bella had sent brightly colored balls soaring through the air. They had been playmates then, mother and daughter, friends who giggled mischievously at secret jokes and played house in their own kitchen even as they cooked real meals. Content within their insularity, their lives had revolved around each other and around Marc, the father and husband, who ruled their enchanted world. They were an isolated, symbiotic trio then, a small family who delighted in their exclusive closeness and reveled in the admiration of all who knew them.

Until.

The single word hung heavily, the fragmented beginning of a sentence to be hesitantly and painfully completed. *Until* she had revealed her pregnancy to them. *Until* they had made their arbitrary demand that she marry. *Until* they had declined to accompany her to the clinic at Neuilly, her mother pleading illness, her father insisting that he had to complete a commissioned canvas.

Until she had returned home, weary and weakened, accompanied by Michel and Elsa, who had remained with her throughout the ordeal.

Their silence afterward had been mutual. Bella and Marc had asked no questions, and she had not told them of her feelings of abandonment as she lay in the sterile white operating room, nor had she spoken of the pain that had overwhelmed her during the procedure.

"Mamochka, Maman, Mamele," she had screamed in all the languages of her despair, but there had been no comforting, caring maternal reply. She lay very still in the recovery room and felt that her vitality, the buoyant exuberance that had always energized her, had been suctioned away even as those unwanted embryonic cells had been aspirated from her womb. Her only comfort had been Elsa's reassuring words in the aftermath of her pain.

"You will never have to endure this again, Ida," her friend had said. "You will take control over your body. You will become pregnant only when you have decided to have a child."

"But how will I do that?" Ida had asked, her voice quivering.

"There is something called a Dutch cap, a small rubber cap. You slide it in before intercourse and it prevents the sperm from reaching the ovum. We are living in the twentieth century. We are fortunate, Ida. Women now have control over their bodies, over their futures."

That Dutch cap was hidden among her negligees. She had not told her mother about it. Bella had rescinded her right to her trust and shattered the wondrous security of her childhood.

Still, watching her mother move through the garden, she was overcome with sadness and regret. She pressed her face against the cold windowpane and acknowledged that she wanted to reclaim her parents' affection, to offer them her own. Michel, a faithful son himself, had urged forgiveness and reconciliation.

"They are still your parents. You are still their daughter," he had insisted.

He was right, she knew. She would have to accept them with a renewed understanding of their strengths and weaknesses and of her own. Their fractured togetherness could be repaired. Within hours, they would escort her to the marriage canopy, her girlhood ended, her new life launched. Ida Chagall would become Ida Rapaport, but always and forever, she would be her parents' daughter.

"I am Ida Chagall," she said aloud, reclaiming her place in their life. "*Mamochka. Papochka. Ma mère. Mon père. Je suis votre fille.*" The very words comforted her, cauterizing a gaping emotional wound.

She remained at the window as her father emerged from his studio, carrying a painting. Holding it tenderly, he showed it to her mother who bent her head to study it. How beautiful and vulnerable they appeared to her, both of them so slender, so fragile of form and feature, their faces brushed by the pale autumnal sunlight. Marc stepped back and lifted the painting so that Bella might view it from another perspective.

Ida was seized with an urgent desire to see it for herself. It was, she knew, his wedding gift to her. He had worked on it night after night, often missing dinner. Bella had carried his meals out to his studio. "Your father wants this painting finished for your wedding day," she had said.

Ida, still weak and enervated, still wrapped in resentment, had not replied, nor had she entered the studio to view the work in progress. But that resentment, that anger, had dissipated. Watching her parents enter the house, the painting balanced between them, she felt a surge of love, commingled with compassion. She would forgive them. She had to forgive them. Her life, and now Michel's, was inextricably bound up in theirs. She banished the litany of *untils*. They would once again be reunited, a family scarred but intact.

There was a light knock at the door.

"Ida, may I come in? May I help you dress?"

"Of course, *Maman*. But first I want to see Papa's painting," she said.

She opened the door and kissed Bella's cheek, and together they went into the salon. Marc had placed the painting on a wooden stand beside the bridal chair. It was a faithful rendition of that very chair on which Ida would be seated as she greeted her guests and welcomed her groom.

"It's a beautiful painting, isn't it, Idotchka?" Bella asked.

Ida nodded and knelt so that she might study it more carefully.

Marc had painted the intimate interior of their own salon, dominated by the empty chair shrouded in a stark white covering, a spray of white roses tossed carelessly across the cushioned seat. She saw that the bouquet of fresh flowers placed on the actual chair exactly matched the flowers in the painting. She marveled at her father's attention to detail. He was a fantasist who did not deny reality.

His brush had captured every detail of the room, decorated for the wedding. White roses filled the vases and urns flanking the bridal throne, and candelabra stood on a small table covered with an ivory-colored cloth. He had painted a flickering white memorial candle, an imagined object that gave deference to the dead, the ghostly, vanished grandparents Ida would never know. There was a fringed pink carpet in front of the chair, a small relief from the theme of white upon white upon white. The absent bride, the vacant chair, the monochromatic flowers might have been melancholic had Marc not added a painting that hung on the wall above the table. The painting within the painting was a miniature re-creation of his own work *The Birthday*, his gift to Bella in celebration of their own marriage. Bursting with zest and movement, humor and grace, it depicted an airborne acrobatic lover, his face fused with that of his beloved standing on tiptoe and grasping a bouquet of flowers.

Ida knew that painting well. It had always made her smile, and she smiled now. It was a graphic promise of a kind, her father's wishful assurance that the exuberance of the birthday lovers would be replicated in her life with Michel. *As it might well be*, she told herself. Their marriage was reluctant, but it was not loveless.

"Do you like it, my Ida?"

Marc had entered the room so quietly that she had not been aware of his presence. She turned, smiled, and lifted her hand reassuringly to his anxious face. The tensions between them receded.

They had been mutually disappointed and they were mutually reconciled. Wounds remained, but they would be healed. Standing beside him, the lassitude of the preceding weeks faded, and she felt herself restored and reinvigorated.

"I love it, *Papochka*," she said. "And now I must get dressed. Come, *Maman*."

Together, Ida and Bella left the room. Marc remained. He stared hard at the painting as though viewing it for the very first time. It was his best work, he knew, and yet he was overcome with sadness as he looked at it. His daughter, his Ida, was absent from it as she would now and forever after be absent from their home. But he had not lost her. He would not lose her. That was a loss that he could not bear.

Ida was a radiant bride. Her upswept hair was a coppery coronet to which Bella had affixed a gossamer veil. Her rose-gold skin was aglow, and the white satin wedding gown hugged her full figure. Enthroned on the bridal chair, the bouquet resting on her lap, she smiled at the guests who approached to greet her and wish her well as the klezmer musicians played softly in the background.

Her parents stood beside her, Bella, her black hair a sleek cap, elegant in her signature green velvet gown, and Marc in his high-collared, brown linen jacket and flared trousers, not unlike the uniform of the Soviet Commissar that had been his uniform during the heady days of the revolution, that vanished time before hope turned into despair. A high, brightly colored skullcap was perched on his thick graying curls. He was a swift and lively satyr, his movements both frenetic and graceful, his blue eyes glittering gimlets in his narrow face.

Michel's diminutive sad-eyed parents, his father's black suit frayed at the lapels, his mother's well-pressed silk dress as gray as her hair, smiled shyly. The prominence of the Chagalls, the beauty of their home, intimidated them. Their son had been catapulted into a new and unfamiliar world. They approached the bridal chair tentatively, extended their hands to Ida and her parents, and retreated into a corner with two elderly cousins.

Only a small group of friends had been invited to the wedding. Ida was relieved and grateful that Elsa and André had made the journey. Elsa smiled at her encouragingly, and she smiled back. Theirs was a friendship soldered in affection and complicity.

Henri Matisse stroked his silver goatee and kissed Ida's hand. She had long been his favorite, a laughing mischievous child grown into a beautiful and vibrant young woman. He studied Marc's painting and nodded approvingly.

"A wonderful work," he said. "A pity you did not pose for it, Ida. Perhaps that would have been considered bad luck in your religion. It's true, isn't it, that Jews are prohibited from creating images?"

"But you must realize, *cher maître*, that my father has never observed that prohibition," Ida replied with a sweetness she did not feel. It irritated her that Matisse, so long a friend of their family, still saw them as the "other." In his eyes, Marc would always be a Jew, born into an alien tradition.

Other friends approached to offer their good wishes and then to study the painting of the bridal chair before claiming the seats that faced the marriage canopy. They sat in expectant silence, an attentive audience, anticipating an interesting and unfamiliar performance. Edmond Fleg, the Yiddish poet, watched them resentfully.

"Judaism as theater," he murmured to Joseph Opatoshu, the novelist who was Marc's closest friend.

The klezmer musicians altered the tempo of the music and played the wild joyous tune that signaled the bridegroom's approach. Bella swiftly drew the veil over Ida's face, and then Michel stood before her, tall and grave-eyed, his thick dark hair brushed back from his high forehead. Unlike Ida, he was pale, but that pallor faded when he smiled. Ida's smile beneath her veil matched his own. He bent and lifted the veil so that he might see her face. He nodded, signifying that this indeed was the bride that had been promised to him.

He stared down at his Ida, who had danced barefoot beside him on an alpine hillside, the fiery-haired, laughing girl with whom he had fallen in love in the season of sunlight. Tenderly, he lowered the veil and accompanied his parents to await her beneath the wedding canopy. The musicians played even louder, and the guests clapped their hands excitedly.

Then once again, the music was muted. Only the flautist played a haunting melody as Ida rose from her seat and, supported on either side by her parents, glided toward her groom.

The ceremony was swift. The bearded rabbi had been warned not to prolong it, and he intoned the benedictions, proffered the sacramental wine, and lifted the plain gold wedding band high, so that the witnesses might examine it for any break in the metal. A marriage ring had to be as unflawed as the match itself. A smile wreathed Michel's face as he held Ida's hand in his own and repeated the ancient vow.

"Behold, with this ring, you are consecrated unto me according to the laws of Moses and of Israel." His voice rang loud and clear. There was an outbreak of applause and excited shouts of *"Bonne chance!"* and *"Mazel tov!"*

The musicians played a fiercely joyous tune as Michel's foot stamped heavily on the glass, which shattered into glittering shards. Still playing, exhilarated by their own music, flautist and violinist danced away, preceding the newly married couple who threaded their way through the excited guests.

The music resonated throughout the reception. Marc and Bella danced an elegant waltz and, surprisingly, Michel's parents joined them, moving across the floor with dignified grace. Michel and Ida linked hands with Elsa and André in a lively dabke and were soon joined by other dancers. The joy was contagious. Even Katya was pulled into a wild hora as stomping men and light-footed women circled the room. Marc seized his daughter's hands and they whirled about in rhythmic abandonment, Ida's bright hair spilling loose and whipping tongues of flame about her shoulders. Michel thrust forward and rescued his bride from her father. They danced with abandon, bride and groom, now husband and wife, as the musicians played feverishly, their faces damp with perspiration, their eyes bright with excitement.

Bella stood beside her brother Yaakov, who handed her a flute of champagne. They watched the dancing couple.

"Oh, Yaakov," she murmured. "Did we do the right thing?"

"What's done is done," he replied. "Your daughter is married. *Mazel tov*, Berthe."

She smiled. He had called her by the name of their shared childhood, the name given to her by their absent parents. It reminded her that she was and forever would be a daughter of her people, submissive to the values and traditions of that vanished world.

"*L'chaim*," Yaakov said. "To life.

"*L'chaim*," she repeated.

"To Ida."

"To Ida. To Ida and Michel."

Bella sipped the wine, relishing its sweetness and the comforting pressure of her brother's arm upon her shoulder.

Chapter Ten

*I*da, wrapped in the white cape borrowed from her mother, stood on London Bridge, hypnotized by the blazing lights that streaked across the steel-gray sky and rocketed down onto the dark waters of the Thames. The radiance of the descending fireworks danced across the river in a confluence of brightness. Flashes of flaming orange mingled with the golden hue of the imperial crown of the United Kingdom. Brilliant blues collided with ribbons of scarlet and glittering white stars, the colors of the Union Jack, as they jetted across the gentle waves. The crowd cheered wildly, waved paper flags, and tooted their tin horns as they celebrated the twenty-fifth anniversary of their king's reign.

"I've never seen anything so lovely," she said breathlessly, her face bright with excitement.

Her hostess in London, Lady Clerk (pronounced Clark), smiled benevolently and twirled her lorgnette. The aristocratic Englishwoman, who had become an intimate of the Chagall family when her husband served as ambassador in Paris, was amused by Ida's naive excitement. Chagall's daughter was so young, actually, an adolescent although she had been married for a year. But then perhaps Jews were accustomed to such young marriages, although the Chagalls were not typical Jews.

Lady Clerk, an aspiring artist, was grateful to Marc Chagall, who had so generously allowed her to work in his studio and study his techniques. She had argued against his decision to send Ida to represent him at his first London exhibition at the prestigious Leicester Gallery. Ida, she had predicted, would have difficulty coping with the ingrained snobbery of the London art world. It was understood that she was talking about anti-Semitism, but by tacit agreement, that inference remained unspoken.

"Won't Ida miss her young husband?" Lady Clerk had asked. "And is she experienced enough to negotiate with the collectors and curators interested in purchasing your paintings?"

Marc Chagall remained impervious to her arguments. "Her husband is involved in his studies. And I do not worry about Ida's lack of experience. She is a capable young woman," Marc had replied. "I can rely on her. My wife's frailty at this time prevents me from going to London myself, but I will trust everything to Ida and, of course, to your kind self."

He had smiled his seductive impish smile, and Lady Clerk, who was both his painting student and his acolyte, had at last assented. Few people could resist his charm. And it was well known that Bella Chagall's health was fragile. There were those who said she had grown despondent when her daughter married, and her frequent illnesses, headaches, and mysterious intestinal disorders were symptoms of that depression. It was rumored that she remained at home, wandering aimlessly from room to room, often remaining in peignoir and negligee throughout the day.

Depression was a new word in the lexicon of Left Bank artists and writers. They spoke knowingly of the new theories being promulgated by the Austrian psychiatrist, Sigmund Freud, who claimed that physical illness often sublimated emotional distress. *Sublimation*, they repeated and speculated about the efficacy of psychoanalysis, the new talking cure.

"Bella Chagall is a *malade imaginaire*," Dora Maar, Picasso's mistress, maliciously repeated to Lady Clerk. Dora Maar herself suffered a nervous breakdown only weeks later.

There were those who speculated that Bella's melancholy was a result of the frightening news emanating from Germany and Russia where she had friends and family who were almost certainly in danger. Stalin had launched his reign of terror, and Hitler's threats had escalated into ominous reality. The Chagalls' friends were already leaving Paris. The Opatoshus were in New York, and they wrote urging Marc and Bella to join them.

"I could never leave Europe," Bella wrote in reply. "If I leave Paris, I will die."

She surrendered to her sadness and no longer dealt with either the management of the household or the sales of Marc's paintings, passing those obligations to Ida. The acrimony that had preceded Ida's marriage was forgotten. She was, once again, regnant in her parents' household, a role that Michel accepted in silent resignation.

Ida was happy to be swept up into her parents' orbit, to return to the exciting world from which she had been exiled when she married. She loved Michel (*of course I do*, she told herself repeatedly), but she was bored with her life as the wife of a student, impatient with her own efforts at drawing and painting. Her studio classes were uninspiring, her domestic chores boring. Cooking alone in her cramped kitchen, without her mother's daring experiments with spices and exotic ingredients, was a desultory affair.

She was relieved to be restored to her role as her mother's comforter, her father's charming consort. She accompanied him to the dealers' galleries and the cafés of the Left Bank where she basked in the admiring gazes of the artists and poets who sat for hours over glasses of milky absinthe. Her marriage did not diminish her pleasure in their recognition of her vivacity, her tantalizing sensuality.

She charmed visitors to Marc's studio, smiled enticingly at collectors, spoke knowingly of the value of each painting. When her father suggested the trip to London, she had agreed enthusiastically, and Lady Clerk had at last been seduced by her eagerness.

"We will be happy to host her, but does her young husband agree?" the Englishwoman had asked Marc.

"Michel has his studies and other obligations. He knows that Ida looks forward to visiting London. There is no need to worry about Michel Rapaport."

The astute diplomat's wife understood that his son-in-law's reaction was of little interest to Marc Chagall. His only concerns were for his work, his wife, and his daughter. It was fortunate, Lady Clerk thought, as she drew up a guest list for the welcoming dinner at her

Belgravia home, that auburn-haired, fair-complexioned Ida did not look especially Semitic. She was tolerant of Jews, but she knew that many of her set had ill-concealed prejudices. And, of course, Ida was extremely personable. It was possible, after all, that despite her youth and inexperience, she would manage.

And Ida not only managed but did so exceedingly well. She had swiftly conquered London society with her vibrancy and charm. Royals and artists alike, the intellectuals of Bloomsbury, and the curators of major museums admired the beautiful, stylish nineteen-year-old who smiled with engaging sweetness and conversed with ease in German and Russian, English and French.

She had, with authority, perception, and an eye to space and lighting, supervised the hanging of her father's paintings in the Leicester Gallery. She negotiated with collectors with astonishing shrewdness and spoke knowledgeably with the art critic of the *Times*.

She enchanted London and London enchanted her. Lady Clerk was amused that in Covent Garden, Ida had clapped as enthusiastically as the smallest children at the jugglers and clowns who entertained the crowds, and so she was unsurprised that Ida viewed the fireworks display from London Bridge with childlike awe.

"It's wonderful that King George's Silver Jubilee coincided with your father's exhibition," Lady Clerk said. "This is a happy time for England."

"I know. I can feel it," Ida agreed. "It's such a relief to be gay after all the gloom and doom one feels in Paris."

"Oh, Paris never stays gloomy for long. After all, it is the City of Light," Lady Clerk said dismissively as she linked her arm through Ida's. They left the bridge and strolled along the embankment toward Guildhall, where the king himself would receive the invited guests.

"This has been a very difficult year for France," Ida said carefully. "The Bourse has been so unstable. One day the prices of stocks are up, and the next day they are down. The failure of the American stock exchange should be a warning that the City of Light may go dark very quickly."

"Ida, *ma petite*, I'm surprised that you concern yourself with financial affairs," Lady Clerk said reprovingly. She thought it unseemly for women to concern themselves with such matters. Why should women bother with the boring trivia of the marketplace? The fluctuations of sterling and dollars, francs and marks, the rise and fall of international exchanges, were the precincts of men. She had never understood the suffragettes' struggle for the franchise. She herself never even bothered to vote.

"Ida, my dear," she added gently, "why should you bother about interest rates and bank offerings?"

"Someone in my family must," Ida replied. "My father paints and my mother is disinterested, so I must manage the sale of his work and our family's finances. It is important that we be very careful. We are living in dangerous times. Germany is in the power of a dangerous man."

"My husband assures me that things will soon get better," Lady Clerk protested. "The world does not want another war. Our Anthony Eden and your own Pierre Laval are working hard to appease Mr. Hitler."

Lady Clerk grimaced as she spoke the name of the odious Austrian. He was such a vile little man. But surely the nation of Goethe and Schiller, of Bach and Beethoven, would not tolerate him much longer.

"Monsieur Laval has done nothing to censor the Croix de Feu," Ida said carefully.

It was not her place to offer political instruction to her hostess, whose husband moved in the highest diplomatic circles. Still the headlines of that day's London *Times* had frightened her. The Croix de Feu, an organization with blatant fascist sympathies, had had the temerity to hold a rally at the Eiffel Tower to celebrate the passage of the Nuremberg Laws, which placed draconian restrictions on Germany's Jewish population. The French tricolor flag had been swathed in bunting adorned with swastikas. When she read of the rally in the *Times*, Ida resolved that she would vigorously insist that her parents apply for visas to the United States.

Lady Clerk dismissed her arguments with a patronizing smile.

"Ida, my dear, you don't really believe that fascism can survive in the land of *liberté, égalité, et fraternité*?"

It was true that Lord Clerk himself had expressed concern about the formation of a political party that so closely resembled the Nazi regime in Germany, but she, a consummate Francophile, refused to be intimidated.

"Michel says that the French fascists are quite dangerous," Ida replied and realized, with a pang of guilt, that it was the first time she had thought of Michel since her arrival in London.

She would write to him that very evening, perhaps even send him a telegram. "*Je t'aime.* I love you. I miss you." A simple message, reminiscent of the days of their clandestine courtship. And she did love him, she did miss him, she assured herself. Poor patient Michel, slogging away at his studies, working in his parents' shop, and dashing through the city to care for her parents. He was relieved, she knew, that Marc and Bella had accepted an invitation to visit Vilna in the fall for the opening of a Museum of Jewish Art. Their absence would be a respite from their constant demands. Michel had not said as much, of course. He was so good, so understanding. She felt a surge of longing for her slender, dark-haired husband. She would buy him a jacket, the Norfolk jacket she had seen in that smart haberdashery on Oxford Street. And when she returned to Paris, they would share a candlelight dinner at La Tour d'Argent. He deserved a reward for tolerating her long absence.

"Shame on Michel for frightening you," Lady Clerk said vigorously. "In any case, we are in London and we can forget about what may or may not be happening across the Channel. And tonight's gala should be really wonderful. Just think, Ida. We are going to see the king himself! We must not be late."

She increased her pace, and Ida hurried to keep up with her. Their excitement mounted as they approached the entry of Guildhall and saw the banner of Saint George waving gently in the evening breeze, signifying the presence of the beloved monarch who had ruled England for a quarter of a century.

Since before I was born, Ida thought delightedly.

She surrendered her white cape to the butler, smoothed the skirt of her long green evening dress, and passed her fingers through her tangled curls.

Ambassador Clerk had waited for them, and she followed him through the reception line and curtsied deeply before the royal couple. Lifting her eyes shyly, she noted the king's pallor, his terrible weariness, and the queen's concerned expression. And then, as she had been instructed, she moved on into the ballroom.

Great banks of flowers from the royal gardens and the greenhouses of Kew lined the walls of the room, which was bathed in the dazzling lights of the low-hanging crystal chandeliers. Couples waltzed gracefully across the polished floor to the soft music of a very bored orchestra.

Ida was briefly alone, and she reveled in the luxury of her solitude, committing to memory the colors and styles of the women's fashionable gowns so that she might describe them to her mother. Though she was enthusiastic about little these day, Bella retained her interest in haute couture. Ida made a mental note to tell her about the short, silver-fringed skirts and the feathery boas of the jazz age that seemed to be so popular. Bella would laugh, she knew, and think them amusing but vulgar, definitely inappropriate for a state occasion.

"Ah, here you are, Ida."

Lady Clerk rushed toward her with a flute of champagne. "Isn't this marvelous?" she asked. "Absolutely everyone is here."

Lord Clerk joined them and they circled the room, smiling and nodding. Ida obediently curtsied when her hostess curtsied and nodded pleasantly when she was introduced to other guests, although she immediately forgot their names. She was pleasantly aware that more than one man stared after her as she moved from one group to another. She had not erred when she had decided to wear the closely fitted green silk gown that matched her eyes. As always, she was invigorated by the admiration of others. Suffused with warmth, conscious of the power of her beauty, she listened without interest as Lady Clerk scattered crumbs of gossip.

"There is Lord Somerset. And Lady Margaret, whom you met at the gallery, is dancing with the Swedish ambassador. How odd that she is not dancing with her husband, but I suppose it's all right. Although there are rumors..." Her voice drifted and then gathered strength. "But then there are always rumors, aren't there?"

Ida nodded. She understood that it was not a question that required an answer.

Quite suddenly, the orchestra stopped playing, the dancers stood rigidly in place, and even Lady Clerk fell silent.

"Their majesties are leaving," Lord Clerk whispered.

The conductor waved his baton, and the strains of the national anthem filled the room. Every voice was raised as the loyal and loving subjects of King George V, the grandson of Queen Victoria, lifted their voices in reverent chorus.

"God save our gracious king," they sang. "Long live our noble king."

Their voices were tremulous. Their country had survived one war and they lived under the threat of another. But on this celebratory night, they willed themselves to optimism. Perhaps they might sing their way into peace. Ida stood very still and wondered why it was that tears filled her eyes. The conductor lowered his baton. The men bowed from the waist and the women curtsied. The ornate door opened, and King George and Queen Mary disappeared into the night. There was a brief moment of silence and then the band struck up an engaging tune.

Within minutes, the hall was reenergized. Once again, the Clerks strolled the room, introducing Ida to their friends and acquaintances who all pronounced themselves delighted to meet the daughter of the famous Russian painter. Sir Jacob Epstein, the distinguished sculptor whose work *Ecce Homo* had only recently been unveiled, kissed her hand.

"Please remember me to your father. After all, we have so much in common, he and I, as do you and I," he said and winked at her.

"Indeed," she agreed and flashed him a brilliant smile, acknowledging her complicity. Ida Chagall and Jacob Epstein understood the anomaly of their presence in the brilliantly lit ballroom. They were both the Jewish children of Russian-born parents, who, against all odds, were welcomed and even admired by the aristocracy of England.

"Is your father making arrangements to leave Paris?" the sculptor asked, careful to keep his voice very low.

"Not yet," she replied.

"He should. He really should. There are dark clouds on the horizon." He shook his head sadly and moved on.

The orchestra no longer played waltzes. The rhythms of swing filled the room, a lively rendition of "Begin the Beguine." There was a burst of enthusiastic applause as an elegant couple stepped onto the dance floor. The man wore an impeccably tailored tuxedo and the crimson sash of royalty. The woman's dress was of silver lamé, and a necklace of tiny diamonds glittered about her very long neck. Her eyes were narrow, her features sharp and predatory. They were not young. Oddly the woman was taller than her escort, but they were both slender and graceful, their faces frozen in practiced insincere smiles. They danced with grace and ease, swinging in and out of each other's arms in a circlet of light.

"Who are they?" Ida asked.

Lady Clerk smiled. "Ida, my dear, you are looking at the prince of Wales, who will one day be king of England. And the woman with whom he is dancing is an American divorcée, a Mrs. Wallis Simpson."

"And will she, one day, be queen of England?" Ida asked, although she was certain that she knew the answer to her question.

"Of course not. The royal family would never condone such a marriage. The people of England would never accept it. Actually, he has no choice. He will have to break with her and do his duty. The country will insist, as will his family. He will, of course, accede to their demands, and I am sure he will not regret it. I suppose you find that hard to understand."

"No. I understand it completely," Ida replied.

She stared at the prince and Mrs. Simpson and thought of how she and Michel had sat opposite her parents at their dining room table and listened to Marc's imperial edict, his demand that they marry. Like the Prince of Wales, neither she nor Michel had been offered a choice. They too had acceded to the demands of their parents and their community and done their duty. She shook her head. *Of course, the comparison is ridiculous*, she thought reprovingly. *She and Michel were hardly royal personages.*

She wondered if the weak-chinned Prince of Wales might actually decide to defy his family and his nation and marry the divorcée at whom he looked with such a yearning gaze. And if he capitulated and did indeed give up the throne, would he regret it? The parallel to her own life teased. Did she regret her marriage? Did Michel? She chided herself for the intrusion of such a foolish speculation, even as she realized that she had answered her own question.

The music stopped, and the future king escorted his American lover from the dance floor. Ida watched them and wondered where Michel was at this very moment. Was he lonely? Did he miss her? Did he regret their marriage? Did she? The questions came again, unbidden, and again remained unanswered.

She thought of Michel throughout her journey home to France on the small craft that ferried her across the English Channel. She read and reread the loving notes he had written her during her absence. No, she assured herself, neither of them regretted their marriage. *And yet. And yet.* She repressed the lingering doubt and thrust the letters back into her bag.

Her fellow passengers were a somber group, absorbed in their newspapers whose stark headlines were uniformly ominous. Dark clouds haunted the continent. Adolf Hitler's rants grew more and more bellicose. Benito Mussolini had trained his sights on Ethiopia. Hardly a country in Europe was exempt from financial instability. Three passengers in the somber uniforms of the soldiers of commerce—dark suits, expertly laundered shirts, striped ties, and bowler hats—leaned against the rail of the deck. Fragments of their conversation floated toward Ida. Chamberlain might appease the

German bastard enough to prevent another war... Roosevelt was right to remain neutral... Roosevelt was wrong to remain neutral.

Ida sat on a portside deck chair, buttoned her blue cape against the chill, shook off her beret so that the wind might ruffle her hair, and removed the scrapbook of newspaper clippings from her portmanteau. She reviewed the favorable critiques of her father's work and anticipated his pleasure as he listened to her translate them. The distinguished critics of the leading London papers had been enthusiastic, generous with their praise and honest in their acknowledgment of their bewilderment at the symbolism of some of his themes.

"Marc Chagall presents us with dazzling colors and rabbinic mysteries," the art critic of the *Times* had observed in a not-so-veiled reference to Marc's Jewishness. Ida had not taken offense. Marc's Judaism vested his work with an appealing exoticism. The paintings in which the "rabbinic mysteries" were dominant had sold well, and the payment checks had been duly deposited in the account she had opened in her father's name in the Royal Bank of Scotland. She had deposited her commission in her own account. She had certainly earned the substantial sum. She had answered endless questions, shared snippets of information about her parents' lives, and discussed her father's routine, his constant search for innovative techniques. Her classes at La Palette had not, after all, been a waste of time. She had learned to parrot the glib repartee of the art world. A photograph in the *Tatler* showed her standing in front of one of the larger canvases, and the accompanying caption had been flattering. "How fortunate that Ida Chagall, the artist's beautiful and knowledgeable daughter, was on hand to explicate her father's themes," the generous columnist had written.

Ida smiled. She might officially be Madame Rapaport, the wife of a struggling law student, but she would always be known as Ida Chagall. She decided that she would not show that clipping to Michel but instead present him with the new bank book in her name. She was the guarantor of financial security for her parents as well as her husband.

Carefully, she replaced the scrapbook and accepted a steaming cup of broth from the tray proffered by a solicitous steward. She was wondrously content, excited by her own accomplishments. She recalled with pleasure Lady Clerk's embrace and effusive words as she left the London town house.

"Ida, you were just superb. So independent, so competent. I have written to your father and told him how very proud we are of you. You must come back to London soon, you and your Michel," the aristocratic Englishwoman had said.

"Of course," Ida had agreed.

But, she thought, *what would Michel do in London?* Despite all her urging, he had not learned a single word of English, and he was uncomfortable in the world of art and artists. Even a year after their marriage, he sat in silence at her parents' dinner parties, staring at his watch, impatient to leave for their own small drab apartment. Poor dear Michel, still—and perhaps forever—so ill at ease in the world that had been thrust upon him.

She wondered if he would be waiting for her at the dock. But of course he would be there. She closed her eyes and imagined how he would stride toward her, his arms outstretched, a smile igniting his angular face. He was her Michel, faithful and dependable, and he would look so handsome in the Norfolk jacket she had bought for him at a price that had caused her to gasp. But he deserved the best; of course he did.

Soothed by the rocking motion of the ship, sated with her own success, she imagined the excitement of her return, her husband's affection, her father's pride, her mother's gentle approval. She would not allow the threatening headlines, the whispering of the dark-suited doomsayers, to shadow her contentment. Still smiling, she fell into a pleasant sleep, waking only when the shore of France came into view.

Chapter Eleven

Michel, with a baguette tucked beneath his arm, his green book bag laden with texts and the ledgers of his parents' small shop, trudged up the rue du Bac. He paused at the newsstand and bought a copy of the evening paper, barely glancing at the headlines. There would be no good news. He could not remember when an optimistic headline had last appeared in a Parisian journal. Still, he and Ida read the papers each morning and each evening. It was their compass, each ominous dispatch a flashing needle, pointing them toward the direction they knew they would have to take. The inevitable journey of escape was delayed by the Chagalls' stubborn reluctance to leave Paris and Ida's refusal to emigrate without them. Michel told her repeatedly that they were running out of time, and she assured him again and again that she would impress the gravity of the situation on her parents.

His own mother and father had registered at the British embassy for visas to Palestine. They would be safe in Tel Aviv. It was a Jewish city, and Palestine might become a Jewish homeland.

"Perhaps then we can stop running," his mother had said ruefully as she removed the battered suitcases they had carried from Moscow to Berlin, from Berlin to Paris, from the storage closet.

His aunt and uncle had managed to get visas to the Dominican Republic and two of his fellow students had booked passage to Cuba. He thought of registering at the South American embassies. Uruguay, Brazil. They were alternatives that he knew Ida's parents would scorn, but with the inevitable German invasion of France, they would have to seek any available refuge. It was ludicrous for Marc, who recognized the danger, to insist that his fame would protect them.

He reached the shabby apartment building he and Ida had rented when she returned from England. The rooms were small, the kitchen cramped, and the narrow balcony inaccessible, but the rent was very low.

"We'll take it just for a few months," Ida had assured him, implicit in her words the promise that within that brief period, they would leave Paris. But they had lived there for two years, and all that had happened was that the paint in the bedroom had peeled, the switch that ignited the hallway light had broken, and they were no closer to leaving the city.

He stared up at the narrow windows of their apartment and was not surprised to see that they were dark. Of course Ida was at her parents' new home, their rented villa near the Trocadéro. The move was Marc's restless and foolish defense against the ominous news that assaulted them day after day. He rationalized that the change of address would keep them safe. He spoke of a synagogue service he had attended as a boy in Vitebsk at which a man had stood before the Torah and proclaimed that he was changing the name of his ill son because Jewish superstition had it that when someone was desperately ill, the name of the invalid was changed so that the Angel of Death might be deceived and unable to find his intended victim. Perhaps, he had said with an impish smile, the German angels of death might be deceived by their move and thus unable to find them.

Michel had smiled bitterly at his father-in-law's naïveté. Did he think that the Gestapo would rely on a phone book when they hunted for Jews? *The great artist was a genius*, Michel thought, *but a naive genius*. Unlike the Angel of Death, the Gestapo could find anyone, could kill anyone.

He mounted the dark stairwell slowly, annoyed by Ida's absence. Still, when he opened the door, he was somewhat soothed by the delicious aroma of garlic and onions. Ida had not forgotten that she had a husband. Her note on the table informed him that she had prepared a chicken paprika stew for him. He had only to heat it up. It was, he knew, her mother's recipe, redolent with the scent and taste of Russia.

Ida's culinary skills were the legacy of the long days of her childhood when she and Bella had played house together, cooking the robust stews and soups of Vitebsk for Marc's pleasure and their own.

Michel knew of the loneliness of Ida's early years. He had been witness to her girlhood timidity, her sweet innocence and docility, her playfulness in the alpine meadow where they had come together so sweetly, so tenderly, so rashly. But that innocence, that docility, had vanished. She was a forceful and assertive woman. Her body was possessed of a passion and power that too often overwhelmed him. Her magnetic personality, her animated conversation, her easy laughter attracted friends and admirers who surrounded her in cafés and at parties. Her London success, her father's almost total reliance on her competence, invigorated her with confidence.

"*La belle Ida*," the artists and writers of the Left Bank cafés called her in Michel's hearing, many of them unaware that the shabbily dressed, angular-faced student was *la belle Ida*'s husband.

Michel had noted that Bella's encroaching weakness and melancholy ignited Ida's energy. He vaguely recalled a Russian folk tale, perhaps a Baba Yaga story, in which a daughter sucked away her mother's health and energy and then grew wings of strength that enabled her to fly off into distant climes.

He dismissed the association, shamed by its implied disloyalty. Ida was devoted to her mother whom she resembled in so many ways. Like Bella, her moods soared and plummeted without warning. Too often she bewildered and exhausted him, but his heart beat faster when she drew close; her very presence seduced him.

He wandered into their small salon and glanced up at the painting of *The Bridal Chair* that hung there. It occurred to him, not for the first time, that the emptiness of the painted chair corresponded to the emptiness he felt in the room where he was so often alone.

Wearily, he tossed his jacket onto the frayed sofa and picked up the letter that the postman had slipped beneath their door. It was from Elsa Liebowitz in New York, where she and André lived. He knew that Ida had written to them asking for help and advice about emigration. He felt a surge of hope. Perhaps there was news of a visa or a mention of sponsorship.

He lit the flame on their small stove to warm the chicken stew and opened the envelope. The news was not good. Elsa had contacted various Jewish organizations and learned that there was virtually no possibility that the Chagalls would be granted visas. American law restricted immigration. The authorities adhered to a strict quota system, indifferent to the plight of the Jews of Europe. The quota for Russian immigrants was exhausted. But Elsa suggested that since Michel had French citizenship, it might extend to Ida as his wife. They could then qualify for visas under the French quota. Once in the United States, they might campaign on behalf of their parents. But she cautioned that even if they were granted visas, financial difficulties remained. Money would be needed for their passage as well as a surety of three thousand dollars for each, a guarantee that they would not be financially dependent on the American government. She regretted that she and André could not offer them funds as their combined salaries barely covered their own expenses.

Michel read and reread the letter. Money was not a problem. They had never touched Ida's account in the Bank of Scotland. Clearly, if he and Ida managed to get to America, they would be better positioned to help their parents. But he knew that Ida would never leave without Marc and Bella. Her loyalty to them was sacrosanct. Still, he would try to convince her.

"You cannot judge him as you would judge other men," she often reminded him. "He is a genius."

Only once had Michel dared to assert that even geniuses had their foibles. Her father, he had insisted, was not immune to the judgment of ordinary mortals like himself. She had stared at him angrily and slammed the door as she left the room.

He replaced the letter in the envelope so that Ida might read it when she returned home. He spooned the heated stew into a dish and read his newspaper as he ate. The front page news was predictable. There was a photograph of the coronation of King George VI and a smaller photo of the Duke of Windsor and Mrs. Wallis Simpson emerging from a limousine. Michel had no doubt that the photograph of the renegade lovers would attract more attention than the coronation. It occurred to him that the duke and duchess should receive special recognition for offering the world a diversion from the grim news that emanated from Germany. Glancing at the slender royal and his American paramour, he recalled Ida's almost casual confession that she admired the prince for his ability to resist the demands of the royal family and the prime minister. He had wondered then if she herself regretted her own submission to her parents' demands and their marriage. It was a question he would never pose to her—or to himself.

He skimmed the news stories from Italy and the United States. Mussolini and Franklin Delano Roosevelt were of little interest to him. But his hands trembled when he turned the page and read the critique of an art show in Munich. It was titled "The Nazi Exhibition of Degenerate Art." A single photograph illustrated the article, a black-bordered reproduction of Marc's portrait of a rabbi that had hung for years in a Mannheim museum. Michel read the accompanying text with horror. The portrait was only one of several of Marc's paintings selected for the exhibition that included the works of other artists. Picasso and Matisse had also offended the sensibilities of Adolf Hitler. The führer, the reporter wrote with wry incredulity, considered the artists insane and advocated their sterilization or perhaps criminal prosecution. It was Marc Chagall who was especially singled out for vitriolic condemnation. According to the Nazi curator of the exhibition, he was a Jew who saw the world through the distorted lens of Jewish perception. Goebbels himself had labeled "the Jew artist Chagall" a degenerate.

The writer, a French journalist who had attended the exhibition and observed the hatred and hysteria of the crowds, was at once indignant and horrified. "What is happening in Germany?" he asked in the conclusion of his article.

A stupid question, Michel thought. Everyone knew what was

happening in Germany. Barbarians ruled that nation, and those barbarians would soon be at the gates of Paris. Teutonic evil would move inexorably across one border after another until it devoured all of Europe. That same journalist would soon ask, "What is happening in France?"

No longer hungry, he pushed his plate aside, the stew half eaten. He went to the phone and called the Chagall apartment. Ida answered on the first ring, and he could hear the sound of voices and the clink of glasses in the background. It did not surprise him that the Chagalls' home was crowded with visitors. An informal salon convened there almost every evening. Artists and poets, denizens of Left Bank cafés and Right Bank mansions, would be talking too loudly, their laughter exploding in nervous bursts. This was not a time for Parisians to be alone. They sought comfort in company, in nervous meaningless exchanges, in the relief of too much wine and gossip.

Marc basked in the admiration of his guests, the invited and the uninvited. Ida was his lively and welcoming hostess, a surrogate for her mother who was so often ill with a mysterious *affaiblissement*, an undefined weakness.

Michel imagined the array of wine bottles, the vivacious conversations in a cacophony of languages, French colliding with Russian, English spoken in one corner, German in another. Marc might suddenly break into song, a half-remembered Yiddish ditty or a long, mournful ballad. He might even dance, a spry and graceful elf, waltzing to music that only he could hear, his arms outstretched, as though in readiness to gather in his absent wife. His guests would clap; their applause was the price of admission. At such gatherings, Ida roamed the room, carrying trays of food, bottles of wine.

"Michel," she said breathlessly into the phone. "How wonderful that it is you. Will you be coming tonight? There are so many interesting people here."

"No," he said, struggling to keep his tone even. "Actually, I want you to come home. It is important that we talk. At once."

"Why?" she asked and laughed at something someone in the room had said, one of the "interesting people," he supposed.

"Have you seen the evening paper?"

"No."

"When I show it to you, you will understand. Please leave now."

"My father has guests. Important guests." She lowered her voice. "Sartre himself may be coming. And perhaps de Beauvoir."

"And I am telling you that it is important that you come home. At once."

There was a brief silence. He had surprised her. It was rare for him to make a demand.

"Very well, Michel. I will leave now," she said, and he heard the fear in her voice.

Less than an hour later, she sat beside him on the sofa. He handed her the newspaper, and she read the story and leaned against him, her face pale, her hands trembling.

"We must do something at once," she said. "If the Germans invade, which they will surely do, my father will be their immediate target. We must make him understand that. We'll speak to him together tomorrow."

"Tomorrow," he agreed and held her close. "Everything will be all right, Ida."

It was, he knew, a foolish and futile reassurance. They both knew that everything would not be all right. They came together that night, not in passion but in fear, seeking to comfort each other with the warmth of their bodies and the tenderness of their touch.

Michel and Ida arrived at the Trocadéro apartment early the next morning. A sullen Katya served them croissants and coffee. Madame was sleeping, she said as she slammed cups and saucers onto the table. The maître was in his studio.

"Tell him that we must see him," Ida insisted.

Katya stared at her, hostility and resentment in her pale eyes. A friend had mentioned seeing the maid at a Croix de Feu demonstration in Montmartre waving a paper swastika flag. Ida had not told her parents that Katya was a Nazi sympathizer who should be fired. Marc and Bella feared change and disruption. Katya had long been a fixture in their lives, and they would resist replacing her. Ida anticipated their arguments. They would claim that Katya was a foolish girl, a stupid girl, but her politics did not affect her work and good maids were hard to find.

Ida did not think Katya was either foolish or stupid, but she knew that it was pointless to argue with her parents. Katya would be tolerated because she knew exactly how long to boil Marc's morning egg and when to bring Bella her specially brewed tisane.

"Your father will be very angry," Katya said. "You know that he does not like to be disturbed when he is working,"

"N'importe," Ida replied dismissively. "Go and tell him we are here. Va."

Katya wiped her hands on her apron, shrugged, and left the room. They listened as she knocked too loudly on the studio door. They heard her speak to Marc in a flat indifferent monotone. They heard his angry response and then the heavy door slammed. Minutes later, he stamped into the room and stood before them, his eyes narrowed, his face ablaze with indignation. Katya had been right. He was angry, very angry. Any interruption of his work was a violation, a sin against his talent. He had not removed his smock, and he carried a paintbrush wetly shimmering with vermilion that spattered on the polished floor. Katya trailed after him, wiped up the drops of paint, and smirked smugly before disappearing into the kitchen.

"What is so important that it could not wait?" Marc asked.

He brandished his paintbrush at Ida. As always, he ignored Michel. His daughter's husband did not interest him. He seldom spoke to him and rarely addressed him by name.

"This is what could not wait, Papochka," Ida said.

She thrust the evening newspaper at him, opened to the article on the German art show. Similar articles appeared in the morning editions of *Le Monde* and *L'Express* that Michel had bought that morning.

Marc seized the paper. His face contorted in pain as he looked at the black-bordered photo of the work he had painted so many years ago. It was a painting that he especially loved because it was his second rendition of the portrait of the bearded rabbi. The first one had been among the many canvases he had completed before the outbreak of the Great War, abandoned when he was forced to race back to Russia, and never reclaimed. He had re-created the portrait, calling it *The Yellow Rabbi*, because of the phosphine tone that defined the tortured face. The color symbolized his own vanished world, which he had rescued from oblivion by the power of his brush and the intensity of his imagination.

"It would seem that this poor painting, my unfortunate rabbi, is ill-fated. I am told that the first portrait hangs in the dining room of a Nazi financial adviser. I wonder that it does not disturb him to eat his dinner beneath the gaze of a rabbinic sage. But then I suppose he never bothers to look up at it. It is enough that he owns it. And now my *Yellow Rabbi* has been kidnapped from the Mannheim Museum and vilified by that vicious little Austrian who thinks he will rule the world. It is said that he, Hitler, that fascist devil, is himself a failed painter, and yet that evil mediocrity dares to call the work of Marc Chagall degenerate?"

His voice thundered into fury. He sliced the air with his paintbrush as though it were a rapier with which he could pierce hatred and ignorance. Blood-colored drops spackled the floor.

"History will judge who is the degenerate, Adolf Hitler or Marc Chagall. Adolf Hitler or Pablo Picasso. Adolf Hitler or Henri Matisse. It will be no contest," he shouted. "But meanwhile, we suffer."

"It is only a painting," Ida said. "And perhaps it is fortunate that it should receive such attention. It is a sign to us, a warning. We know that you are in great danger, that you will surely be a target when the Nazis invade France. Your life, our lives, are more important than any painting. We must leave Europe, Papa. Our departure must be arranged as soon as possible."

She held the morning papers out to him, open to the descriptions of the Munich art show. Marc sat down heavily and read each article, a bitter smile playing at his lips as he turned the pages.

"I see that I am in excellent company. The Spaniard is also a degenerate. Also Mondrian. And Grosz. Grosz and I share a special distinction. We are both Jewish and degenerate. We are indeed blessed. I must call and congratulate him," he murmured. He shrugged and tossed the newspapers aside.

"Papa, don't make light of this. The situation is urgent. We must try to get visas to the United States, to Cuba, to Argentina, to Palestine. Anywhere."

Her voice trembled. It was her father who had monitored Hitler's rise to power, yet he refused to understand his terrible vulnerability and their own.

Marc strode to the window and pulled back the draperies. Sunlight flooded the room, and he leaned forward and looked out at the broad plaza. At its center, the French tricolor, hoisted on a tall white flagpole, fluttered in a gentle wind.

"I do not see a swastika flying there," he said.

"Not yet," Michel said grimly. "Give the Nazis a few weeks, a few months. They are only biding their time, and then the swastika will fly over the Arc de Triomphe itself."

"And you, of course, have a crystal ball, Michel," Marc retorted caustically. He turned to his daughter. "You know, Ida, if I were to actually consider leaving France, I would not choose to go to America. No. I would return to my motherland, to Russia."

She stared at him in disbelief.

"You cannot mean that. You know what happened to your friend Gorky when he returned to that so-called Mother Russia. He was murdered. And so was your teacher, Yuri Pen. You yourself read André Gide's report of his trip to Moscow. Although he is a communist, he warned against the evil of Stalin's regime. How could you even contemplate returning to such a country?" Her eyes blazed with indignation.

"Gide, André Gide," he said dismissively. "How can a Frenchman, a writer, understand the Russian mind, the Russian heart? Ah, my Ida, I have such longings, such yearnings. If only I could see the Western Dvina River again. When we were in Vilna two years ago, your mother and I, we were so very close to Vitebsk. I felt like the Moshe, the Moses of our Torah. I was so close to my promised land and yet I could not enter it."

Ida laughed harshly. "But of course you know that although your parents named you Moshe, you chose to be Marc. Vitebsk is gone. You live in Paris. Today's Russia, the Russia of Stalin and his thugs, is not your promised land. The only land that can offer you any promise of survival is the United States. You must stop denying what is happening in the world you live in. You are neither Russian nor French. Paris is not Mount Nebo from which Moses looked down on the promised land. You and *Mamochka* are stateless Jews, without passports, without *cartes d'identité*. You know how dangerous that is, especially now. We have to act at once. There are letters to be written, people to be contacted. Do not waste any more time with your fantasies. *Assez*. Enough."

He stared at her in shocked disbelief. How dare she speak to him in such a tone? He stood immobile, his anger matching her own, his face frozen, his eyes narrowed into slits of glacial blue.

"Do you really think that they will dare to threaten Marc Chagall?" he asked arrogantly.

Ida stared at him, her face flushed with rage. Michel placed a restraining hand on her shoulder, but her fury would not be contained. She seized the scattered newspapers, ripped them into shreds, and flung them at her father. The ribbons of newsprint fell to the floor, but the black-bordered photograph of *The Yellow Rabbi* remained intact and rested at his feet.

"Your question should be 'When will they threaten Marc Chagall?' And then 'Will they kill Marc Chagall or send him to a concentration camp?'" she hissed. "Wake up, *Papochka*. Wake up before it is too late."

Michel took her arm, and together, they left the room.

Chapter Twelve

*O*ne season followed another. Paris rested beneath blankets of snow, then awakened to the fragrance of spring and the budding blossoms of the trees that lined the broad avenues. The air glowed golden in the summer sunlight and then, too swiftly, the autumn sky was darkened by the moody cobalt of *l'heure bleue*, the twilight hour. Ida barely took note of the changing clime. She sat at her desk hour after hour, day after day, and wrote letters, always meticulous in her phrasing. She was careful. She wrote and rewrote. She knew she must not appear to be desperate, that she must not appear to be pleading. But she was desperate. And she was pleading. The letters went to the friends she had made in England, to influential art critics, to Lord and Lady Clerk, to the English Rothschilds who had enthused over her father's work at the Leicester Galleries, and to the French Rothschilds who had purchased more than one canvas from the Ambroise Vollard gallery in Paris.

She sent an urgent letter to the Reinhardt Galleries in New York, which had hosted Marc's first American exhibition. She wrote to Solomon Guggenheim, who had purchased her father's work and for whom she had arranged generous reductions in price. Might she expect such generosity to be reciprocated for the family of the artist whose work hung in his home? Mr. Guggenheim, of course, had read accounts of the Nazi Degenerate Art Show in Munich and knew how vulnerable her father would be in the event of a German invasion of France. Surely he would help an artist he admired who was also his coreligionist? She was careful not to use the word "Jew."

She wrote to Eric Cohen, the owner of the Goodman's Matzo Company, because she knew he was a collector with great interest in her father's paintings as well as a committed Jew. She complimented him on his taste in art. His collection was receiving recognition. How wonderful it would be if the Chagalls could come to America and Mr. Cohen could meet her father. This could happen if he somehow might manage to expedite their entry into the United States.

Her letters received polite replies. Lord and Lady Clerk, writing separately, assured her that her anxiety was unfounded. The ambassador wrote that Mr. Chamberlain himself, their astute prime minister, had assured them that he had met with Mr. Hitler, who had promised that the Sudetenland would be his last territorial claim in Europe. Lady Clerk wrote in her delicate hand, on notepaper embossed with the family's crest, that the prime minister was absolutely certain there would be peace. "We have complete faith in Mr. Chamberlain. Do not fret, dear Ida," she added.

But Ida did fret. The replies to her appeals were discouraging. Solomon Guggenheim was circumspect. He assumed that Ida knew that the American government would not relax its quota restrictions, that absolutely no exceptions would be made. He, as well as other influential American Jews, thought it was important that their community not be overly visible in their efforts on behalf of the Jews of Europe. Any hint of partiality might invoke an anti-Semitic reaction, and American Jews also had their problems.

"We don't want the people of the United States to feel that the Jews have pushed them into war, which is something that Charles Lindbergh and his 'America First' movement are already saying," he wrote. He added that he hoped the money he had paid for his Chagall acquisitions had been wisely invested.

Ida had, in fact, deposited his substantial check into her father's account at the Royal Bank of Scotland. She did not share this information with Solomon Guggenheim but wrote a polite reply and asked him if he could think of any influential non-Jewish Americans to whom she might turn for help. She remembered then that Guggenheim, that respectable German Jewish millionaire, had a mistress, Hilla Rebay, an artist her parents had known when they lived in Berlin and who had once visited their family in Paris. The day had been warm and they had gathered in the garden, where Bella served tea from a samovar and Hilla Rebay had talked and laughed. It was her musical and generous laugh Ida remembered. She found Hilla Rebay's address among her father's papers and wrote her a letter, asking if she could use her influence with Guggenheim to help her parents. She expected no answer, and none arrived.

Eric Cohen, however, replied cryptically that there was a plan under consideration that would aid notable artists and intellectuals, her father among them. Unlike Lady Clerk, he did not advise her "not to fret."

"We are working with the State Department and have organized a distinguished committee. We will be in touch," he promised, and Ida understood that he feared to be more explicit lest his letter be intercepted.

She wrote to Pierre Matisse, Henri Matisse's son who had opened a gallery in New York and offered to represent her father in that city. He was slightly more encouraging. He had heard there was an unofficial group charged with considering the plight of "special cases." Given his talent and achievements, Marc Chagall would surely be considered such a special case. He wrote regretfully that it was not politic for him to be more specific. She assumed that he referred to the "committee" Eric Cohen had hinted at and that he too feared censorship.

Only slightly reassured, she intensified her efforts. Michel often returned home to find her still seated at her desk, her fingers stained with ink, her face pale, her bright hair flowing about her shoulders because she could not be bothered to put it up.

Michel himself spent long hours pounding the pavements of Paris, wandering from embassy to embassy, standing in one line after another. Masha, his mother, worried that his shoes would wear out. She glued cardboard to the leather soles, darned his socks, and patched the sleeves of his jackets.

Diminutive Masha Rapaport had, through the years, worried and worked her family into survival. She had worried their way out of

Russia to Germany and then from Germany to Paris. She had worried Michel into law school. Masha worried her way through the present. She wrapped sandwiches for Michel and filled thermoses with hot tea to sustain him as he made his rounds.

His marriage had surprised her, but it had not disappointed. She recognized Ida's energy and ingenuity. The Chagalls lived in a world apart from her own, and she wasted little time thinking about Bella and Marc. It was Ida who was important. She recognized her determination and saw her as a dependable accomplice in desperate times.

The Rapaports went to their little shop in Le Marais each day. There was little business. The shelves were depleted, and they did not order new stock. Their suitcases were packed, their small savings account closed, their few pieces of jewelry sewn into the hems of their winter coats. They would be ready to leave when the British issued their visas to Palestine. They were veterans of flight, cognoscenti of survival.

Michel was persistent. He visited and revisited the American embassy on the avenue Gabriel, veered off to the New Zealand embassy on rue Léonard de Vinci, turned the corner to the consulate of Costa Rica, and stood in line in front of the offices of the Dominican Republic. *Where was the Dominican Republic?* he wondered. South America? Central America? It made no difference. It was far from Germany. He filled out visa applications for Marc and Bella, for Ida and himself, and for his parents, although he knew they would not be dissuaded from their hopes for Palestine. He met with bored embassy bureaucrats who reviewed his papers and offered little hope. He confronted hostile clerks who barely looked up when he stood at their counters. There were days when he thought himself invisible and days when he wished that were true. But he was tenacious. Exhausted when he returned to their little apartment, he nevertheless insisted that Ida leave her desk, join him for an aperitif, and listen to the jokes he had heard in one line or another.

A Jew applied to the American embassy for a visa and was told that the quota was filled but there might be places in five years' time. "Should I come in the morning or the afternoon?" the applicant asked.

Ida laughed obediently.

Another Jew went to a relief agency where an official spun a globe and advised that there were no visas for Canada, the United States, the United Kingdom, or any South American country, then asked if the applicant had any other requests. "Yes," was the answer. "Perhaps you can find another globe."

Ida listened, but she had used up that day's ration of laughter.

She was newly intent on obtaining French citizenship for her parents. She besieged every friend and acquaintance in Paris to assist her. Letters were written; calls were made. André Malraux interceded with various ministers, but reports drifted back to Ida that the French government was hesitant because Marc had served as a commissar of art in Vitebsk. It did not seem to matter that he had been ejected from that very dubious position and was now hated by the Soviets.

She decided on another tactic. Dousing herself in perfume, she dressed in a smart black suit and a white silk blouse that revealed her rosy cleavage. With her hair twisted into an elegant chignon, a single flame-colored curl kissing her neck, she made her way to the Ministry of the Interior and into the office of a senior deputy. She smiled her most brilliant smile, proffered her parents' dossiers, and asked in the gentlest of tones how French citizenship could be denied to a Russian émigré who was persona non grata in the land of his birth. Her father had been stripped of his commission, and he was unwelcome in Russia.

"This is ridiculous, *n'est-ce pas*? You, who are so discerning, so sensitive, can see that such a position is ridiculous, monsieur," she told the pale, weak-chinned bureaucrat, inviting his agreement, his complicity. She leaned forward, moved closer, and brushed his hand with her own. "How sad that you and I must meet in such a place," she said. "I can feel that you are so simpatico. Perhaps we can meet for a tisane."

He blushed. He nodded.

She smiled again; she would seduce him into compliance.

"I will see to it, madame," he said. "Just leave your parents' file with me."

He did see to it. Marc and Bella became naturalized citizens. Marc showed Ida his passport.

"It is issued to Moise Chagall," he said disconsolately.

"That should please you," Ida teased. "You are Moshe once again, looking across into your promised land."

She saw the displeasure that flickered across his face. He did not want to be known as Moshe or Moise, the Jewish artist whose surname, written in the Hebrew letters *sin, gimel, lamed,* could also be read as Siegel. He was not Moshe Siegel. He was, and always would be, Marc Chagall, *un artiste Parisien.*

But the names on the passports were unimportant. They were valid documents to be held in readiness as the news grew more and more ominous. On a cold November night, as Parisians sat in cafés blue with cigarette smoke, sipped their glasses of *vin blanc,* and listened to the wistful voice of Edith Piaf, the war against the Jews exploded into violence in Germany.

Fires burned, glass was shattered, and pools of blood filled the streets. Parisians read the morning edition of *Le Monde* in disbelief, unable to comprehend the brutality taking place in the land that bordered their own. The newspaper trembled in their hands and they whispered the dreaded words: *La nuit de cristal fracassant. The night of breaking glass. Kristallnacht.* The windows of Jewish shops, synagogues, and homes were shattered, Jewish-owned buildings were burned to the ground, and boys wearing the uniforms of Hitler Youth danced around bonfires, feeding the flames with Torah scrolls and holy texts snatched from synagogues.

Parisians, Jewish and non-Jewish alike, shuddered. The cafés and restaurants of Le Marais and Montmartre were empty that evening, and no one came to the Chagall home on the Trocadéro. The inevitable could no longer be denied. The citizens of the City of Light knew that darkness was imminent and that they would soon be confronted by their own nights of shattered windows and blazing fires. Marc slept with their passports and *cartes d'identité* beneath his pillow. Ida sent telegrams, urgent pleas for help that fell soundlessly onto desks in London and New York. She received no replies.

Marc stopped reading the newspapers, stopped listening to the radio. He spent hours in his studio, painting feverishly.

"Your father is like Nero," Michel said sarcastically as he and Ida left her parents' home one night and walked through the dark and silent streets of the city. "He paints while Europe burns."

"What would you have him do?" Ida asked angrily.

"Clearly he doesn't have to do anything. You and I do everything for him," Michel replied drily.

Ida stared at him. She knew Michel resented her involvement with her father, but she had not realized the toxicity of his resentment. She stood very still for a moment and then lifted her face to his and kissed him on the lips. He held her close and saw that her eyes were closed. He understood that her kiss was an apology of a kind.

"It's all right, Ida," he said, all bitterness drained from his voice.

He took her arm, and they continued on their way, their footsteps echoing down the deserted streets.

It was at last decided that Marc and Bella would leave Paris. Ida found a house in the Loire Valley offered for rent by a taciturn farmer named Jacques LaSalle. Within weeks, it was clear that Monsieur LaSalle resented their presence.

"It appears that in his book, I have committed two crimes," Marc complained to Ida in a hastily scribbled letter. "I am both a Jew and an artist. *Tant pis*. More's the pity. He is more than happy to take my money. It seems that the francs I give him for the exorbitant rent he charges us have not been tainted by either my occupation or my religion."

"Pay him no mind," Ida wrote back. "Try not to alienate him."

The farmhouse would provide refuge in the event of a German invasion. The landlord, despite his aversion to Jews, was a man who could be bribed into silence.

She found herself alone in Paris because Michel, suddenly and without warning, was drafted into the French army. He came home on a brief leave, and Ida stared at him in his ill-fitting uniform, his thick hair tamed into a military cut that emphasized the narrowness of his face. Their eyes locked, but they did not speak.

Slowly they undressed and came together in silence, their intimacy laced with sadness, complicit in their loneliness. She stood at the window when Michel left and watched him walk down the street, his back bent beneath his duffel bag. She struggled to remember the graceful, dreamy youth in the leather cloak who had walked by her side through the alpine meadow. She turned to her mirror, loosened her hair, and wondered if he saw her still as the enchanting young girl who had walked beside him in the waning days of summer. She shook her head wearily. How foolish she was. Of course they had changed. They were no longer young lovers, their bodies drenched in golden sunlight. They were a married couple facing a world grown dark and unfamiliar.

"I love you," she whispered to her absent husband, the youth become a man, the student become a soldier, and she knew that to be the truth. But she knew too that the love she felt for him was no longer forged by ardor; rather, it was a tenderness drained of passion.

───

She visited Michel's parents and helped them organize the depleted stock in their small store, helped his mother to sort through her collection of tattered photographs—sepia prints of Michel's grandparents, snapshots of Michel as a small boy, of Michel on his graduation day from the Lycée, Michel and herself on their wedding day, posed beneath her father's painting of the bridal chair.

"I had thought that one day I would have a photograph of a baby, your baby and Michel's," Masha Rapaport said daringly.

She had envisioned a grandchild with Ida's bright hair and Michel's soft, thoughtful eyes.

"Perhaps one day," Ida replied gently.

It was not impossible, she told herself as she walked home in the late afternoon. She and Michel might yet have children. She had been careful, ever mindful of Elsa's advice, but she would not always have to be so cautious. A love that had changed could change yet again. But not now. She would not have a child when the clouds of war darkened the sky. And not here. Not on this continent that she knew would soon be engulfed in flames.

She paused in the Tuileries Garden and watched a group of children at play. A very small boy wearing a sailor suit rolled a large blue ball toward her. He was fine-featured, with deep dark eyes, and his hair was a mass of carrot-colored curls. She rolled the ball back to him and smiled at his young mother.

"How old is he?" she asked pleasantly.

"Almost four," she replied.

"He is a handsome child," she said and walked on, her heart heavy with a sadness she had long forbidden herself.

Her calculations were simple, their implications clear. The child she might have birthed would have been almost four and, like that merry boy who chased after his ball, such a child might have had deep dark eyes like Michel's and hair like her own.

The reflection came unbidden, unwelcomed. She had, from the moment she left the clinic in Neuilly, willed herself not to think of what might have been. She had done what she had to do; she and Michel had decided on that together. They had thought then that there was no other choice, and perhaps they had been right. They never spoke of the *avortement*, the abortion that she had exiled from memory. She had not wept in the Neuilly clinic; she had not wept on her wedding day. But at this twilight hour, as she walked alone through the darkening street, tears filled her eyes. She allowed them to fall; sorrow was the smallest of luxuries. She wept for herself and for Michel, for the unborn child, and for Masha Rapaport, who treasured memories and photographs but had yet to stare lovingly at a snapshot of a grandchild.

Chapter Thirteen

*M*ichel, aware of her growing despondency, wrote encouraging her to visit her parents in the Loire Valley.

"They surely miss you and you miss them. And I know that you want to see your father's new work. It is still safe to travel to the south," he added cryptically, and she wondered if he had real intelligence about the probability of an invasion.

It was a relief to travel south. Paris was slowly becoming a fortress, its windows shuttered, its museums surreptitiously emptied, the shelves of groceries stripped by housewives preparing for a siege. Ida relaxed as she stared out the train window at the sylvan landscapes untouched by the prospect of war. The branches of trees swayed against the gentle breezes, and the foliage shimmered in the bright sunlight. Farmers tended their fields, and flocks of sheep meandered lazily through meadows rich in purple clover. It was difficult to believe that this was a country on the threshold of disaster.

Marc and Bella were elated at her arrival, delighted with the wine and cheese she had managed to coax from reluctant shopkeepers.

"Ah, Idotchka, we can always depend on you," Bella said.

Ida smiled and wondered when it was that their roles had been reversed, their dependencies transposed, the pampered daughter become the concerned caregiver.

In the farmer's outbuilding her father used as a studio, she marveled at his new works.

"I paint my way out of sadness," he said drily.

She wandered through the makeshift studio where the odors of damp hay and manure mingled with the studio scents of turpentine and linseed oil, fascinated anew by the varied worlds on her father's canvases. He had reverted to the circus motif that had always intrigued him. Once again, he created graceful acrobats and leering clowns, exotic figures whose implied innocence seemed to render them incapable of evil. The circus paintings, executed in charming pastels, contrasted with the main focus of his larger works. During the recent months of heightened existential terror, it was the Judeo-Christian theme that engaged him; crucifix and sacrifice haunted his thoughts, invaded his dreams, sprang to life in his paintings. Daringly, in an impasto of layered oils, he commingled the testaments, Old and New, Jewish and Christian. The two religions collided with each other in a riot of colors and phantasmagoric imaginings. He mined the biblical sources and melded them with modern images, the suffering of ages past corresponding to the suffering of his own world, past and present coequal, evil matching evil.

He had been named for Moses, but it was Christ he painted. Ida studied his *White Crucifixion*, a portrayal of the suffering Christ on the cross, his emaciated body covered by a *tallit*, a Jewish prayer shawl, his lips and eyes closed in death. Above his halo was a Hebrew inscription—"Jesus of Nazareth, King of the Jews"—and at his feet, weeping mourners knelt, surrounded by fearsome enemies. He painted modern storm troopers and uniformed soldiers brandishing red flags, chasing after terrified women and vulnerable children. It was a chaotic scene of fleeing Jews burdened by awkward bundles, the scavenged remnants of their endangered lives. Marc's message was clear. History moved on, but suffering and persecution remained.

There were other crucifixion depictions, fanciful and disturbing, in which he painted his own image as that of a suffering Jew. "Marc Chagall, King of the Jewish Artists," was scrawled angrily across one such canvas.

Ida moved from one painting to another, pummeled with memories, overwhelmed with sadness. That night, for the first time in years, lying in her narrow bed, the nightmare recurred. Once again, she ran the desperate race to freedom, but she was no longer a child clutching her parents' hands. Dressed in a bridal gown, clutching a bouquet of wilting white roses, she was a solitary fugitive on an unfamiliar road, surrounded by threatening strangers who spoke mysterious, incomprehensible languages. When she awakened, her cheeks were wet with tears. She lay very still and wondered if she was destined to run for safe haven all the days of her life, in wakefulness and in sleep. Oh, she was tired, so very tired. Fatigue weighted her body. She closed her eyes but feared to sleep, feared that invading dream of chaos and terror.

"Did you sleep well, Idotchka?" her father asked the next morning. He glared at Katya who had managed to stain the tablecloth as she poured the coffee. The maid ignored him.

"Very well," Ida lied, but she met her mother's gaze, saw the sadness in her eyes, and knew that Bella, who sensed her every mood, had guessed the truth.

Ida's vivacity, her aggressive determination, did not deceive Bella. Ida was her daughter, inheritor of her moods and fears although better equipped to combat them. Of course Ida had not slept well. Michel, her husband, was a soldier during a time of war. Ida was alone in Paris, struggling to find a way to save all their lives. How could her sleep be undisturbed? In this frightening time, no one slept well.

Bella's brother Yaakov wrote that his Paris medical practice was dominated by weary insomniacs in search of elusive rest. Yaakov dispensed sleeping pills and anodynes to exhausted men and women, but still they lay awake through the long nights. Hitler had murdered the sleep of the Jews of Europe.

Bella remembered their flight from Russia, their stays in hostels and inns where mothers and fathers approached nightfall uneasily, placing clean clothing, sturdy walking shoes, and winter cloaks near their children's beds while they themselves lay awake, fully clothed. She and Marc had placed small Ida between them on narrow beds, her breath warm and sweet upon their faces. She remembered too the rituals of survival—jewels and money sewn into the hems and sleeves of garments or concealed in the insteps of shoes, documents blanketed in the linings of overcoats. Always they had been prepared for the inevitable moment when their lives would change forever and their wanderings would begin.

How foolish she had been to imagine that they were safe, that their Ida, raised in the City of Light, would be spared the fear that had rimmed their lives. She knew that her daughter's sorrowful race to survival—and their own—was just beginning, and there was no comfort to be offered.

Ida lowered her head; her bright hair tumbled loose from its pins and curtained her face. Slender Bella, enfolded in a white robe worn almost to transparency, its wide sleeves waving across her arms like gossamer wings, moved across the room and embraced her. Ida melted into her mother's arms, relieved to abandon her self-imposed bravura, her uncertain certitude, even for the briefest of moments. Together then, hand in hand, mother and daughter followed Marc into his makeshift studio. Bella was to pose for him that morning.

Bella took her place. Her white robe was supposed to be a wedding gown, but her face was so wreathed in sadness and her body was so inert and lifeless that the loose garment seemed more like a shroud. Marc was not deterred. He had decided on a bridal scene, and it was a bridal scene that he would paint.

"I will call it *The Betrothed*," he announced as his brush flew across the canvas.

"If it is finished before I leave, I will take it back to Paris. There is an American collector who pays in dollars. I am told that he is partial to wedding scenes," Ida said.

They would soon need money, a great deal of money. There would be bribes to be paid, tickets to be purchased, visas to be negotiated. Portraits of brides were easier to sell than studies of corpses. The money in the Bank of Scotland was their only security, and she would not touch it.

She watched as he worked and wondered to whom, in her father's artistic perception, her mother was being betrothed. Was Bella being consecrated to an unseen lover or to the invisible Angel of Death who might appear in a corner of the canvas, perhaps waving a swastika rather than a scythe? As always, her father's imaginings remained impenetrable enigmas that both fascinated and frightened her. She struggled to anticipate him, but she knew that she could not match the pace of his brilliant and mysterious fantasies.

She went into the house to study the accounts, to speak with taciturn Monsieur LaSalle, offering him several hundred francs for the purchase of fresh eggs and butter for her parents.

She hugged Bella, kissed Marc on both his cheeks as she waited for the taxi that would carry her to the small rural train station.

"Take good care of *Mamochka*," she whispered to her father. Bella's pallor and listlessness worried her. "Tell Katya to prepare soups, cassoulets."

Ida looked across at the fertile fields of the farm. The warmth of the late spring days would mean an early vegetable harvest, and the neatly plowed furrows were already covered with tender shoots. Beets sprouted and wild sorrel covered the verdant meadows.

"Borscht," she added. "And schav." The remembered sustenance of her mother's childhood, the recipes she had treasured and cooked with pleasure. "Katya must prepare them for you."

"That Katya," he said dismissively.

Ida had noticed that the Polish maid was openly indolent, that she spent a great deal of time with the farmer, neglecting dirty dishes that accumulated in the scullery and not bothering to sweep the floor. It was time to get rid of Katya. She could not be trusted. A village woman could be found to take her place. She would deal with that on her next visit.

"*Au revoir, Papochka.*"

She stood beside him, startled to realize that they were almost of an equal height. She had never before thought of him as a small man.

"*À bientôt.*" He kissed her on both her cheeks and waved her into the waiting taxi.

It was wonderful, Ida thought as she drove off, that the farewells of the French were optimistic pledges of anticipated reunions. The English "good-bye," so heavy in its finality, always filled her with sadness. She relaxed on the train that sped her home to Paris. She needed to be alone, to recoup her strength, to resume her campaign of writing letters that she knew would remain unanswered. Still, she could not surrender hope. It was not in her nature. Perhaps there would be a letter from Michel, a loving letter assuring her that he was safe. She struggled to lift her own spirits, to fight her exhaustion. All she needed was a little rest, a brief solitude.

But there was no respite. Tragedy was compounded. A week after her arrival in Paris, Ambroise Vollard, the Chagalls' art dealer who had been an important source of their income, was killed in a traffic accident.

The money that he owed them from sales already transacted would not be forthcoming until his estate was settled. The funds to which they had ready access were very limited. Her only comfort was the knowledge that their accounts in the Bank of Scotland were secure.

But there were new and more ominous developments. Ida trembled as she listened to the radio. German Foreign Minister Joachim von Ribbentrop and Joseph Stalin had signed a horrific pact that ensured that neither country would attack the other nor would assistance be offered to any third party at war with the other. It was said that Lithuania, enlarged by the Vilna area, was assigned to Germany. The impossible had happened: fascism and communism, the strangest of bedfellows, had entered into a deadly and brutal consortium. Ida thought of her father's naive fantasy of returning to Mother Russia and shuddered to think of his reaction to this new dark betrayal. Her heart was heavy as she journeyed southward again.

Her fears were not unfounded. Marc barely looked up when she entered the farmhouse. Pale and unshaven, he wore the bewildered expression peculiar to mourners struggling to assimilate the reality of a death. His blue eyes were faded as though hours of weeping had blanched their brightness. The news had overwhelmed him, reduced him to a sorrow he could not fight with brush and canvas. She placed her hand on his, lifted her fingers to his cheek, and brushed away a single tear.

"My Russia—it is gone forever," he murmured.

He would never return to the land of his birth. The fate of Vilna compounded his desolation. He wept for the beautiful city that had welcomed him so enthusiastically only three years earlier. Vilna, the Jerusalem of Lithuania, the intellectual capital of his exiled people, was lost.

"Tell me it's not so, Ida," he pleaded.

Ida shook her head and spread the Paris newspapers across the kitchen table, pointing to one story after another that confirmed the sinister alliance.

"It is so, *Papochka*," she said. "But it may not be as dangerous as you think. This Hitler-Stalin pact may only be diplomatic maneuvering. You know, a military game of chess."

She did not believe her own words, but they were all she had to offer. She unpacked the baguettes and cheeses she had brought from Paris, the croissants her mother favored and the sweet cherries that had only recently appeared in the markets at Les Halles. She opened the icebox and frowned at the empty shelves. The sink overflowed with dirty dishes and the counters were slick with congealed fat. No meal had been prepared for her parents' lunch, and she suspected that they might not have had breakfast.

"Katya!" she called angrily.

Her father shook his head warningly.

"Don't call her. It is pointless. She does nothing for us. She spends all her time with LaSalle. They are plotting against us. They plan to murder us in our sleep and steal all our money. They plan to lead the Nazis to us when they invade."

He spoke in a whisper and his blue eyes were wild with fear. He paced the room and pointed with a trembling finger to the door that led to the farmer's quarters. Ida, who had entered through the garden, saw that he had pushed a bureau against it, erecting a barricade that was as futile as it was, in all probability, unnecessary. The farmer was unpleasant and patently anti-Semitic. It was likely that he and Katya, who was also unpleasant and anti-Semitic, were lovers, but she did not think they were murderers or thieves. She realized that her father, sleep-deprived and malnourished, had lost his grip on reality and submitted to a latent paranoia. Irrational fear obscured reason. But it was transitory, she assured herself.

She steeled herself to action. She would help him to overcome it. He needed sleep, food, and reassurance. He would be fine.

She led him to a chair and spoke to him with a calm that she did not feel.

"I see that you are frightened. This has been a difficult time. I understand that. Of course we will make other arrangements. I will find us a new place to stay and I will get rid of Katya. I should have done that a long time ago."

She would not tell him that the maid had been seen at pro-Nazi rallies. Such knowledge would only feed his paranoia.

"It will be all right. We are not in any danger," she continued, her voice very soft.

She poured him a large glass of vodka, sliced the baguette, and covered it with the chèvre cheese he favored. This she cut into small pieces as though preparing a snack for a child. She offered him one bite at a time, encouraging him to eat slowly, to chew carefully. Obediently, he ate and drank. His hands stopped trembling and he nodded, willing himself to believe her. She smiled encouragingly and patted his shoulder as she handed him the food in the manner of a mother feeding a hungry but reluctant toddler.

"Eat, *Papochka*, eat," she coaxed.

She turned as her mother entered the room and rushed to her side.

"Oh, Idotchka. We have been so upset."

Bella's voice quivered, and her breath came in small gasps. She had rouged her very pale cheeks and circled her eyes with kohl. She wore her rainbow-colored robe, and her jet-black pomaded hair was a glistening helmet, giving her the look of the emaciated gypsy women who wandered the streets of Paris. Ida embraced her and imagined that she could feel her mother's heart flutter beneath the flimsy fabric.

"Everything will be all right, *Maman*. I promise," she said softly.

She had, she realized, assumed Bella's own tone, parroted the words her mother had so often uttered, copied the patient cadence of maternal reassurance, the daughter now the mother.

The next morning, she found lodgings for her parents at a pension in Saint-Dyé-sur-Loire. The proprietor, Madame Duval, was a widow whose husband had been killed in the First World War. She wore only the black serge dresses of the perpetual mourner. Day after day, she nourished her grief with hatred.

"*Les Boches.*"

She spat out her detestation of the Germans and showed Ida the gold-framed photograph of her very young husband in uniform. He had been twenty-five years old at his death. How old was Ida's soldier husband, she asked, and her eyes filled with tears when Ida told her that Michel had not yet celebrated his twenty-fifth birthday. Ida told her that she was Jewish and she wept again. She was proud to welcome Jews into her home.

"Ah, the poor Jews. *Les pauvres juifs.*" She sighed. "*Jésus*, poor *Jésus*, was himself a Jew." She fingered her crucifix.

Madame Duval kept the lights very dim. The rooms were cold, the kitchen small and crowded, but Ida was undeterred. Here there would be no fascist landlord, no slovenly, Jew-hating serving girl.

She returned to the farmhouse, paid the farmer more rent than was due him, and gave Katya two months' wages. She did not give them Madame Duval's address. Katya looked at her scornfully.

"You cannot buy my good will, Madame Rapaport," she said. "You and I recognize each other for what we are."

Ida did not reply. Katya's enmity, her hostile intimacy, was no longer of any importance.

"I wish you *bonne chance*," she said curtly and continued her packing.

—

Summer ended, and on the first day of September, a somber newscaster interrupted a radio broadcast of Mahler's Fourth Symphony with the announcement that Hitler had invaded Poland. The Chagalls stared at each other in stunned silence.

"What does this mean?" Bella asked fearfully.

Ida looked out the window at the clear sky, the shaded pathways ribbed with sunlight, at the children skipping beside their kerchiefed mothers who carried string bags laden with vegetables through the streets of the village. It was a scene of sylvan peace. If Michel was with her on such a day, they might have walked along the river, reveling in the brilliant sunlight, the cool breeze. But Michel was a soldier in an army that was surely preparing for battle. France, like England, was a signatory to the pact that promised to protect Poland and would therefore soon be at war with Germany.

"We don't yet know what it means, *Maman*," she said, struggling for a straw of reassurance, but her father shook his head wearily. His narrow face was frozen into the death mask of hopelessness. He switched the radio off. There was no need for additional news.

Two days later, Madame Duval knocked urgently on their door. Her face was flushed and she clutched her crucifix as though desperate for whatever comfort it might offer.

"*Mesdames, monsieur, c'est la guerre, la guerre,*" she told them, her voice so soft that they strained to hear her. "*La guerre, la guerre,*" she repeated and swayed from side to side.

Ida reached out to steady her, and Marc turned on the radio. Together they listened to the melancholic voice of the BBC announcer who informed his listeners that at eleven o'clock that morning, Prime Minister Chamberlain, who had promised Lady Clerk that there would be peace in their time, had informed the citizens of Great Britain that their country was at war with Germany.

"May God bless you all. May he defend the right. It is the evil things that we shall be fighting against—brute force, bad faith, injustice, oppression, and persecution—and against them I am certain that the right will prevail," Chamberlain concluded.

Riveted to the radio, they listened to Prime Minister Édouard

Daladier reveal in sad and muted tones that he had called on the Chamber of Deputies to authorize the declaration of war on Germany.

"The peace has been lost," the announcer said sadly.

"As though it had ever been found," Marc muttered and impatiently switched the dial to another station as though another broadcast might be more optimistic. They heard an even more sober report, and then there was a brief silence as a recording of "La Marseillaise" filled the airwaves.

In their small room in Saint-Dyé-sur-Loire, the Chagalls and Madame Duval stood and sang the anthem of their beloved country. The landlady's voice was frail but touchingly lovely. She held Ida's hand tightly as they lifted their voices in defiance of the grim news. "*Le jour de gloire est arrivé,*" they sang, and Ida wondered how many months, how many years, would have to pass before the day of glory would indeed arrive.

Marc switched the radio off, and Bella sank into the easy chair.

"Oh, not again," she said softly, and tears streaked her cheeks.

She had been only twenty-five years old when the guns of August sounded in 1914, and now, in her fiftieth year, Europe was at war yet again. Would every quarter century of her life launch another catastrophe? She wept in silence, and Marc and Ida looked at her helplessly. It was Madame Duval who sat beside Bella and took her hands in her own.

"*C'est la vie, madame,*" she said softly. "*C'est la vie.*"

"*C'est la vie,*" Bella repeated, her broken voice so soft that they could barely hear her.

Chapter Fourteen

*M*a *chérie*, how strange this war is," Michel wrote to Ida. "My lieutenant calls it the *drôle de guerre*, a war of falsity. No shots are fired. No bombs fall. I do not even bother to refill the magazine of my rifle, and I probably would not know how to fire it. The army has given us no training at all. Our officers seem to rely on their well-tailored uniforms and their smart berets for protection. They continue to assure us that the Maginot Line is impenetrable, and I hope that they are right, although I doubt it. Ida, they say that Paris is still quite peaceful, but be vigilant. I know that your father will have an exhibition at Galerie Mai, and while this is good news, it worries me that you will be traveling so often from the Loire to the city. I confess to being pessimistic, but I fear that the *drôle de guerre* will become *une guerre actuelle*, a real war. Please do what you can for my parents. You are in my thoughts, *ma chérie*."

Ida read and reread his letter, recalling the loving notes he had written her during the days of their courtship. Always he had ended with the tender assurance, "*Tu es dans mes rêves, dans mon coeur.* You are in my dreams. You are in my heart." Those words had vanished. She placed the letter in her drawer. At least she was in his thoughts if not in his dreams. She wondered if they were still in each other's hearts.

She followed his advice. She was vigilant as she and her father journeyed to Paris to prepare for the exhibition. A driver recommended by Madame Duval drove them to the city and back, their passports and identity cards within easy reach.

Paris was a joyless city. Christmas was approaching, but there was no appetite for festivity. No *Père Noëls* stood on street corners in scarlet costumes. Few wreaths were hung in shop windows or on front doors.

Everyone was suspect in a city gripped by fear. The cafés were empty, the restaurants deserted. Distrust contaminated friendships. Neighbors looked askance at each other. Accents were remarked upon and questioned. Marc, with his shock of wild curls, Russian peasant shirts, and loose linen suits, and Ida, with her red-gold hair, close-fitting, gem-colored dresses, and determined stride, attracted attention. Twice they were stopped by gendarmes and asked to produce their papers. A clerk in a patisserie ignored them. When Ida complained to the owner, she was told that his shop did not welcome foreigners.

"But I am French," she protested.

He stared at her in stony silence, and she left without purchasing anything. Rumors abounded. Gertrude Stein and Alice Toklas had left the city for unknown precincts. No one feared for their safety. It was known that they had a great deal of money as well as contacts among fascist sympathizers. But there was great concern about Chaim Soutine, George Grosz, and other Jewish painters and writers who had vanished. All Jews were in danger.

Traveling back to the Loire Valley, their hired car moved slowly down traffic-clogged roads. Trucks and cars, loaded with valises and trunks, and clumsy moving vans crammed with furniture formed a grim cortege. The faces of the drivers were wreathed in anger. Sullen children stared out of the grimy windows of crowded vehicles. Weeping women held their infants close. Ida dreaded yet another journey to Paris to prepare the catalog for the exhibition. She did not want to leave her parents during the holiday season, but she had no choice.

Alone in Paris, Ida worked on the exhibition, careful to avoid contact with anyone she did not trust. There were whispered rumors about suspected collaborators, speculations about when Paris itself would be invaded.

She visited Michel's parents and stood between them as they lit their Hanukkah menorah and sang the blessings very softly. The potato pancakes that Masha Rapaport prepared were overly salted, and Ida thought that she could taste her mother-in-law's tears in the crisp edges. Walking home, she stared up at the windows of strangers and glimpsed the soft lights of Christmas trees. Her own apartment was dark. She turned on the radio. Bach's "B Minor Mass," long her favorite, was being aired. She switched the radio off. She could not bear to hear the choir sweetly singing in German, the language of a nation that threatened her very life. She stared up at the painting of *The Bridal Chair* and wondered where Michel was on this cold starlit night.

The new year brought a brutal winter. Marc's exhibition at the Galerie Mai was sparsely attended as rumors as thick as the falling snow flew across Paris.

The Maginot Line would not hold.

German forces were moving west.

Paris was in danger.

Paris was safe.

The French military would take no action until they could count on British intervention.

The French military would launch an offensive regardless of British support.

In Saint-Dyé, the Chagalls read the papers obsessively and listened to the hourly newscasts.

They sat at Madame Duval's scrubbed wooden table and struggled to separate rumor from fact, to formulate a plan. Where should they go? What should they do? Their options were limited. There was no place to go. There was nothing to do. Ida continued to write her pleading letters. She no longer bothered to mask her desperation. Someone had to help them. If the Germans invaded, their death warrants, hers and her parents', would be sealed.

She haunted the Saint-Dyé telegraph office, sending urgent wires, and awaited replies that never came. Bella, ghostly pale, remained in bed throughout the day and wandered barefoot from room to room during the night. A spectral figure in her white nightgown, she paused occasionally at a window to stare into the darkness, her lips moving soundlessly until either Marc or Ida, sleepless themselves, walked her back to bed.

The Daladier government fell. The new prime minister, Paul Reynaud, seemed weak and ambivalent to Ida, strong and determined to Marc. Nothing was certain. Nothing was predictable. Food was being hoarded and money withdrawn from banks. Ida and Marc studied maps and train schedules as Bella grew weaker and more morose. Madame Duval planned to move to the home of relatives in the south.

"The war will come to the Loire," she said. "I do not want to see blood on the streets of my Saint-Dyé. I do not want to see Nazis sleeping in my beds, drinking my wine."

One night she carried the bottles stored in her cellar into the garden and emptied them one by one onto the frost-hardened earth. Ida helped her, gagging at the acrid odor and the finality of the gesture.

The landlady's decision resolved their own uncertainty. They too would move further south. They hired a driver who took them to Avignon and registered in a small hotel. Ida chose rooms that overlooked the boulevard and then she herself traveled to Paris, promising to return as soon as possible.

"I'm worried about Michel's parents," she said. "And I want to visit the American embassy. They may have news for us."

"Surely your in-laws can manage. Your mother and I need you," Marc objected sullenly. "And the Americans worry only about themselves. They will not help us."

She ignored his protest. He no longer had power over her. She was not the vulnerable adolescent girl he had forced into marriage. She had control of her own life and of theirs.

The United States Embassy in Paris was in a state of chaos. Crates filled the reception area and the air was heavy with the odor of burning documents. It was clear that the Americans were planning to evacuate immediately if the city fell to the Germans. A marine reluctantly admitted her and a harried cultural attaché barely looked up from his mountain of files to listen to her request for visas for her parents.

"Persons of note," she said. "My father is an artist of international distinction."

"Of course I know of your father. I know his reputation. But he is a Russian. The quota for Russian immigrants has been filled," he replied.

"My father now has French citizenship."

"The quota for France has also been filled. But in the unlikely, the very unlikely, event that places are found, remember each of your parents will have to put up a three-thousand-dollar bond to ensure that they will be able to sustain themselves in the United States. And of course they will have to pay for their passage."

"That will not be a problem," she assured him.

Her father's account in the Bank of Scotland would suffice.

But the attaché was no longer listening, his attention diverted by a shower of memos that a pale secretary dropped on his desk. Ida left the embassy without looking back.

She arrived at the Rapaports' apartment where they were preparing to travel to the southern coast and helped them pack their meager possessions. Before leaving, Masha Rapaport looked around the barren flat and thrust the key into her worn black leather purse. Metal struck metal. She smiled bitterly.

"Key against key," she said. "The keys of all the homes I have left. My house in Moscow. Our dacha in the Crimea. My flat in Berlin. And now our little shop and flat in Paris. How many more keys will I gather in this life of mine, Ida? Another and perhaps another, if we are fortunate. We pray for a miracle. Will there be a miracle, Idotchka?"

Ida shook her head. "We can hope. We can pray," she said, her voice flat, devoid of hope, indifferent to prayer.

She kissed her in-laws good-bye. Her mother-in-law's cheek was papery and her father-in-law's unshaven skin bruised her lips.

"*Au revoir.*"

They whispered the words in unison and she hurried away before they could see her tears.

Back in her own small apartment, she packed their few belongings, relieved that Michel, during a brief leave, had crated the painting of

The Bridal Chair and shipped it to Saint-Dyé. She thrust her sketch-book and drawing pencils into her already bulky portmanteau. She paid the concierge the rent that was due and told her that she and Michel were leaving Paris.

"Will you be returning, Madame Rapaport?" the kindly woman asked.

"I think not," Ida replied.

"Where will you be going?"

"That is uncertain."

She trusted no one. Not even this pleasant woman with whom she had occasionally shared a glass of *vin ordinaire*.

"I understand," the concierge said sadly.

They shook hands solemnly and Ida hurried away, eager suddenly to catch the next autobus to Avignon.

During that long journey, she opened her sketchbook for the first time in months. She drew, in odd geometric design, an uneasily balanced tower composed of oddly shaped keys, at the apex of which a shawled woman stood, her arms outstretched. She stared at the completed drawing, surprised at her own skill. She had all but forgotten that she too was an artist.

Exhausted, she fell asleep, awakening only when the bus reached Avignon.

The church bells tolled as she made her way down the cobble-stone paths of the ancient city, hurrying to the small hotel where her parents had lodging. The proprietor stared at her in surprise.

"But Monsieur and Madame Chagall are not here. They left some days ago. They have moved to their new home."

"Their new home?"

She stared at him, stunned by his words.

"Yes, madame. They live in Gordes. It is beautiful, the little village of Gordes. Of course they made a strange choice of *maison*, very strange choice, but they were determined. Here is the letter they left for you with their new address. They are so kind, your parents, so charming. Look, your father gave me this drawing and I have framed it."

He pointed to a framed charcoal drawing of his hotel that Ida knew her father had dashed off swiftly and thoughtlessly, remembering of course to scrawl his name in a corner.

"Yes. They are. Very kind. Very charming," she agreed.

She took a taxi to Gordes. It was, the driver told her, an impoverished village with very little to recommend it.

"Here in Avignon, we have the Palace of the Popes and the Bridge of Saint-Bénézet. What do they have in Gordes? Poverty and more poverty. Madame, the streets there, the *calades*, are so narrow and so hilly that it is impossible to walk from one to another without stopping for breath."

She read out her parents' address.

"The Fontaine Basse quarter. Why should your parents choose to live there?" he asked disapprovingly. "Of course property there is cheap, very cheap. Your people like cheap, *n'est-ce pas?* And they know how to bargain. *Les juifs.*"

He turned, looked at her slyly, and fingered the large Saint-Bénézet medallion he wore around his neck.

Ida flushed. How could he have known that the Chagalls were Jewish? But then, of course, how could he not have known? Marc Chagall was famous in France, celebrated throughout the country as *l'artiste juif,* the Jewish artist, despite his yearning to be known as *l'artiste français.* If a taxi driver in Avignon knew he was Jewish, then his religion was known to everyone in France. He would be a marked man in the event of a German invasion.

She stared out the window as the driver maneuvered his way upward from the *calades* past the narrow pink stone houses. He zigzagged through the meandering streets and alleyways, cursing under his breath as shadows obscured his vision.

"This is the Fontaine Basse quarter," he muttered at last, driving more slowly and coming to a halt before a large, rectangular-shaped stone building. He consulted the address she had given him and turned to look at her.

"There must be a mistake, madame. Surely your parents would

not live here. It was once a school run by the nuns. My own sister studied there. It's been deserted for many years. The rooms are huge and very difficult to heat. My poor sister shivered throughout her lessons. And the windows are large and there are many of them. The holy sisters spent hours and hours cleaning them. Who would want such rooms, such windows? You must have mistaken the address."

"My father may rent it for a short time," Ida replied. "He is an artist and needed room for his paintings until we make other arrangements."

The words soured her mouth. What other arrangements could they make? She paid the fare and added a very large tip.

"You see, monsieur," she said as he looked at the generous franc notes in surprise, "we are a generous people, *les juifs.*"

He cringed and helped her remove her bags. "Of course. I meant no harm, madame."

"I understand. No one means any harm," she said wearily.

She did not knock but thrust the heavy door wide open so that sunlight flooded the room. Bella and Marc, startled by the sudden radiance, wheeled about and rushed to greet her. Their faces were aglow, their voices strong.

"Idotchka. How wonderful that you are here. Isn't this marvelous? So much room, such magnificent light. It is a miracle that we found such a wonderful place," Marc said excitedly.

He embraced her with new strength.

Bella, all lassitude banished, kissed her on both cheeks. She wore the uniform of their many moves. Ida recognized the familiar coverall she always wore to unpack, the faded scarf that covered her dark hair.

"*Ma chérie.* My darling. Such a surprise we have prepared for you. Come to the window. Look at what a view we have," she exclaimed, pulling Ida across the room.

She brandished a feather duster as though it were a scepter, waving it about the huge, many-windowed room; she was the queen of her newly claimed domestic kingdom. No longer a lodger, she once again had a home. Ida knew that her mother was happiest when she created an attractive and welcoming domestic fortress over which she had dominance. The world around her might fall into chaos, but her home would be orderly and filled with beauty.

She led Ida to a wide open window, its panes glinting in the afternoon sunlight. Ida stared out at fields covered with lavender, the fragrance of the delicate blossoms suffusing the room. She looked up and saw the dramatic outcroppings of mica-silvered rocks that jutted from the sky-hugging hills of the Vaucluse range.

"Yes. The space is wonderful," she agreed. "And the view is marvelous. I can see why you rented it."

Her father looked at her in surprise. "But we didn't rent it. It was not available to lease. We bought it."

"You bought it?"

She was incredulous. How could her parents buy property in a country they would soon be forced to flee? This was a time to buy jewels and diamonds, portable and concealable, baubles that could be traded for currency, used for bribes, offered to counterfeiters in exchange for false papers. Jews did not buy houses they might have to leave, clutching keys to doors they would never again open. Her parents, like Michel's mother, had keys to abandoned homes and studios in Vitebsk and Berlin, in Paris and Montchauvet. And now there would be keys to a convent school in Gordes. She stared at them, flushed with anger.

"Yes, of course, we bought it," Marc said dismissively. "Why not? We both loved this building. There is room to store all my paintings and I have a wonderful studio. And you haven't seen all the rooms. There is a suite for you and Michel. We thought you would be pleased."

Ida struggled to keep her voice calm, to contain her fury. "What did you pay for it?" she asked, already fearing the answer.

He walked over to a cluttered desk and rummaged through a pile of papers. "I have it right here. One moment. Ah, this is the deed. Do you want to see the deed?"

"No. I want to know how much you paid for it," she repeated.

"Wait. I will find it. The receipt." He fumbled through the papers, ignoring those that fluttered to the floor. Invoices were mingled with correspondence, newspaper clippings with scrawled shopping lists. He would, as always, rely on her to put them in order, she thought bitterly. She was, after all, both secretary and bookkeeper.

"All right," he muttered, "I can't find the bill of sale. But I entered the payment in the register of the checkbook just as you always ask me to do."

He beamed at her like a small boy anticipating congratulations for doing the right thing and flourished a leather-bound checkbook. Her heart sank as she recognized the scarlet insignia of the Royal Bank of Scotland. Of course, she had left both the bankbook and the check-book with him. It had never occurred to her that he would look at it, and certainly she had never imagined that he would write a check against their account. She paid their bills and balanced their accounts. Marc claimed indifference to money. His art consumed him. He had no time to deal with financial trivia.

Ida was a skilled bookkeeper. She kept careful records, studied and calculated bank statements. She knew exactly the amount that had been on deposit in Edinburgh, which included the receipts from the Leicester Gallery exhibition, the Guggenheim purchase, and remittances from the Vollard sales. She knew that there was enough sterling on deposit to cover their passage and the three-thousand-dollar bond each of them would need to obtain American visas. That money was their only insurance, their guarantee of survival.

She took the checkbook from him with trembling hands and studied the entry of the check he had written to an estate agent in Avignon to cover the purchase of the abandoned Catholic school. It was in the amount of six thousand, seven hundred English pounds. Her breath came in tortured gasps, and vomit soured her mouth. She sat down and gripped the arms of the chair, a new chair, she realized, upholstered in red velvet. More money had gone for the purchase of furnishings. She smiled bitterly and stroked the fabric. What would her father do with this red velvet chair when he had to flee Gordes? She knew the answer. He would, of course, leave it behind. He had the habit of leaving things behind. Things and people. Furniture languished in storage in Paris, in Passy, and in Berlin. There were his sisters in Vitebsk, his teachers and friends in St. Petersburg and Berlin, all left behind, their addresses unknown.

She sighed deeply. She should not have left the checkbook with him. She knew that despite his professed indifference to money, he always bought what he wanted, spending lavishly on his own wardrobe and on Bella's, on furnishings and travel. His money was not limited to material purchases. And money was his weapon, his emotional cudgel. She remembered how he had bought her compliance to the abortion and to her marriage by threatening to deny her financial support.

She handled the sales of his paintings, but although he did not question her judgment, he always quizzed her with studied disinterest about the prices she had agreed to and the amount of her own commission.

"I am making you a rich woman, Idotchka," he had said more than once with wry affection.

She saw with new clarity that his self-proclaimed indifference to money was a feint. He had always been aware of the exact amount on deposit in Scotland and had not hesitated to use it to buy the property in Gordes and to furnish it with his usual extravagance.

Ida stared hard at him, as though seeing him for the first time. He averted his eyes from her penetrating gaze, and Bella hurried to his side and placed her hand protectively on his shoulder.

"Why are you so upset, Ida?" he asked impatiently. "You see how much this house has meant to your mother. And it was my money, after all."

"Of course it was your money," she replied. "I should have thought that you would want to use your money to protect *Mamochka*, to protect me, to protect Michel and perhaps his parents. Now we are without funds for bonds if our visas to America are, by some miracle, granted, no money to pay our passage. You have wasted it all on this house, on this abandoned school."

She waved her arms and looked around the room, dimly lit because a storm was gathering in the Vaucluse hills.

"We don't need visas," he retorted. "No one will arrest Marc Chagall. No one will dare. We will not have to leave France. We will be protected here. We are citizens of France."

"Other so-called citizens of France, artists and writers as famous as you believe yourself to be, have already left or are making plans to leave or to find hiding places. Chaim Soutine has left Paris. Picasso told me that Gertrude Stein and her friend Alice are gone. Max Ernst, Franz and Alma Werfel, Lion Feuchtwanger, even Golo Mann, Thomas Mann's own son—all of them are seeking refuge, all of them understand the danger. If Golo, the son of a Nobel Laureate, doesn't believe that his family's fame will protect him, you think we will be safe because you are the great Marc Chagall? How could you have gambled away our survival?" she asked bitterly.

"There is still money," he said, shrugging his shoulders. "Your own account is still intact."

"The funds from what you call 'my own account' have been sustaining us for all these months." Her voice dripped sarcasm, then rose in anger. "I never thought of that money as 'mine.' I thought of it as a family account and I spent it on our family."

Ida crossed the room and stood before an open window. Rain was already beginning to fall, and she leaned out and allowed the droplets to cool her face, moisten her hair. Her anger dissipated into resignation. She breathed in the sweetened air.

All was not lost. Time was still on their side. The Germans had invaded Belgium and the Netherlands, but France would continue the fight for freedom. Hadn't Prime Minister Paul Reynaud assured the nation that Paris would not fall? She had memorized the words with which he had charged his people "to be worthy of the grandeur of the hour...to rise to the misfortunes of our country." Help might yet come from the United States where a committee to assist artists had formed. She had written to Lord Clerk about obtaining British visas. Palestine was a possibility. She turned to her mother and forced a smile. She nodded to her father, a reluctant gesture of forgiveness.

Bella breathed a sigh of relief. She had feared that Marc's temper and Ida's fury would strike against each other, like flint against a rock, creating an irrepressible conflagration. That, at least, had been avoided. She kissed Ida and smoothed away the tendrils of damp hair.

"Come, Idotchka. Let me show you the lovely room I have prepared for you," she said. "It's so wonderful to think that we own a place of our own, that we are safe in this lovely house."

Ida followed her into the airy bedroom. She dutifully admired the woven purple coverlet and brightly patterned cushions Bella had placed on her bed. *The Bridal Chair* was in place on the whitewashed wall. She stared up at it and then bent to sniff the white roses Bella had placed in a black ceramic vase that rested on the bedside table. The fresh wide-petaled blossoms might have been plucked from the beribboned bridal bouquet of snow-colored roses in her father's painting of the monochromatic bridal chair that lacked a bride. Bella had placed a silver-framed photograph of Michel on the bureau. Ida studied his thin face, his sad dark eyes.

Where was he? she wondered. *Where was her alpine lover, her weary husband?*

"Thank you, *Mamochka*. The room is beautiful," she said at last.

There would be no more recriminations. What was done was done. She would find a way; she would contrive a new agenda for survival.

Chapter Fifteen

The days in Gordes passed slowly. Ida resumed her letter-writing blitz, focusing on the escalating peril the Chagalls faced. Elsa answered Ida's letters, although the help she could offer was limited. She and André had a small son and they were both working double shifts at the hospital.

"But, Ida, all your concerns seem to be only for your parents. You must worry about yourself and Michel," she cautioned.

"Michel and I are young and strong," Ida wrote in reply. "We will be able to manage. My parents are old and my mother is very fragile. Neither of them has as yet confronted the dangerous reality of their situation, so I must fight for them. I know that I can count on you to help."

A cryptic letter from Elsa offered hope. André had a patient, a man of considerable wealth, who was active in a committee concerned with aiding artists and writers trapped in Nazi-dominated Europe. There was, Elsa wrote cautiously, reason to be optimistic.

Ida understood that Elsa could not be more specific. The rumors of censorship were well founded. Every envelope that reached the family in Gordes was opened and indifferently resealed. She continued her efforts, her pen tightly clutched, ink staining her cramped fingers.

Marc worked at a furious pace. In the wide-windowed studio, he alternated his tortured depictions of crucifixions with paintings of ripe peaches, jeweled clusters of grapes, plucked and dressed poultry. He countered martyrdom with nourishment, the cruelty of man with the enduring beauty of nature's bounty.

Bella cooked. The fragrant aroma of simmering soups and stews drifted through the house. Food was still abundant. They ate well, seated at the long refectory table, a convent legacy. A vase of fresh flowers that Bella arranged each morning was always on the sideboard. They were actors on a stage of peaceful domesticity, clicking cutlery against china, filling their wineglasses, talking softly to each other. They did not speak of the war. They did not speak of Michel whose battalion had been posted to a distant garrison, probably along the Somme. Ida prayed for his safety each night and then wondered to whom she was praying. She envied her Uncle Yaakov his perfect faith.

"I am praying to Yaakov's God," she told herself.

Each morning, Bella wandered through the peaceful garden, filling her basket with sprigs of lavender that she distributed throughout the house, mingling them with the first roses of the season. The sweet scent wafted through every room, battling the stench of fear leaching through doors and windows.

On a glorious June afternoon, Bella called to Ida from the garden, her voice vibrant with delight. A lilac bush had burst into bloom.

"We have lilacs," she called. "Wonderful white lilacs. Ida, come at once. You must see them."

But Ida did not stir from her desk. She sat as though in a stupor, her hand resting on the dial of the radio. As always, she turned on the news hourly, resuming the habit her father had abandoned. On this morning, when lilacs burst into bloom, the broadcaster thundered disaster. German invasion! German assault! Paris, the City of Light, had fallen to the Nazis. Waves of nausea washed over her. She had anticipated the worst, and yet she was unprepared for it.

No, she thought in despair. *Oh no. It cannot be. It has not happened.*

The news paralyzed her. The unthinkable was an actuality. Even with British support, the French army had surrendered, their resistance even briefer than that of Poland, whom they had so sanctimoniously mocked. Prime Minister Reynaud's brave and beautiful words had fallen on deaf ears. His people had not, in fact, heeded his plea and risen to the grandeur of the hour. Neither lilacs nor lavender could insulate Marc and Bella Chagall from the dangers that they had refused to acknowledge.

"Ida," Bella called yet again.

Ida went to the window. She looked up at the sunlit sky and glanced at the lilac bush heavy with alabaster blossoms. The beauty of the day broke her heart. She struggled for breath and then called to Bella, who cradled a bouquet of the lovely flowers.

"Get Papa. Get Papa and both of you come in at once."

And so they sat together, Marc in the red velvet chair wearing his paint-spattered smock, a streak of carmine paint bloodying his cheek, Bella hugging her white lilacs, and Ida with her ink-stained fingers clasped. In silence, they listened to the terms of the armistice that was clearly not an armistice at all but a humiliating acceptance of defeat. The Nazis would occupy two-thirds of the country. The south-central region would be governed by Marshal Pétain, who was headquartered in Vichy.

"Vichy?" Bella asked in surprise. She knew the town. She had taken the curative waters at the spa there. A beautiful place, a landscape unsuited to war.

"Yes. Vichy," Ida repeated.

The charade was over. Her parents could no longer ignore the danger of their situation. Picturesque Vichy was now the grim seat of fascism. Every French port except Marseilles was sealed. Ida's own wary optimism had been misguided. They had, in fact, run out of time. Masha Rapaport had been right. Only a miracle could rescue them. She feared for Michel's parents. Had they reached the Riviera, which might still provide a brief haven? And what of her Uncle Yaakov's family trapped in a defeated, Nazi-dominated Paris? She went to the window and stared out at the lilac bush where the innocent blossoms trembled in a gentle breeze.

Hand in hand, Marc and Bella left, closing the door softly behind them.

In her room, Ida lifted the photograph of Michel from her bureau. Where was he now, her soldier husband, her Michel, *ami* and *amant*?

Was he alive or dead, free or a prisoner? She glanced at the calendar. She would not soon forget the date. On June 14, 1940, her life as she had known it had ended.

"Michel," she whispered, and she collapsed onto her bed, his framed portrait heavy upon her breast.

Chapter Sixteen

pring ended and the heavy heat of summer descended on Gordes, broken now and again by a teasing wind, sea-scented and cruelly brief. Marc painted in his underwear, sometimes working indoors and sometimes beneath a palm tree, in the shade of its heavy fronds. His body glistened with pearls of sweat that mingled with the droplets of paint that fell from his brush. The tales of suffering as hordes of refugees fled Paris, the news of concentration camps and deportations, impacted his work. He painted with anguished ferocity, mixing his colors carefully, creating an odd albescent white, the noncolor of innocence, for his painting of *The Madonna of the Village*. He saw Gordes as Calvary and the Jews of Europe as martyrs at the stations of the cross. In his febrile imagination, France became the Holy Land beleaguered by barbarians. Paris was Jerusalem, Hitler was Pontius Pilate, and the Jews, like their coreligionist Jesus, were once again the victims.

He ignored Bella's pleas that he wear proper clothing. It worried her that the goyim of Gordes might see him at work outside in his dingy underwear.

"Are we expecting company? Are we entertaining the artists of Paris?" he asked sarcastically. "Who comes to see the pariah Jewish artist in this primitive town? I will paint naked if I want to."

Bella sighed and offered no further argument. She dressed each day in the colorful, long, loose gowns of gossamer fabric she had favored in Paris, but she knew it was useless to argue with him. She spent hours on the chaise lounge beneath the window. The aroma of the newly blossoming lemons and citrons wafted toward her. With a damp cloth covering her eyes, she drifted into a melancholic daze, anesthetized by sadness and despair.

Each day, Ida walked into the village. She posted her own letters and hoped for a letter from Michel or even a response to one of her urgent appeals for help. She would not let her hope die. Each day, Yvette, the weary young postmistress, shook her head sadly, and each day, Ida nodded and shrugged her shoulders.

"*À demain*," she said. "Till tomorrow."

"*À demain*," Yvette agreed.

They were coconspirators, she and the slender postmistress, whose thin fingers sorted through stamps and aerograms. They were engaged in a pact of mutual reassurance, convincing themselves that perhaps the next day or the day after that would bring news that would lighten their hearts. Yvette's husband was also a soldier and, like Michel, his whereabouts were unknown. Ida knew his name. Pierre. His picture, taken in uniform, stood on Yvette's counter, just as Michel's photograph stood on her bureau. The faces of their absent husbands vested the young wives with memory and hope.

Ida struggled to recall the sound of Michel's voice, the scent of his body, the power of his passion. She said his name as she looked at his photograph. "Michel. Michel, *mon mari*." She imagined that Yvette turned to her own husband's picture from time to time during the day and murmured, "Pierre, *mon mari*—Pierre, my husband."

Always she walked home slowly, savoring the peace of the village and her own solitude. She stopped at the shops to scavenge provisions for their dinner. Vegetables and fruits, fish and meat were scarce. Hoarding had followed the news of the defeat of the French army. Flour, sugar, and coffee had disappeared from the shelves of the grocery store, but Ida smiled engagingly at the greengrocer, batted her eyelashes at the baker, and complimented the fishmonger on the beauty of his newborn daughter. With luck, she arrived home with wilted greens, a stale baguette, and a pale fillet of sole. A farmer whose picture she sketched, telling him how handsome he was, sold her eggs and confided that he had a fondness for redheaded women. She thanked him and whispered coyly that her soldier husband shared his taste.

"Survival by seduction," she told herself bitterly as she prepared their dinner.

They ate in silence. Bella no longer cooked. She ignored the food that was set before her, managing a few bites only when Ida insisted. Marc greedily emptied his own plate and then scooped up the remnants of Bella's meal. He wondered each evening why Ida could not have managed at least a small sweet for dessert.

"I will try, *Papochka*," she said coldly. "But there are no sweets in Gordes."

Her annoyance curdled into a silent anger. She would not try. He asked too much of her.

He returned to his studio after dinner, and Ida and Bella sat in the dimly lit room and listened to the gloomy newscast. Italy was allied with Germany. London was being bombed. The Vichy government was intensifying its anti-Semitic agenda. Pétain redefined French citizenship, nullifying the papers of all individuals who had been naturalized since 1927. The Chagalls' precious and hard-earned passports and identity cards were invalid. They were classified as "undesirables."

"Still, it is better than being called an enemy alien," Ida said dryly.

So-called enemy aliens were being rounded up and confined to secure prison camps. Ida knew that Feuchtwanger, the great novelist, was at Camp des Milles, a former tile and brick factory, now a fortress ringed with barbed wire. She shivered. Camp des Milles was only kilometers from sleepy, gentle Gordes, where lemons were still peacefully harvested and stamps were offered for sale in a well-run post office. Her family's daily existence was surreal. Her daily reply to Yvette, "*À demain*," till tomorrow, might well be "*Jamais*," never.

Bella remained in the salon each evening until Marc returned from his studio. Ida left her sitting in the half darkness, pleading fatigue.

"I am tired, *Maman*," she said. She kissed her on both cheeks, always saddened by the papery texture of her mother's pale skin.

"Sleep well, Idotchka," Bella murmured each night.

She did not sleep well. Once again, frenetic dreams caused her to toss and turn, to awaken gasping for breath, her body awash in the sweat of nocturnal terror. In that nether world, she was racing, as always, but she was no longer a child clinging to her parents' hands. It was her adult self, grown to a monstrous size, who propelled her much-diminished parents forward, their slow and belabored pace hampering her own progress. She lurched forward, hobbled by the burden of her father's rolled canvases and the small awkwardly shaped bundles of her mother's sorrows strapped to her back. Now and again, she tried to run, stooped though she was beneath her burdens, fearful of her pursuers who grew closer and closer. The hooves of their horses pounded as they gained ground.

"Don't leave us, Idotchka. Don't abandon us," the parents of her dream pleaded. Their voices were wisps of sound drowned out by a sudden storm. Rain fell and lightning exploded in a blaze of light. A thunderbolt crashed deafeningly as the dream ended. Always she awakened then, relieved that the night was, after all, quiet, that the storm's crescendo had no reality. She touched her face then and understood that the raindrops that fell upon her face were her own tears, that her flight was illusory, that she was safe in a bed scented with lavender.

On a hot July night, when her room was silvered by moonlight, she again awakened to the familiar cacophony of that imagined storm. But the dream's ending was altered. There was now an unfamiliar and insistent knocking, the sound of iron against wood. She opened her eyes, thrust herself into dream-free wakefulness, but the pounding continued. It was real. Someone was knocking at the front door, repeatedly, desperately.

She glanced at her clock. It was two in the morning. Her heart beat rapidly as she sprang from her bed. There had been frightening reports of nocturnal home invasions by the Vichy police, sometimes accompanied by Gestapo troopers. Such terror squads were in fierce pursuit of "enemy aliens" or "undesirables," who were summarily arrested, thrown into trucks, and transported to the prison at Camp des Milles.

"Jews," the townspeople whispered to each other. "That's who they're after."

The good citizens of Gordes assured themselves that they were safe. It was only the Jews and the gypsies who were in danger. They whispered about rewards offered for information about such alien undesirables.

Ida knew that it was common knowledge her family was Jewish. Gordes was a very poor village. Anyone might betray them for the price of a dozen eggs, a bushel of potatoes. And it seemed that someone had.

The knocking continued, louder now. She trembled and ventured toward the window. A tall man, the epaulettes of his uniform glinting in the moonlight, stood there, his arm extended, his booted foot kicking the heavy oaken door.

He pounded once with great ferocity and then again. She imagined that her parents were cowering in their bedrooms, fearful and trembling. Swiftly, she brushed her hair, shrugged into a peignoir, choosing one that was sheer enough to reveal her breasts. With shaking hands, she applied lipstick, perfume, a dash of rouge.

She hurried to the front door, freezing her face into a mask of indignation, struggling to rehearse the indignant words she would hurl at the invader. "How dare you disturb decent people's sleep at such an hour? Have you no consideration for my elderly parents who are not well? Leave at once."

Or perhaps she would smile in beguiling confusion. "Surely you have the wrong address. But would you perhaps like a cold drink on such a hot night?" She would smile and toy with the ribbons of her dressing gown.

The danger both energized and calmed her. She braced herself, opened the door, and stared into the darkness at the tall, gaunt man whose clenched fist was raised high. Dizzied, she struggled for breath, steadied herself, and looked at him, unable to speak, unable to move.

He stood on the broad stone step. His creased and filthy uniform hung loosely on his gaunt body. His beret was askew. Roadside dust silvered his thick dark hair, and his narrow face was pale with fatigue. A duffel bag caked with mud was on the ground beside him. Her heart stopped. Her hands trembled.

"Michel," she whispered, fearful that if she raised her voice he would disappear. "Oh, Michel, is it really you?"

He opened his arms wide and she collapsed into them. "Yes, my Ida. *C'est moi.* Michel."

His voice was so soft she could barely hear him, but she lifted her hand to touch his lips, to trace the contours of his face, the roughness of his unshaven chin, the tiny scar at the corner of his mouth. The pressure of her fingers confirmed his reality. She remained in his embrace, her ear pressed to his chest so that she could hear the beating of his heart. He was alive; her prayers to the God she did not believe in had been answered.

She felt his lips on one cheek and then the other. She removed his beret, threaded his hair through her fingers, and led him to her room. They did not speak. They had no need for words. Their relief was palpable, their exhaustion profound. They stretched out across her bed and fell asleep in each other's arms. No dream invaded her sleep that night. She was protected; she was safe.

———

She awakened the next morning to the gentle pressure of his hand upon her head. He smiled as she turned toward him. They spoke softly then, in the half-light of dawn, of all that had happened during the long months of their separation. She told him of the moves from the Loire farmhouse to Saint-Dyé, to Avignon, and at last to Gordes. She marveled that he had found them.

"My parents knew that you had been in Avignon. They managed to get a letter to me, so when I was demobilized, I went from one inn to another in Avignon until I found the hotel where your parents had stayed. The concierge there told me that you were in Gordes. There was no transport so I walked here, catching a ride for a few kilometers with a truck driver and for another few kilometers with a milkman. Short rides and very long walks."

He rubbed his bare feet, and she saw the broken skin and angry blisters on his heels.

"Where are your parents?" she asked.

"They managed to get to Nice. They think that they will be safer there because it is under Italian occupation. There is a great difference between the Italians and the Germans."

"Is there?" she asked bitterly. Mussolini, after all, had joined forces with Hitler, and the Italian army had laid siege to France from the south.

"No one is as brutal as the Germans," he replied bitterly.

She cringed at the harshness of his tone, muted into sorrow as he spoke of his own brief and terrible war. He had fought in the triangle bounded by Amiens on the Somme and then in the Oise Valley. The German onslaught had been vicious. The badly trained, inadequately armed French troops had confronted a superior, well-trained force, an army without mercy.

"I had a rifle, but I barely knew how to load the magazine. I shared a trench with a boy named François, a sixteen-year-old from a farm near Le Havre. He had never shaved, never made love. He cried for his mother when he threw his grenades, sometimes forgetting to remove the pins. *'Maman. Maman.'* I don't think I will ever forget his voice. We both ran out of ammunition, but he had one last grenade. He stood up to throw it, and an enemy bullet hit him. He fell back, onto me, bleeding so heavily that his blood soaked my shirt. I touched his wrist and felt his pulse, very faint but still a sign of life. A German soldier tumbled into our trench and, without blinking, shot him in the head and then leapt out waving his pistol. The Nazis weren't taking prisoners. I heard their officers shouting. 'Shoot! Shoot to kill! No prisoners!' And that is what they did. The bastards."

Michel sighed and closed his eyes.

"And yet you survived," Ida said wonderingly.

"Yes. Because I didn't move and because I was covered in François's blood, so that damn Boche assumed that I was dead. And at that moment, lying there, I wished that I was."

But he had survived and somehow found his way to a base where he was issued a clean uniform, given a fistful of francs, and demobilized. He was on his own. A defeated France had no further need for its soldiers. He had concealed his demobilization papers in his underwear and set out to find his wife, his Ida. Her name had become his mantra.

"And that is what I did. I found you," he said triumphantly and held her close.

There was a light knock, tentative, hesitant. Ida and Michel lay very still and said nothing as the door opened. Bella and Marc, avian figures enveloped in their oversized, wide-winged nightclothes, stood in the doorway. They stared at their daughter and her husband.

"Michel came last night," Ida said.

"Yes. We heard him," Marc said. He held out his hand, and Michel lifted himself up and grasped it. "*Shalom aleichem.* Peace be with you." Marc offered the traditional greeting one Jew extends to another.

"*Aleichem shalom,*" Michel replied dutifully.

"Welcome, Michel," Bella whispered.

They left the room as silently as they had entered it.

Michel reflected on the brevity of their greeting. They had not asked him a single question about where he had fought and what he had seen. He understood that they did not want such knowledge. They preferred that the war remain an abstract. Its reality was too frightening.

He sighed and turned to Ida, grateful to lie beside her in this strange, oddly constructed house. He thought of how they had stood together in the moonlit darkness, how she had melted into his arms. It was enough that their reunion had been suffused with affection and gratitude, with touch and caress. It was of no importance that it had been oddly devoid of passion.

"Because we are so tired, so very tired," he said aloud and wondered if he believed his own words.

The two couples settled uneasily into their shared life in Gordes, entangled in a familial snare, trapped by bonds of love and resentment, their roles defined.

Each morning Marc retreated into his wide-windowed studio. He had furnished it with a large table, wicker chairs plundered from a garden shed, and a small cot. It was flooded with sunlight throughout the day and he was reluctant to leave it, even for meals. More often than not, he ate alone, barely acknowledging Ida when she set the tray of food down on the table cluttered with brushes soaking in turpentine. She cleared away pots of paint and linseed oil, carefully capped distorted tubes. Painting supplies were in short supply, and she guarded them closely, aware that they were as necessary to her father's survival as food and drink.

Bella continued to work on her memoir, filling notebook after notebook with her memories of Vitebsk. She wrote of Sabbath dinners at the candlelit table, of festival preparations, the scent of the citron at Sukkot, the crimson wine stains on the white Passover tablecloth. Sleeping and waking, she heard her parents' voices, her brothers' boyhood quarrels. She occasionally wandered into the studio and shared a meal with Marc. They spoke softly in Yiddish and sang half-remembered songs, occasionally with Ida. Never with Michel.

"It is not that I do not like your husband," Marc told Ida one day as she cleared the dirty dishes and glasses from the studio table. "It is simply that he does not interest me."

Ida was silent. She did not tell him that for Michel, the reverse was true. He did not like Marc, but he found him intriguing. But of course, who would not be intrigued by her father, that elfin narcissistic genius whose imagination soared and whose faith in his own power and prestige was indomitable? After all, she herself had revered him as an artist, marveling at the enormity and eclecticism of his talent. It had taken her years to confront his flaws, to recognize his foibles and frailties. She loved him still, but she saw him with a disturbing clarity.

When the two couples were together, they discussed only the progress of the war. The news was never good. Britain stood alone against the Nazis. The German war machine moved steadily across the continent, and with each fascist victory, the Jews of Europe were increasingly endangered. The rumors of concentration camps were no longer rumors. They were stark reality. The neutrality of the United States was bewildering.

A letter from Elsa offered a glimmer of hope. "We worry about you and Michel, but there may soon be good news. A letter will come to you from the American Consulate in Marseilles. Read it carefully."

In yet another letter, Elsa wrote of a man named Varian Fry.

Elsa's cryptic words gave Ida hope. She continued her own daily routine of constant correspondence, her walks into Gordes, occasionally accompanied by Michel whose presence attracted dangerous attention.

"We must be careful," she told him, but he had left his fear in the trench, drowned in the blood of the sixteen-year-old boy who had never kissed a girl or passed a razor across his chin.

"What will happen will happen," Michel said. "I am done with running."

Daringly he traveled to Nice to visit his parents. The resort city was crowded with refugees. Bewildered throngs of sad-eyed families teemed through the narrow streets. Their clothing was worn, their bodies unwashed. Hunger soured their breath. The refugees slept beneath the boardwalk, in abandoned cabanas. Whole families shared a single room in dismal *pensiones*.

Michel's parents, veteran survivors, had somehow found a hovel in which to live and scavenged scraps of food. They urged him to bring Ida and join them.

"Nice is farther south than Gordes, closer to Marseilles, and the port of Marseilles is still open. There would be more hope for you here," his father pleaded as his mother continued to fold scraps of red crepe paper into the poppies she sold on the street.

"I have heard that the American consul in Marseilles is sympathetic to Jews and has granted visas on compassionate grounds to French citizens. You and Ida might be eligible," she said, twisting a wire about the flimsy paper blossom. "Once in America, you would be able to help us, to help Ida's parents," she said. "You might as well try. What is there left to lose?"

The wire pierced her finger, but she ignored the droplet of scarlet blood.

"I doubt that we would qualify for such visas, but even if we did, Ida would never leave her parents, and the Chagalls insist that they are safe in Gordes," Michel said sadly.

And he, of course, would never leave Ida, not to save his own life, not to save the lives of his parents. Ida was his bride, his wife, his love, whom he soothed in the darkness of her dream-haunted nights.

He kissed his mother's hand and tasted her blood upon his tongue.

Chapter Seventeen

*A*s the summer dragged on, the bad news grew worse. Anti-Semitic legislation in Vichy, the arrests and deportations of prominent Jews, the German advances and victories, thrust the Gordes household into a paralyzing depression. Bella moved like a somnambulist, a silent, spectral figure in her flowing white gowns. Marc exploded in anger at the slightest annoyance. A tube of paint disappeared; he could not find his palette scraper. He shouted and cursed until Ida soothed him and restored order to his studio, coaxing him into a calm that she herself did not feel. She cajoled her mother into taking short walks, persuaded her to eat a bit of cheese, to drink her morning café au lait. She brought Michel an English primer, offered to teach him the language.

"You will need English when we go to America," she said, smiling bitterly at the hopelessness of her hope.

Michel marveled at her strength, although he knew that she too was unnerved by the uncertainty of their days and nights. Her dreams, like his own, were tumultuous. They awakened and clung to each other, entangled in the sweat-stained bedclothes, listening as the rustling wind brushed the silver leaves of the olive trees that rimmed their garden.

"We must do something, anything, Michel," Ida whispered to him one night as they lay awake in heat-heavy darkness. Her voice was barely audible against the rumble of distant thunder, a teasing storm that threatened but did not arrive.

He threaded his fingers through her hair, drew her closer, but she lay passively in his embrace. He turned his face to the wall. She was right. They had to do something, anything.

"I will try," he said at last. "I will go to Marseilles. My mother heard that the American consul there is sympathetic to Jews."

"We have nothing to lose," Ida said, but her voice, like his own, was devoid of optimism.

He left for Marseilles early the next morning and traveled through the brutal heat to the port city, grateful that the journey, however futile, offered a respite from the palpable tensions of Gordes. The mutual uneasiness intensified with each passing day.

Once in Marseilles, he headed immediately to the American consulate. The tall American marine who stood guard at the gate, aglow with health, his posture erect, his uniform immaculate, looked at him dispassionately. Michel, in his dust-spattered trousers, worn army boots, and ragged brown serge student jacket, observed him with envy. *How wonderful it must be*, he thought, *to be an American, a citizen of a country that was secure and unthreatened*. He approached the marine tentatively and lowered his voice to the respectful tone of the supplicant in search of even the flimsiest document of hope.

"I want, if you could arrange, to speak to someone about a visa?" he asked in his broken English.

"This is the consulate. The visa department is in Mont-Redon," the marine replied and then, to Michel's surprise, he smiled reassuringly. "Mont-Redon is not far," he added helpfully. "And the trolley just across the street will take you there."

Michel understood only the words "Mont-Redon" and "trolley." Ida was right to insist that he learn English. It was the language of survival. Once in America, he thought whimsically, he would learn English and learn to smile broadly and confidently. He recognized the absurdity of his fantasy. It was unlikely that he would ever reach the United States. His future, if indeed he had one, was obscure and uncertain.

He nodded gratefully to the marine, raced across the street, and boarded the blue-and-cream-colored trolley that had announced its arrival by blowing a foghorn. The plaintive sound reflected his own deflated mood. He fumbled for the fare and stumbled toward a window seat. He gazed out at the narrow streets, his attention

riveted to the colorful crowds that surged in great waves of purpose-
ful humanity, each hurrying passerby seemingly intent on an important errand, a defined destination.

In the lassitude of rural Gordes, in the isolation and melancholy
of the Chagall household, he had forgotten that there was a bustling
urban world, vested with vitality and the urgent demands of daily
life. Housewives carried net bags bulging with brightly colored vegetables, gleaming maroon eggplants and bloodred tomatoes, feathery
wands of bright green dill. Baguettes were tucked under their arms.
He envied them the normalcy of their lives and imagined them in
their orderly kitchens, preparing soups and salads; the war had not
yet invaded their lives.

At a crossing, the trolley paused and he caught sight of a fair-
haired young woman walking arm in arm with an officer of the
Vichy police. The tilt of her head, a peculiar clumsiness of her gait,
seemed familiar to him. *Katya*, he thought instinctively, but the trolley moved on before he could see her more clearly. He dismissed the
thought. Katya, who had not bothered to conceal her Nazi sympathies, had surely left France for Germany.

Refugees stumbled into the crowded car at each stop, obstructing
the aisles, speaking too loudly in Yiddish and French, in German and
Ladino. Their hair was matted, their weary faces inked with soot,
and their unwashed bodies reeked of sweat. Michel gave his seat to a
gaunt, large-eyed woman who held a small dark-haired baby in her
arms. She whispered her thanks, and he saw the outline of a Jewish
star on her threadbare gray jacket. She had, he surmised, escaped the
precincts of the Vichy government where Jews were compelled to
wear the yellow star of David and ripped it from her garment.

"*Tikvah*," he said softly to her and wished he could offer her
something besides the Hebrew word for hope.

"*Toujours l'espérance*," she replied softly. "Always the hope," and
he was comforted.

The trolley rolled on through limestone hills, into the shade of
date palms, and then proceeded to the coast, its route ending at a

driveway lined with plane trees. Beyond the manicured pathway was a fortress-like building. An American flag on its parapet fluttered in a gentle breeze. The trolley disgorged its ragged passengers and they surged toward the building, joining the crowd that already waited restlessly, desperate pilgrims all, jostling each other in their search for the holy grail, the magical visa applications that might grant them entry into the promised land. The refugees were indifferent to the beauty of the cerulean sea and the earth-colored mountains that bordered the consulate, indifferent to the heat of the day, indifferent to each other. Michel pitied them, an irony, he realized, because he himself was pitiable.

He looked up at the imposing entry to the building and watched as a slender, bespectacled young man wearing a beautifully tailored gray suit, a homburg perched on his dark hair, exited and hurried toward a waiting car. He was clearly an attaché of some importance, Michel supposed, and he turned away indifferently. He waited for an hour, and then another hour, until a consulate official stood on the steps of the building and bellowed through a bullhorn that the visa office was closing until later in the day. The crowd groaned, but Michel was relieved. He had, he decided, endured quite enough for one day.

He took the trolley back to the center of the city and, on impulse, entered a small sidewalk café on the boulevard d'Athènes. An aperitif was within his budget, he assured himself, and he ordered the anisette liqueur that Ida had favored during the clandestine meetings of their Paris courtship. The cloudy liquid was a reminder of dreamy hours spent in a distant land. The nervous youth he had been, the shy girl she had been, were strangers to him now. He touched the ragged edge of his worn jacket and remembered that he had once worn a leather cloak.

Sipping his drink, he stared across at the Basilica of Notre-Dame de La Garde and thought how easy it would be for the church fathers to hide endangered refugees in their vast fortress. Perhaps Marc could offer them one of his crucifixion paintings in return for a safe haven. He smiled bitterly. This was his day for absurd thoughts and haunting memories. He took another sip and turned his head and watched an elderly couple leave Le Splendide Hôtel, just across the way, and make their way across the street and hesitantly to the café. He wondered why they looked so familiar and suddenly realized who they were. Franz and Alma Werfel. He had seen them at the Chagall salons in Paris and more than once at the Sorbonne literary forums he had occasionally attended to please Ida. He stood hurriedly and approached them. They stiffened perceptibly. The elderly woman paled and her husband gripped her hand.

"Monsieur Werfel, Madame Werfel," he said deferentially. "I did not mean to startle you. I hope you remember me. I am the son-in-law of Marc Chagall, Ida's husband."

They stared at him and the tension faded from their faces.

"Of course. You are Michel. Ida's Michel. I do remember you," Franz Werfel said. "May we join you?"

"It would be an honor," Michel replied honestly.

This, at least, was something he could report on happily when he returned to Gordes. The Chagalls would be duly impressed by the fact that Michel had shared a table with the world-famed Franz and Alma Werfel. Franz Werfel was a distinguished novelist and his wife, the legendary Alma, was a famous beauty, an enchantress who was previously married to Gustav Mahler, the composer, and Walter Gropius, the architect. She was said to have been the mistress of Oskar Kokoschka, the Austrian painter of whom Marc spoke half admiringly, half contemptuously.

As Alma Werfel sat opposite him, Michel saw vestiges of her legendary beauty in her flashing dark eyes and her haggard, fine-boned face. Franz Werfel, on the other hand, was short and potbellied, his pate a shimmering pink beneath a very thin layer of gray hair. Marc, so proud of his own abundant curls, who always compared himself to others, would be pleased to learn that Werfel was balding, Michel thought.

He wondered why the Werfels were in Marseilles. Their fame should have shielded them from the Nazis, but then, of course, Ida was right. No Jew, no writer or artist, no matter how famous, was safe in German-occupied lands.

"Is your Ida still so beautiful?" the writer asked benevolently.

"She is indeed," Michel replied. "The war, of course, has been very difficult for her. Difficult for all of us."

"And for us as well," Alma said, her voice husky and sensual, her eyelashes brushing her high cheekbones. Her tongue shot out to moisten her thin, carefully painted lips. Michel understood how she had served as muse to so many men of genius. She exuded a feral sexuality, a confident awareness of her own magnetic charisma.

"We escaped from Austria, just ahead of the arrival of the storm troopers, and somehow we managed to reach Paris. From there we went to Lourdes, but no miracle awaited us there and finally we came to Marseilles," she continued.

"Are you safe here?" Michel asked.

"No. Who is safe in Nazi-occupied territory? But we are hopeful. We have American visas, but we do not have French exit visas so we cannot leave France legally," Franz Werfel said. "We are like Alice who was lost in a not-so-wonderful wonderland, but like her, we may yet find our way through the maze."

The waiter hovered, staring too closely at them, and Franz Werfel ordered brandy for Alma and himself, the sustaining liquor of the weak and elderly. As their drinks were placed on the table, Michel saw the dapper American who had left the visa office at Mont-Redon take a seat at a nearby table. He nodded almost imperceptibly at Franz Werfel and turned his attention to the *International Herald Tribune*.

"Who is that man?" Michel asked.

The writer leaned closer and lowered his voice. "He is the source of our hope and possibly of your own. His name is Varian Fry. He is an American who represents a committee organized by American Jews who hope to rescue writers and artists trapped in Europe. He will establish an American Relief Center here in Marseilles, and he has a list of those who are endangered and a fair amount of cash to be used as he sees fit. Mostly for bribes and to pay counterfeiters, I would assume. Alma and I have already met with him, and he has promised to assist us."

"But then you must introduce me to him. Perhaps he can help our family," Michel said eagerly. He half rose from his seat, but Alma Werfel placed a restraining hand on his arm.

"We dare not approach him or even acknowledge him in public. All his activities are secret, and the Vichy police and their informers are everywhere."

Michel glanced at their waiter, a young Algerian, and noticed for the first time that his eyes were everywhere as he absently wiped off a nearby table. It was true. No one could be trusted. But it was desperately important that he contact Varian Fry.

"I will give you some reassurance," Alma said gently. "When we met with him earlier in his room at the Splendide Hôtel, the American vice consul in Marseilles, a Mr. Harry Bingham, came in to see him. A very handsome man, I must say, this Mr. Bingham. Such wonderful eyes. Wasn't he handsome, Franz?" She smiled teasingly.

"I did not notice Mr. Bingham's eyes. I was concentrating on trying to save our lives," the novelist said drily.

She shrugged and continued. "This Mr. Bingham had a letter that he showed to Varian Fry. I glanced at the letterhead. It came from the Museum of Modern Art in New York."

"My wife has the unfortunate habit of often glancing at documents that do not concern her," Franz Werfel observed and smiled the smile of a man amused by his beautiful wife's unfortunate habits.

She ignored him again. "Although they spoke very softly, I heard a single name mentioned. Mr. Bingham said that the daughter of Marc Chagall had written repeatedly to Alfred Barr, the museum curator, pleading that he help her parents. He was speaking of your wife, Ida, was he not?"

Michel nodded. "I know that she has written more than once to Mr. Barr," he said and smiled bitterly. "She has written more than once to everyone in the world who might help."

"Then, of course, the Chagalls must be on Mr. Fry's list," Alma Werfel concluded.

"I hope so. But how do I make certain of that? Should I try to speak to this Varian Fry?" Michel asked. He deferred to Alma's expertise. She clearly knew how to charm her way through a diplomatic maze. But it was Franz Werfel who answered him.

"To make direct contact with Varian Fry will endanger him. You must wait. And hope. That is all any of us can do. We are prisoners of the *pagaille*, this terrible chaos in which we live. But I am optimistic. I am certain that your family will soon hear either from Mr. Fry or Mr. Bingham," he said. "They will know when and how to contact you when the time is ripe. You must rely on them as Alma and I do."

He drained his glass, licked his lips, and helped his wife rise from her seat.

"*Bonne chance*, Michel. Our good wishes to your loved ones. Perhaps we will meet in happier times, in a happier place."

Michel lowered his head respectfully, gratefully. "I hope so," he said.

Supporting each other, the world-famous writer and his wife, whose beauty had entranced geniuses, made their way slowly out of the café.

He glanced at the table where Varian Fry had been seated. The American had left. His carefully folded newspaper remained on the table next to his empty glass.

Michel too left the café, aware of the waiter who watched him as he crossed the road. He bought a bottle of Pernod for Marc and then impulsively entered a small boutique on the boulevard d'Athènes where he purchased a delicate, sea-green silk scarf for Ida. It was pointless, he knew, to return to Mont-Redon and stand in the line of the desperate.

He was more lighthearted than he had been for months as he traveled home to Gordes. Ida had been right. His journey had not been futile. Nothing had been lost and, however serendipitously, there had been a gain. The meeting with the Werfels had offered him a modicum of hope. "*Toujour l'espérance*," the weary young mother on the bus had murmured. He appropriated the word that sustained her. *Tivkah. Espérance.* He smiled. Hope. That was the gift he would bring to his Ida, that and the beautiful sea-green scarf. He imagined the gossamer fabric draped about her graceful shoulders, capped by her thick and radiant hair.

Chapter Eighteen

*M*ichel told Ida about Varian Fry, and she spoke of him to Marc.

"Varian Fry? I do not know the name. Who is this Varian Fry?" Marc asked dismissively as he sat in the garden sipping the Pernod, which he had accepted only after glancing contemptuously at the label.

"He is a man who may help us get to the United States," Ida said. "Michel told you what the Werfels said. And my friend Elsa has written me about him."

"Ah yes, Elsa. Your doctor friend in New York whose advice was sadly lacking when you needed it," Marc replied sullenly and refilled his glass.

"Her advice was, in fact, excellent then," Ida replied coldly.

It infuriated her that Marc blamed the blameless Elsa but never expressed regret for his own arbitrary behavior, nor did he acknowledge any error. Other men made mistakes, but Marc Chagall was never wrong.

"And it is excellent now," she continued. "She told me what she knew about this Mr. Fry. He is a gentile, the son of a very distinguished family, a graduate of Harvard University. He was a journalist, and when an assignment took him to Germany, he became aware of the situation there."

"The situation?" Marc asked sarcastically. "Is that what your friend Elsa, so safe in America, calls the Nazi plan to exterminate the Jews of Europe? A 'situation'?"

He snorted derisively. His mouth leaked a milky driblet of Pernod, and Bella, who sat between them, wiped it away, patting his lips as though he were a small boy.

Ida ignored him.

"Elsa writes that he is an idealist, impelled to do what he can to help certain individuals escape Nazi Europe and reach America. Elsa's husband, André, is the physician at a private girls' school where Mr. Fry's wife teaches, and he was able to speak to her about our family. Mrs. Fry promised to write to her husband about us. Given that connection and the intervention of Mr. Barr at the Museum of Modern Art, I think Varian Fry will do what he can to help us."

"We do not trust idealistic gentiles," Marc retorted. "Bella, do you believe that an American goy really wants to help a Jewish artist?"

Bella shrugged indifferently. "Goy, Jew, trust him, trust him not," she said, her voice so faint that Ida could barely hear her. "It is of no importance to me. This Mr. Fry may say what he will, do what he will. I will never leave France. I will never leave Europe. I know that if I go to the United States, I will die." She lowered her head and lifted her arms in despair; the long, loose sleeves of her white gown fluttered like the wings of a pale and wounded bird.

"Do not trouble yourself, *Mamochka*," Ida said. "We have not yet heard from Mr. Varian Fry. There is no need for you to come to a decision."

"I doubt that we will ever hear from your too-righteous gentile," Marc added sourly.

Ida did not argue. She understood that her parents had been conditioned to suspect and distrust strangers. They were prisoners of their own chronicle of despair, always anticipating betrayal. She poured her father another drink and draped a shawl about her mother's shoulders, grateful that she had avoided the contagion of the fear and pessimism that haunted and enfeebled them. She would not abandon the last vestiges of trust and hope.

That trust and hope did not betray her. A week later, a letter arrived from Alfred Barr of the Museum of Modern Art in New York, offering to host an exhibition of Marc's work.

Marc tossed it aside. "How does Mr. Barr imagine that I might arrive at such an exhibition? How does he imagine that my paintings will be transported to New York? This is a foolish letter, a foolish invitation."

"No, Papa," Ida said firmly. "Mr. Barr is not naive. He knows that you are in danger. This is a letter that you can show to the French authorities. It gives them an excuse to offer you a visa." She took the letter from him and placed it in a clean white folder on which she carefully printed the words "Exit Documents."

"You are being unduly optimistic," Marc said. "A letter of invitation to an exhibition that will never take place is certainly not a document of any value."

Ida did not reply. Weeks later, as a balmy autumn drifted into the first chilly days of winter, there was another letter to be added to her folder. It was from Varian Fry, who wrote that he was anxious to be of assistance to the Chagalls. His phrasing was circumspect.

"Mr. Barr, the director of the Museum of Modern Art, is anxious to welcome you to New York," he wrote. "Perhaps you have already received a letter of invitation from him."

Ida recognized that this was his way of telling Marc that there was a coordinated effort in progress, a confederacy of individuals committed to helping the Chagalls escape from France. She was newly optimistic.

"Papa, Varian Fry can be of great help to us. He can arrange visas to the United States and exit visas from France," she said urgently, gripping the precious letter. "He has already assisted many of our friends. Max Ernst and Jacques Lipchitz have accepted his help."

Letters had arrived from friends in Paris, telling her as much in the cryptic language of the endangered.

Marc stared at her impassively. "And I know that André Gide and Henri Matisse have refused it," he retorted. "My friends in Paris also keep me well informed."

"Gide and Matisse are not Jewish," Michel reminded him. "They are not in the same danger as you and Bella, as Ernst and Lipchitz."

Marc spat out his rebuttal, his face flushed with anger. "Jacques Lipchitz and Max Ernst are not Marc Chagall. They do not have my fame or prestige to protect them," he insisted. "I am safe here in Gordes. No one has threatened me. If I leave now, the canvases I have been working on will remain unfinished."

"And if you do not leave, the Vichy police arrest you, and you will not live to finish them," Ida said harshly. "Even the great Marc Chagall will be unable to paint in a concentration camp, and certainly he will not be able to paint from beyond the grave. There are no studios in the world to come."

"Ida, how dare you speak to your father like that?" Bella asked, her voice quivering, but Ida strode out of the room, Michel trailing after her.

Marc wrote to Varian Fry, curtly thanking him for his efforts.

"But I am not ready to leave France. It is, you know, my adopted country," he added. "I am a citizen of the Republic."

Ida grimaced as she showed his note to Michel. "He may think that he is a son of France," she said bitterly. "He does not realize that the Vichy government of his France has disowned him."

"He is not alone," Michel replied. "All the Jews of Europe are orphans now. Our adoptions have been rescinded by the order of Adolf Hitler and Marshal Pétain."

Ida copied her father's reply to Varian Fry and added it to her file.

Weeks passed. The news grew more and more ominous. The Vichy government declared Jews "a foreign people" and passed anti-Semitic legislation. As had happened in Germany, Jews were dismissed from government service and had to register with local authorities. Jewish-owned businesses were to be placed in the hands of trustees. Gentiles were forbidden to accept employment from Jews. Jeanne, the buxom village girl who had worked in the Chagall household for months, sent her small brother to collect the wages that were due her. The boy explained that her parents had forbidden her to work for Jews. It would be breaking the law.

"*Whose* law?" Ida asked harshly, but the boy dashed away, clutching the handful of francs she had given him without bothering to count them.

There were rumors of impending deportations and even darker rumors that the concentration camps were actually death camps. Marc read the papers with trembling hands. Bella awakened in the night, her face wet with tears. They could no longer deny the danger that threatened them.

Ida's file of exit documents grew. In January she added a letter from Varian Fry confirming that he had obtained visas to the United States for both Marc and Bella using the invitation from the Museum of Modern Art as a pretext.

"Wonderful news, *Maman*," Ida exulted, disguising her disappointment that there was no mention of herself and Michel.

"It is not wonderful," Bella replied morosely. "And we will not leave France unless we have reentry visas. France is our home."

Marc nodded in agreement.

Michel glared as they swept out of the room.

"They are mad, both of them," he said angrily. "My own parents cannot even hope for American visas, and King Marc and Queen Bella, like spoiled children, dare to negotiate, to make demands. Do they really think that they can get their way in all things? They cannot rule governments as they ruled us."

Ida remained silent. Michel had never before spoken so harshly of her father's imperious edicts, but for the first time, she did not argue with him. Did he regret that they had obeyed Marc and married? Did she? Of course, their years together had not been easy. Their marriage had been strangled by history, by the advent of the war, by their obligations to their parents. They had been separated and reunited. Resentments had mounted, hers and his, unarticulated and unreconciled. And yet they were together, husband and wife, and they cared for each other. They would sort it all out at another time, in another place. But of course, that no longer mattered. Not now, when it was their very survival that absorbed them.

She shook her head wearily, exhausted by the convergence of conflicting thoughts, conflicting feelings. That night, as though to atone for them, she draped the sea-green silk scarf over her naked shoulders, but Michel sat up late reading and she fell asleep at last, the scarf lost among the bedclothes.

The very next day, she accompanied Marc to Avignon where he delivered a letter to the prefect of Vaucluse, stating that since entering France in 1910, he had considered himself a French citizen and, even more importantly, a French painter. He wanted that citizenship legally affirmed so that if he left the country, he had the right to reentry. He added that his wife, also a lover of France, was his partner and had worked with him on his exhibitions, and she wanted similar reassurances.

It did not surprise Ida that his plea was received without comment. She had dressed carefully for the visit, brushed her hair so that it fell about her carefully made-up face in coppery folds. She wore a white sweater that hugged her breasts; she was prepared to seduce the prefect into compliance. Seated behind his ornate desk, pomade glinting on his carefully trained black mustache and his black hair, a tiny gold swastika pinned to the lapel of his dark jacket, he did not raise his eyes from the documents spread before him. He did not look at Ida. The prefect of Vaucluse could not and would not concern himself with the plight of the artist and his wife, whose French citizenship had already been rescinded. The daughter's beauty did not interest him. They were Jews, and therefore "foreign people."

"I regret that I cannot offer you any such assurances," he said stiffly. "My government does not consider you and your wife to be citizens of France."

Ida did not bother to glare at him as they left. She did, however, place a copy of Marc's petition for the reentry visa in her exit file.

A week later, Varian Fry wrote of his intention to visit the Chagalls. Harry Bingham of the American consulate in Marseilles, who collected contemporary art and admired Marc's work, would accompany him. Ida understood their hidden message, coded to deceive the Vichy censors. She wrote in reply that the Chagalls looked forward to the visit. Mr. Bingham might be particularly interested in her father's series of crucifixion paintings.

Varian Fry and Harry Bingham arrived in a limousine on a brisk March day, and the streets of sleepy Gordes erupted in excitement. The villagers left their shops and workplaces and stood beside children on the rutted curbsides to stare at the enormous car. Housewives emerged holding brooms and dust mops and clustered in doorways, their hands shading their eyes against the pale sunlight as the driver negotiated the narrow roadways. Curiosity abounded.

"Who could be in the car?"

"Men of importance, probably Americans."

"But they might be officials from Vichy. Possibly even Marshal Pétain himself."

"*Non.* The car had the license plates awarded to *les diplomates.*"

The car had passed, leaving clouds of dust in its wake, and finally a small boy reported that it had stopped at the former convent school where *l'artiste juif* lived with his family. The Americans had carried baskets of food and wine into the building.

"Meat, cheese, baguettes," the child announced. "Fruits, wine." His list grew longer as the afternoon wore on and his listeners drifted away.

The villagers shook their heads and muttered angrily to each other. Of course, the home of *les juifs* would be the destination of the Americans. Jews had connections, contacts. It had been said that the American president, Franklin Roosevelt, was himself a Jew. Perhaps what the Germans and Pétain were saying was true. Jews wanted to control the entire world. It was the Rothschilds' fault that the American stock market had failed, that the Bourse was unstable.

Ida greeted Varian Fry and Harry Bingham, and Michel showed them to the best bedroom in the house, a sunny room that overlooked the garden. Ida rushed into her father's studio to tell him that their guests had arrived, but Marc did not move from his easel. He wiped his brush on his creased and faded pants, rolled up the sleeves of his tattered dark blue shirt, and concentrated on finishing the halo about the head of yet another crucified Jesus.

"My suffering Jew," he muttered as he sprayed a fixative across the gleaming wet paint.

He shuffled back from the canvas and stared at it, then shrugged and followed Ida into the house.

"Perhaps you should put on a clean shirt, a jacket," she suggested.

"I am who I am," he retorted. "Marc Chagall has no need to impress American bureaucrats." He did, however, thrust his fingers through his mass of graying curls, arranging them so that they fell becomingly above his ears. His vanity, as always, both amused and irritated Ida.

However, he greeted the Americans with the charm usually reserved for dealers and patrons. He minced gracefully toward them, his narrow face wreathed in a smile that was oddly boyish. His blue eyes glinted as he shook their hands, his grasp strong, as though to demonstrate that he had eluded the weaknesses and ravages of age. He spoke in French, which both the Americans understood.

"Monsieur Fry, Monsieur Bingham, how good of you to come to our humble home in this little village," he said with mock humility.

Bella stood beside him, her overly rouged cheeks emphasizing her pallor, her dark eyes encircled with kohl. Her black hair framed her delicate face, and she wore a flowing rainbow-colored gown. She smiled shyly as Marc introduced her with disarming pride.

"This is my beautiful wife, Bella. It does not surprise you that Marc Chagall has such a beautiful wife, such a beautiful daughter? He has been blessed with such beauty because he is a creator of beauty. I say this only because it is true."

Ida winced and Michel frowned, but Marc was unembarrassed by his own vanity.

He invited them into his studio, and they looked about the large disorderly room, taking note of the huge kitchen table piled high with brushes and paints, the smocks and oversized oil-stained shirts that dangled from battered wooden chairs. A screen encircled two easels, works in progress on each. The room was heated by an inefficient coal stove, and finished canvases leaned against every wall. Marc chose several and placed them on the floor to be scrutinized.

"Are they not magnificent? Are they not beautiful?" he asked proudly.

He held up one crucifixion painting after another then, grinning mischievously, he led them to his more lighthearted depictions of circus life, the still lifes of fruits and vegetables, and his large and fanciful portmanteau scenes dominated by sad-eyed bovines.

"See my wonderful cows," he exulted. "They dance on rooftops; they glide through the heavens. Cows are my favorite animals. They are so placid, so accepting. I paint them again and again. Perhaps because I understand them. They are like myself, like my family, like my people. They are wonderful creatures whose survival depends on the will of others. They are so dignified, so lovely, these dumb beasts who are led to pasture, who flood buckets with the sweet milk of their udders. We too, we Jews, must follow those who would herd us, who would milk us dry. The milk of cows nourishes those who drink it just as my paintings nourish the imagination. My wife's writing will nourish the thoughts of those who will read her words. We are very productive cows, my Bella and myself. In your America, we too will be dumb animals, our tongues muted. How will we talk? How will we be understood? We speak no English. Will Americans understand Yiddish? Will they understand French? Tell me, are there cows in your America? How will I live in a land without cows, my very own compatriots?"

He laughed derisively. He had spoken not to amuse his visitors but to amuse himself.

Varian Fry coughed delicately into his silk handkerchief and answered quietly. "I can assure you, Monsieur Chagall, that there are many cows in my country."

"I am relieved to hear that. Perhaps I will soon see those cows. My daughter, Ida, is now the manager of our lives. She insists that we leave Europe." His voice suddenly broke, and the two Americans looked away in embarrassment.

In the evening, they sat in the salon and sipped tea that Bella brewed on the samovar, sweetening it with the last of the honey from the hive at the bottom of their garden. The village grocer refused to sell them sugar, claiming that it was forbidden to sell comestibles to "foreign people."

Michel stirred his tea and asked the question that had teased him since the Werfels had first told him about Varian Fry's courageous and hazardous campaign. "May I ask you, Mr. Fry, why a man like yourself is concerned with the difficulties of our people?"

The American stared at him as though surprised by the question. He replied in the flat tone of a teacher explaining the obvious.

"Perhaps you should ask how it would be possible for a man like myself, a Christian American, to ignore the suffering of those who are the victims of injustice and cruelty, Jews as well as non-Jews. I did not come to this work suddenly. Back in 1935, I was a journalist working in Berlin. I was walking down Kurfürstendamm when suddenly a crowd attacked an innocent Jew, an ordinary man who had simply been shopping. He held a gift-wrapped parcel, perhaps a birthday present for his wife or his child. The hoodlums knocked him to the ground, kicked him, and then turned against any passerby they assumed to be Jewish, even pulling drivers out of passing cars. They beat them with clubs and shouted words that I had never heard before. 'The best Jew is a dead Jew.' They sang their anthem: 'When Jewish blood spurts from the knife, then everything will be fine again.' The street was red as though a rainfall of blood had fallen. That gift-wrapped parcel was soaked by the blood and trampled on by booted feet. I could do nothing on that day. I was alone and no match for a mob. I knew then that not only were the Jews of Germany in mortal danger, but all of civilization was also threatened. As a civilized man, as a Christian, as a fortunate American citizen, I knew that I had to do something. Artists and writers are the guardians of our civilization. They must not be victims of the barbarians at the gates. That is why I am in France as part of the Emergency Rescue Committee. Here in France, in 1941, I have the opportunity to do what I could not do in 1935. You speak of 'your people,' Michel, and you mean the Jewish people, but my world is not divided between Jews and gentiles. I see only human beings, men and women who must be helped.

That is why I am here in Gordes. Does that answer your question, Michel Rapaport?"

Michel nodded, awed by his courage and his humanity.

Varian Fry smiled the thin, modest smile of a teacher, satisfied that a lesson has been learned. He opened his briefcase and removed a sheaf of papers. "I have good news for you," he said. "We have managed to obtain American visas for both Monsieur and Madame Chagall. You know that my government requires a bond of three thousand dollars for each new immigrant, and Hilla Rebay has convinced Solomon Guggenheim to guarantee most of those funds. She was very moved by a communication she received from Madame Rapaport."

Ida clasped her hands and breathed deeply. Her letter to Guggenheim's artist mistress had been answered, not with words but with action.

"Hilla Rebay. We knew her in Berlin. She played with watercolors. Her work was interesting. Some of it," Marc murmured disparagingly.

Michel frowned. It was like Marc, he thought bitterly, to disparage a woman who was now his benefactor. He had not thanked Harry Bingham and Varian Fry for their strenuous efforts on his behalf, nor had he acknowledged Ida's persistence. Marc Chagall, the self-proclaimed emperor of art, was an indifferent recipient of their tribute. *Damn him*, Michel thought.

"It is very good of Madame Rebay," Marc said stiffly and rose from his seat to shake hands, first with Varian Fry and then with Harry Bingham.

"I am also pleased to tell you that money has been raised in America for your passage. There were generous contributions, including several hundred dollars from Madame Helena Rubinstein," Varian Fry continued. "But now that all this is in place, there is no time to waste. You must travel to Marseilles immediately and be ready to leave France as soon as we can arrange passage to Lisbon for you. The visas have an expiration date."

Marc stood and pounded on the table, his cheeks flushed with anger.

"Do you expect us to leave without our daughter?" he asked. "Why have you not arranged a visa for Ida?" He waved his arms, an imperious spoiled child whose will would not be denied.

Harry Bingham glanced at Varian Fry, who patiently assembled his documents, indifferent to the artist's outburst.

"We are still working on behalf of your daughter and her husband," the American consul said coldly. "And we are hopeful that we will obtain both the visas and the funds that they will need. But you cannot wait for this to happen. Time is of the essence. You are in danger in France. The Vichy government speaks of establishing a department of Jewish affairs. That is the first step toward the deportation of French Jews. You do not want to risk deportation, Monsieur Chagall. We all know what happens in those concentration camps."

They fell silent. Marc sat down, his shoulders slumped in defeat.

"But what about my paintings?" he asked in a broken voice. "How can I abandon my life's work?"

Ida placed her hand on his shoulder. "Do not worry about your paintings, *Papochka*. Michel and I will take care of them. We will somehow manage to get them out of France and bring them to you in America," she said. "I promise." She spoke in the patient cadence of a mother soothing a spoiled child with a promise that she might not be able to keep.

Michel stared at her. He turned away so that she would not see the anger that darkened his face.

"You promise us that?" It was Bella who asked—Bella, so fragile and withdrawn, who summoned the strength to impose her will on her daughter.

"I promise," Ida said solemnly. "We both promise, don't we, Michel?"

He nodded because he did not trust himself to speak, suffused as he was with resentment. He knew that all their resources, all their energies, would be directed to the rescue of Marc's work. Ida seemed to have forgotten that he too had parents, a gentle mother, a weary father, who needed their help. They too were vulnerable, and Fry's Emergency Rescue Committee would do nothing for them. They were not, after all, guardians of civilization. They were only ordinary Jews, struggling to survive. Were their lives less important than Marc's canvases?

"Very well then," Varian Fry said, snapping his briefcase closed and polishing his steel-framed spectacles, their lenses clouded by the steam of the samovar. "Everything is settled. We look forward to your speedy arrival in Marseilles. I will arrange for lodgings."

"*Merci. À bientôt*," Ida said very softly, and she stood beside Michel as the two Americans left the room.

Bella knelt before Marc, her head resting on his lap. She sobbed quietly as he stroked her dark hair. "I cannot bear it. I cannot flee again," she whispered. "I am not strong enough. How can I leave France? How can I leave Europe?"

"You must accept it, *ma chérie, ma belle Bella*," Marc said. "If we are to live, we must leave France."

With his hand still resting on her head, he sang softly in Yiddish. It was a song Ida remembered from her childhood, a mournful song about a calf being led to slaughter. He sang chorus after chorus until Bella no longer wept but added her trembling voice to his. Arm in arm, still singing, they left the room.

Chapter Nineteen

*D*ays after Varian Fry's visit, Yvette, the sad-eyed postmistress, Ida's only friend in Gordes, beckoned her into her office. Their embrace was tentative. They were awkward confidantes whose intimacy had been forged in shared grief and anxiety during the early days of war when their soldier husbands fought on distant battlefields.

"It will be all right," they had assured each other then, but for Yvette, it had not been all right. On the day that Ida saw the black bunting on the window of the post office, she had wept, and that evening, she had carried a casserole and a bouquet of primroses and lavender to Yvette's home, where a votive candle flickered in the window. The young widow had clutched the flowers to her breast.

"Pierre. His name was Pierre," she had murmured, and Ida had thought that but for the grace of God, their positions might have been reversed and she would have been such a mourner, whispering, "Michel. His name was Michel."

Yvette shuttered the small window, blocking any view from public space. She turned to Ida and although they were alone, she spoke softly, glancing fearfully toward the closed aperture.

"Ida, my father has a cousin in the Vichy police. He told him that they are rounding up younger Jews and sending them to Camp des Milles. They say that from there, they will be deported to work camps in eastern Europe. They are offering a reward to anyone who leads them to such Jews. There are those in Gordes who are poor enough and hungry enough to betray even their own families. Your parents are too old to interest them, but you and Michel are in danger. I have heard your names mentioned more than once. You must leave this village as soon as you can."

She handed Ida a letter and glanced nervously at the shuttered window. Through the slats, they heard the impatient muttering of villagers annoyed at the delay.

"Yvette should be attending to her duties instead of gossiping with that redheaded Jew," a woman said querulously.

Ida overheard her and shook her head sadly. "Is it now forbidden to speak with Jews?" she asked.

Yvette smiled wanly. "Goodness is forbidden. You see what is happening, Ida. Do not delay." She fingered the small silver cross that hung about her neck. "I will pray for you."

"And I for you," Ida said and wondered to whom she would offer her prayers. She was the daughter of a man who painted crucifixion scenes in the morning and portraits of sad-eyed rabbis in the afternoon. The crucifixion scenes frightened her; the sad-eyed rabbis filled her with tenderness. She knew only that she was a Jew, daughter and granddaughter of Jews. The God in whom she might believe but to whom she would pray was, for her, a Jewish God.

The two friends embraced and kissed each other's cheeks. Ida hurried out through the rear door. She licked her lips and tasted the salt of Yvette's tears.

The letter Yvette had given her was from Varian Fry. "The weather is turning treacherous," he wrote cryptically. In view of the changing climate, he had arranged for the crating and transport of certain valuables to Marseilles. "The truck driver and his helpers who are in my employ are reliable," he assured her. "Do not be alarmed if they arrive very late at night. Their routes are complicated. They will take you and Michel to Nice. It really is important that you have a holiday before the storms begin." His signature was indecipherable and there was no return address.

Ida told Michel what Yvette had said and showed him the letter. He read it and handed it back to her.

"We know what those storms will be. Varian Fry is telling us that we are in danger," he said, confirming what she already knew. "We must be on that truck."

"But it will mean leaving my parents here. How are they to get to Marseilles without our help?"

"Will we be able to help them if we are in a concentration camp in Poland?" he asked harshly. "You cannot protect your father's work if you are deported from France. Yvette knows that there are those in Gordes who will betray us for a few sous or a dozen eggs. Your parents will be safe. They are protected by both their age and their fame. If Varian Fry made arrangements for us, he has surely made arrangements for them."

She nodded. His arguments could not be ignored. Both Marc and Bella agreed with him.

"We are not novices at escape, Idotchka," Marc said. "We managed to get from Russia to Berlin, from Berlin to Paris. Surely we will manage to go from Gordes to Marseilles."

Ida's sleep was restless during the nights that followed. The dream recurred, altered yet again. Her desperate race toward a mysterious refuge was solitary. Unprotected by her parents, Michel a ghostly shadow trailing behind her, she ran, wearing her mother's diaphanous white gown and fearful that she might trip over the long skirt. Her hair was in disarray, a tangle of copper-colored curls tossed by a vicious wind. She clutched the painting of the bridal chair to her bosom, the wooden frame cutting into her tender flesh like the nails of a crucifix, but she did not loosen her grasp. She awakened; her trembling hands felt her breasts and she sighed with relief to find them firm and unbloodied.

She was lost in that dream on the night that Varian Fry's truck driver arrived. Bewildered by the sound of the heavy truck on their gravel path, she leapt out of bed. Michel was already dressed and busily thrusting their documents into a worn leather briefcase.

"Hurry, Ida," he urged. "We must be ready to leave when they have finished crating and loading your father's works."

She dressed quickly and removed the painting of the bridal chair from the wall, wrapping it carefully in the woven purple coverlet from the bed that had been so briefly her own.

The driver showed them Varian Fry's card, but he did not reveal his own name. Anonymity was a protection against betrayal. They stood uneasily in the doorway until all the crated paintings were carried into the vehicle.

Marc and Bella did not weep. They embraced Ida, whose eyes were tightly closed, locked against the threatening flood of her sorrow. Bella held Michel's face between her trembling hands and kissed him on each cheek.

"You will take care of our Ida," she said, her words a plea.

"Of course I will, *Maman*," he assured her. He had never before called his wife's mother *Maman*.

Marc shook Michel's hand absently, his eyes riveted to a crate that he did not deem securely closed. The driver added a nail and another hasp and Marc grunted his satisfaction. He did not wait for the truck to lumber out of the yard but took Bella's arm and went into the house, now divested of his work, every wall bare, every corner vacant, its soul gone. It had ceased to be their home.

Neither Ida nor Michel looked back, nor did they speak as the truck continued on to Nice where Michel's parents awaited them.

Every morning, Masha Rapaport mopped the stone floor of the tiny, sparsely furnished hovel in an endless battle against the rats and vermin that haunted the port city. She roamed the streets all day, hawking the paper flowers she crafted and the bits of lace she tatted by the light of guttering candles. She sold the sad bouquets on street corners to Italian soldiers and to the owners of cafés and restaurants who placed them on the tables they could no longer afford to cover with proper cloths. Michel's father had mysteriously become a cobbler, mending the Italian soldiers' boots and replacing the heels and soles of children's shoes.

"Who taught you to mend footwear?" Michel asked him.

"Necessity is a wonderful teacher," his father replied as he lifted the well-honed knife and sliced into a bit of leather.

The Italians were benign occupiers. They offered Masha vegetables from their battalion kitchens, and they brought pungent cheeses when they reclaimed their mended boots. The Rapaports learned their names. Masha brewed coffee with chicory and offered steaming cups to Marcello and Luigi and Guido who, in turn, showed them pictures of their wives and children. She mended their uniforms and washed their shirts and underwear. They rewarded her with stale baguettes and smiles and a few francs.

"We will not starve," she said as she prepared watery stews with the vegetables and crumbled the cheese into a sauce. The Rapaports were veteran survivors.

Ida and Michel rarely ventured out. The beautiful city, the capital of the Maritime Alps, overflowed with refugees. Forty thousand Jews sought sanctuary in the coastal city. Families shared single rooms in unfashionable hotels. Desperate mothers brought their children to the seashore and bathed them in the surging waves, but still the rancid odor of sweating bodies and unwashed clothing mingled with the scent of orange blossoms. Ida averted her eyes from the large-eyed children whose lank hair hung about skeletal faces.

Occasionally, desperate for air, for the sight of sea and sky, they walked along the Promenade des Anglais, stared out at the clear blue waters of the Mediterranean, and paused to peer into shop windows. France was at war, but the merchants of Nice stoically maintained a facade of normalcy. Gowns of shimmering silk draped the blasé mannequins in the windows of stylish boutiques. Ida saw a cape of the exact blue of the cape she had bought in Paris all those years ago on an afternoon when her life had changed forever.

"Do you remember my blue cape?" she asked Michel.

He drew her close.

"Of course," he replied and adjusted the sea-green silk scarf, his impulsive gift to her.

"I have it still, that cape," she said wistfully.

They walked on past shop windows that displayed slender vials filled with the heady perfumes derived from the bright floral beds that sparkled throughout the Riviera. It was strange, Ida thought sadly, that tender and beautiful flowers flourished amid the ugliness of war. Strange too that the sun continued to rise each day in a blaze of glory and sink so slowly into the sea, that the birds continued to sing. Nature was so oddly unperturbed by war.

One evening, they strolled beneath the arbors of orange and olive trees in the Albert I Garden where young people gathered for evening picnics. A giddy soccer game was in progress, the ball soaring high into a sky tinged with the melancholy pastel hues of a seaside sunset.

Ida looked at Michel, who was slowly and methodically stripping the frond of a date palm. The longing in his eyes matched her own. His youth, like her own, had been forfeit to war. *Pauvre Michel. Pauvre Ida.* She pitied him even as she pitied herself.

"Michel," she whispered and kissed him on the lips, a kiss of passion and yearning. He held her close, and hand in hand, they strolled to the esplanade that led to the sea where Ida plucked rose-gold primroses from a wild bush that hugged the rocky incline. She brought them back to Michel's mother.

Masha Rapaport pressed a fragrant blossom to her lips, and a single tear crept down her withered cheek. "It is a very long time since I held something beautiful in my hand," she said apologetically.

———

March drifted into April. A letter from Bella told them that they had, at last, arrived in Marseilles and were registered at a small hotel. Bella's spidery script was blotted by tears.

"Your father is very unhappy here. Our room is small and ugly. We do have a balcony, but it is so narrow that if we stand on it together, we must press against each other. It is just as well because the view is so depressing. We look down on an alleyway where prostitutes walk up and down as soon as darkness falls. On every corner, horrid men stand selling pieces of paper to each other. Forged baptism certificates, forged exit visas. When will you come to us, Idotchka? Will we see you before we leave Marseilles? Mr. Fry tells us that we will have to go to Lisbon by train and you know how *Papochka* and I hate trains. Come soon, Idotchka. Come as soon as you can. Your parents need you. You must help us during these terrible days of waiting."

Ida handed the letter to Michel, who read it, his face dark with anger. Bella's complaints were trivial, her demand unconscionable. How could her parents consider placing Ida in such danger?

"You cannot go to them. It is too dangerous. The Vichy police have *rafles*, roundups of Jews in Marseilles every day. They say that young Jewish women who are arrested are sent to brothels," he protested.

"I know, I understand," she replied sadly. "But still…"

"But still, although you are my wife, you are first and foremost your parents' daughter," he completed the sentence, his words laced with bitterness.

He packed a small bag for both of them. He would go to Marseilles with her. He had to protect her.

He looked at his own mother and father, knowing that no matter what they felt, they would remain silent. His mother shrugged and prepared sandwiches for their journey. His father hammered a wooden heel onto a battered shoe and spoke very softly.

"You must be careful." Grief edged his words of warning.

They were careful. They sat apart from each other in the crowded carriage of the train. "So many Jews on this train," the heavy over-dressed woman who sat next to Ida remarked. Her breath was sour. She pointed to Michel. "Look at him, so dark, so greasy. I can always smell them. And I am never wrong. *Parfum de ghetto*, we call their odor."

"Yes. It's disgusting," Ida murmured and thought that she would like to kill the woman and throw her from the train. The ferocity of her own thought frightened her. Hatred had never been in her nature.

In Marseilles, they left the train separately as they had agreed. If one of them should be accosted by a Gestapo agent or the Vichy police, the other would escape. They raced down side streets, walking close to buildings and avoiding the lights of the street lamps until they reached the Chagalls' hotel. A disgruntled concierge looked up from his newspaper and muttered a room number, waving them toward an unswept stairwell that led to the second floor.

Marc and Bella were huddled together on a narrow bed pressed against the wall of their tiny room. The dingy curtains were tightly drawn as though the darkness itself threatened them. Ida was shocked to see how profoundly they were changed. Marc had abandoned his role as the impudent, elfin artist, arrogantly confident of his ability to charm. He crouched on the unmade bed, his hands twitching nervously, his eyes darting from the window to the door. Bella, her delicate face waxen, her helmet of dark hair streaked with silver, embraced Ida too tightly. She complained of the journey from Gordes to Marseilles. She spoke nervously of all that had to be purchased before their departure for Lisbon and protested the need to go to Portugal.

"Why must we go to Lisbon?" she asked plaintively. "Doesn't Monsieur Fry realize how difficult it is for us to travel?"

"The port of Marseilles is now dangerous. Portugal is still a neutral country where ships embark for the United States," Michel replied impatiently. "You will sail on such a ship."

He masked his annoyance and went out to the balcony. Ida listened to Bella's requests. There were cosmetics she needed, a particular French face cream and kohl, which she had heard was unavailable in America.

The war, Ida reflected, had not impacted her mother's vanity.

Bella insisted that they would need food to sustain them during the journey. She had heard that shipboard food was barely edible, and Ida knew how particular her father was, how he craved dried apricots and almonds, chocolates and marzipan. And of course they would need warm coats, heavy sweaters.

"I would do all the shopping myself," Bella said apologetically. "But your father says it is dangerous for us to leave the hotel, and I am not well, Idotchka."

She chronicled her symptoms. Her weakness, her insomnia, her faintness when she awakened each morning, the headaches that assaulted her throughout the day. And the nausea, the terrible nausea. All foods disagreed with her. She retched after eating.

"I am sick," she moaned. "You have a sick mother, Idotchka."

Ida nodded. She was familiar with her mother's illnesses, both real and imagined. "Don't worry, *Mamochka*," she said patiently. "Michel and I will buy whatever you need. We will go to the markets tomorrow."

"It is dangerous," Marc said warningly. "Jews are being arrested each day. I leave the hotel only to buy the newspapers. But you are safe, I am sure. You have papers. Of course you have papers."

Michel turned away. He knew that Ida would not tell her parents that their papers were no longer valid. Their French citizenship had also been invalidated. They were subject to arrest at any moment. But that danger would not deter Ida. Her mother needed cosmetics, warm clothing, dried fruits and nuts, and Ida, now and forever the most dutiful of daughters, would supply them. Somehow she had managed to find the funds to pay for them. He suspected that she had sold her own few pieces of jewelry, but he had not asked her.

She insisted that they would be safe. Given her bright hair and fair complexion, she could pass as a gentile. She laughed when she spoke of the woman on the train who had assumed her to be a Christian although she had recognized that dark-eyed and dark-haired Michel was a Jew. He did not laugh. He knew himself to be vulnerable, but he had no choice. He would not allow Ida to go into the streets of Marseilles alone.

Early the next morning, they hurried to the market square. Ida raced from shop to shop while Michel remained outside, staring intently into display windows so that his face would not be seen. At last her purchases were complete. Relieved, she turned to him.

"Let's treat ourselves," she said. "Let's pretend we are normal people living in normal times and go into a café for croissants and coffee."

He nodded. The sidewalk café nearby was relatively empty, and if they sensed any danger, they could rush out and hop onto the trolley that traversed the street. He pulled the brim of his hat low and they sat at a table near the entry. As they studied the menu, another couple entered.

The woman strutted in importantly, the heels of her high black boots clicking in military rhythm. Her straw-colored hair was tightly curled and her fleshy cheeks were dotted with rouge. She wore a purple silk dress, cut low enough to reveal the rise of her ample breasts. A much shorter man, in the uniform of the Vichy police, held her arm proudly. As they walked past Ida and Michel, the careless swing of her oversized black purse grazed Ida's arm. Ida grew very pale. She waited for them to pass and then reached for Michel's hand.

"Did you recognize her?" she whispered. "It's Katya. Our Polish maid."

He nodded. "I thought I saw her when I was last in Marseilles, but I wasn't sure. All right. Don't look at them. I don't think she noticed us. We will drink our coffee and eat our croissants and then leave. Quietly, slowly. See, she is not even looking at us."

"Too busy seducing her Nazi," Ida said bitterly.

They sipped their coffee, keeping their heads averted, and left the café. They took a circuitous route back to the hotel, but as they rounded a corner, Ida heard footsteps hurrying after her. She turned but saw no one. But as they entered the hotel, Michel swerved and saw Katya. She stood across the way staring at them, a spiteful smile on her lips.

They rushed up to the Chagalls' room and locked the door. Marc was on the balcony, and Michel pulled him back into the room and drew the curtains. He did not bother looking down at the street. He knew that Katya would still be there.

"What are you doing?" Marc asked indignantly.

"We are in danger," Michel replied angrily. "We must leave this place. Ida, you must go to Varian Fry at the Splendide Hôtel, tell him about Katya, and ask him to find another safe house. Quickly."

She nodded, but even as she walked toward the door, it was forced open. Three burly Vichy police officers in bottle-green uniforms burst into the room, brandishing clubs of lacquered wood. Their leader waved a document in the air.

"We have a warrant here for the arrest of Marc Chagall, an alien in France."

Marc trembled and Bella clung to his arm.

"Do you know who my husband is?" she shrieked. "He is a world-famous artist."

"We know who he is," the officer replied. "He is a world-famous degenerate Jew, an enemy of the Reich. We have been told about him."

Ida escaped the room as Bella's protests became wild wails of grief. She ran down the road but turned at the corner to see her father, an unresisting rag doll of a man, being thrust into a police van. A voice called mockingly after her.

"Madame Ida, run, run for your life. You and your people no longer rule the world."

"Damn you, Katya," she muttered.

Her heart hammering, she increased her pace, gasping for breath but never pausing until she reached the Splendide Hôtel. Crowds of refugees filled the hallways that led to offices of the American Relief Center. Their voices were a cacophony of desperation, their faces tight masks of anxiety. They congregated on landings and sat on the steps of stairwells, ferociously defending their places in the waiting line. A sallow mother changed a baby on a landing. The stench of the soiled diaper mingled with the odors of sweat, unwashed clothing, and sour breath. Ida circled past two wailing toddlers who were briefly calmed when their weary, gray-faced father handed them crusts of moldy bread to chew on. She ignored furious cries of protest.

"There is a line, madame. Wait your turn, madame!"

She did not line up; she did not wait. She raced into the Relief Center office and ran past the astonished receptionist who rose from her seat in protest. Her breath labored, her body drenched in sweat, she burst into Varian Fry's office.

He peered at her across his desk, its surface covered with neatly arranged stacks of documents. He wore a well-tailored dark business suit, the inevitable silk handkerchief tucked neatly into his pocket, the calculated uniform of a fastidious man, intent in defying the chaos that surrounded him. He carefully moved aside the mountain of papers before him.

"What has happened, Madame Rapaport?" he asked, his voice calm and controlled.

"My father has been arrested by the Vichy police," she said, struggling for breath. "Perhaps half an hour ago. They came to the hotel. Three men. Vichy officers."

"Half an hour ago," he repeated and glanced at his watch. He reached for his telephone. "Miriam, please connect me to the police department at the bishopric here in Marseilles," he said. He set the receiver down and repositioned his papers, methodically stamping and signing document after document. Ida stared at him. Why had she placed so much faith in this nondescript businessman, this fussy bureaucrat in his Savile Row clothing? He could not arrange for her father's release. All he could do was sign letters and stamp forged documents. They were lost. All their efforts had been in vain. Her eyes burned, but she did not weep.

He looked up from his work. "A glass of water, perhaps," he offered.

She shook her head, and he smiled apologetically and opened yet another folder. "Visas," he explained. "They must be completed today."

She grimaced. She had no interest in his damn visas. All she cared about was her father, who was in a prison cell, and her mother, who lay weeping on her unmade bed. She wondered if Michel was safe. He too might have been arrested. But she was certain that it was only her father who interested those arresting officers. Katya must have told them what a prize catch the great Marc Chagall would be. She sank into a chair and wondered wildly what she could do next.

At last a voice crackled through the receiver and Varian Fry lifted it.

"Good morning," he said cordially. "This is Varian Fry of the American Relief Center. Do I have the honor of speaking to the prefecture in charge?" A silence and then he continued. "Your honor, I speak for myself and for Mr. Harry Bingham, the American consul here in Marseilles. I understand that you have taken the world-famous painter, Monsieur Marc Chagall, into custody. My government, and indeed Eleanor Roosevelt herself, the wife of the president of the United States, are very concerned about the safety of Monsieur Chagall. I assume that you have not forgotten that the United States has given full diplomatic recognition to the Vichy regime. You would surely not want to jeopardize that recognition that is so important to Marshal Pétain by ignoring our feelings about the detention of this important artist. I must warn you that if he is not released within the hour, I will call David Anderson of the *New York Times* in London and tell him about the arrest. You know that such a news story will cause an international scandal that will please neither President Roosevelt nor Marshal Pétain. So you will agree that it is in your best interest to arrange for Monsieur Chagall's release. I assume you will need to consult your superiors about this. I will wait on the line for your reply."

He removed the cap of his gold fountain pen and resumed his work, signing the documents he had stamped. Again the receiver rested on his desk. Ida sat at the edge of her chair, fighting a wave of nausea. At last he lifted the receiver again, listened, and then spoke, his voice laconic although his hand trembled.

"Thank you. You have made a sensible decision. My government is grateful to you. A car will be at the police station within the half hour to receive Monsieur Chagall." He turned to Ida. "As you see, all will be well, madame," he said. "Your father is safe. You will want to go to him, of course. My car is just outside the hotel. It will take you to the police station."

She grasped his hand. "How can we ever thank you, Mr. Fry?" she asked.

"Oh, don't thank me," he replied. "Thank the stupid Vichy police officer who believed that I could actually manage to reach a *New York Times* correspondent in London and that he would actually care enough to write about it. The *New York Times*, you may know, has not been a great advocate for the Jews of Europe."

Ida paled as he laughed the mischievous laugh peculiar to confident tricksters of fate.

"I would not have had the courage to play such a dangerous game," she admitted ruefully.

"You have courage enough, Madame Ida. You saved your father's life today. But there is no time to waste. We were lucky today, but luck is fickle. Tell your parents that they cannot delay any longer. They must leave Marseilles for Lisbon as soon as possible. I only regret that I cannot arrange visas or funds for you and your husband. Still, I have no doubt that you will somehow manage. I will help you get the paintings to America. You are a survivor, madame, a brave and resourceful survivor."

He rose from his desk and kissed her on both cheeks. His lips were cold and dry as they brushed against her flushed and burning skin.

Chapter Twenty

*M*arc was safe. He and Bella sat on their narrow hotel bed, holding hands like frightened pale children. Ida repeated Varian Fry's warning.

"There is no time to be lost. You must leave Marseilles at once," she said.

He nodded his agreement and immediately added conditions.

"Yes," he said. "We must leave as soon as possible. But arrangements must be made. I will not leave without my paintings."

"Damn your paintings," Michel hissed angrily. "Paintings do not bleed. They do not breathe. Human lives, yours, Bella's, Ida's, and mine, are worth more than your damn canvases."

Marc looked at him contemptuously. "You do not understand the importance of great art, Michel. Let me explain it to you. You have perhaps heard of the Italian sculptor, Benvenuto Cellini?" he asked.

"Of course, I have," Michel replied irritably.

"Here is a story about Cellini. It seems he was simmering a cauldron of metal for the casting of a medallion while his small son played nearby. The solution was not to his liking. It had reached the boiling point, but it lacked a sufficient amount of calcium to achieve the color he envisioned. He picked up the child and tossed him into the mixture so that his bones would provide the missing calcium. The cast was successful and the finished work exquisite. It was, supposedly, the gold medallion depicting Leda and the swan that is now in the Vienna Museum. That medallion is immortal. What was more important—the life of an insignificant child or a masterpiece that has endured through the ages? An interesting riddle, *n'est-ce pas*?" He smiled, a teasing and taunting smile.

They were silent. Marc's question was not a question; his riddle was not a riddle. It was a statement, frightening in its certainty. He had answered Michel's question. Yes, he was saying. His paintings were more valuable than all their lives.

Ida was pale with disbelief. "You cannot mean that you would sacrifice all of us for your work?" she asked.

"Of course not," Marc said, shrugging mischievously. "I just told a little story. I thought it might amuse you."

Michel frowned darkly. Marc's "amusing story" was a statement.

"You cannot stay in Marseilles," Ida persisted. "Michel and I promise that we will bring your paintings to America. Mr. Fry has said he will help us."

She made plans for their departure. Michel barely listened as she spoke of her efforts to arrange for the shipment of the paintings.

He traveled to Nice to reassure his parents that he was safe and to be certain that they themselves had not been arrested in the daily *rafles* and deported to the concentration camps at Drancy or in North Africa.

"You must not worry about us, Michel," Masha Rapaport said.

He reflected that Ida's parents had never spoken those words to her. "You must worry about us," was their unspoken charge.

He was relieved when Marc at last agreed to leave for Lisbon at the beginning of May. Ida, with Varian Fry's help, had arranged for the crates of paintings to be transported to Madrid.

Dark clouds canopied the sky on the day of their departure. Bella wept in the cab on the way to the train station. "If I die in America, promise that you will bring my body back to France," she pleaded.

"You will not die in America," Marc said harshly.

"Promise," she insisted.

"We promise," Ida interceded. "But you must not think like that, *Mamochka.*"

She knew that her words were futile. Bella was death-haunted and would not be consoled.

As their cab sped through the narrow streets of Marseilles, sirens sounded and police trucks passed them. The driver cursed as he took circuitous turns, screeching to a halt and then accelerating as he drove in the wrong direction down one-way streets.

"It's the damn Jews," he told them. "The police are finally getting rid of all those stinking refugees. They cleaned Marseilles out this morning. No more *parfum de ghetto*. We'll be able to breathe again."

"Where are the Jews being taken?" Michel asked casually.

"A cargo ship is waiting for them in the harbor. Maybe they'll cart them out to sea and sink the lot of them."

Michel and Ida, Marc and Bella, looked at each other. Another day and they might have been herded onto that ship. Michel did not tip the driver who cursed them as he drove away.

At the station, their farewells were tearful. Michel was startled when Marc hugged him, shocked to see that his father-in-law's eyes were bright with tears.

"Take care of our Ida," he said.

They embraced her, holding her tightly in the vise of their fear and love.

"Will we ever see you again?" Bella whispered.

"Of course you will, *Maman*." Ida's voice was calm, although her heart raced and her hands trembled.

Michel pried her loose from their grasp as the conductor shouted the last boarding call. Marc and Bella reluctantly mounted the steps that led to their carriage.

"*Au revoir*," they called to each other, their voices rising above the train's piercing whistle. Bella stood on the platform of her carriage as the train left the station. She waved a white handkerchief. It fluttered in the wind, a small flag of surrender.

Ida and Michel returned to Nice. Ida charted her parents' progress from the postcards they sent. They had reached Spain without incident, but the crates of paintings had been impounded by Spanish customs at the insistence of the German embassy. Helpless, without friends to intercede for them, they had no choice but to continue their journey to Portugal. Marc sent Ida a frantic telegram from Lisbon, pleading with her to arrange for the Spanish government to release the paintings. She showed it to Michel, who crumpled it and tossed it away.

"We must do something," she pleaded.

"We've done enough," he retorted. "Their lives are saved. And we are still here, trapped like mice in a cage. Jewish mice. Did your father ever paint mice, Ida?" His bitterness morphed into cruelty.

Letters of complaint followed. The Portuguese capital was unwelcoming. Their hotel was dilapidated. They were exhausted. Bella was ill and mired in depression.

"I do not eat. I do not leave this hotel room," she wrote. "Your father cannot paint here so he writes. He writes letters that he does not send and Yiddish poems that no one will read. Ah, Idotchka, it would have been better if we had never left Vitebsk, if we had died in our village."

Her mother's words congealed into a palpable bitterness that settled heavily on Ida's heart. She wrote to Varian Fry and to the curator of the Prado in Madrid. She received halfhearted promises of assistance from both of them.

Marc wrote that passage had been arranged for them on the Portuguese freighter SS *Pinto Basto*, sailing in mid-June. The ship was old, but it would not be a lonely voyage, he added sarcastically. Hundreds of other Jews would be their traveling companions, plucked from the streets of Lisbon. He recognized them. The bearded men and bewigged women had stepped out of his own paintings.

"It pains us to leave Europe," he wrote. "But we look forward to welcoming you and Michel when you arrive in New York with my paintings. You will not forget my paintings, Idotchka."

Ida passed the letter to Michel, who glanced at it and thrust it back at her.

"And if we come without the paintings, will he welcome us?" he asked harshly.

She did not reply. She circled June 21 on her calendar. That was the day the SS *Pinto Basto* would arrive in New York. She would know then that her parents were safe.

Ida willed herself to optimism and breathed a sigh of relief when Varian Fry's secretary called to report that the Chagalls were in New York and had passed through immigration without incident. The secretary had other good news to report. In a lilting voice, pleased because she so seldom had good news, she told Ida that her father's paintings had been released and awaited her in Madrid.

The weight of months of worry slipped from Ida's shoulders. She rushed home, kissed Michel on his forehead, and pulled him to his feet, urging him into a small dance of joy. Startled, he whirled her about the room, pleased at her pleasure.

He did not ask how they would reach Madrid or how they would lay claim to the paintings. He did not ask how they would pay for their visas or for their passage to America, if by some miracle they managed to reach an open port in Spain or Portugal. He would not darken the flash of joy that lit up his wife's lovely face for the first time in months. He marveled at her refusal to understand the gravity of their own situation as she celebrated her parents' escape to freedom.

"She does not see that every door is closed to us," he told his mother that afternoon as they walked along the beach. Masha was collecting shells that she fashioned into small ornaments she sold on the streets. "Our citizenship has been revoked. We could be arrested any day," he continued.

"Not every door is closed," Masha replied quietly. "See what I have for you."

She set her basket down on the damp sand and removed a cloth-wrapped packet concealed beneath the shells she handed to him. She had not dared put it in her purse because she had been stopped more than once by the Vichy police, who had searched through it and examined her documents. He opened it and gasped as he stared at two exit visas, one for him and one for Ida, their names beautifully inscribed and a gold seal affixed to each document.

"This is fantastic," he said. "How did you get them?"

She smiled.

"Guido, the Italian soldier, the one with that fine black mustache, asked me to sew some buttons on his uniform. As I mended it, he asked me why I was so sad and I told him about you and Ida and how we feared for your lives. Guido is a good man. He hates fascism. He is a clerk to the general in charge of arranging for arrivals and departures of Italian nationals, and he managed to steal blank exit visa forms from his desk. His friend Carlos was a lithographer in Florence and he filled in your names. Guido was especially proud of the seal. He found it in a file drawer. It is meaningless, of course, but it is impressive. Which is fitting, he said, because this whole terrible war is meaningless. He asked me to promise that when the war is over, I will tell the Allies how Guido Mercurio and Carlos Mangelli helped a Jewish family. Such testimony will exempt them from any punishment. And I promised, of course."

She bent to pick up a large, beautifully shaped nacreous shell, her eyes bright with pride in her achievement.

"Do you think it will work?" he asked, his elation suddenly diminished by doubt. "And if we do manage to get out of France, how will we manage passage to New York?"

Again she smiled.

"Your father wired money to Moshe Rapaport, our cousin in Seville, who purchased two tickets for you on a ship called the *Navemare*. It will sail from Seville to New York. You will use the exit visa to reach Madrid and then go on to Seville to Moshe's apartment. That is how you will get to New York," she replied.

He had known of a well-connected Rapaport cousin in Seville, but his parents, so fiercely independent, had never wanted to impose on him. Not for themselves. But they would do anything for him, their Michel, for their Michel and Ida, his wife.

"But how did you pay for the tickets?" he asked.

"My mother's cameo. Your grandfather's diamond tie clip. We sold them." She shrugged. "We saved them carefully, but what use will they be to us now? The British have slammed the gates of Palestine shut. We will remain in France. But you and Ida are young. You have a future. You can save your lives."

"Oh, *Maman*," he moaned, overcome with love for her, for his father, awed by their selflessness and generosity. "How can I leave you?"

"But you must," she replied. "We will survive, your father and I. We are experts at survival. We will be together again when this war, this terrible war, is over."

He embraced her, felt the fragility of her small body, inhaled the very scent of her love, the lavender-tinged aroma of her papery skin mingled with the sweet-smelling breeze that blew in across the crashing cobalt waves of the Mediterranean.

Chapter Twenty-One

*I*da and Michel reached Madrid on a sweltering August day, grateful to have crossed the border into Spain but nervously aware that they had yet to pass through Spanish immigration. Conditioned to fear and uncertainty, they trembled as a Spanish officer boarded the train and demanded to see their documents. Michel handed them to him, and his heart sank as the man examined them and frowned.

"Italian. They are written in Italian," the immigration officer said irritably. "I cannot read Italian. I will have to find someone who can translate these papers for me."

Michel stared at him helplessly, but Ida smiled and loosened the buttons of her blouse.

"It is so very hot, isn't it?" she asked and dabbed at the beads of sweat that trailed down her neck to her breasts. "Please, senor, do not trouble yourself to locate a translator in this heat. I will translate them for you."

He hesitated. He was a very young man, and he wanted nothing more than to complete this tour of duty and retreat into his favorite cantina. He reflected that given the heat and his overwhelming thirst, he could easily down an entire pitcher of sangria. But he did not actually mind lingering in this particular carriage of the train. The senorita was very beautiful, her hair the color of copper and her smile so inviting. He did not see many smiles on the faces of the frightened refugees whose papers he examined day after day.

"Very well," he said at last. "Please translate them for me."

Ida nodded. "Of course. It will be my pleasure."

Michel stared at her in surprise. He knew Italian was not in Ida's linguistic arsenal. He stared straight ahead as she studied the documents and informed the officer that the government of Italy authorized safe passage for Michel and Ida Rapaport, who were students of art and would remain only briefly in Spain in order to study the paintings on exhibit at the Prado.

"This is a special student visa," she explained. "See the seal, the gold seal. It is issued only to students. But you must know that, of course, as an officer of your rank. Surely you are familiar with such documents."

Again she smiled at him seductively, licked her lips, and twisted a curl about her finger.

"Of course I know that," he agreed. "And you and your husband are both art students?"

Ida looked at Michel and laughed. "But he is not my husband," she said. "He is my brother. He has friends in Madrid so I will be often alone. You will find me on any day of this week in the El Greco gallery of the Prado. Perhaps you can show me your beautiful city if we should happen to meet."

"Oh yes," he said eagerly and handed the papers back to her.

Suddenly the day did not seem as hot to him. He was not on duty the next day, and he thought of how pleasant it would be to wander down the cool corridors of the museum with this beautiful woman, whose long, fiery lashes almost brushed her high cheekbones.

"Welcome to Spain, senorita," he said and helped her down the steps of the train carriage, smiling benignly at Michel who trailed after her.

"I congratulate you," Michel muttered as they trudged through the streets of Madrid, but there was no pleasure in his voice. "You all but stripped naked for him."

The naive girl he had married had become a woman who knew all too well how to exploit her beauty. He had loved his bride, but his wife, this determined woman who relied so recklessly on her sensual beauty, sometimes seemed a stranger to him.

Ida shrugged.

"I took a chance and it worked," she said. She would not apologize for using the only weapon at her disposal.

"You were lucky." His voice was muffled by a sudden sadness.

"We were lucky," she corrected him.

They hurried to the Spanish customs office and arranged for the crates of Marc's paintings to be shipped to the port of Seville where they would be held until they could be loaded onto the *Navemare*. Ida made certain that *The Bridal Chair* was placed in the largest of the crates.

"These crates must be handled very carefully," she cautioned the shipping agent.

"Senora, they weigh over a thousand pounds. It will be impossible to be careless with them," he replied and laughed harshly.

Within hours, they were on an express train to Seville. For the first time in months, they were safe from danger. Mysteriously, Franco's fascist government was unthreatening to Jews. Michel had heard it rumored that the dictator's father was Jewish, or perhaps it was his mother, but the truth was of no importance. They would not be in Spain for very long.

Ida smiled and took his hand. "You see. Everything is working out," she said.

"Is it?" he asked wearily and turned away to study the sere landscape as the train sped southward.

They were welcomed into Moshe Rapaport's tiny apartment and assigned a sofa in the living room. Two other young couples, Hannelore and Leon Herzberg and Claire and Henri Dreyfus, who also awaited passage on the *Navemare*, slept on the floor in nests of blankets Moshe had scavenged from neighbors. Michel and Ida liked them at once. Hannelore and Leon, both engineering students, had managed to escape from Germany while Claire and Henri, a doctor and a nurse, had been on the run from the Nazis since their hasty wedding in Alsace. Both couples had family in the United States. They traded place names. New York. Chicago. Boston. Cities of hope, cities of freedom. The very names soothed them. The similarity of their situations, their youth, and their optimism created an immediate intimacy.

Moshe Rapaport was a rotund little man, his fleshy face deeply lined, as though new furrows had been carved into it with each new flight. He and Leah, his pleasant plump wife, could no longer count the places they had lived in since fleeing Russia. Leah seldom left the impossibly tiny kitchen where she cooked huge pots of cereal and stews for her young guests whose names she never bothered to learn. Moshe and Leah were awaiting a ship that would carry them to Palestine where their two sons lived on a kibbutz.

"But how will you get into Palestine?" Michel asked. "The British have a quota on Jewish immigration."

"Should I worry about the British?" Moshe asked and laughed again. "I am a Jew. If I can't come in through the door, I will climb in through the window."

They did not argue with him. Ironic merriment, they realized, was his defense, hope his only weapon.

The *Navemare*, a Spanish cargo ship that had been swiftly converted into a passenger vessel, finally steamed into the harbor. The young people gathered their possessions and hugged Moshe and Leah, who thrust parting gifts on them—packets of food and a parcel of brightly colored bandannas that Moshe had found on the floor of yet another abandoned apartment.

"Who knows? You may find a use for them," he said. "A Jew can find a use for anything."

They laughed, promised to write, and rushed down to the pier, where they presented their papers and boarded.

They saw at once that the condition of the ship was appalling. Compact columns of bunks crammed the foul-smelling hold, which was crowded with elderly German Jews who had taken advantage of a special dispensation for those over the age of sixty-five. They were allowed to emigrate if they took no more than the equivalent of five American dollars with them. The disoriented elderly passengers in the cramped steerage area looked around in bewilderment and mumbled anxious queries.

"Moshe was right. We should have opted for Palestine," Michel said ruefully.

"Oh, we'll be all right. We'll pretend that we're on our honeymoons," Leon said, and they laughed.

Ida went to the deck where cargo was being unloaded, her eyes fixed on a crate containing her father's paintings that was being hoisted by several seamen toward a passageway.

"Where are you taking those crates?" she shouted. "They are my property."

"They'll be stored in the lowest hold," a burly stevedore called back.

"No. They belong on deck. There. Over there." She pointed to an area just above the prow.

"Who says?" he asked belligerently.

"I say."

She rummaged in her purse and pulled out the Italian exit visas, which she waved at them. "These documents are special authorization from the director of your shipping line. Don't you see his seal?"

He looked at her blankly and reached for the document that she knew he could not read. He fingered the gold seal and nodded.

"As you say, senora," he agreed and instructed that the crates be lowered onto the deck.

She sighed with relief. The storage area in the hold might flood during the crossing, and she could not risk water damage to her precious cargo.

She and Michel stood on the deck and breathed free for the first time in months as the *Navemare* moved with surprising grace out into the open sea. He held her close as the coast of Europe receded from view.

"When will we return?" he wondered aloud.

"I will be back," Ida promised.

It occurred to him, only hours later, that she had said "I" rather than "we," a realization that neither surprised nor discomforted him.

Chapter Twenty-Two

The dangers that lay ahead assaulted them on their very first day out to sea. A rumor circulated that there was a shortage of drinking water, and passengers, in the grip of panic, scrambled to seize the containers of potable water. Distraught women clawed and shoved as they claimed bottles for their children. Two old men pummeled each other as their weeping wives attempted to separate them. Children crawled beneath the legs of adults and emerged waving carafes of the precious liquid.

Ida turned to Michel and her friends. "We must stop this," she said.

She sprang into action. She stood on an upturned barrel, flanked by Michel, the Dreyfuses and the Herzbergs, each of them waving an improvised banner crafted of the brightly colored bandannas. Moshe had been right. They had found a use for his improbable gift.

"Stop this. Stop this at once," she shouted.

Her voice shrilled authoritatively above the melee, and the warring passengers turned to her. Miraculously the riot was quelled. The desperate crowd stood in expectant and obedient silence.

"Form lines. One line in front of each banner," she commanded, and they obeyed. "You will stand on these lines whenever water or food is being distributed," she said.

There were murmurs of dissent, but the lines were formed. Day after passing day, as the *Navemare* plowed through the waves, they stood in their assigned places. The three young couples took their places each day, their banners fading in the harsh sunlight and stiffened by the salt-scented winds. Ida remained in charge. She herself carried food and drink down to the hold for invalids, and when her self-imposed duties were accomplished, she wrapped herself in her blue cape and perched protectively on the huge crates that contained her father's paintings.

Michel occasionally sat beside her, sometimes fingering the fabric of her cloak. He remembered the long-ago day when she first wore it. She had sailed into the Left Bank café, her arms outstretched, the matching beret perched on her bright curls. "My blue-winged love," he had thought then. The cape had become faded and threadbare. His alpine Ida, his tender lover, his sad-eyed bride, was now a regal woman whose features were chiseled into a fine sharpness, her skin wind-burnished. She ruled with impunity from her deckside throne.

The ship could not sail a direct course. The German navy had turned the Atlantic Ocean into a maritime battlefield. Their submarines lurked beneath the rising and falling waves, stalking freighters and passenger ships. The *Navemare* radio operator brought hourly reports to the captain who altered course, now turning westward, now turning eastward, to avoid the deadly torpedo fire that had already sunk so many other vessels.

"We will be at sea forever," Claire Dreyfus murmured to Ida as they sat together atop her pyramid of crates.

Ida laughed bitterly. "I think 'forever' has already passed," she said.

She wandered across the deck with her drawing pad, clutching her diminishing supply of graphite sticks. She drew ragged toddlers playing circle games, an old woman huddled in blankets, a man wrapped in a prayer shawl swaying devoutly at first light.

Day drifted into night and night into day. The sea grew turbulent and the ship plowed through a storm, heaving dangerously from side to side as the gusts of wind grew more and more powerful. It seemed to the frightened passengers that the sea itself had also declared war on them. They huddled below deck as bullets of rain spewed down and angry waves soared onto the deck. Shafts of lightning scissored their way across the heavens, and thunderbolts exploded deafeningly.

Exhausted sailors sloshed their way from station to station, seawater spilling out of their high boots.

Throughout the horrific tempest, Ida, wrapped in her blue cape, her hair drenched beneath the rain-soaked, green silk scarf, scurried across the deck, cajoling sailors to cover her crates with tarpaulins. She and Michel secured the makeshift covering against the increasingly fierce gale winds. When at last the crates were safely covered, she fell into Michel's arms and allowed him to carry her to her bunk.

The storm ended, and the Jewish high holy days began. The weary congregation stood on deck, their faces dampened by sea mist commingled with tears, and prayed their way through Rosh Hashanah, the Jewish New Year. They toasted each other with dregs of sacramental wine that tasted like vinegar.

"Next year in New York," they said bitterly.

Dreams of Jerusalem were futile. Survival was their minimalist goal, New York their Zion, and the United States their promised land.

On the eve of Yom Kippur, the Day of Atonement, the worshippers gathered again. Their bodies swayed in rhythm with the newly gentle waves. An elderly cantor intoned the Kol Nidre prayer in quivering tones. Ida watched him, moved by his dignity and devotion, reminiscent of her father's portrait of a rabbi that the Nazis had called an example of "degenerate art."

He stood before them again the next day and chanted the awesome *Unetanneh Tokef* prayer.

Ocean spray pearled his white beard, and his blue eyes glistened as he sang the familiar, poignant words.

"*Mi yichye, umi yamut?* Who will live and who will die?"

"Save us. Save our children," they prayed.

Ida and Michel also prayed. They asked the God in whom they might believe to protect them, to offer them some small hope for the quiet happiness that had for so long eluded them.

Ida saw how the prayer shawls of the men were lifted by vagrant winds. She watched a father lift his small son and daughter and hold them close, drawing his tattered white *tallit* over their shivering bodies. The little girl's hair was lemon yellow. Her father had a tube of oil paint in that exact shade. She wondered how Marc might paint this synagogue at sea. She wondered if he would be moved to lift his own voice in prayer. But he would have no need, she decided with a flash of insight. His paintings themselves were prayers.

The day drew to a close. Sunset spread its melancholy pastel rays across the upturned faces of the exhausted congregation. Mysteriously, a shofar was produced and the cantor blew the triumphant resounding notes.

"*Shanah tovah.*"

"A good year."

Their whispered wishes drifted through the windswept darkness.

Disease continued to sweep through the ship. Henri Dreyfus, their doctor friend, opened his medical bag and displayed its meager contents.

"Aspirins. Alcohol. Liniment. These are our weapons. How can we fight typhoid? It is as though we are shooting arrows at huge cannons."

His voice was somber, his face drawn. He had stayed up all night, darting from one sick passenger to another.

"You're certain that what we're dealing with is typhoid?" Michel asked him.

"Classic symptoms. Headaches, vomiting, elevated temperatures, bloody diarrhea," Henri replied. "I've seen only a few cases. I did my residency at a private hospital in Paris, which is hardly a breeding ground for typhoid. The rich are more susceptible to syphilis and gonorrhea."

Claire remained at his side, refilling basins of water for compresses, offering soothing words of hope to the hopeless. Pale and exhausted, she stretched out on a narrow bunk, her hands resting protectively on the gentle rise of her abdomen. Ida realized that her friend was pregnant.

"There must be other doctors and nurses on board. We need their help," Ida said.

She raced onto the deck and spoke to group after group, urging anyone with a medical background to offer assistance. There were those who came forward willingly, others who responded tentatively.

"You must help," Ida told them adamantly, and they reluctantly agreed.

"Who can say no to that redheaded devil?" an elderly internist muttered to his wife as he followed Ida.

A psychiatrist who had worked with Freud circulated among the patients with a thermometer and a stethoscope.

"I hope I still know how to use it," he told Henri and offered him the contents of his own medical bag, which consisted largely of laudanum and valerian.

The deaths began. The cantor was the first to succumb to the disease, his prayerful Yom Kippur query answered. He had died and the ocean was his grave. His sallow, bewigged wife trembled uncontrollably as she stood at the rail of the ship and watched as his body, wrapped in his worn prayer shawl, was lowered into the sea. A quorum of ten men chanted the Kaddish and Ida was surprised to see that Michel was among them. She wondered sadly if he was rehearsing for his own role as a mourner.

She knew that his restless sleep was haunted by dreams of his parents. He awakened, calling their names, and grasped at the fetid air as though he might pull their ghosts into his arms. She dared not comfort him. She was all too familiar with the power of nightmares. She herself awakened exhausted from the nocturnal races she ran endlessly during the brief hours of her slumber.

Day by day, the death toll grew. The deckside funerals were swift, the emaciated bodies scarcely creating a splash as they were dropped into the sea.

Ida, making her rounds of the hold, saw that the small girl with lemon-yellow hair was ill. She carried damp cloths to the distraught parents and she wiped the child's face. It was a flower of a face, she thought, the tiny mouth a rosebud, the skin petal-soft beneath the lucent layer of sweat.

"Shayna, her name is Shayna," the mother said, her cheek pressed to the child's feverish forehead.

"And she is *shayn*, a beauty. How old is she?" Ida asked.

"Seven, just seven."

Ida's eyes filled. She might have been the mother of a child who would now be seven years old. She chastised herself for the thought; it was obscene to mourn the ghost of her unborn child, not when the living, breathing child before her so desperately needed her help. Fatigue was playing vicious games with her imagination. She shrugged herself free of the thought as she ground a precious aspirin into water and fed it to Shayna. She moistened yet another cloth and wiped her spindly limbs, but the child's temperature soared. She shivered although her body was slick with sweat. As Ida watched, her rosebud of a mouth opened in a smile, and her eyes fluttered closed as though a sweet dream had eased her way into death.

"No! *Nein!* *Nein!*" her father shouted and cradled his daughter's small inert body in his arms.

Her young brother wept and his mother held him close.

"Shayna, Shayna." She whispered his sister's name into her surviving child's ear as though mandating him to remember her always.

"Shayna, Shayna," he repeated, his voice breaking.

She was buried within the hour, and it was Ida who stood with the small group of mourners and intoned the Kaddish, wishing fervently that she could believe in her whispered prayer. Was it a great and sanctified God who allowed a child with hair the color of lemons to die such a sad and terrible death?

Shayna's death was the final loss of life on the *Navemare*. The illness had run its course. The voyagers had survived and dared to contemplate the new lives that awaited them. The children played circle games, lovers sought sweet privacy in the lifeboats, and even the demeanor of the seamen softened.

Hannelore and Claire joined Ida on her usual perch atop the crates. Michel scavenged blankets and canvas sacks and created a nest for the three friends who lifted their faces to catch the fleeting rays of light. Claire's pregnancy was now apparent and she told them that she had felt the child move within her womb. Shyly, the two young women touched the soft swell and felt the tender flutter of the nascent life.

"You were very brave to proceed with the pregnancy," Hannelore said. "My sister became pregnant just as she and her husband finally got visas to the Dominican Republic. She couldn't bear the idea of carrying a child during such a dangerous voyage into such a dangerous world."

"What did she do?" Ida asked, although she knew the answer.

"She had an *avortement*, an abortion," Hannelore replied. "She is young. They'll have other children."

"We thought of abortion," Claire admitted. "I'm a nurse, Henri is a doctor. We understood that we had that option and that it wouldn't pose any real danger. We knew that if a pregnant woman was swept up in a *rafle* and sent to concentration camp, she would immediately be killed."

"Why didn't you do it?" Ida asked.

"I didn't want to give Hitler another victory, another Jewish death. Henri said he would accept whatever decision I made, but I know he was relieved when I decided to carry our child. We had already taken so many risks that we decided we could take one more."

"You don't regret it?" Hannelore asked.

"No. Do you think your sister will regret her decision?" Deftly, Claire tossed the question back at her.

It was Ida who replied.

"She may regret it and she may not. But she will never forget it."

They looked at her and reached out to cover her hands with their own, but no questions were asked, no answers volunteered. Ida stared straight ahead, out to the sea where quite suddenly a flock of gulls appeared, swooping down and sailing gracefully on the crests of foam-laced waves.

"Gulls," Hannelore said wonderingly. "We must be approaching land."

"New York," Ida said softly, and she wondered if her parents would be aware of the *Navemare*'s arrival. She realized that it was the first time in weeks that she had thought of Marc and Bella and she wondered if she should feel guilt or relief, acknowledging that she felt neither. Soon enough, she would be swept back into the orbit of their love, their needs, their demands.

She awakened the next morning to sounds of jubilation, to clapping hands and stamping feet, to the excited laughter of children and shouts of gladness. Ida and Michel, hand in hand, rushed onto the deck and stared at the majestic statue that reigned over the harbor.

"Lady Liberty," Michel said. "We're in America." His voice broke. "Idotchka, we are in America."

She pressed her face against his chest and wept, moistening his shirt with her tears. He held her close, his hand resting on her shining hair. She leaned against him, too faint to support herself, her cheeks burning, her head spinning.

Chapter Twenty-Three

They disembarked and plunged into the turmoil of immigration, answering questions, extending their documents for official scrutiny. The customs officer examined the crates that contained Marc's paintings and vigorously stamped the import forms.

"Lucky for you this stuff was on deck," he told her. "Everything that was stored in the hold of that floating coffin they call a ship was waterlogged and rotted. We had to toss it all out."

"Yes," she agreed. "I was lucky. I was indeed fortunate."

She marveled at her use of the words. It had been a long time since she had felt herself to be either lucky or fortunate. Her spirits soared.

"Lucky," she repeated. "Fortunate."

Michel took her arm and they walked slowly through the gates and plunged into the tumultuous crowd in the arrivals area. Michel's eyes raked the anxious throng, searching for his in-laws, overcome with bewilderment by the clamor of competing sounds, the sea of faces, the incessant honking of horns, and the shrilling of sirens. He looked frantically about and suddenly heard their tremulous voices, miraculously soaring above the deafening cacophony.

"Ida! Michel!" Marc and Bella were shouting in unison.

Michel waved his hat in the air and called their names again and again. They caught sight of him and battled their way forward, thrusting themselves through one group and then another, as always skillful maneuverers. Marc's gray curls bobbed up and down.

"See there they are, your mother and father," Michel told Ida reassuringly.

She turned and trembled with excitement.

"*Mamochka, Papochka!*" She rushed toward them and fell into her father's outstretched arms.

Bella clung to Michel, her face wet with tears. Her hand rested briefly on her daughter's brow.

"My child, my *zeis*," she whispered.

Ida smiled wanly, but she did not open her eyes and Marc didn't release her from his embrace.

Bella gripped Michel's arm.

"Michel, we are so happy that you are here at last. Was the voyage very difficult? Our Ida looks so tired. You should have seen that she rested more. And what of the paintings, Marc's paintings? Are they safe? Oh, you don't know how anxious he has been."

She spoke breathlessly, punctuating each question with a fierce pinch of his arm that caused Michel to recoil and wrench himself free.

"Yes, Ida is tired," he replied curtly. "She's exhausted. We're both exhausted. But the paintings, the damn paintings are safe." He willed himself to patience as they organized their baggage and arranged for the storage of the crates and then took a cab that drove through the city.

The Chagalls had established themselves in an apartment on Riverside Drive that overlooked the Hudson River. Ida marveled at how her mother had managed to re-create the ambience of the world she had left behind. The heavy dark furniture and the upholstery of the sofa and chairs, the flower-filled Chinese vases, were reminiscent of the textures and scents of her Parisian homes.

Ida looked down at the traffic that streamed down the drive. She marveled that the pedestrians who hurried across the wide thoroughfare never slowed their pace to look down at the gleaming water or paused to notice the small craft that drifted so gracefully across the gentle waves.

"Why is everyone in New York in such a hurry?" she asked Michel.

"They have places to go, things to do," he replied and smiled bitterly. He himself had nowhere to go, nothing to do.

The apartment was a magnetic destination for the Chagalls' small community of friends and acquaintances. Refugees from France and Germany, Yiddishists from eastern Europe, artists and writers, the famous and the unknown, sat at Bella's dining room table, sipped tall glasses of tea, sucked on sugar cubes, and traded questions.

When would the United States enter the war?

When would Roosevelt come to the aid of the allies?

They sighed over battles being fought in the meadowlands of their childhoods; they wept when the towns and cities of their birth were mentioned. Their continent was ablaze; fires incinerated their friends and relations, their homes and their books, the Torah scrolls and prayer shawls of vanished worshippers. The women wept. The men grew red-faced with anger.

Michel listened to them impatiently.

"They do not realize how fortunate they are," he told Elsa, who visited them on afternoons when she was not on call at the hospital. "They are alive in the land of the free."

"It is difficult for them to recognize how much their world has changed," she said.

"Everything has changed," he agreed. "We are not as we were when you first knew us, Elsa. Ida has changed. I have changed."

He glanced across the room to where Ida sat, half listening to an old man whose name he did not know. She nodded occasionally, but her eyes were glazed and her face was very pale.

"She is still very tired," Elsa said. "She has not yet recovered from the voyage."

"Neither of us have," he admitted.

Only that morning, he had stood before the mirror and stared at his own face as though he were looking at a stranger. When had he become so gaunt? Why did his eyes seem so dull, his skin so ashen?

"You must take care of her." Elsa spoke very softly. "I say that as a doctor and as a friend."

"I will take care of her, of course I will, but I must find a life for myself, a way to survive, a way to help my parents."

Melancholy thickened his voice and Elsa placed a comforting

hand on his shoulder. The import of his words had not escaped her. He had spoken in the singular. He had not spoken of finding a life that they would share. She knew that they no longer shared a room. It was, Ida had explained, because her nights were restless and dream-haunted. She did not want to disturb Michel. She slept alone in a high white bed beneath her father's painting of *The Bridal Chair*. Elsa recalled Ida as a joyless bride sitting motionless on that white-sheeted chair, clutching her bridal bouquet. Perhaps the sadness of that wedding day had been a prequel to this marriage that now seemed drained of all vitality.

"Things will get better, Michel," she assured him.

"Will they?" he asked and smiled wistfully.

"I am sure of it," she said. "You must visit us soon. André looks forward to seeing you. And we want to introduce you to our son."

"I will visit. Of course I will."

He helped her on with her coat. She crossed the room to embrace Ida and nodded to Marc and Bella, who had barely acknowledged her presence. Elsa noted their clothing with some amusement. Marc was debonair in a purple velvet jacket, and Bella wore a loose, jade-green kimono of shimmering silk. Elsa understood that these were the costumes of their new roles. They dressed as a couple to be admired and courted as much for their tragic lives as for their talents. Elsa kissed Michel on the cheek and closed the heavy door very quietly behind her.

Elsa, always wisely stoic, was right. Things did get better. Ida's strength was restored. Newly energized, she began to explore the city. Her parents thought New York ugly, inhospitable. Their English was limited. Marc was comfortable only on the Lower East Side where he spoke Yiddish to the shopkeepers and bought the staples of his Russian childhood. But the rushing and bustling city excited Ida, and she trawled it with great eagerness. She accompanied Marc to the Garden Cafeteria on East Broadway where they shared a table with Yiddish writers and poets and traded stories of their vanished worlds. She smiled as he bought herring plucked from barrels, cucumbers pickled in brine, black bread, and pot cheese. Her father, she realized, was capable of re-creating his world anywhere. She, however, would have to forge a new life in this new land.

She fashioned her hair into a single long braid and bought dark skirts and wide, colored blouses.

"You look like a schoolgirl," Michel said.

"Do I? I never was a schoolgirl, you know," she replied.

It occurred to him that she was trying to reclaim the girlhood that had been denied her, but he said nothing. He had not returned to her bed. She did not visit his room. They did not speak of their nocturnal separation. Silence served them well. Unuttered words could not be regretted.

Ida wandered through the room Marc used as his studio. It was flooded with sunlight throughout the day, but his new works were dark, unaffected by the optimism of America and the energy of New York. War-torn Europe haunted his imagination, invaded his canvases and sketch books. He painted scenes of suffering; his landscapes were moonlit and misty. He depicted Vitebsk trapped in dancing flames.

"Sad paintings," she said.

"These are sad times," he replied. "But Pierre Matisse manages to sell much of my work."

"His gallery here in New York is successful then?" Ida asked too quickly. As always, the business dimension of the art world engaged and excited her.

"He works hard and he is fair. He represents Fernand Léger, Jacques Lipchitz, Max Ernst, André Breton. So you see, I am in good company. We are a brigade of fortunate exiles."

"Excellent company," she agreed. "But perhaps, Papa, you might think of brightening your palette. Paintings with sharper colors, on lighter themes, are easier to sell."

"Still the businesswoman, Idotchka," he said wryly.

"My business sense has worked well for you, has it not?" she replied. "I think that I managed your affairs quite well in London. In Paris."

She spoke daringly. She knew that he resented the reminder that she was partially responsible for his success. Michel had remarked that he had never thanked them for transporting his paintings to New York. Those very paintings that had claimed so much of her energy and enterprise were now part of Pierre Matisse's inventory.

She would visit the Matisse gallery. Pierre, she knew, would welcome her. After all, she had been his father's favorite. He surely knew how expertly she had negotiated sales and commissions for Marc in Europe. She could do as much in New York, working through the gallery. The very idea energized her. She was poised at a new beginning. She would explore every opportunity, use all her resources and talents. She had earned the right to lay claim to her own life, to be the architect of her own future.

She studied the drawings she had done aboard the *Navemare* and decided that they were better than she had thought. She could surely work as a portraitist. She would ask Pierre for his advice. Middle-aged, introspective men like Pierre Matisse were always pleased to offer advice to beautiful young women. She smiled at herself in the mirror. Yes, she was still a beautiful young woman.

Impulsively, she called James Johnson Sweeney, the curator of the Museum of Modern Art, with whom she had corresponded, and arranged to meet with him.

That appointment was scheduled for a day when she and Michel had been invited to visit Elsa and André.

"I am too tired to go," she claimed plaintively. "I have a headache. They will understand."

Michel frowned and offered to stay home with her, but she waved him away.

She wondered afterward why she had not simply told him the truth. She could have explained that Sweeney was an important contact for the Chagalls, for Marc as well as herself. But Michel would be disinterested and she resented his reluctance to enter the orbit of the art world that so engaged her. They did not speak of that reluctance.

A discussion might prove dangerous. It would be a clear articulation that her world was not and never would be his.

Michel went alone to visit Elsa and André. He brought a small toy, a hand-carved wooden wagon, as a gift for their son Daniel, who delighted in rolling it across the kitchen floor.

"It's charming," Elsa said. "Where did you find it?"

"I made it," Michel said. "It gave me something to do." He smiled wanly. "The days are very long," he added. "I look for work, but I know that my search is almost impossible. My English is terrible. I have no skills. Two years of studying law at the Sorbonne qualifies me for nothing in New York. I even applied for a job as a messenger and the man at the employment agency laughed at me. I don't blame him. I could barely read the addresses on the packages he showed me, so how could I hope to deliver them? I walk through Times Square and I see the large poster of Uncle Sam with his finger pointing and saying 'Uncle Sam Wants You.' That much English I understand and then I think, 'Uncle Sam does not want me. No one in this country, this promised land, wants Michel Rapaport.' So to fill the hours of my day, I carve a toy for your sweet Daniel. I deliver my father-in-law's paintings to the Matisse gallery. I go to the French consulate and to the Hebrew Immigrant Aid Society and ask if there is any news of my parents, although, of course, I know that there will be none. Evenings I attend English classes at a public school where I sit at a very small desk with other refugees. We students do not look at each other when we arrive and we do not look at each other when we leave. We are ashamed, I think because we are grown men and women who sit in seats that are meant for children."

"No need to be ashamed," André said. "We sat in such seats, Elsa and I, when we first arrived in this country. And now we have our jobs, our little home, our magical son." He hoisted small Daniel onto his lap and tickled him beneath the chin until the child laughed, slid down, and dashed back to his new toy.

"Ah, but you had something that I do not have," Michel said quietly.

Elsa held her breath. She did not want to hear Michel say that she and André had had each other while he was trapped in a dying marriage. His answer relieved her.

"You had your medical degrees. You had credentials to offer an employer," he said.

Elsa looked at him with new respect. He would not impose the deeper sorrows of his life on them. He was stronger than she had thought.

"But you too have something to offer," André said. "Listen to me, Michel. You have a wonderful speaking voice. So clear, so smooth, so pleasant to listen to. Elsa has told me how you would recite poetry during your days at the encampment and how everyone was impressed with your fluency. My friend Pierre Lazareff represents the Free French. He works with the Voice of America, a U.S. State Department program that broadcasts to Europe. They want to increase transmission to France. Pierre is in search of French speakers who can read the news and create radio programs that will offer encouragement to listeners in France so that they will know that they are not alone, that they have allies in the free world. It would be an important job and one that I think would suit you well."

"It is especially important now," Elsa added. "The United States is not yet at war, but that day is very close. Everyone in this country expects it to happen—next week, next month, next year. Washington cannot remain much longer in the waiting room of history. The president will not abandon American allies. He is only waiting for an excuse to enter a war that he already knows he must fight. The Voice of America will be an important agency when that happens."

"That is why Lazareff is in search of newscasters who can raise French morale and encourage the people to resist the Nazi occupation," André said.

"And would he hire me?" Michel asked hesitantly.

"Why would he not hire you?" André replied gruffly. "I will call him this very moment and arrange for you to meet him."

He went to the phone, spoke briefly, and then passed the receiver to Michel.

Pierre Lazareff would be delighted to meet him. Could Michel arrange to come to the Voice of America office the next day? It was in Rockefeller Center, a convenient location.

"You will know how to reach it, *n'est-ce pas?*"

"*Bien sûr,*" Michel said. He did not know how to reach it, but he would find it, just as he had found embassies and consular offices in Paris and Nice, in Madrid and in Lisbon. Necessity had made him a skilled navigator of foreign streets.

"At noon then. There is a wonderful French restaurant nearby. I imagine you would not be opposed to eating a fresh-baked croissant. *Au revoir. À demain.*"

"*À demain,*" Michel repeated. He set the phone down and smiled gratefully at his friends.

Pierre Lazareff was an amiable man. Portly and florid, he emanated a contagious confidence and optimism. He had fled Paris just before the German invasion and made his way to London, where Charles de Gaulle had encouraged him to go to America. The war to free France would be fought on many fronts, de Gaulle had assured him, and an important front would be that of effective propaganda. Washington was in agreement. Pierre Lazareff had a budget, a broadcasting studio, and fields of transmission, but he needed effective newscasters.

"We must fight the Nazis on the airwaves. Our people must know that they are not alone. You will give them news, encourage and engage them, urge a viable resistance movement. Can you do that, Michel Rapaport?" he asked.

"I can," Michel replied. He bit into the croissant. Pierre Lazareff had not erred. The croissant was fresh-baked and flavored with anise.

Lazareff ordered omelets and discussed hours, expenses, and salary. Michel chewed slowly and nodded.

"One last thing. Your name. You must assume an alias for the broadcasts."

"My name?" Michel asked, disconcerted. "Do you object because my name is Jewish?"

"No. Of course not. But your parents are in France. If the Gestapo monitors your broadcasts, and they will, they will be in danger. You understand that."

"All too well," Michel agreed. "And so I will not be Michel Rapaport." He thought for a moment. "I will be Michel Gordey," he said without hesitation.

"A quick decision," Lazareff said approvingly. He too made swift decisions. It had taken him only minutes to recognize how valuable an addition to his staff this young man, this Michel Rapaport, would be. He had a voice that was at once sonorous and gentle, that both soothed and inspired confidence. "Why Gordey?" he asked.

"My wife and I lived in Gordes, our last home before fleeing France. I am hopeful that if my parents are alive, they will recognize my voice and make that connection. And they will find a way to contact me."

He closed his eyes and thought of his resourceful mother, his sad-eyed father. *If* they were alive, he had said. *If. Si.* The monosyllable of uncertainty weighed heavily upon his heart.

"A wise choice," Pierre Lazareff said. "I will see you at the office tomorrow then."

He paid the bill and left, pausing at the cashier's station to fill his hand with peppermint candies. His craving for sweets had begun during the early days of this bitter and terrible war.

Michel remained at the table and stared down at his coffee cup. He was overwhelmed by his good fortune. He had a job, an important job, a job that would pay a salary and release him from accepting the dollar bills that Marc counted out so grudgingly. He had a new name, a new profession. He would no longer be known only as Ida Chagall's husband, Marc Chagall's son-in-law. He was now Michel Gordey, newly his own person with his own mission.

He walked energetically across Central Park, breathing in the clear chill air of early winter. It seemed to him that he was filling his lungs with hope. He was exhilarated when he returned to the Riverside Drive apartment. There was a new buoyancy in his step, a new assertiveness in his voice. That evening, with barely muted pride, he told the family about his appointment. Ida hugged him, proud and relieved. His depression had weighed heavily on her. His new independence ensured her own. Marc said nothing. His silence did not surprise Michel. He had learned, over the years, that his father-in-law rarely took pleasure in the success of others.

Ida's quiet smile of pride sufficed. He took her hand and led her from the room.

They slept together that night, her body pressed against his own, their limbs entangled. When they embraced, it was with gentleness; when they came together, it was with ease rather than with passion. Their movements were practiced, the touch of their hands tender and comforting, the sweetness of their mingled breath familiar. But even as her body arched toward his, even as they laid claim to each other, there was no surge of joy, no cry of delight.

Exhausted, they leaned back against the pillows, their eyes closed, but they were reluctant to surrender to sleep. They did not speak. It occurred to Ida that they were not unlike dear friends, reunited after a long separation, newly surprised that their affection had endured. Like fairy-tale characters, they had wandered through a dangerous forest, evading danger, struggling to survive, but without a trail of bread crumbs to guide them home. Together they had raced across borders and crossed an ocean, mutually dependent, mutually supportive. No matter what else happened, they would always be bound up in bonds of affection. They would always be linked by shared memory.

And Michel, as though reading her thoughts, lay quietly beside her and took her hand in his own. They fell asleep at last, with their fingers intertwined.

Chapter Twenty-Four

*L*ife in New York settled into a routine. Bella worked on her autobiography day after day. She wrote and rewrote in Yiddish, her pen moving rapidly as she raced to capture the world of her childhood, as though fearful that it might be obliterated in memory even as it had been destroyed in actuality. Her chronicle of Vitebsk denied Hitler a victory, she told Joseph and Adele Opatoshu, the Chagalls' closest friends, who listened as she read from a completed chapter in a voice trembling with emotion.

"You must not work so hard, Bella," Joseph Opatoshu, an accomplished novelist, advised. "Writers need time to reflect, to replenish their imaginations."

Bella shrugged and continued to work at a frenetic pace.

Re-creating the ambience of their life in France, each Sunday the Chagall apartment, high above Riverside Drive, became a salon to which friends and acquaintances flocked. Marc reveled in the roles of both the generous host and the guest of honor at his own party.

He was voluble about his new works. He was painting with a new intensity, in anticipation of his first New York exhibition. He spent every day in his studio, his brushes flashing across canvases large and small, his palette gleaming with fresh pools of paint. He was determined to make his mark in the city of his exile. Pierre Matisse and Ida, working together, shrewdly predicted that the war and his own personal history would ignite a renewed interest in his work.

Ida too worked with fierce concentration. She dashed across town each morning to help select paintings from the early period in Paris. She prepared the catalog, spending long hours proofreading, and updated the guest list. She supervised the positioning of each painting.

"You are exhausting yourself," Michel warned her, although he himself was also working long hours, leaving for his Voice of America office at the crack of dawn and returning late in the evening. The hours of transmission were geared to Paris time, and between each broadcast, newspapers and journals were scavenged for material, musical selections had to be decided on, and interviews arranged. Michel introduced new concepts. It was his idea to open each program with a robust rendition of "La Marseillaise," igniting patriotism, and to conclude with a gentle Piaf chanson, inspiring nostalgia. He traveled to meetings in Washington and conferences in Montreal.

He and Ida lived parallel lives, their worlds disparate, their interchanges increasingly swift and perfunctory.

The exhibition opened in November. Ida was the reigning hostess, meeting with critics and dazzling patrons with her analysis of her father's work, pointing out the bold colors and themes of fantasy and wonderment, making quotable statements.

"My father was a pioneer. His work sowed the seeds of surrealism," she declared with a charming toss of her head and a brilliant smile. Her pleasure in her own words and her delight in her father's work was contagious. Her London success was replicated. Her elegance and charm were celebrated. She designed her own clothes, selecting shimmering, bold-colored fabrics, royal blue silks and jade-green satins, that offset the coppery tones of her thick hair. She mingled effortlessly with seasoned collectors and moneyed dilettantes alike, now speaking French, now speaking English, tossing off snatches of German and Russian.

Her dramatic and hazardous escape from Europe, her horrendous journey on the *Navemare*, mutated into fascinating anecdotes. Her courage was admired, the drama of her life applauded. Young women envied her adventures; young men thought her glamorous and courageous.

Charles Leirens, a Belgian photographer visiting New York, came to the apartment and Marc and Bella posed for him. He saw Ida standing in the doorway and trained his camera on her, intrigued by her full-featured generous face, the graceful arcs of her eyebrows. She smiled, frowned, stared at him gravely, and laughed, a willing and quiescent subject.

"Are you also an artist, Mademoiselle Ida?" he asked.

"Madame," she corrected him. Though she and Michel barely saw each other, he would not have her marriage ignored. "Yes, of course. I too am an artist."

She had not abandoned her own work. Somehow she found time to attend studio classes. She filled the pages of her sketch pads with portraits and landscapes, still lifes and free-floating designs, now working in charcoal, now in pastel chalks. She never showed her efforts to her father, nor did he ask to see them. Bella glanced at her drawings, but it was Ida's marriage, not her art, that concerned her.

"You and Michel must spend more time together," she said worriedly. "Your father and I were never apart so often."

Bella's fear for their marriage was palpable. She would forever adhere to the values of Jewish Vitebsk where divorce, like an unmarried daughter who had lost her virginity, meant a loss of respectability.

Ida sighed. She would not remind her mother of Marc's wanderings alone through the French countryside in search of new landscapes or of the long hours he spent in his studio.

"My marriage is different from yours, *Maman*," she replied impatiently. "This is a different time. Women live their own lives. Our husbands and fathers do not define us."

Even as she spoke, she acknowledged inwardly that her very name defined her. The world knew her as Ida Chagall, daughter of the artist.

"*Plus ça change, plus c'est la même chose.* The more it changes, the more it remains the same. Marriages are vulnerable. You must be careful," Bella warned.

"Don't worry. When the exhibition is over, Michel and I will have a holiday," Ida promised.

The exhibition ended on the first Friday in December. Pierre Matisse declared it a significant success. He was increasing the regular income he sent to Marc each month, and substantial amounts would be forthcoming as the paintings sold. He wrote a generous check to Ida in recognition of her assistance. In celebration, the Chagalls invited their friends to brunch on that Sunday. It would be, Bella decided, more elaborate than their usual Sunday salons.

She began to bake at dawn, and by midmorning, the air was heavy with the sweet scents of cinnamon, allspice, and nutmeg. Her face flushed, a large white apron covering her green silk dress, she darted from oven to counter, arranging her babkas and slices of apple and banana cake on serving dishes. Flakes of confectioner's sugar jeweled her cheek, and Marc, in his peacock-blue velvet jacket, playfully licked them off. Bella laughed and swatted his hand. Ida stood in the doorway and watched them, at once amused and envious. For that brief instant, she saw them as the carefree and charming lovers of her childhood. She smiled and went into the dining room where Michel stood at the window, staring down at the bleak street.

"You're not working today?" she asked in surprise.

"There is a popular theory among journalists that no news of any importance occurs on a Sunday. Generals and politicians also need their day of rest," he replied drily. "So I have leave to relish your mother's apple tart."

Ida laughed. "Then you must help me prepare for this very important brunch," she said, pleased by the unexpected lightness of his tone.

They stood at opposite ends of the table and draped it with a heavy white linen cloth. Michel carried in the samovar he had discovered in a shabby secondhand shop. It was silver plate, darkened by neglect, but Bella had polished it so that it gleamed in the soft light of the winter morning. He placed it next to the platter of artfully arranged cut fruit, russet pears leaning against blushing apples, interspersed with golden segments of orange. Bella, always the aesthete, was particular about appearances. Her home, the table that she set, clearly stated that the Chagalls had survived, their dignity intact, their prosperity assured. They would live as graciously as they had always lived, impervious to adversity, Hitler be damned.

Ida and Michel set out the china and cutlery. She found it oddly comforting that they shared this small domestic effort. It had been weeks since they had done anything together, caught up as they were in the separate currents of their new lives.

Gratefully, she took his hand in hers and pressed it to her lips. He looked at her in surprise and thought to tell her how beautiful she looked at that moment. He marveled at how the copper-colored wool dress that hugged her slender body almost exactly matched her bright hair. But he remained silent even as the color rose to her cheeks. He knew their emotional balance to be tenuous, easily upset by even the most casual words.

Ida turned away and went into the spacious living room, so carefully furnished with heavy dark cabinets, deep leather chairs, and patterned carpets. The tasseled sofa was upholstered in a green and gold brocade not unlike that of the very uncomfortable divan that had dominated their Paris living room. Some of the furniture was borrowed from friends; other pieces had been purchased at consignment shops. The sofa was on loan from an artist in the throes of a divorce; the bookshelves had once stood in Pierre Matisse's gallery. Marc and Bella were skilled and resourceful scavengers, experienced at creating effective stage sets on which to play the roles thrust upon them by history.

Ida lit the lamps against the gloom of the wintry morning. She studied her father's paintings, moved anew by his landscapes and circus fantasies, his gouache of the floating village of Vitebsk, and the pen and ink drawing of a synagogue that would illustrate her mother's still-unfinished memoir. A portrait of herself as a sad and pensive child in a French garden stared down at her. She wondered what she had been thinking as she posed on that distant day. Had her thoughts been happy or had she been reflecting on the evasive dreams that even then had so often stayed with her during her waking hours?

"Where is my laughing Ida?" Michel had asked the first time he saw that portrait. It was not a question that he would ask. He was all too familiar with the source of her sadness.

The doorbell rang, and she shed her melancholy reverie and hurried to answer it. The regular guests entered in convivial clusters, their faces bruised by the cold wind, their ill-fitting heavy coats tightly buttoned. They were eager to escape the grim solitude of a wintry Sunday in a city not their own. Meyer Schapiro, the tall, fine-featured art critic, presented Bella with a bouquet of lilacs purchased from an overpriced florist. It was an extravagant gesture, but he knew the flowers to be her favorite. She kissed him on both cheeks in gratitude and placed the blossoms in a vase of clear blue glass that she set at the center of the table. The fragrance of the delicate blossoms filled the room, and each new arrival inhaled it deeply, perhaps remembering their own gardens abandoned in distant lands, where lilacs grew in abundance.

They filled their teacups, nibbled bits of cake and fruit, and settled themselves in the living room, choosing seats in circlets of lamp-light. They spoke softly, in a gentle hum of languages—Yiddish and French, German and English, Russian and Polish.

On the hour, Marc turned on the radio and all conversation ceased. The hourly news broadcast was integral to their Sunday ritual. They sat in silence as they sipped their tea and nibbled their pastries, waiting for the newscaster to tell them what was happening on the continent of their birth. There was unusual static and then, with sudden clarity, the voice of the newscaster, hoarse and trembling, assaulted them with an onslaught of horrific news. They struggled to comprehend his words, their faces pale with fear, their eyes wide in disbelief, as the distant war invaded their quiet afternoon.

Anguished, confused, they plucked single words from the abrasive narrative and tried to arrange them into a cohesive whole.

"Attack," they heard.

"This very morning."

"Pearl Harbor."

They stared at each other in wonderment. Who had been attacked? Where was Pearl Harbor?

"Japanese planes," they heard. "The American fleet bombed. Horrendous loss of American lives."

Each word was a jagged piece of a verbal puzzle whose meaning eluded them.

"Why are Japanese bombs killing Americans?" Bella whispered to Marc, who squeezed his eyes shut.

He could not answer because he did not know. Their war was in Europe, across the Atlantic Ocean. The Pacific, Hawaii, the continent of Asia, were beyond their imagination.

"With this unprovoked attack, the United States of America has been plunged into war," the announcer continued, his voice heavy with grief. "This Japanese aggression is an act of war."

They turned to each other. These were words that they understood. They were familiar with acts of war. They were the victims of acts of war. They sat in silence as he repeated the ominous words, pronouncing each syllable with great care. Marc turned the volume up. Teaspoons clattered against china plates, the delicate sound offsetting the heavy words. They learned that Pearl Harbor was in Hawaii. The battleship *Oklahoma* had been bombed in Honolulu. The Philippines were under attack. There were unconfirmed rumors of German involvement.

"The Germans, the goddamn Germans," Marc muttered.

Bella dropped her teacup. She did not look down as it shattered into delicate shards on the hardwood floor. "Another war," she said, tears streaming down her cheeks.

"No. The same war," Michel corrected her, and they nodded in unison.

This was the war they had awaited, the war they had hoped for and dreaded. They had never factored Japan into their equation, but that did not matter. The United States, the land of their refuge, was at war with a German ally and so would soon be at war with the Nazis. Marc switched the radio off, and they sat in the awkward silence of visitors in a house of mourning.

Michel sprang to his feet and rushed to the hall closet for his winter coat.

"I must get to the studio," he said to Ida, who followed him. "It seems that I was wrong. News of importance does occur on a Sunday." His voice was laced with bitterness.

"But you will come home as soon as you can?" she asked, and he recognized that her question was a plea.

"I will."

He placed his hand on her head, and she felt the pressure of his comforting touch even as the door closed behind him. She returned to the living room and stood beside her parents at the window, startled to see that cars continued to move at an unhurried pace down Riverside Drive although passersby looked up at the sky and quickened their steps.

Chapter Twenty-Five

Winter drifted into spring, spring into summer, each season dominated by news of the European theater, news of the Pacific theater. The war consumed Bella and Marc. It shadowed their days, filled their nights with fear. Ida bought black shades for the windows, mandated for use in air-raid drills, but they never raised them. The darkness of the apartment reflected the darkness of their mood.

The unremitting heat of the Manhattan summer and the discouraging war news unnerved them. They listened in heavyhearted silence to Hans von Kaltenborn's rich gravelly voice reporting that there were unconfirmed rumors of mass murders of Jews in eastern Europe. The anonymous victims of those unconfirmed rumors might well be their relatives and friends, Marc's sisters and their children, Bella's brothers and their families. Names crowded Bella's mind and memory. Was Mendel in Siberia? Where was Abrashka? Had Yaakov found a hiding place in Paris? The questions sapped her energy. Marc's lips moved silently, mouthing the names of his sisters, his friends.

Ida avoided the apartment. She left early each morning, rushing from her art classes to Pierre Matisse's gallery and then to the hospital where she volunteered. She went to parties given by new friends, young men and women she met in her classes or at the hospital. She returned home with her color high, the ghost of a smile lingering on her lips. Parties and friendship were new to her. Laughter in these desperate days was a gift.

She remained her parents' mainstay, shopping for them, opening their mail, paying their bills, and answering her father's correspondence. She arranged for their ration books from the newly organized

Office of Price Administration, counting out the tiny color-coded stamps for the requisite amounts of sugar, coffee, meat.

She arrived home one summer evening, and sorting through the mail, she set aside an envelope emblazoned with Mexican stamps.

"Do we know anyone in Mexico?" she asked her father.

He shrugged.

"There are people everywhere who Marc Chagall does not know who think that they know Marc Chagall," he replied enigmatically. "So perhaps there are such people in Mexico. It must be from someone who wants something from me. Something for nothing, I suppose. 'Cher Monsieur Chagall, can you send us perhaps a small print for our charity's auction.' 'Can you send us a small donation for our kosher soup kitchen?'" His voice rose to a mimicking falsetto, but he hovered close as she read the letter.

It did not surprise Ida that neither Bella nor Marc had dared to open the envelope. Any unfamiliar correspondence filled them with fear. Unexpected phone calls frightened them. They allowed the phone to ring until Ida answered it; they left letters unopened until she read them. She was their buffer against a frightening world. The compliant daughter, the once vulnerable child whom they had so obsessively protected, was now their protector.

"What is it? What does the Mexican want?" Marc asked impatiently.

He knew that with Ida's aptitude for languages she had been able to translate the Spanish without difficulty.

"It's an invitation, *Papochka*. A wonderful invitation. The government of Mexico invites you to Mexico City to work on the stage sets of *Aleko*."

"Give it to me," Marc commanded.

He seized the letter from her and stared at it impatiently as though the Spanish words might morph into Russian, Yiddish, or French. He discerned names and dates and understood their impact. *Léonide Massine*. Of course, Léonide, his old friend, the Russian choreographer he had met in Paris and then again, by happy coincidence, in New York. Their reunion had been productive. Throughout the spring, they had worked together, Marc designing sets for the Russian-inspired ballet as Léonide perfected his choreography. *Aleko.* The name of that ballet jumped out at him, repeated in each paragraph. "Palacio de Bellas Artes," he read, silently mouthing the unfamiliar Spanish words. He remembered that Massine had told him that would be the venue for the ballet's premiere.

His blue eyes glinted, and his narrow face glowed with pleasure. He grasped Bella's wrists and waltzed about the room with her.

"To Mexico, Bella *meine*," he sang. "To Mexico, *un pays magique*, a magical land."

She laughed and tossed her head back, her graceful steps matching his. The depression of so many months was abandoned. They sang softly, a Russian song that Ida did not recognize. It was, perhaps, a song that they had sung as young lovers walking across the bridge that spanned the Western Dvina River.

Ida watched them with a twinge of envy and wondered when she and Michel had last shared such a moment. She watched her parents glide across the room, her father humming, her mother's head resting on his shoulder. When their impromptu dance ended, she clapped as they sank down on the sofa, their smiling faces glistening with perspiration. Bella threaded her fingers through Marc's gray curls and Marc wiped the beads of sweat from her face.

He picked up the letter.

"Massine will be overjoyed," he said. "He often said that he wanted me beside him when the ballet went into rehearsal."

"Of course," Bella agreed. "He needs you. What would Léonide's choreography be without your set designs? Don't you agree, Idotchka?"

"Of course," Ida said although she did not agree.

Ida knew that her father's set designs were dependent on Massine's translation of Pushkin's poem and Tchaikovsky's music into the inspired fluidity of dance. But of course, Marc, like a greedy child, with Bella's encouragement, would claim the dominant role. She shrugged. Their reaction was irrelevant. What was important was that they had been invited to Mexico City, that they would bask in its brilliant sunlight, accept the adulation of its cultural elite, and immerse themselves in the theater work they had always loved. They would create sets and costumes, replicating their long-ago experience at the Jewish Theater in Moscow. She wanted them to sing again, to regain, however briefly, the world that had been lost to them, to emerge from the carapace of depression that held them prisoner in New York. And, she acknowledged, she herself wanted to be liberated, however briefly, from the burden of their melancholy, their constant neediness.

"But, Ida, how will you manage all alone? Michel is so often away," Bella said worriedly.

It was true that Michel was rarely home. Since the United States' entry into the war, Radio Free Europe had intensified its operations, and several times a day, listeners in occupied France tuned their clandestine radios to the station outlawed by the Gestapo and heard his reassuring introduction: *"C'est Michele Gordey, de La Voix d'Amerique."* He traveled from state to state, conducting interviews, gathering information, offering insights. Even when he was in New York, he often slept on a camp bed in his office. When night fell in America, the light of dawn crept across embattled Europe. The war progressed at a frenetic pace, crisis following crisis, news stories exploding day and night. Michel was constantly on call, his work his priority. He and Ida, by mutual if unspoken consent, were no longer at the center of each other's lives. When they shared a meal, it was more often by chance rather than design.

"I will manage," she assured them. "Perhaps Michel will be able to spend more time at home."

She did not tell them that his absence did not trouble her, that, in fact, she relished the idea of waking in an empty apartment, relieved of all responsibility, accountable neither to her parents nor to her husband. How wonderful it would be to be alone!

Within a week, Marc and Bella left for Mexico. They sent Ida exuberant letters. The journey, exhausting as it was, had energized them. They were working with Alicia Markova, the brilliant English ballerina, who loved the wonderfully imaginative scarlet costume Bella had sewn for her. They had had dinner with the Mexican artists Diego Rivera and Frida Kahlo. Bella had found some marvelous woven fabrics of subtle jade and brilliant blue, perfect colors to offset Ida's fiery hair and radiant complexion.

Ida shared their letters with Elsa as they sat in the courtyard of Beth Israel Hospital where Elsa was on staff and Ida volunteered.

"Do you miss your parents?" Elsa asked. She herself choked on her loneliness. André had enlisted and was working in a field hospital "somewhere in Europe." She understood that he could not tell her where. Silence on the home front was a weapon. Signs everywhere reminded them that "loose lips sink ships."

"It is the least I can do for this country that has given us so much," André had said when he told her of his commission, and she had not objected. Still, she missed him desperately. She took refuge in her work at the hospital, in her small son Daniel, who went to sleep each night with his father's picture beneath his pillow and the small wooden car that Michel had fashioned for him clutched in his hand.

"No," Ida said honestly. "I miss them not at all. This is the first time in my life that I have ever had the luxury of living my own life, of doing as I pleased. If I want to have a party, I have a party. If I want to stay out all night, I do just that. No excuses. No explanations. I eat when I please, I sleep when I please."

"And do you sleep with whom you please?" Elsa's tone was mischievous.

"If it should come to that, why not?" Ida replied defiantly. "I was eighteen when I married Michel. I was a child bride, a child wife. But I am no longer a child. I am a woman and I want to live a woman's life. I want to dance. I want to laugh. Why should I not have the experience of other men, other lovers? I am not like you, Elsa. There is no André in my life. No Daniel. We are at a new place in our marriage, Michel and I. Together yet separated. Connected yet independent. Friends. Best friends. I haven't taken a lover yet, but I'm not saying that it is not a possibility. Do I shock you when I say that I am not sure that Michel himself would object? You need not answer. I shock myself." She fingered the button on the blue jacket of her uniform, her eyes bright with tears.

"You must be careful, Ida," Elsa said. She understood that Ida's words reverberated with loneliness.

"You gave me that warning once before," Ida reminded her and the two young women smiled. Memories of their European past briefly banished the sadness of their uncertain present.

Ida's hair fell across her shoulders in a cascade of radiance. Elsa smiled with the wistful benevolence that plain women often accord their more beautiful friends. But she did not envy Ida. She, after all, had her child, her career, a husband who was both lover and colleague. André would return to her. He had to return to her. She clung fast to that certainty. She pitied Ida for her restless yearning, her poignant need to dance, to laugh, to retrieve a life and love that had been denied her.

—

The parties, the desperate attempts at gaiety, continued. Ida danced herself into exhaustion. And she laughed; her forced merriment was nervous and high-pitched. She bought the short, brightly patterned skirts and sleeveless, pastel-colored blouses that were newly fashionable, a thought to be patriotic because fabric was needed for uniforms. Her long, graceful legs were bare because nylon and silk were needed for parachutes. She hosted parties, floating through the apartment barefoot, setting out plates of chips and dishes of sour cream and onion dips. In Bella's absence, no cakes were baked in the Riverside Drive kitchen. Sugar and eggs were rationed and so was time. Everyone on the home front was either working or volunteering for the war effort. Ida's new female friends took jobs in the post office, ran elevators, drove taxi cabs. The frivolity of their evenings and weekends was hard earned. They were determined to seize whatever fun they could. The soldiers and sailors with whom they danced in smoke-filled apartments and at USO clubs held them close and gave them their APO addresses. They dutifully wrote letters on flimsy V-mails as one troop after another was shipped overseas.

Ida's parties were crowded. Friends and the friends of friends filled the room. Music blared from the phonograph. Bella's oriental rugs were rolled back, the heavy furniture pushed aside as the young people danced Lindies and fox-trots on the hardwood floor. Ida learned to jitterbug to "Chattanooga Choo Choo." She collapsed onto the brocaded sofa and joined in the wistful singing of "The White Cliffs of Dover" and the lustier "Praise the Lord and Pass the Ammunition." GIs in uniform arrived carrying raffia-wrapped bottles of Chianti that they poured into paper cups. Officers brought their PX purchases of scotch and vodka. They drank, but they did not get drunk.

One night, a young marine trailed Ida into the kitchen and pressed up against her, his lips seeking hers.

"Please," he said. "Please, Ida. I'm shipping out next week."

She heard the desperation in his voice, allowed him to kiss her, all the while wondering how it was that he knew her name when she had no idea who he was.

She smelled fear on his breath. How old was he? Twenty-one, perhaps twenty-two? She remembered the very young French soldier whose dying hemorrhage had saved Michel's life.

"You'll be fine," she assured him and allowed his hands to travel nervously across her body.

His kiss, his touch, had not been unpleasant. They had merely been meaningless. She neither savored nor regretted them.

She occasionally went to dinner or a film with one young officer or another, but they soon bored her. They were so young, these Americans, untouched by life, unscarred by history. They were smooth-cheeked, innocent-eyed boys who wore the uniforms of men, players in a fantasy masquerade that would all too soon become a tragic reality. She pitied them and allowed them to touch her breasts, press their lips to her neck.

"But I have nothing to say to them," she complained to Elsa. "And I am not interested in what they have to say to me."

Elsa smiled. She wondered when Ida would find a lover, a man who would match her experience and passion.

Michel appeared at the apartment occasionally when a party was in progress. Ida danced with him, relaxed in his arms, surprised at his easy grace. They had been lovers who had never danced, a married couple who had seldom laughed. They sat in the kitchen together and traded fragments of their days with the ease of their long intimacy. She showed him her parents' letters from Mexico, which he read with slight interest.

"Soon they will begin to complain about Mexico," he said knowingly.

She agreed. She and Michel often spoke of Marc and Bella as though they themselves were the parents, amused by their childish vagaries, Marc's restlessness, Bella's yearnings.

Michel had not yet had any news of his own mother and father, although he inserted hints to them in his broadcasts. Daringly he had invented an interview with a son whose mother fashioned paper flowers that she sold on the streets of Nice. "If that mother hears this broadcast, she might try to send a message to her son through yours truly, Michel Gordey," he had said, but no message had been received.

"They may not have heard the broadcast. They may not know how to communicate with you. No news is good news," Ida assured him.

He shook his head wearily. Worry lines creased his avian face. She worried that he was not eating well. He had lost weight; his clothing hung loosely on his angular frame. He, in turn, worried that she was not getting enough rest.

"Not that you don't look beautiful, Ida," he assured her. Always and forever, he knew, she would look beautiful to him.

He arrived one evening and stood in the doorway and watched as she danced with a sailor whose friend stood beside him. Ida's bright hair was braided into pigtails. She wore tan slacks and the loose khaki shirt a GI friend had given her. She laughed as she danced, laughed as her partner led her through intricate steps and swept her into a dip, color rushing to her face.

"She's a great girl, that Ida," the young naval officer said. "How do you know her?"

"She's my wife," Michel replied shortly, and he wondered if she still wore her wedding ring.

He fell asleep in her bed that night, beneath the painting of *The Bridal Chair*, and awakened at dawn to find her beside him, her eyes closed, her voice a whisper.

"Please, please. Don't let them catch me. Please, please, put out the fire."

The whispered words floated through the half darkness. He recognized them. Her recurring dream had been part of the life they had shared. Her sleep-bound body trembled and he held her close until she lay still and slept quietly in his arms.

He took her hand in his, saddened but unsurprised to see that she no longer wore the ring he had placed on her finger beneath their wedding canopy in an autumnal garden where the fragrance of late-blooming roses had filled the air.

Chapter Twenty-Six

*M*arc and Bella returned from Mexico elated by the reception his work had received. Their spirits soared when *Aleko* was next performed at the Metropolitan Opera House and Marc's sets were acclaimed by the elite art critics of New York. But once the ballet closed and their stay in the limelight ended, they again imprisoned themselves in a dark and suffocating pessimism.

Bella burst into tears suddenly and inexplicably. Marc shut himself in his studio, but his canvases and sketchbooks no longer interested him. He felt that the scope of his paintings and drawings was limited after working on the splendid amplitude of the stage sets.

"How can I work on such a small scale?" he asked Ida, kicking aside a canvas.

He longed to create murals, to decorate ceilings and places of worship. His crucifixion paintings no longer satisfied him. He needed space to re-create his tortured martyrs, space to re-create biblical scenes. He dreamed of Michelangelo's Sistine Chapel. He yearned to paint his own vanished village on the ceiling of the long-destroyed great temple of his people, envisioned only in his dreams.

"The war will end and you will explore new horizons," Ida assured him. *As will I,* she thought and wondered what those horizons might be.

Spring arrived. Marc and Bella ventured outside and felt the soft wind upon their faces.

"It will soon be Passover," Bella said. "Should we have a seder?"

"Who would we invite?" he asked bitterly. "My dead sisters? Your dead brothers? Will their ghosts sit around our table?"

And then he held her close because his words had caused her to weep.

It was the Opatoshus who hosted the Passover seder, but there was little joy at their festively set table. The assembled guests were haunted by the grim news of the war. The Japanese had captured Bataan, and Germany was sending huge units of planes and tanks to the Russian front, testing the strength of the Red Army. The émigré Jews dutifully turned the pages of their Haggadoth as Joseph Opatoshu read the story of the cruelties endured in Egypt and the miracle of liberation.

"Isn't Michel coming?" Bella whispered to Ida as she turned a page.

"Of course he's coming," Ida replied. "He called and said he'd be late. Some important news was breaking and he had to deliver a broadcast."

"Important news is always breaking," Marc said bitterly. "Bad news and worse news. Your Michel cannot come to the seder because he must tell the people of France that their world is on fire, that German bombs are falling on London, that Jews are being killed in gas chambers. The Voice of America might do better to remain silent."

"Please, Marc." Bella placed a restraining hand on his arm. "You are ruining the seder for everyone."

"God is ruining the seder," Marc retorted as Ida stood and helped Adele Opatoshu clear the soup plates.

"Michel is doing his job, *Papochka*," she said calmly. "He will be here soon, I'm sure."

Minutes later, Michel flung the door open and burst into the room. His face was pale, his dark hair unkempt, his eyes flashing. Although the spring night was cool, his sweat-stained shirt clung to his body and his jacket was slung over his shoulder. He panted, struggling for breath.

"Michel, what's happened? What's wrong?" Ida asked, running toward him.

He stared at her and sank into a chair.

"Everything is wrong. Everything has happened. The worst, the very worst."

They listened in shock and sorrow as he told them that the Warsaw ghetto was surrounded by the Waffen-SS. German tanks were moving through the streets and troops were going from house to house. Houses and factories were on fire.

"But the Jews are fighting back," he said. "Oh yes. They are dying, but they are fighting back. That is what I've been saying again and again in every broadcast. The world must know that the Jews are fighting back." He closed his eyes. His arms fell loosely to his sides. "I'm tired, Ida. So tired. I've been reading communiqués for hours. Hours and hours. And still we don't know all that happened and all that will yet happen. Our Washington office says it may take days before the ghetto is totally destroyed."

She brought him a glass of wine and held it to his lips. He sipped slowly, as Joseph Opatoshu lifted his Haggadah and in his strong voice invited Elijah the prophet into the room. Bella, her face white, her hands trembling, ran from the room. Marc followed her into the bathroom where she stood over the toilet bowl, vomiting out her terror and her grief.

"*Gotenu,*" she murmured between spasms. "My God."

"God?" he asked and wiped her pale face with a damp white cloth. "God is busy. He's playing his fiddle on the roof of a burning house in the Warsaw ghetto. Ah, but perhaps the ghetto is no longer. Where then has God taken his fiddle? When will we know? How will we know?"

They walked slowly back into the dining room where the guests, pale and sad-eyed, were nevertheless singing the concluding song of the Haggadah. Marc added his voice to theirs. "One kid," he sang. "One only kid, that my father bought for two farthings. Poor little kid. Poor little kid."

The knowledge of events in the Warsaw ghetto paralyzed them. The ghetto was destroyed. The Jews had mounted a courageous but futile defense.

The stories filed by international news services were unsatisfying. "The Associated Press says 'victims.' Did these 'victims' have names, faces? Reuters talks about the destruction of the ghetto. Tell me, Mr. Reporter, how did that destruction take place?" Marc asked bitterly. He tossed aside the Yiddish newspapers that he read obsessively and angrily each day. "I want to know. I want to hear from witnesses, from Jewish witnesses."

"Ghosts do not speak. I do not think we will soon hear from any of the Jewish survivors," Ida said wearily.

She was wrong. On a still June evening, the quiet of the apartment was disturbed by three sharp knocks at the door. Marc and Bella looked anxiously at each other, frightened as always by any unanticipated invasion of their increasingly solitary life. Ida, her hair still damp from a swift shower and braided into a single plait, stared at her immobile parents, shook her head wearily, and opened the door. She stared dubiously at the cherubic, pink-faced man who stood at the entry, smiling with the confident awareness of a man always certain of his welcome no matter the time, no matter the place. He strode into the apartment and embraced her without hesitation.

"Idotchka, you must be my little Idotchka. So grown up, so beautiful."

He spoke in a booming Yiddish, and his smile grew broader as he planted a kiss on each of her cheeks. His eyes glinted brightly behind his rimless glasses. She felt the strength of his embrace, inhaled the tantalizingly familiar scent of his skin, and eased herself free as her parents rushed toward them.

"Itzik, Itzik Feffer. My God, I don't believe it. Itzik Feffer, here in the United States." Marc's voice trembled and the two men hugged each other, both of them openly weeping.

"Ah Bella, my Bella." Itzik Feffer turned to Bella, took her hand, and lifted it tenderly to his lips. "As beautiful as ever. The beautiful mother of a beautiful daughter."

Bella laughed. "And you haven't changed. You are still the Lothario of the steppes. Come in, come in. You must be hungry."

"Don't you remember that I was always hungry? I could finish one meal and begin another one at once. I used to eat the food your Idotchka left on her plate, and now your Idotchka does not even recognize her Uncle Itzik."

He laughed and took Ida's hands in his own. She wondered at the softness of his skin, the gentleness of his touch.

"I'm sorry, but that was so many years ago," she said apologetically. "I must have been a very little girl."

"So many years ago. So many lives ago," he amended. "So many wars ago," he added. "I was so young then. 'Uncle Itzik' you called me then although I was only twenty."

He laughed again and took a seat at the table, eating swiftly as Ida watched him with growing curiosity. All his movements were vested with urgency; she sensed that he was a man with no time to waste, a man whose energy never flagged. He spoke rapidly as he ate, anticipating the questions they had not yet asked. He told them that in the years since Marc and Bella had fled Russia, he had worked as a reporter and risen to the rank of lieutenant colonel in the Red Army. He was also vice chairman of the Jewish Anti-Fascist Committee, and in that capacity, he had been sent on an unprecedented mission to the United States. There were still Jews in the Soviet Union, and his government had asked him to help raise money in the United States for his threatened community.

"But isn't it the Soviet Union itself that threatens the Jews?" Ida asked caustically.

"Ah, little girl, why did you grow up? When you sat on my knee in Moscow with your hair in pigtails, you never asked such cynical questions." He smiled benignly at her, lifted her long braid playfully. "You must not believe such propaganda, my Ida. Mother Russia loves her Jews. And I think her Jews continue to love Mother Russia. Isn't that true, Moshe?"

Marc cringed. He disliked being called by his Yiddish name. Still he nodded his assent.

"This poor Jew, at least, loves his homeland," he said. "I splash my canvases with red, the red of revolution, the red of hope."

"The red of blood," Bella muttered.

"Surely, Papa, you remember that when you were in Vilna, the Soviet government refused to allow you to cross the border into Vitebsk," Ida said irritably.

"That was in 1935. The war has changed all that. In these terrible times, Russia is the only nation that protects Jews. Isn't that so, Itzik?"

"I am here, am I not?" he replied. "The Soviet government has sent a Jew as an emissary to plead for other Jews."

Bella brought Itzik a slice of babka, which he ate with relish.

"Your favorite, I remember. But what of your poetry, Itzik?" she asked. "Do you still write?"

"A poet never stops writing. And a Yiddish poet, in these times, has an obligation to write. Do you know what Simon Dubnow said as he lay dying in the streets of Riga? His last words were 'Jews, remember, Jews, write!' I will not forget. I have written and will yet write more." He reached into his pocket and removed a dog-eared Yiddish pamphlet. "This is how I remember. This is what I have written."

He flipped it open and read a few lines in mellifluous Yiddish. The murmured verses fluttered through the room, winged words beating against the sadness of their silence.

Itzik sighed and handed the pamphlet to Bella. She read the title aloud in Yiddish and in English.

"'*Di Shotns fun Varshever Geto.*' 'The Shadows of the Warsaw Ghetto.' May we borrow this, Itzik?" she asked.

"You may keep it," he said. "I have other copies. Too many. Who wants to buy and read the work of a Yiddish poet? And will you read it, Idotchka? Do you know some Yiddish?"

"It is still the language of my heart," she replied softly and studied his reaction. She wondered why it was so important to her that this rotund, energetic man approve of her.

"I hope that your heart will not break when you read my words. My own heart broke as I wrote them," he said and he did not smile.

He told them then how he had written it after encountering survivors of the ghetto who had somehow made their way out of Warsaw. The ghetto, they told him, became a sea of flames. "Can one drown in a sea of flames?" he asked sadly, and Ida closed her eyes and envisioned small children swimming through tides of fire as sparks rained down from heavens set ablaze.

Their mood lifted as Itzik Feffer tossed out crumbs of gossip, speaking of the love affairs and divorces of distant friends, peppering his stories with amusing dollops of malice.

"And you, Itzik, you are still married?" Marc asked.

"In my own fashion," he replied enigmatically. "I have a favor to ask of you," he said to Marc as he rose to leave. "Will you lend me your little Ida so that she may introduce me to New York? I need her to explain the different neighborhoods to me, to tell me where the subway goes and where I can find a decent knish and a bowl of kasha."

Ida blushed and spoke before her father could reply. "I am no longer 'little Ida.' You do not need to ask my father's permission, nor my husband's for that matter. I decide how I spend my days. And it will be my pleasure to be your guide through New York, Itzik Feffer."

"Of course. Of course. You are an independent woman. I like that. I respect that," he replied. "Your husband is to be congratulated. He is a very lucky man. I look forward to meeting him."

"Michel's work with the Voice of America keeps him very busy," Bella interjected hastily.

It worried her that Michel, so immersed in his work, was hardly ever at the apartment, hardly ever with Ida. No longer the shy student who had sat so uneasily at their table in Paris, Michel was now a highly respected journalist, recording the dramatic and tragic times.

Itzik Feffer nodded.

"The Voice of America is indeed very important," he murmured.

He shook hands with Marc, kissed Bella on both cheeks, and lifted Ida's braid, brushing it across his mouth.

"It is the color of firelight," he said. "I had to see if it would burn my lips."

He laughed, and they all laughed with him. His charm was magnetic, his laughter contagious.

"I will see you tomorrow then," he said.

"Yes. Tomorrow," Ida agreed.

They met each day that week in the early afternoon and wandered through the streets of the city. Ida introduced him to the Automat and smiled at his childlike delight as he plunged nickels and dimes into the slots and watched the windows slide open. He removed the soups and salads that he favored hurriedly, as though fearful that the panels would slam shut.

"In Russia," he told her, "everything is rationed. Bread, milk, potatoes."

"Here too we have rationing," she said.

"Ah, but there is rationing and then there is *rationing*," he retorted.

She taught him the recipe for "Automat wartime lemonade," adding the free slices of lemon to cold tap water. He pronounced it delicious and she smiled. Everything he tasted was delicious. Everything he saw was *wunderbar*, wondrous.

They went to Central Park where the trees wore the tender leaves of early spring, the newly blossoming forsythia glowed golden in the sunlight, and on the playground, children scrambled merrily across jungle gyms and raced toward swings and seesaws.

"A country at war, a city at peace," he murmured, and there was admiration rather than bitterness in his voice.

One afternoon they strolled through the halls of the Museum of Modern Art where she showed him two of her father's lithographs. They bought pretzels from a street vendor. Grains of salt glistened on her lips and he wiped them off, smiling benignly. In Coney Island, they rode the Ferris wheel and hugged each other with the delight peculiar to small children. Neither of them had ever before ridden on a Ferris wheel.

Ida went to hear him speak at fund-raising rallies and applauded vigorously. She noticed that the same two bored-looking young men, wearing identical cheap gray suits, their hair cut short, turned up wherever they went.

"FBI agents," he explained. "They think that I am a spy. Do I look like a spy, Idotchka?"

She thought for a moment, took off his glasses, and replaced them. "A very plump, nearsighted spy, perhaps. But spies are never plump and nearsighted. They're supposed to look like Clark Gable or maybe Humphrey Bogart," she said.

"Who is this Clark Gable? Who is this Humphrey Bogart?" He waved his hand dismissively.

"A good spy would have to know who they are," she said sternly, and they both laughed.

At a party in Harlem, handsome Paul Robeson embraced him.

"We are together in this war against racism," the tall, muscular black singer said. "Your people and my people have much in common."

"But Robeson's people aren't getting gassed," Ida murmured as they left.

"He is a good man. Naive, like all Americans, but essentially good," Itzik retorted.

In the Garden Cafeteria on East Broadway, he ordered borscht and kasha varnishkes and spoke Yiddish to the elderly waiter whose hands trembled when he brought them a platter of onion rolls for which he refused payment.

Itzik broke off pieces of the roll, which he fed to Ida.

"You are my little bird," he said. "I am feeding my little bird."

"That is what my father used to call me," she said. "In fact, you are very like my father."

He laughed.

"No. I am, in spite of everything, a happy man. Your father, in spite of his good fortune, is a melancholy soul."

"I think more discontented than melancholy," she protested. She doodled on the paper place mat, wrote her name, Itzik's name, her father's name, and encased them in a jagged square.

"But, of course," he added, "we are both passionate about you. In very different ways." All lightness left his voice. "Can I say that much to you, Ida?"

He looked hard at her, as though to memorize every contour of her face—the arch of her eyebrows, the curve of her lips, the subtle gold the spring sunlight had brushed across her skin. She did not flinch from his gaze. She matched it with her own. Their eyes locked. He took her hand and laced his fingers through hers. She trembled and leaned toward him, aware of the sudden hardness of her breasts, the tympanic beat of her heart.

They took the subway uptown and walked across Broadway to his small hotel.

"Room three forty three," he told her. "Wait five minutes and then come upstairs."

She waited then walked through the small lobby, her head held high, her step determined. She entered the small room and walked into his open arms. He undressed her swiftly, knowledgeably, a careful paternal lover who folded her blouse so that it would not crease and draped her skirt over the chair. She unbuttoned his shirt, stroked the graying hair of his chest; he slipped his trousers off and she marked the narrowness of his hips although he had the round stomach of a middle-aged man partial to food and drink. Her father had the beginnings of such a paunch, she thought absently as she stretched out across the narrow single bed.

He traced her body, each touch of his fingers tender and restrained. He kissed her gently, now on her forehead, now on her cheeks, and then, with a swift surge of daring strength, on her lips, his tongue entering her mouth even as he plunged deep into her welcoming and compliant body.

He was a swift and skillful lover, his cry of triumph exultant.

"*Meine liebe maidele*," he said in Yiddish as he lay back in exhaustion against the pillow. "My beloved little girl."

The endearment was poignantly familiar. Throughout her girlhood, in the quiet of the night, she had heard her father say those very words to her mother, his voice penetrating the thin walls that separated their rooms.

She rested her head on his chest, fingered the strands of gray hair that covered it. She had taken a lover who was as old as her father, who shared his background, and she understood, with sudden clarity, that that was why she had chosen him. The new reality they shared banished her dark and dangerous fantasies.

"Idotchka," he murmured.

"Don't call me Idotchka," she said peevishly. "I am not a child. I am a woman, a married woman."

"Yes. Of course. You are married."

"In my own fashion," she said, tossing his words back at him.

They were inseparable for the rest of that summer. They spent long afternoons in his small hotel room. He came and went from the Chagalls' apartment as though it was his own home. Bella mended the pastel shirts he favored, the pink ones that matched his cheeks, the pale green ones he selected with great care, the color close to the celadon of his eyes. Marc and Bella welcomed his presence, listened avidly to the stories he told in the languages of their childhood. He assuaged their loneliness, soothed their longing. They praised Ida for helping to make his stay in New York pleasurable. They did not speak of the obvious closeness between their daughter and their old friend.

Michel arrived one evening at the dinner hour and slid with ease into his own chair at the table. He smiled at Itzik, asked him questions about events in Russia, and invited him to be interviewed on a Voice of America broadcast.

"Perhaps you could mention that you were pleased to meet the son of your old friends, the Rapaports, here in New York," he suggested. "I know, of course, that you never met my parents, but it might be a way of letting them know that I am alive."

"I would be pleased to do that," Itzik agreed. "I am not opposed to telling the occasional white lie when it can do some good. Deception is one of my talents."

Ida dropped her fork. It clattered against her plate, but neither her husband nor her lover glanced at her, lost as they were in a heated political debate. Itzik argued that Churchill was bluffing when he warned the Axis that an intensive Allied assault would soon be launched. Michel insisted that the British prime minister rarely bluffed. The Allies were advancing; the second front was successful. Sweden reported that women and children were being evacuated from Berlin.

"We are winning the war," Michel said.

"But the Jews have already lost it," Marc countered bitterly.

Itzik and Michel shook hands cordially at the door. Itzik, as always, kissed Bella's hand and placed his hand lightly on Ida's head.

"I knew your wife when she was a beautiful little girl," he told Michel.

"And now you know her as a beautiful woman," Michel replied and pulled her close.

"He is very charming, this Itzik Feffer," Michel said when he and Ida were alone in her room, seated beneath the painting of *The Bridal Chair*.

"Yes. Everyone says so," she answered carefully.

"He is very like your father, don't you think?"

"Yes. I suppose he is," she said softly. "He is a very good poet, Itzik Feffer."

She turned away so that he could not see her face, but he heard the tenderness in her tone as she said the name.

"You must be careful, very careful." His voice was heavy with concern. He drew her close and she rested her head gratefully on his shoulder. It was Michel, she acknowledged, who understood her, who discerned her secret yearnings, her nocturnal fears. He intuited her feelings for Itzik, but he did not resent them. His silence was eloquent. They had reached a new crossroads in their odd and ill-starred marriage.

"I am careful," she assured him. "He leaves New York in October."

"Another chapter closed," he said.

She nodded.

He looked up at *The Bridal Chair* and wondered who would take possession of it when he and Ida parted. That time would come, he knew. He would be sad, she would be sad, but their hearts would not be broken. They would always and forever remain connected. *The Bridal Chair* would be Ida's. He would never want to own an artifact of a wedding at which he, the bridegroom, and Ida, the bride, had been reluctant ghosts.

Ida slept in his arms that night and she did not dream.

Itzik prepared for his return to Russia as an autumnal chill spread across the city. Bella made a farewell dinner in his honor. A bowl of autumn foliage was her centerpiece. The brilliant red and gold leaves, so brittle and vulnerable on their slender branches, matched her mood. She wore her favorite green velvet gown and frowned when Ida swept into the room in a dress of bridal white, a spray of baby's breath wrapped around her long braid.

"White is for summer," Bella said reprovingly.

"White is for when I choose to wear it," Ida replied. She did not tell her mother that Itzik loved to see her dressed in white, that he had more than once presented her with a white flower for her hair, a camellia or a lily, that inevitably lay nestled between her breasts in the peaceful aftermath of their coupling.

The dining room was crowded, the table laden with platters of pirogen, tureens of borscht, bowls of compote, the foods of all their childhoods. Michel did not attend. Ida noted that he had never arranged for the promised interview with Itzik.

The invited guests were the Yiddish- and Russian-speaking artists and writers, Marc's coterie of intimates in exile. New York was their Babylon, Paris their Jerusalem. The women wore the gem-colored velvet and satin gowns of another continent, another era. Their husbands smelled of liquor and tobacco, neither of which erased the sadness in their eyes. They offered extravagant toasts to Itzik and lifted their glasses; they proclaimed their commitment to peace and friendship, to brotherhood and solidarity, then downed the vodka in single gulps. Itzik, as always jovial and smiling, his cherubic face pink with pleasure, thanked them for their hospitality and generosity. He turned to his hosts and beamed.

"I thank you for all that you have done for me," he said. "We will see each other again when peace is restored."

He walked around the table and kissed each of them in turn. Ida sat very still as his lips brushed her cheek, as he lifted her braid playfully. She loved him and hated him for his joviality. He was anticipating his return to Russia. She was dreading his departure from her life.

Gifts were exchanged. Itzik gave them specially bound copies of his poems. Marc gave him a charcoal drawing of Ida.

"I will treasure this. I will always treasure it," Itzik said.

"Of course you will," Marc said.

Ida wondered how much her father knew, how much he had guessed. Whatever his speculation, he would not share it with her mother, that dutiful daughter of Vitebsk, forever concerned with convention and respectability.

It was Bella who walked Itzik to the door. She wept as he embraced her one last time.

"Will I ever see you again?" Bella asked plaintively. "Will I ever see Europe again?"

"Strength, Belloshka. Strength," he said and bowed his head.

The door closed behind him, and Ida and her parents stood in silence, a trio of lonely mourners whose last comforter had departed.

"Itzik never answered me," Bella said softly. "Because he knew. He knew that I will never return to Europe. Poets see the future." Unshed tears glinted in her eyes as she walked slowly into her bedroom.

Ida cleared the table, weeping as she worked. Her father touched her shoulder, but she brushed his hand away.

"Are you all right?" he asked.

"I'm fine," she said bitterly. "I am always fine, am I not?"

"You are," he agreed. "And you are strong."

She turned away and opened and closed the book that Itzik had given her. He had not inscribed it. She lifted the glass that remained at his setting and licked the clear beads of vodka that clung to its rim.

Chapter Twenty-Seven

*B*ella's sadness deepened as the seasons drifted by and the war in Europe continued unabated. She remained indoors except when Ida persuaded her to leave the apartment for short walks. She worked for hours on the memoir, writing with a febrile verve, her pen racing across page after page as though she were in a race against time. She wrote and revised, wrote and revised, working until she was exhausted, and then fell onto her bed and turned her face to the wall, willing herself to an evasive sleep. She drank tonics in pursuit of strength, but weakness overcame her. Marc, once again painting furiously, paid her little attention.

Ida returned home on a May evening to find Bella in bed, still wearing her faded nightgown, her face parchment pale, dark circles beneath her eyes, her black hair oily and uncombed. Manuscript pages littered the night table; the cup that had contained her morning coffee remained half full and the single slice of toast that Ida had placed there in the morning was cold and stiff as cardboard.

"Have you been in bed all day?" Ida asked, her voice trembling with both fear and anger.

"I was too tired to get up," Bella said. "Too tired to work. Too tired of life."

She pointed to the scattered pages, words blotted, paragraphs crossed out.

"The words do not come, and when they do, they do not say what I want them to say," she continued. "I am writing through a fog, struggling to write of that which is no longer. Vitebsk is gone. I see it only as a shadow." Her voice lilted in the cadence of a sorrowful prayer.

"But Vitebsk has been liberated. The tide of the war has changed," Ida said impatiently.

"Yes, I know. But what does that liberation mean to me, Idotchka? What is left of my father's house, of the synagogue where your father and I were married? Is the Hotel Brozi still standing, do farmers still sell their produce in Padlo, our poor little market square? Last night I dreamed that brides, still in their wedding dresses, sat shivering around a fire. Their bodices were torn, a symbol of mourning, because they were widowed only minutes after they became wives. They sat amid the embers of the synagogue, the embers of the bridal chair. Why should I have dreamt such a dream? What does such a dream mean?"

Ida knelt beside the bed, took Bella's hands in her own, and struggled to find words of comfort.

"It was only a dream. It means nothing. You are exhausted because you have been working too hard. You are doing your best, *Mamochka*, as you always do. And your best is wonderful. You are a good writer, a marvelous storyteller. I still remember the stories you told me when I was a little girl. Your book will be important. When you are rested, the writing will come easier. Give it time." She spoke with a certainty she did not feel, but Bella grew calmer.

"But do I have time?" Bella asked. "I think that the embers of my dream are the words I need to kindle the burning lights of my story. But I cannot reach them. I am too weak, too tired." She leaned back against the pillows, her face as white as the counterpane.

"Soon you will be strong enough," Ida replied, and very gently, she helped Bella out of bed.

She eased her into the shower, startled by the pallor of the flesh that hung so loosely on her skeletal frame. She sponged her milky skin, shampooed her dark hair, and helped her into the colorful robe Marc had bought in Jerusalem, a garment he had said was fashioned for a Semitic queen. Ida had recognized the narcissistic implication of his words. If Bella was a queen, then he himself was a king, and Ida was, of course, a princess.

"Tomorrow, *Mamochka*. Everything will be all right tomorrow," Ida promised.

Softly, she repeated the lying mantra. She knew, as Bella knew, that nothing would be all right, not ever again. Fighting her own tears, she heated a pot of soup, ladled it into a bowl, made sure that Bella ate it, and then sought her father out in his studio.

She saw that he had been working for hours. The room was harshly lit, and streaks of varicolored paint ribbed his oversized shirt. Bright droplets had rained down from brushes impatiently shaken, speckled his cheeks, and rimmed the edges of his thick gray curls. Oblivious to her entrance, he stood motionless before his easel, absorbed in his work. She waited until he lifted his brush and dipped it into the puddle of aniline black on his palette then leaned closer and stared at the work in progress. He had painted Bella, her face deathly pale, her eyes wide with fear, her body mysteriously attached to a sleigh. Ida watched as he deftly wafted his brush and darkened the hair to the exact jet shade of Bella's layered bob. Suffused with anger, she lurched forward and planted herself in front of the easel.

"You should be taking care of *Mamochka*, not painting her," she shouted harshly.

He turned and looked at his daughter, his gaze desperate rather than angry.

"I try," he said sadly, placing his brush carefully in a jar of turpentine. "Do you really think me so heartless, so uncaring, Idotchka? I go to her and she closes her eyes. She turns away from me. She says she is sick. She says she is weak. I have no medicines to give her. It is this war that sickens her. What can I do for her, Ida? Can I end the war? Tell me what it is I must do and I will do it."

She heard the naked pain in his voice and spoke more softly.

"She needs to go out, to leave this apartment."

He sighed. "She does not want to go out. She hates the city, this New York with its noise, its crowded streets. You know that yourself. Everyone hurrying on their way to nowhere. The cars with their headlights painted black, the newsboys shouting the headlines of this battle, that battle. She cannot bear to see the gold star banners in the windows of the apartments. Every star means death and she imagines weeping mothers, keening wives. She told me that she can hear the screams from the death camps. And I believed her. Sometimes I hear them too. Sometimes I think that I myself am screaming. She says that the very air she breathes in this New York chokes her. Can I rebuild New York so that my Bella can walk down quiet streets?"

He sat down, his shoulders hunched in defeat, and lifted his paint-stained shirt to his face. His voice broke. He, the great Marc Chagall, wept.

Ida glanced around the studio, focusing on the watercolors balanced against the walls, the series of landscapes in gouache. Scenes from Cranberry Lake in the Adirondacks, the sylvan enclave where her parents had vacationed the previous summer. She had spent a few days with them there. Bella had been happy there. They had strolled together beneath the birch trees beside the shores of the sparkling lake that reminded both her parents of the Western Dvina River in Vitebsk. The answer to her father's question came to her. He had to take her mother back to the quiet of the forest, the beauty of the gentle lake. Peace and beauty were what her mother craved.

"This is what you must do," she said with quiet certainty. "You must take her back to Cranberry Lake. She herself said that the countryside in the north reminded her of Russia, of her family's dacha. She will feel the cool mountain breezes, walk in the shade of the trees, the quiet of the forest. She is sure to feel better there."

"All right. We will go to Cranberry Lake," he agreed, but there was no hope in his voice.

He turned back to his painting.

Bella was resistant. She complained that the long car ride was tiresome, claustrophobic. She had felt ill during their journey the previous year.

"It was as though I were in a coffin," she said. "As though I was being driven to my own burial. I am not yet dead. Soon but not yet."

"Don't be foolish," Ida retorted. "A car is a car, not a coffin. Don't indulge yourself with such foolish ideas. I have found a wonderful hotel. Everything will be done for you. Your meals, all the housekeeping. Fresh linens each day, and you know how you love the scent of sheets that have been dried in the summer air."

Bella nodded.

"The sheets in my mother's house always smelled of sunlight," she said dreamily.

Ida sensed triumph and spoke more quickly.

"Think of the cool winds, think of the wonderful woodland. Think of the lake, your Western Dvina River here in America."

"But what of my work?"

"You can take your work with you. You can take your pens, your ink, all your manuscripts. They sell writing paper in the Adirondacks," Ida assured her, coaxing forth a smile and, at last, reluctant acquiescence. They left the city, Bella weeping, Marc's face frozen into a stoic mask of acceptance.

Ida remained in New York. She had her classes, her volunteer work, invitations to dinners and to parties. She was once again in pursuit of gaiety.

She had felt oddly emancipated since Itzik Feffer's departure. She would never regret loving him. He had gifted her with a latent vibrancy, awakened her to the excitement of sensuality. Their togetherness had been a catharsis, a release from forbidden yearnings. Her girlhood had ended with Michel. Her womanhood had begun with Itzik.

Newly aroused, newly confident, she lived at a frenetic pace. She went to parties and basked in the admiration of young officers, danced until dawn with men she would never see again. She slept late each morning, her curtains drawn against the new brightness of June sunlight.

She was deep in such a late morning slumber when the ringing of the phone jarred her into wakefulness. It was Michel, his voice electric with excitement.

"It's happened. It happened this morning. D-Day, Ida! Allied troops have landed on Normandy. Europe is going to be liberated. We are going to win this damn war!"

"Oh, Michel. Is it true? Tell me it's true." Trembling, she clutched the phone.

"It's true. I heard Eisenhower's broadcast. Thousands and thousands of ships, planes, American, English, Canadian, all on the attack. De Gaulle himself is in London. They say that within months, perhaps within weeks, all of France will be free. *Vive la France!*"

His voice broke and she knew that he was weeping. All of France included Nice, where his parents might still be alive.

"*Vive la France*," she repeated as her own tears fell.

"I will call again when I can," he assured her. "It will be difficult because I will be broadcasting nonstop today. Pierre is flying to London to meet with Free French leaders. I may go with him. Everything is uncertain. *Au revoir*, Ida."

"*À bientôt*, Michel. Be careful, stay safe," she rejoined, but the phone was already silent.

She called Marc and Bella, who had heard the news on the hotel radio.

"How long will it take until Paris is liberated, until it is safe for us to return home?" Marc asked excitedly. "As soon as that happens, we will go back to France, your mother and I."

"Home. Home to Paris," Bella added in a quivering voice. "Think of it, Ida. We will see our Paris again."

"The invasion has just been launched. It will be some time before Paris is liberated," Ida warned. "But we are on our way to victory. Our France, our Paris, will soon be free."

"*Vive la France*," they said in unison.

Ida called Elsa, who was joyously effusive. She knew only that André was somewhere in Europe. The invasion meant that the war would be over sooner rather than later and he would be demobilized.

"Your parents must be ecstatic," Elsa said.

"They are strangers to ecstasy, as you know. Pessimism is what they know best. But yes, they are happy. As happy as they know how to be," Ida agreed.

She went to the window, looked down, and saw that the boats sailing down the Hudson had hoisted American flags to their masts. Men and women, meeting along Riverside Drive, embraced each other. A young girl hurried up to a GI, offered him a full-petaled rose, and planted a kiss on his astonished face.

Tears filled her eyes. She wept for all the young soldiers who would never feel a young girl's lips against their cheeks, for all the gold star mothers whose mourning would never end. She wept for the Jews of Europe, for the aunts and uncles and cousins she had never known. And then she dried her eyes, dressed quickly, and hurried to the hospital. The war was not yet over. There was work to be done.

Chapter Twenty-Eight

*A*t Cranberry Lake, Bella and Marc listened to the hourly newscasts obsessively. As the Allied victories continued, the anxiety that had haunted them for so long abated. Marc returned to his sketching and painting, Bella to her writing. In the late afternoon, they abandoned themselves gratefully to the beauty of the landscape and took quiet walks along the shores of the shimmering lake. They walked slowly, in the gait peculiar to invalids recuperating after a long illness. They would be completely healed only when Paris was liberated and the Allies' victory in Europe was a reality.

That reality burst joyously upon them on a balmy August day. They turned the radio on and heard exultant broadcasters announce that Allied troops had entered Paris. The strains of "La Marseillaise" emanated from every station, followed by breathless updates. French and American troops had smashed through to the heart of the city, receiving a tumultuous welcome. The German commander had surrendered. De Gaulle was en route to France.

Michel called to give them the latest news. Although he and Ida were separated, his connection to the Chagalls, in all its complexity, remained intact.

"Troyes is free. The Fighting French patriots are on the Île de la Cité. I am waiting for news from the Riviera, from Nice." They heard the tension in his voice.

"I pray for your parents," Bella said, and it occurred to Michel that this was the first time since his arrival in America that either Marc or Bella had mentioned his mother and father.

"As do I," he said softly. This was no time for recriminations.

Glued to the radio, they listened to the news in Yiddish, in

French, and in English. Ida called, breathless with excitement. She was hurrying to a party at the French consulate.

"Isn't the news wonderful? Are you happy, *Maman*? Is it beautiful in the mountains on this beautiful day?" she asked.

"It is very beautiful. Your father and I are going for a walk. We want to tell the trees and the mountains the good news," Bella assured her.

Ida smiled, relieved to hear the lilt in her mother's voice, the whimsy of her words.

Marc and Bella walked through the forest; lifting their faces to the warmth and brilliance of the late autumn sun. Bella paused beneath the tallest of the birch trees and Marc held her close.

"You are so beautiful, more beautiful than the day I met you," he said and he touched her face lightly, startled to find that her cheeks were wet with tears. "Ah, you are weeping with happiness," he said and she did not contradict him.

"You know that your beauty is engraved on my heart," he continued. "Before we left the city, I finally finished the painting of you that I began so many years ago. I called it *À Ma Femme – To My Wife*.'"

"I know." Bella smiled. "I stole into your studio the night before we left and I saw it. The colors stopped my heart. Even the dull brown you used to paint the houses of our poor upside-down Vitebsk that you hid in a corner of the canvas. And the red divan. I tried to remember if I had ever posed for you on a red divan or if you had only imagined it."

"But you know, Bella mine, my imagination is my reality," he protested. "You realize, don't you, that you will live forever in my heart and in my paintings?"

"Do you think I want to live forever?" she asked.

She lifted her hand to a low-hanging branch and plucked a leaf, which she twirled through her fingers. Its green matched that of her loose batiste blouse, a gift from Ida who knew how Bella loved the lightest of fabrics against her skin.

"It's strange," she said sadly, "that we Jews call our burial ground *Bet Chaim*, the House of Life. What do you think that means, Marc?"

"I don't know," he replied harshly. Her sudden melancholy on this joyous day frightened him. He took the leaf from her and threaded it through her hair. Green became her. She had been wearing a green cape on the day they first met. He closed his eyes and saw her as she had appeared to him all those years ago, her delicate face flushed to a rosiness that matched that of the wildflowers she carried. Her girlish laughter had been musical, her step light as she skittered across the bridge and mischievously urged him to chase her.

But now his Bella, the beautiful woman who now walked beside him through the Adirondack woodland, was pale, slow of step, her gaze distant. Why, when Paris was free, was she descending yet again into a frightening melancholy? He feared for her; he feared for himself.

"It is getting cool," he said, although it was a warm wind that brushed their faces. "Let's go back to our room."

"Yes. Of course. I want to do some work before dinner," she agreed.

Slowly they made their way back. They walked with their heads down, avoiding the radiance of the declining sun as though they feared what its brilliant light might reveal. Bella paused and looked up at the gold-streaked sky across which violet-tinged clouds scudded.

"Such colors," she murmured. "Such beauty."

She took the leaf from her hair and tossed it away. They watched as it was wafted aloft by a vagrant wind and then continued on their way.

They decided, that night, that they would spend another week at Cranberry Lake, organizing their possessions. They would return to New York and stay there only for as long as it might take them to arrange for their return to Paris. Marc looked around their hotel room, cluttered with their clothing, their books, his painting paraphernalia and sketchbooks. Bella's pale stockings hung over the back of a chair and her dressing table was littered with containers of powder, pads of rouge, lipsticks, and jars of her many face creams, some still sealed, others uncovered. He counted two combs, three hairbrushes. He reflected, with wry amusement, that Bella's moods might vary but her vanity never waned.

He removed a suitcase from the closet and began to sort through his own drawers.

She remained seated at her desk and made no move to help him.

"What are you doing?" he asked irritably.

"I am organizing my manuscript," she replied, shifting the piles of pages. "Here are drafts. Here are copies. I have put my final rewrite in this folder. Remember that."

"You are wasting time," he replied. "Leave it for when we return home. You should be working with me, helping me. Why this sudden concern with your papers?" he asked.

"I want you and Ida to know where everything is," she answered calmly. "I am marking each folder. In case."

"Foolishness," he said angrily, but he did not tell her that her ominous words seared his heart, that his anger was fueled by his fear. *In case of what?* It was a question he would not ask. He told himself that in the morning, her mood would improve and she would help him.

But the next morning, she felt too weak to leave her bed. She complained that her throat hurt, that her head ached. He brought her a cup of hot tea and assured her that she would soon feel better. The landlady offered her own tonic of honey and brandy, which Bella swallowed with difficulty.

She remained weak and listless throughout the day. She was no better by nightfall and moaned in her sleep. She awakened with a frightening suddenness, disturbed by dreams she could not remember. Marc bathed her burning forehead with cold cloths. He removed her sweat-soaked nightgown, dressed her in her sheer white robe, and spooned more of the tonic into her mouth. But her fever did not subside. Her eyes were glazed and she babbled incoherently.

"I see the smoke. The smoke from the trains. The smoke from chimneys. *Mamele, Tatele*, where are you? The future is written in the smoke. Marc, we must save our little Idotchka. Run, Marc, run, Idotchka, run!"

He knew that she was delirious, but he decided against calling Ida. She would be better soon, very soon. He remained at her bedside as she slept briefly and then sat upright. She raised and lowered her arms so that her wide white sleeves fluttered like wings and shouted, "We must leave this place. They hate us here because we are Jews. We must go back to Vitebsk. When does the boat leave for Vitebsk?"

Frightened, he summoned a taxi that sped to Tupper Lake where there was a Catholic hospital. Marc helped Bella to the admitting desk, and she looked up at the wooden crucifix that hung above it. A group of nuns huddled in a corner, fingering their rosary beads as they reviewed charts. Bella stared at their black garb, their snow-white wimples, the heavy gold crosses that dangled from their necks. Her eyes grew wild and she clung to Marc.

"They are crows, vultures, eaters of carrion. They will kill me because I am Jewish," she moaned.

"No. No. They are nursing sisters. They will help you," he said and took the form that one of them handed him. "See, they want only to know your name, your age, your religion."

"Don't tell them, don't tell them," she begged. "They must not know that I'm Jewish. I cannot stay here. I will not stay here. Take me back to the hotel. I must finish my book."

She staggered to the door and he followed her. Reluctantly, he ordered the driver to return to Cranberry Lake.

He called Ida.

"She is sick, our Bella, very sick. Her fever is high, her words confused. I took her to Mercy General Hospital at Tupper Lake," he said in a quivering voice, "but she would not stay. The nuns, the crucifixes on the walls, everything frightened her. What should I do, Idotchka?"

"Take her back to the hospital at once," Ida said decisively. "She must be treated. I am leaving New York. I will meet you there. Everything will be all right, *Papochka*."

She did not believe the words even as she spoke them. Hurriedly, she seized her coat, remembered to put all the cash in the apartment into her purse, and jumped into a cab, where she urged the driver to speed to Grand Central Station.

"Don't worry about a ticket. I will pay it if we are stopped."

They were not stopped. She thrust a handful of bills at him, not pausing to count them, glanced at her watch, and sped through the terminal. There was just enough time to catch a train for the Adirondacks. She tried to remember if the journey took ten hours or twelve, and she prayed that she would not be too late.

But she was. Exhausted, her heart pounding, wet to the bone from a torrential rain, she burst into the hospital. Marc stood in the entryway, peering out into the darkness, his pale face unshaven, his blue eyes dulled by misery. He fell into her arms.

"She is gone," he sobbed. "My Bella, your *mamochka*, she is gone." He drifted into Yiddish. "*Meine kleine Belloshka, nisht mit uns.* My little Bella, she is gone."

Ida rocked him gently back and forth, his head pressed to her breast, her own grief delayed so that she could offer him the fullness of her solace.

It was a nun who told her, in the gentlest of voices, that it was a streptococcus infection that had killed her mother.

"We could have saved her if we had penicillin, but all the available penicillin is sent to military hospitals. I am so sorry. Would you like to see her?"

Ida nodded. She followed the nursing sister to the small, white-washed room where Bella lay on a narrow bed. Her delicate face was blanched of all color and yet her expression was strangely serene. Ida wondered who had so carefully brushed her mother's dark hair into a lustrous, jet-colored cap. She placed her hand on Bella's and felt the rigidity that was slowly seeping into the long, slender fingers. She removed her mother's plain gold wedding band and kissed the rosebud of a mouth, the cheek so pallid, so cold and clammy.

She looked up and saw the mark of a crucifix on the wall above the bed although the space itself was empty.

"The crucifix upset your mother so I removed it," the nun explained gently.

"That was very kind of you. I want to thank you for all you did for her," Ida said.

She fingered the death certificate that the nun handed her.

"If it was not for the war, we would have had the penicillin that could have saved her life," the nursing sister repeated and crossed herself.

"Of course," Ida said. "The war."

The war that had pursued Bella from Paris to Gordes, from Marseilles to Portugal, and then across the Atlantic Ocean, had triumphed at last in the peaceful mountains of upstate New York.

Bella's funeral in New York was held on a bright September day when the seasons of summer and autumn commingled and a gentle wind whistled through sunlit warmth. It was, Ida thought sadly, the kind of day her mother would have loved. Her heart was heavy with the knowledge that circumstances and history had made it impossible to fulfill their promise to Bella that she would be buried in France. The émigré community who came to the chapel watched a weeping Marc, supported by Ida and Michel, take his seat. His heartrending sobs punctuated the service, occasionally rising to a wail of despair.

"My Bella, my beautiful Bella has left me, has left this world," he moaned.

Ida held him close, her arm about his shoulders, his head resting against her, as though he were a small boy in danger of falling. Like a solicitous mother, she wiped his tears with her own handkerchief. She and Michel stood beside him at the conclusion of the service as friends offered their condolences. She accepted kisses and embraces, nodded at their comforting words, while Marc stood immobile and silent, paralyzed by his grief.

Sheets draped the mirrors of the family apartment during the shiva, the seven days of mourning, and Marc also insisted that Ida turn all his paintings to the wall.

"We are only required to cover the mirrors," she protested wearily.

"But my paintings are mirrors, reflections of the life we lived, my Bella and I."

At the end of the week of mourning, the mirrors were uncovered, but the paintings were not turned back. He was not yet ready to surrender his grief. Ida's own heart was heavy, laden with tears unshed. She could not weep. Her father had a monopoly on sorrow.

For weeks, he refused to answer the phone. It was Ida who acknowledged the mountain of condolence notes written in Russian and Yiddish, French and German, English and Hebrew. He ate very little and wandered through the apartment, his lips moving soundlessly. He was a prayerful mourner in the solitary synagogue of his grief.

She feared that he would fall, that he would go mad, that he would drive her into madness. In desperation, she placed the carton of Bella's notebooks and file folders on the dining room table in front of him. He lifted one notebook and then another, his hands trembling.

"I will translate them," Ida said. "And you will illustrate them. You will see. As we work, we will hear her voice, we will see her face, her smile. She will come alive for us."

He stared down at the page open before him, the delicate Yiddish script dancing through his tears.

"Yes. Yes. That is what we must do," he agreed. He took Ida's hand in his own and pressed it to his lips. "You are a good daughter, Idotchka," he said.

"I try," she said. "I have always tried."

She turned away. His words and her own filled her with sadness. She had tried so very hard to be a good daughter. *Perhaps too hard*, she thought as she sat in a circlet of lamplight and watched Marc slowly turn one page after another, his finger clutching a pencil as though he might begin to draw at any moment.

Chapter Twenty-Nine

*B*ella had titled her manuscript *Brenendike Licht, Burning Lights*. Ida translated it into French as *Lumières Allumées*. She studied each draft and notebook, working her way methodically through her mother's complex literary jigsaw puzzle, re-creating the Jewish world of Vitebsk through the prism of tender memory. Marc organized each entry according to the rhythm of the Jewish calendar, and as he created the graceful line drawings for each chapter, the melancholy that had haunted him since Bella's death dissipated. The afternoon that he completed his final sketch of Bella as a young girl reading in the Vitebsk clock tower, he walked through the apartment and turned the paintings away from the wall. His long mourning was at an end.

Eventually, the apartment once again became the scene of parties and impromptu gatherings. Their guests included the older writers and artists, the French- and Yiddish-speaking émigrés who were Marc's friends and acolytes. Ida was the welcoming hostess; Marc, dressed in one or another of the brightly colored shirts and striped jackets he favored, sat regnant in a blue velvet easy chair beneath his painting of a nude Ida floating above the village of Vitebsk.

Michel came and went, a guest in the apartment where he still lived in a room of his own. The Voice of America, even more important now that Europe was in a state of flux, occupied all his time. He traveled back and forth to Washington, always rushing to catch a train or a plane. He worried obsessively about his parents and used every contact, however remote, in his urgent efforts to determine their fate.

He dashed in one evening, his avian face ablaze with excitement.

"I've finally had news of my parents, Ida," he exclaimed. "They're alive! They survived the war, both of them. But they were ill and disoriented and they did not know how to find me. It did not occur to them that Michel Gordey was actually Michel Rapaport. I leave for Paris tomorrow to be with them and to deal with Voice of America business. Pierre wants us to expand our operation there and in Berlin. Most probably, I will be away for some months."

"How wonderful, Michel," Ida said and kissed him on both his cheeks. "You know how fond I've always been of your parents, how grateful I am to them."

"I do know that." A memory teased him and blossomed into recall. "I remember how you brought my mother those wild primroses; they were rose-gold, I think. They made her so happy. That was good of you, Ida."

"I loved her." She lowered her head so he would not see her tears.

She helped him pack and gave him gifts for his parents, a cashmere cardigan for his mother, a long woolen scarf for his father who had always complained of the cold, a box of chocolates that a GI had given her, a bottle of cognac Marc had received from a patron. She pressed a slip of paper into his hand.

"This is the address of my mother's brother, Isaac. We believe that it is possible that he and his family also survived. You remember that their little daughter is named Bella? We thought it strange that they would choose the name of someone who was still alive, but what a blessing it is that there may be another Bella in this world," she said. "Please see if you can find them. They haven't answered my letters. They may not even know that my mother is dead."

"I will try to find them," he promised. "And Ida, you must take care of yourself."

He put her hand to his lips and hesitated for a moment. She thought that he might kiss her, that he might caress her face, finger tendrils of her hair, hold her close, but she knew that such gestures belonged to another time. Still, they remained bound to each other. They had shared so much, endured so much. He would bring her gifts to his parents. He would seek out her relatives. She might cease to be his wife, but she would always and forever be his Ida, just as he would always and forever be her Michel.

He left. The apartment door slammed behind him.

She sniffed a handkerchief that he had forgotten, inhaled his scent, and wondered when she would see him again. Their separation, long anticipated, had begun. She flung the window open and watched him walk down the street.

She would not grieve, she promised herself.

It was not difficult, she realized, to keep that promise, to condition herself to gaiety. The war was ending and the season of celebration was beginning. Ida drifted from one gathering to another and invited friends to her own exuberant parties. Her frenetic socializing kept loneliness at bay.

On V-E Day, Ida flung the windows open and her exultant guests tossed armloads of confetti onto Riverside Drive. Champagne bottles from a mysterious source appeared and corks were popped, glasses lifted to catch the sparkling spray. The war in Europe was over, Japan would soon be subdued, and a bright and peaceful future awaited them. They had earned their music and their laughter and the right to enjoy the bubbling drink that tickled their noses and lightened their hearts. They hugged each other in the happy certainty that theirs was the last generation that would ever have to fight a war.

Michel returned from France, sobered by the devastation he had seen, exhausted by his work and his efforts to establish his parents in a comfortable home. His father was ill, his mother fragile; their dream of Palestine would never be fulfilled. He was very thin. His sleep was restless. Elsa warned him that he would soon be very ill if he did not take a vacation.

"The free world will survive for a few weeks without Michel Rapaport," she said wryly. "Don't you think so, André?" she asked.

André looked up from his medical text, nodded, and limped

over to the window. The heel of his right foot had been blown away during the Battle of the Bulge when his medical unit had been attacked. Unable to stand for long hours in the operation room, he had abandoned surgery and was qualifying as a pediatrician.

"We all need a vacation," he agreed. "The whole world needs a vacation."

Small Daniel, a handsome and playful child, rushed up to him.

"Play with me, Papa. Uncle Michel brought me a new game."

André waved him away. He stared down at the scene on the street below, at children returning from school and women hurrying home, hugging their brown bags of groceries. The quiet patterns of daily life slowly dispelled his depression.

Elsa sighed. His war was over, but André needed time, she knew. They all needed time. Herself. Michel. Ida.

She turned to Michel.

"I'm worried about Ida," she said. "She's working too hard. Every housekeeper she hires quarrels with Marc. He cannot speak English and they, of course, cannot understand his French, so he shouts and the poor women storm out. So it is Ida who cleans the apartment and prepares the meals. Who does the laundry and carries the trash to the incinerator? Certainly not the great Marc Chagall. And still she continues to work at the gallery. She is heading for a collapse. You are both in need of rest."

Michel nodded. "I know. I see that, but what can we do? Even the daily cleaning women cannot tolerate his behavior. He points and draws pictures and explodes in anger because they fail to understand what he wants. And he complains that there are holes in his socks and he's too cheap to buy new ones. Ida has no time to darn them, but he keeps tossing the damn socks onto her bed. I suggested that she tell him to go barefoot."

He spat the words out. He no longer bothered to conceal his anger at Marc.

"Something must be done. I am meeting Ida tomorrow. I will talk to her then," Elsa assured him.

She and Ida met the next day in Central Park. Daniel skipped along beside them, carrying the large red ball Ida had brought him as a gift.

"You look tired, Ida," Elsa began cautiously.

Ida shrugged, but before she could reply, Daniel rolled the red ball down a path and raced after it. A small girl, her straight brown hair draping her shoulders and neatly fringing her high pale forehead, picked it up and tossed it to him.

"Good girl, Jean," the child's mother said gently.

Elsa turned and looked at her.

"Virginia," she said. "How nice to see you. Please meet my friend Ida Chagall."

Ida held her hand out to the tall, slender young woman, intrigued by her subtle beauty.

"I met Marc Chagall, the painter, when I was an art student in Paris. Are you related to him?" she asked.

"He's my father," Ida replied.

"I remember him well. I am glad to hear that he is in New York."

Ida understood that she meant that she was glad that he was alive, that he was one Jew who had not fallen into the hands of the Nazis.

"I'm taking Jean over to the swings," she said to Elsa. "Would you like me to take your son as well?"

"Yes, thanks," Elsa agreed. "We'll get coffee and meet you there. A coffee for you?"

"No. No. That's all right." She shook her head. "Come, Jean. Come, Daniel."

"Poor thing. She can't afford the coffee," Elsa said as they walked on. "We'll buy her one."

"How do you know her?" Ida asked.

"She came to my clinic, desperately worried that she might be pregnant. Fortunately she wasn't. She had apparently stopped menstruating because she was malnourished. Her husband is a much older man, an impoverished Scots painter, on the verge of a mental breakdown. They get by on what she earns cleaning houses and doing some sewing. I gave her some vitamins, but there wasn't much else I could do," Elsa said sadly.

"If she studied in Paris, she must speak some French," Ida said musingly.

"I know she does. We've spoken in French. She's fluent," Elsa agreed. "Ida, it occurs to me that she might solve your problem. She sews, and she keeps house. She speaks French and would understand your father. It would be a good arrangement for you and good for Virginia, who needs steady employment."

"But will it be good for my father?" Ida asked.

"Why not?" Elsa replied indifferently.

They bought three coffees and half a dozen doughnuts, carrying them to the swings where Virginia was pushing the laughing children.

"I'll take over," Elsa said and handed her the coffee and a doughnut.

Virginia smiled gratefully and went to stand beside Ida.

"I was wondering," Ida said carefully, "if you could do me a great favor. Our family, my father, my husband, and myself, are in great need of a housekeeper, someone who can clean and cook and do some mending."

Virginia sipped her coffee. She hesitated before replying.

"I would be glad to take such a position," she said. "But I would have to bring Jean with me. My husband is not capable of looking after her."

"That would be fine," Ida agreed. "Can you come to meet my father tomorrow morning?" Ida asked.

"Of course."

Ida scrawled her address and phone number on a scrap of paper as the children bolted toward them, followed by Elsa.

Ida held the bag of pastries out to them and they munched happily and ran to the slide.

"I will see you tomorrow then," Ida said to Virginia.

She kissed Elsa on the cheek and hurried home where she told her father about Virginia. He nodded indifferently.

"As long as she's honest. And quiet. And as long as her child does not bother me," he said.

"She said that she met you in Paris," Ida added.

"Everyone says that they met Marc Chagall in Paris," he replied sarcastically.

Virginia arrived the next morning. Ida ushered her into the studio where Marc was already at work. He wheeled about as they entered, flashed his brilliant smile at Virginia, and, to Ida's relief, held out his hand.

"My daughter tells me that we met in Paris," he said. "And now that I see you, I do recall you."

Ida smiled. She was certain that her father had no memory of Virginia. She was all too familiar with his ability to charm and dissimulate.

"Yes. It was at an atelier on the rue Campagne Première, Bill Hayter's atelier. I was studying there and you sometimes visited," Virginia replied. "I remember you well."

"Do you find me much changed?" Marc asked teasingly.

He pulled up his oversized trousers, fumbled with the buttons of his brightly striped, paint-streaked shirt, and, with a boyish gesture, smoothed his unruly gray curls.

Virginia blushed. "Not so very much," she said softly.

"Ah, you are lying. I know that you are lying," he said, his eyes bright with flirtatious pleasure.

He took her arm and escorted her from the studio, his footfalls gliding lightly in his worn slippers. Ida trailed behind, oddly disturbed by the swift attraction she sensed between them.

Small Jean waited in the dining room, turning the pages of a tattered picture book. She had the resigned patience of an only child of difficult parents, conditioned to tread lightly and speak softly. Ida felt an instinctive sympathy for the little girl. She understood isolated childhoods.

"You and Jean look so much alike. Almost like sisters," Ida said to Virginia.

"Did you and your mother look alike?" Virginia asked.

"No, not at all."

Ida pointed to her father's portrait of Bella as a slender wraith of a girl that hung above the fireplace and then waved toward the painting in which she was portrayed. She had posed in the nude, her red-gold hair draping her shoulders and falling across her firm full breasts.

"As you can see, we were very different, my mother and I." She picked up her sketchpad and a stick of charcoal. "Would you mind posing for me with Jean for just a few minutes?" she asked and Virginia nodded in agreement.

Ida worked swiftly and held her pad out to Virginia. Her drawing was skillful. She had captured the similarity of their features, their heads tenderly inclined toward each other, Virginia's hand resting protectively on Jean's shoulders.

"It's very good," Virginia said, looking at it carefully.

"I wish that I had a drawing of my mother and myself." Ida's voice was heavy with sadness, but almost at once, she sprang to her feet, banishing regret, racing away from memory.

The mood was broken; there was work to be done. She moved authoritatively through the apartment, showing Virginia where the cleaning supplies and linens were kept, the mending basket that over-flowed with undarned socks, the kitchen with its sticky floor and counters. She advised her to clean her father's room when he was in the studio, the studio when he ate, and then to straighten her own room and Michel's.

"You must think it strange that my husband and I sleep in separate rooms," she said.

"Not at all," Virginia replied. "I do not share a room with my husband."

They stared at each other, two young women who did not sleep with their husbands, who understood the world of art, who might have been friends in another time, another place.

"Everything is understood then?" Ida asked. "My husband and I are leaving for a brief vacation. Will you manage?"

"I will," Virginia assured her, her tone carefully submissive.

Ida and Michel left for their vacation that evening.

"One last shared holiday," Michel murmured.

"Perhaps," Ida said sadly. "But perhaps not."

Their years together had been suffused with uncertainty. There was no certainty even now.

Virginia arrived early the next morning and began her life as Marc Chagall's housekeeper. Within days, she was also his lover.

Chapter Thirty

*A*fterward, they could not tell when it had begun.

Marc claimed he had recognized their shared destiny the very moment she entered his studio.

He had thought, he said, that Bella had sent Virginia to him. Bella, in death, was his guardian angel. She would not cease to protect him. Virginia speculated that their intimacy could be traced to her third day in the apartment when he asked her to join him when he ate because he felt lonely in the large dining room. Such intimate meals then became a pattern. Small Jean napped on the living room couch as her mother and Marc ate and sipped their wine. They spoke of their disparate childhoods, her early years in Venezuela and later in Dorset and Paris, as the lonely and unhappy daughter of a British diplomat. He reminisced about his youth in Vitebsk, his studies in St. Petersburg, his life in Paris, so cruelly aborted by the war. They pitied each other and offered each other comfort with the softest of gazes, the lightest of touches.

In a more relaxed mood, he gossiped about the artists they had both known in Paris. He was ambivalent about Picasso, dismissive of Giacometti and Miró, hostile to Max Ernst.

Virginia listened to his stories, both awed and amused. He invited her into his studio and she reveled in the time she spent in the large, wide-windowed room with its familiar scents of drying brushes dipped in turpentine, linseed oil, and the acrid odor of fixatives. Ida had furnished it with huge potted plants and suspended a swaying mobile from the high ceiling. It was, Marc explained, a gift from Alexander Calder, intended to console him after Bella's death.

"But why should I be consoled by such a creation, the body of

a man with the head of a goat?" he asked. "Calder doesn't understand me. There is no one who understands me now that my Bella
is dead."

"I will try to understand you," Virginia murmured daringly.

She punctured his sadness by telling him about her own Bohemian
student days in Montparnasse, describing the masquerade balls at
which students and artists, models and prostitutes, danced until dawn
and slept in each other's arms.

"And did you sleep in the arms of many young men?" he asked
teasingly. "Or perhaps you are intrigued only by older men."

"I am intrigued by you," she admitted.

She did not add that she had also been intrigued by her husband,
the weak and elderly John McNeil. Her family had condemned that
marriage as an unhealthy obsession with the weak and infirm, similar to her childhood nursing of birds with broken wings, hares with
injured legs.

But this was different. Marc Chagall was neither weak nor infirm.
Age had not affected his amazing energy, his formidable talent. He
was the opposite of her ill and impoverished husband.

She kissed him gently on the lips, entwined her fingers in the
tangle of his gray curls, amazed at how soft they were to her touch.

It was not long before he entered the bedroom while she changed
the linens. It was not long before they collapsed together onto the
unmade bed. She unbuttoned his shirt and buried her head in his
chest. Through the closed door, they could hear Jean babbling happily to herself as she played with the small toys she crafted out of bits
of clay and stray buttons. The child's prattle vested their midday coupling with an aura of innocence. They turned to each other, smiled,
and dressed very swiftly.

Ida sensed their new and daring intimacy when she and Michel
returned to New York. She realized at once that the relationship
between Virginia and Marc excluded their daughters, herself and
small Jean who was enrolled in a nursery school at Marc's insistence
and expense.

"Perhaps you should spend more hours at your studio classes, Ida," Marc suggested to her. "You must not spend so much time in the apartment."

"He wants to be rid of me," Ida told Elsa. "It's a pity that there is no nursery school for the adult daughters of fathers engaged in afternoon love affairs with their housekeepers."

She did not blame Virginia. She knew that Virginia was desperately poor, trapped in an unhappy, loveless marriage, and estranged from her own father. Of course she would be enticed by a relationship with the world-famous and prosperous Marc Chagall. But she resented Marc.

"He might have waited until the first anniversary of my mother's death," she complained to Michel, who smiled bitterly.

"He is a dependent man who has no capacity for solitude," Michel replied coldly. "Surely you know that."

Ida nodded. She had always known that.

She did not speak to Marc about Virginia but remained complicit in their domestic charade. Virginia ate alone in the kitchen. She addressed Marc as Monsieur Chagall and was never introduced to their guests. She glided silently through the room at parties or gatherings, balancing trays of glasses, removing dirty dishes, a compliant servant who knew her place. When Ida gave a small dinner party, she invited Virginia into the dining room and offered her a glass of vodka, which Virginia drank standing up and wearing her housekeeper's apron.

Ida was careful to set boundaries. Virginia's weekly wages were placed discreetly on the kitchen table. When she was in the room, Ida spoke to Marc in Russian, which Virginia did not understand. Virginia ignored them as she swept the floor and dusted the furniture.

But tensions within the apartment mounted. Marc and Ida argued. They disagreed about household matters, about negotiations for the sale of his paintings, even about the food and liquor bills. Their angers, however heated, were brief. Inevitably Ida spoke soothingly to Marc, called him *Papochka*, pressed her lips to his forehead.

She loved him and feared for him, feared for their togetherness. She watched Virginia disappear into his studio. She watched him follow Virginia into the kitchen. Virginia was usurping her place, but she was also freeing Ida of her worries about Marc.

"You cannot have it both ways, Ida," Michel said when she complained. He reflected passively that she was, after all, used to having all things her way.

She spent less time at the apartment and concentrated on working more closely with Pierre Matisse.

"This is the time to exploit your father's fame," the art dealer said. "He wants new venues for his work. And with the war over, there is a hunger for new and exciting experiences in art, in dance, in theater. The New York City Ballet is interested in his work."

She immediately met with a director of the Ballet and showed him the file of reviews of her father's sets and costumes for *Aleko* in both Mexico City and New York.

"You are staging *The Firebird*," she said. "He knows and understands Stravinsky's work."

Dates and deadlines were discussed. Honorariums were offered, rejected, and renegotiated. At last, terms were agreed upon. The commission was in place. Contracts were signed.

"It's a great honor, *Papochka*," Ida enthused. "Pierre Matisse says it will be of major importance to your reputation. Your work must be exemplary. We dare not disappoint."

"Has any work of mine ever disappointed?" he asked laconically as he flipped open his sketchpad and listened to the recording of *The Firebird* that blared from their phonograph day after day, hour after hour.

"Everything depends on your absolute concentration. You must be able to work without distraction," she said and stared hard at Virginia, who blushed and left the room. "You know how you hate the city in the summer. It is too hot, too noisy. You will have difficulty working and so I have rented a house in Sag Harbor, a large house with a studio that overlooks Long Island Sound. You will be able to work in peace there," Ida continued.

Marc frowned.

"I work quite contentedly here. Virginia brings calm and order to my life. I don't want anything to change," he replied. "I cannot manage without Virginia."

Ida recognized defeat.

"Of course we'll ask Virginia to join us in Sag Harbor," she said. "She will keep house, and her little Jean will love the ocean and the beach."

"I'll speak to her," Marc said without looking up from his pad. "Perhaps she will agree."

"Oh, I'm certain she will," Ida replied.

She did not glance at Virginia who entered the room just then, carrying a glass of tea for Marc that she set down, careful not to disturb his drawing pad and pastel chalks.

Chapter Thirty-One

*V*irginia did agree. She did not want to be separated from Marc and it had been a long time since she and Jean had had the opportunity to be at the seaside. Her husband, whose depression had deepened, raised no objection. He knew that they needed the money she earned working for the Chagalls. It was their only source of income.

The white-shingled house on Sea Cove Lane was run-down, its furnishings shabby and sparse, but it was large. The second floor had a sprawling wraparound balcony, and each bedroom had a door that opened to a view of the sea. Free of the heat and noise of the city, they reveled in the brilliant sunlit days and the cool evenings. Salt-tinged breezes brushed their faces as they looked up at the brilliant stars.

The fierce sunlight bronzed Marc's skin and his blue eyes glittered with agate brilliance. Ida, wearing broad-brimmed hats and pastel-colored sleeveless dresses of gossamer fabrics, haunted produce markets and invited friends to extravagant picnics on the beach. She wore daringly cut bathing suits that revealed the sun-gilded beauty of her shapely body and smiled teasingly at the men who stared at her as she sprinted gracefully into the sea.

She taught Jean to swim and helped the child to gather shells, but when she spoke to Virginia, it was only to plan the menu of the evening meal or to remind her that fresh linens were needed in the bedroom when Michel was expected on one of his rare visits. Each conversation, superficially pleasant, reminded Virginia that although she slept in Marc's bed every night, she remained a servant.

Stravinsky's music swirled through the house as Marc immersed himself in the score, committing the powerful rhythms to memory and then working feverishly to capture the elusive images in pencil or watercolor. By nightfall, he was exhausted and rested in Virginia's arms, leaving the balcony door in their bedroom open because he found the sound of the crashing waves soothing.

Ida fell asleep swiftly on those summer nights, but too often she was thrust into wakefulness, ensnared once again in the silken web of a half-remembered dream. Her eyes still closed, she recalled only that she was running down that all-too-familiar road, but now she was alone and unprotected. Marc and Virginia raced behind her, Jean between them, their hands grasping the hands of the child when, without warning, the three of them soared skyward through the welcoming sky, studded with pastel-colored flowers. Ida was left behind, bewildered and terrified. It was that bewilderment, that terror, that caused her to sit up in bed and struggle to re-create the dreamscape, to reach for the sketchbook on her bedside and clutch a charcoal stick that she never applied to the pristine white paper.

She was startled then, as she awakened one night, to hear Jean's terrified scream.

"I'm scared, Mama. I'm so scared." The child's shrill voice pierced the nocturnal silence.

Ida sprang from her bed and raced out to her balcony, only to meet Virginia running from Marc's room. They stared at each other, their white nightdresses silvered by moonlight.

"It's Jean," Virginia murmured. "She must have had a nightmare." She hurried to the child's room.

Ida stared out at the sea, overwhelmed by a sudden inexplicable loneliness. She thought, quixotically, that her own dream, in an odd contagion, might have invaded the child's sleep.

That awkward nocturnal encounter eased the tensions between Ida and Virginia. All pretenses were abandoned. Their casual exchanges were newly pleasant, the household chores shared. When Virginia and Jean took the train into New York to visit John McNeil, Ida did the cooking and the cleaning without comment or complaint.

"Today I am once again your only daughter," she teased Marc

as they sat together during one of Virginia's absences. Stravinsky's celestial wedding music soared through the room.

He looked up from his pad. "I have only one daughter, my Idotchka," he said reprovingly. "I will always have only one daughter."

Late one evening, Virginia and Jean returned from New York visibly upset. Virginia's hair was in disarray and both her skin and Jean's were coated with a noxious dark purple powder. Jean wept uncontrollably as Virginia ran a bath and immersed her in the sudsy water.

"Someone threw a can full of this horrid stuff through the train window. Probably a schoolboy playing a stupid prank. But it was really frightening," she told Ida.

When Jean was bathed, dressed in clean pajamas, and comforted with a cup of cocoa and a bedtime story, Virginia went into the bathroom, surprised to find Ida running a fresh bath for her.

She undressed swiftly and sank gratefully into the steaming water to which Ida had added her own lavender-scented bath salts.

"My mother's recipe," Ida said. "She loved lavender."

She knelt beside the tub, shampooed Virginia's hair, and then sponged her slender, milk-white body with a new loofah.

"You are so beautiful," Ida said admiringly. "*Très belle.*" Gently, caressingly, she passed the sponge across Virginia's firm small breasts. "How does that feel?" she asked.

"Wonderful," Virginia said. "The water is exactly the right temperature. Share it with me."

Ida nodded, slipped off her own robe, and climbed into the tub. They sat facing each other, tall Virginia, her newly shampooed brown hair falling in silken swathes to her shimmering shoulders, and full-figured Ida, her damp titian curls piled high, her skin rosy with warmth and spattered with beads of moisture.

Marc, in search of one or the other, opened the door and stared at them.

"My beautiful girls," he murmured. *"Mes belles demoiselles."*

It occurred to him that they would make an ideal subject for Henri Matisse. He closed the door gently behind him, and as they held towels out to each other and dried themselves, they heard the strains of *The Firebird*, the volume turned even higher than usual.

The idyllic summer days drifted into melancholy autumn. They returned to New York.

Once again they were ensnared in secrecy. Marc worried that his friends might disapprove and see his relationship with Virginia as an insult to Bella, who had so recently died. They might be scandalized because Virginia was not Jewish. Ida worried that the relationship might damage her father's reputation and tarnish her mother's memory.

Virginia understood their reticence. Reluctantly, she and Jean returned to their dingy apartment, to the husband whom she both pitied and resented. She feared John McNeil's volatile and violent moods, but she feared Ida's displeasure even more. She knew that it was Ida who controlled her future.

She was relieved when *The Firebird* went into rehearsal and Ida asked her to help fashion the costumes. Seated side by side, their silver shears flying as the tissue-paper patterns fluttered, they sculpted Marc's intricate designs onto shimmering fabric. Marc worked feverishly on the sets, flourishing his long-handled brushes to create the fairy-tale landscape, the magical woodland, the enchanted dragon. He was transported into Stravinsky's imagined world, his own Russia, the land where he and Bella had lived and loved. Virginia was a stranger to that world yet she worked beside him, her needle flashing. He thought of Bella, felt her presence in the room, imagined her spirit guiding Virginia's hand.

"Your mother is looking down at us. She is happy that Virginia is helping us," he told Ida. "She does not want me to be alone."

His loneliness had come to an end. He felt himself reborn. Virginia had vested him with new life. He studied her sad pale face and marked her grace as she stood and held a piece of brilliant crimson fabric to the light.

Ida was silent. He was, she knew, painting a mental picture, a fantasy that would justify his new life, his new love.

The costumes were fitted directly on the dancers, and Marc painted his designs onto the fabric as they stood submissive and immobile. Balanchine, the choreographer, watched and nodded his approval, but it was Virginia to whom he turned as he worked, as once he had turned to Bella. He sought her admiration, her approval of his work. Virginia was, Ida knew, the secret sharer of all their lives.

"Are the colors strong enough?" Marc asked Virginia as the dancers Maria Tallchief and Francisco Moncion stood on point before them. Virginia offered no criticism, no judgment.

It was Ida who urged him to render the prince's cloak more Mephistophelean, to use more gold to gild the trees of the enchanted forest.

Her criticisms, always accurate, incurred his annoyance.

"You presume," he told her harshly. "Do you think you have your mother's eye? Do you think you can take your mother's place?"

"No, her place is already taken," Ida retorted angrily.

Her cheeks burning, she gathered up the sketches for the costumes that she would offer for sale. Virginia tried to help her smooth out the long sheets.

"I can manage," Ida said coldly, and Virginia shrugged and returned to her needlework.

The Firebird opened at the Metropolitan Opera House, and Ida, radiant in a magenta gown, her hair fashioned into a coppery chignon, entered on her father's arm.

"Chagall's wife is beautiful but so much younger than he is," she heard a gawking bystander say, and she smiled and thought to shout out that she was his daughter, a daughter who ran his household and managed his affairs, a daughter with a wifely role in her father's life.

Marc, wearing a green velvet jacket, his gray curls rakishly combed, his elfin face wreathed in a brilliant smile, nodded regally at the applauding and appreciative crowd. It had not occurred to either of them to ask Virginia to join them.

At home in her dreary apartment, Virginia listened to Stravinsky's music as it was broadcast on WQXR. John McNeil watched her.

"I suppose you'll go to live with the great Marc Chagall now," he said bitterly. "If his bitch of a daughter will allow it."

Virginia was silent. He was right, of course. She would live with Marc if Ida allowed it. Ida ruled her father; Ida mandated every decision.

Virginia bought all the morning papers the next day and carried them to the Riverside Drive apartment, eager to show Marc and Ida the enthusiastic reviews. But it was Michel who opened the door.

"Ida's left," he told her. "She's left the apartment and she's left me. Of course, she left me long ago. As I suppose I left her. But I'm sure you know that."

His voice was calm, his gaze steady. His sadness was palpable, as Ida's had been, but their separation had long been inevitable.

The premiere of *The Firebird* represented a closure of a kind for Ida. She had returned to the apartment infused with a new decisiveness. It was time, she had told Michel, in the hushed stillness of dawn, that she claim her own life. She wanted to live alone, neither with him nor with her father.

Michel had offered no argument. He watched her pack, carried her suitcase down to the street, and kissed her on the cheek as he helped her into a cab. Marc awakened late in the morning. When Michel told him of Ida's departure, his face crumbled in sorrow and disbelief.

"How could she be so cruel? She has left me alone," he moaned.

"You will not be alone," Michel had assured him. "You have Virginia."

"Yes. Virginia. She will live with me. She must," he murmured.

Michel repeated his words to Virginia as she stood there clutching her newspapers.

"Will you and Jean come here to live?" he asked her.

"I don't know," she said and walked past him into the bedroom where Marc stood at the window. He turned to her. She read the fear and sadness in his eyes. Wordlessly, he opened his arms, and wordlessly, all indecision vanished, she walked into them.

Their new life began. The configuration of the Riverside Drive apartment shifted. Michel remained, an odd occupant, neither guest nor resident; he came and left without explanation. Virginia and Jean moved in.

Ida appeared regularly and sat at her desk to deal with the flood of correspondence, with contracts and invoices. Wary and watchful, she occasionally asked Virginia about a bill or discussed the sale of a painting with Marc. Father and daughter were cold and polite to each other, careful acrobats balanced on the dangerous high wire of their uneasy relationship.

Occasionally Virginia and Ida discussed household matters. They recognized that they were discretely bonded to Marc, who dominated both their lives.

"Jean will soon be going to a boarding school in New Jersey," Virginia told Ida one afternoon, her eyes lowered. "We think it will be best for her."

"You mean my father thinks it will be best for him. But do you think it will be good for her to live apart from you?" Ida asked. Jean, who reminded her of her own lonely childhood, had always aroused her sympathy.

"I want to make your father happy," Virginia replied. "Jean will adjust."

"Perhaps you should think about making yourself happy," Ida retorted. "Women, even the great Marc Chagall's women, have the right to their own happiness, the right to make their own choices. I learned that, but it was a hard lesson."

"I am happy," Virginia insisted. "And soon I will be happier still."

Ida stared at her, studying her with a penetrating gaze. She had noticed the subtle changes in Virginia, the new fullness to her slender form, the pallor of her fine-featured face newly aglow. Of course. Virginia was pregnant. Her father would be the father to another child. All their lives would change yet again.

"Does my father know that you are expecting a child?" she asked.

Virginia shook her head.

"Not yet. But I will tell him soon."

"You mean when it's too late."

Virginia averted her eyes. Ida knew the reason for her delay. Abortion was illegal in the United States, although with the right contacts and enough money, illicit arrangements could be made. But after the first trimester, the procedure was too dangerous. No doctor or midwife, however corrupt or compassionate, would attempt it. Clearly, Virginia did not want an abortion.

"I understand," she said. "You are waiting until there is no possibility for termination. How brave you are, braver than I was."

She remembered her mother's barely audible question. *"How many monthlies have you missed, Idotchka?"* She had been too naive then to understand the implications of the question.

"You won't tell Marc, will you?" Virginia asked.

"Of course not. You yourself must tell him. As for me, I have another difficult matter to discuss with him today."

"Thank you," Virginia said.

Ida watched as she left the room, noting that she walked balanced lightly on her heels, her arms crossed over her abdomen. She had already assumed the rocking gait and the instinctive protective gesture of a pregnant woman.

She thrust the pile of unanswered letters aside and reached for the ledger, opening it to the last entries of debits and credits, and pondered the figures. She added up one column then another, finally taking up a clean sheet of paper onto which she copied the figures. They did not surprise her. She wondered if they would surprise her father.

As she cleared her desk, she wondered idly how her relationship with Virginia's child might be defined. Would the unborn child be her half sibling or her stepsibling? Neither, of course, she realized. Her father and Virginia were not married, and they could not marry until Virginia and John McNeil divorced. Even then, there would be no marriage unless Virginia converted to Judaism. Marc Chagall might sleep with a gentile woman, he might impregnate her, but he would never marry her. And would Virginia agree to convert? The unanswered questions dizzied her. She turned again to the ledgers on her desk.

She left the apartment that day without seeing either Virginia or her father.

"*Au revoir*, Papa. *Au revoir*, Virginia," she called from the doorway.

"Good night, Ida." Virginia's voice was muffled. Marc was silent.

Over the next several days, she studied the figures she had copied from the ledger sheet. She did not doubt their accuracy, but she doubted her ability to confront her father with them.

"But I must," she told herself sternly.

"You must not be afraid," Michel, always and forever her confidante, told her gently when she told him what she planned to do. "You are doing what is right."

He offered to go with her, but she shook her head. "No," she said. "This is something I must do alone."

She took a cab and arrived at the Riverside Drive apartment just as twilight dimmed the light in the studio. Her father did not work in such half darkness. She knew that he would have turned his easel to the wall and rinsed his brushes in turpentine, as fastidious in his studio as he was careless in his home.

Marc sat in the dining room, sipping vodka and turning the pages of a Yiddish newspaper. The scent of frying garlic and onions drifted in from the kitchen where Virginia was preparing dinner, valiantly striving to replicate the taste of Bella's pirogen.

"Quite the domestic scene, *Papochka*," Ida said. "I've brought you some pot cheese and sour cream from the dairy on Ludlow Street."

"You can give it to Virginitchka," he said, pointing to the kitchen.

"Virginitchka indeed. So now she is your Russian sweetheart. When will she become your Jewish wife?" Ida teased.

"It has not been discussed," he replied angrily and she knew that Virginia had not yet told him of her pregnancy.

"But there is something you and I must discuss," she said and sat down opposite him. "As you know, Michel and I have parted and he will be returning to France. I can no longer count on him for support."

"As though he ever offered you support. He was always weak, weak as a youth, weak as a man," he said dismissively. "What does he earn? Can his income even compare to mine? You lose nothing with the end of this marriage."

He had always considered Michel a mere appendage to their lives, a husband when propriety demanded that Ida have a husband and then a transient figure easily ignored, easily forgotten.

"And yet it is a marriage that you insisted on," she retorted. "And as it turned out, he is not weak at all. Because of him, because of his parents, I escaped from France. Because of him, your paintings, your precious paintings, were rescued. And it is not true that he did not support me. When he began working, he always gave me an allowance. He will, of course, no longer do so. When we are divorced, he will be under no financial obligation to me. But I will need money to live on, money with which to plan my own future."

"You have your commissions. And if you need more money, just ask me for it," Marc said.

Her color rose. Her eyes were dangerously bright. "Commissions do not guarantee a steady income. I need security, a nest egg, money that I can invest. I am a grown woman, not a child. I don't want to run to my papa because I need a new dress, new shoes, carfare. I want my independence, money that is rightfully mine. I want my share of my mother's estate," she replied. "The paintings that rightfully belong to me."

He stared at her as though she spoke in a language that was foreign to him. His cheeks were mottled with anger, his blue eyes slivers of ice.

"How dare you? What right do you have to my paintings, my money? What inheritance are you talking about? The only painting that belongs to you is *The Bridal Chair* and I wish to God I had never painted it." His voice grew louder and louder as his anger gathered momentum and exploded in a new paroxysm of fury. "Every kopek that has ever been earned for the support of this family was earned by me, by my work, my art. The chutzpah of you to make such a demand."

"My mother would have wanted me to have a portion of that which would have been hers. And I too have earned money. I too have brought kopeks into the household. Kopeks and francs, sterling and dollars. Have I not acted as your representative? Have I not arranged for sales and contracts?" she countered, her anger matching his own. "Who managed to get your paintings out of Europe? Who arranged for sales, exhibitions?"

She pulled the ledger sheet out of her purse and placed it between them. Dates, names, figures. A record of every transaction she had handled. He swept his arm across the table, knocking over the containers of food she had brought. He seized the lined paper with its neat authoritative columns, crumpled it into a ball, and tossed it across the room. The white cheese and the thick sour cream puddled on the table, formed hillocks on the polished wood floor.

"You see what you have made me do?" he shouted and rose, lifting his chair and brandishing it threateningly over her head.

Virginia ran into the room. Appalled, she wrested the chair from him. "Marc, Ida, what is happening here? What are you saying? Ida, what is happening? Marc, you must calm yourself," she pleaded.

Virginia trembled. Explosions of rage were alien to her. Her parents had not argued. They had simply withdrawn from each other into a cold English silence. Her husband had sublimated his rage and disappointment into depression. They were different, this Jewish father and daughter, Marc and Ida, who shouted out their deepest feelings, who wept and shook their fists at each other. She gripped the chair that he had raised so threateningly, the weapon of his rage and disappointment, and stared at Ida's clenched fist raised high as though to defend herself or perhaps to strike him in turn. Their fierce and dramatic declamations in Russian, that passionate incomprehensible language, bewildered her. She slammed the chair down, at a remove from Marc.

They looked at her, shamed by the fear they saw in her eyes, shamed because she turned away from them and went into the kitchen to gather rags with which she slowly and methodically mopped up the white curds of cheese, the tear-shaped drops of sour cream, the snow-colored detritus of their fearful exchange. Exhausted, Marc sat down and Ida turned to go.

"It is not right that we spoke in this way," he said to her, shifting to Yiddish.

"No. It is not right. But I will have my money, *Papochka*. I will have what I have earned," she replied, also in Yiddish.

The tenderness of that language of the heart did not diminish her determination.

And yet she turned, knelt beside him, and kissed him on both cheeks. He in turn curled tendrils of her bright hair about his paint-encrusted fingers.

"*Meine tochter*, my daughter," he murmured.

"*Mein vater*, my father," she replied.

Their anger would not, could not, deplete their love.

Virginia stared at them, as confused by their swift reconciliation as she had been by their violent acrimony. She would never understand them, the man she loved and his passionate, unpredictable daughter.

Chapter Thirty-Two

The first snow fell in November. A light windswept scattering of delicate flakes danced against the huge windows of the studio. Marc stared out at them, recalling the snows of his Vitebsk childhood that had turned the small village into a shimmering wonderland. Virginia sidled up to him and held out his striped jacket. She helped him pull his arms through the sleeves and adjusted the collar as though he were a small boy.

"It is cold in here. I don't want you to get sick," she said softly.

"You are a good mother to me, Virginitchka," he said.

"As I will be a good mother to our child," she replied.

Her words, so quietly uttered, fell like a stone upon his heart.

"What child? What are you saying?"

He stepped away from her, his eyes ablaze with anger, his body rigid. He put his hands to his ears as though to block out her words.

"I am pregnant, Marc." Her cheeks burned, her hands trembled, but her voice was calm. "We are going to have a child."

"Are you mad?"

He spat out the question and she cringed, her face pale, her eyes wide with fear. He stared at her and saw the new gentle rise of her abdomen, watched as she placed her hands protectively across it, the maternal gesture instinctive and undeniable. He bit his lips.

"You can't be certain."

"I am certain. I've seen a doctor. There have been tests."

"Think carefully. We are not married. I am not a young man. The situation is impossible. You are not a child. There is an alternative. You know what must be done."

His mind raced back to that long-ago morning in Paris, when

Ida, young, naive Ida, dressed in virginal white, had revealed her own pregnancy. There had been a solution then. There was the same solution now. *Avortement*. Abortion. Of course America was not France, but with enough money, there was always a way to arrange things.

She turned away.

"It is too late for an alternative, too late for an abortion. And I would never consider terminating this pregnancy, even if it were not too late. This is our child, conceived in love. And I will have our baby. I will not change my mind." Her voice was soft but firm, her gaze unflinching.

He had not thought her capable of such determination, such stubborn resolve. He struggled against his own anger. When he spoke, it was with a cold calm.

"It is not too late. There are ways. I can contact doctors, surgeons."

"I don't care about your doctors, your surgeons. I know what I must do. It is my decision."

Once again, her hands moved across her abdomen; the soothing gesture ignited his fury.

"Very well then. If you will not listen to reason, I will not be responsible," he shouted. "You will bear this child alone and raise it alone. It will not be our child. I will not support it. It will be your child, yours alone."

He went to the window, his hands balled into fists, and waited, willing her to acquiescence, but she remained silent, although he heard the quiet sound of her weeping. He did not turn. He did not want to see her tears.

Virginia walked across the room. He saw her shadow, saw her bend to pick up his handkerchief that had fallen to the floor. She placed it on his worktable beside the carafe of water she carried in each morning because she knew that he grew thirsty as he worked. She was caring and obedient, his Virginia; surely she would care enough to obey him now. Still at the window, he waited for her submission, his attention riveted to a sudden swirl of whiteness as a wild wind tossed the falling flakes. He did not turn even as he heard her leave the studio and close the door quietly behind her. It occurred to him that Ida would have slammed it shut, that Bella would have stormed out. But passionate rage was alien to gentle, well-bred Virginia. He took a sip of water. His eyes burned; he plucked his handkerchief from the table and saw that she had folded it carefully into a neat square.

Unable to work, still hypnotized by the storm that threatened to become a blizzard, he remained at the window and saw her leave the building. She walked down Riverside Drive, erect as always, a faded shawl draped over her shoulders because her tweed winter coat was worn thin and she had not allowed him to buy her a new one. She carried her pathetic cardboard valise, tied with the same rope that had held it closed when she had carried it into his apartment.

Where is she going? he wondered forlornly. How cruel she was. Didn't she care that she was leaving him alone on this lonely wintry day?

He turned to his easel, his brush held high, but he could not paint. He sank down on his worn sofa, touched the Calder mobile, and allowed the swaying metal pieces to rock him to sleep.

He awakened when he heard the front door open some hours later.

Ah, she is back, he thought with satisfaction. She had understood his objections; she had come to her senses and returned just as he had known she would.

"Virginitchka, my foolish girl," he called.

He would forgive her; he would appease her. He would buy her a new winter coat, perhaps even a new valise.

He hurried to the vestibule, but it was Ida, cocooned in a white fur jacket, who stood there, clutching a brown bag of groceries, her face wind-ruddied, snowflakes clinging in crystal buds to her flame-colored hair.

"It's me, Papa, not Virginia. She has gone away. She came to see me. She was worried that you would not have enough food. She asked me to make sure you were all right," Ida said, shedding her coat.

"Gone away? Where has she gone?" he asked despairingly. "She has no money. She has nothing."

"I gave her some money. She wanted to go to the mountains, to the country. She said she needed quiet, time to think, to plan." Ida went into the kitchen, carrying the bag of food.

Marc followed her. "Did she tell you that she was pregnant?" he asked.

"I knew," Ida replied. She removed the vegetables from the bag and formed them into a bright pyramid, emerald green cabbage, scarlet peppers, golden onions. He slashed his hand across her careful arrangement, thrusting the vegetables to the floor.

"What kind of an ungrateful daughter are you? How could you have betrayed your own father?" he shouted. "You should have made her understand. You should have told her how foolish she is being. How can she have this child? What will people think when they learn that I conceived a child with a gentile woman, even before the year of mourning for Bella was over? Everyone will know that I have broken Jewish law."

Ida picked up the vegetables and calmly rearranged them as she answered him.

"When did you begin to worry about observing Jewish law, *Papochka*? No one expects it of you. Do you go to the synagogue? Do you observe the Sabbath? Does a religious Jew paint crucifixions? Your friends all know that Virginia McNeil is living with you, sleeping with you. When they learn of her pregnancy, they will know that Marc Chagall is human, and that a child, his child, will be born to his gentile lover," Ida replied. "And be assured, Virginia will have this child, with or without your support. She is not a frightened eighteen-year-old. She is not your daughter. You have no dominion over her. She is a strong woman. She defied her parents and married her husband. She defied her husband and had Jean. She defied him yet again and came to live with you. She will defy you, and her child will be born. She will manage. As she has managed until now. She may be poor, she may be fragile, but she is a survivor. She will survive and so will the baby that she carries. Your child, *Papochka*, Marc Chagall's child, blood of his blood, bone of his bone."

Marc put his hands to his ears and stamped out of the kitchen into the shelter of his studio. He was dizzied by Ida's reaction, by the truth of her words, furious that she had known of Virginia's pregnancy. Her defense of Virginia was a betrayal. Was this her revenge because he had insisted, all those years ago, that her own pregnancy had to end? He had been right then, as he was right now. He and Bella had rescued her from shame, had restored her to respectability. She was still young, divorced, but not saddled with a child. She was free to forge a new life. How ungrateful she was, this daughter on whom he had lavished such love and largesse. She had wrested what she called her share of his money from him; she conspired with Virginia against him. Was this the daughter he had raised with such love, such tenderness?

He willed her to leave, but he trembled at the thought that he would be alone in the vast apartment as the storm shrouded the city in whiteness. He pitied himself, a man no longer young, snowbound and abandoned by the two strong young women upon whom he depended and loved. They had formed an alliance against him. Grief and anger throttled him as he stood again at the window. The snow had ceased, but the panes were frozen. He waited for Ida to leave, listening for the sound of the door closing behind her, but instead the scent of sautéed garlic and onion drifted into the studio. Ida was cooking.

"I don't want your food," he called petulantly, although because the door was closed, he knew that she could not hear him.

She knocked, told him that dinner was ready, sat opposite him at the kitchen table, and ladled out the ratatouille she had prepared following Bella's recipe, a food he had always loved. She sliced a pumpernickel loaf and handed him the heel of the bread. He and Bella had laughingly called it "the kiss," because it began the loaf and ended the loaf. He did not smile as he took it from Ida, nor did he thank her.

"Pierre Matisse wants to organize a retrospective," she said calmly as he began to eat. "The Museum of Modern Art is eager to be the venue, and then Pierre hopes to transfer the entire exhibition to the Art Institute of Chicago."

She switched roles expertly, morphing from his passionate daughter into his calculating representative. She had said all that she would say about Virginia. There was business to discuss and she was newly confident, having so recently triumphed over him in the matter of her mother's estate.

"I suppose you will be collecting commissions on sales from such a retrospective," he replied drily. He too was skilled at switching emotional gears.

"As is my right. You will recall that I rescued many of those paintings or they might have been looted by the Nazis. I think I have earned such commissions."

"We will speak of this another time," he countered. "Now I am concerned only about Virginia. She is alone on this cold night."

Ida did not reply. She understood that what concerned him was the chill of his own loneliness, the silence that he would confront the next morning and perhaps on all the mornings to come. She poured him a cup of tea, cleared the table, and shrugged into her coat.

"Virginia will be fine," she assured him. "You will hear from her, I am sure."

"Perhaps I will talk to her about converting to Judaism," he said hesitantly.

She laughed.

"Why? Can you see Virginia McNeil in shul? Can you see her waiting her turn in the kosher butcher shop? Can you see her at Uncle Isaac's seder table?"

He shook his head wearily.

"I cannot marry a gentile woman," he said. "If we are to marry, she must become a Jew."

"And she cannot marry you at all. Have you forgotten that she has a husband?"

"But I want her back," he murmured. "I need her."

"And she needs you. Now more than ever. Haven't you already lived together and conceived a child without marriage? Nothing has changed. Wait. She will return."

She held the sugar bowl out to him and he took a cube, placed it on his tongue, and sipped from his glass of tea. The warmth and sweetness comforted him as she had known it would. She smiled wryly at the thought that at this moment, she was both mother and nurse to her father.

"You are right," he agreed. "She will be back."

Virginia did come back. Two weeks later, she entered the apartment. Her hair hung lankly about her shoulders, the bangs that fringed her forehead were uneven, her face was pale, and, because she had lost weight, the protuberance of her pregnancy beneath a loose gray shift was obvious. She stood hesitantly in the doorway, but Marc sprang up from his chair and took her cold hands into his own and rubbed them gently.

"You are back," he said. "My Virginia. I knew you would not desert me."

"Of course I would not desert you." She echoed his words. "And I cannot desert our child. I am full of love for your son. I am blessed to be his mother."

She had rehearsed the speech, framed it and reframed it during the long, rainy days she had spent in a shabby boardinghouse in the foothills of the Catskill Mountains, but now the words sounded childish, stilted to her own ears.

He smiled and patted her head, an affectionate acquiescent father. He could afford such gentleness because he knew that he held all the power; the ultimate decision would be his.

"You already know that this unborn child is a boy?" he teased. "Foolish child, foolish girl."

"To me, he is my son. I am certain that I carry a boy. I even know his name. I will call him David."

"David," he repeated, and his face crumbled.

David was the name of his beloved younger brother who had died in the Crimea. Marc remembered his mother telling him that when a Jew dies and remains without a namesake, his soul cannot rest. He had dismissed the idea as superstition born of shtetl ignorance, and yet there were nights when his sleep was haunted by memories of his brother. In that nocturnal restlessness, he heard again his mother's whispered words. *A premonition perhaps*, he thought as he looked at Virginia, so certain that her child would be a son, so committed to calling him David. He smiled. How could he deny his brother the possibility of serenity in the hereafter?

"David." He repeated the name aloud and placed his hand on the swell of Virginia's abdomen. He thought of a painting he had completed years earlier in which an infant lay curled within the exposed womb of a reclining woman. It occurred to him that he had, presciently, painted his own future.

"All right," he said at last. "We will have a son named David. Dovidl, my mother called my brother. I was in the room when he was born. I heard his first cry. My mother's face was shining. Will your face be shining when you give birth to our son, Virginitchka?"

"I think it is shining now." She pressed her lips to his mouth, his cheeks, his eyes.

They were reconciled and determined to forge a new beginning. Marc wanted to give up the Riverside Drive apartment. It was redolent with memories of Bella and too large for his diminished family. Michel had already left for France and Ida would also soon be working in Paris on his retrospective exhibition. He yearned for the peace of the countryside, a respite from the tumultuous streets of New York, and Virginia longed for a landscape similar to the gentle hills and green meadows of her Dorset girlhood. She found it in the Catskill region and in the village of High Falls where she discovered a small wooden house nestled beneath a beautiful catalpa tree. The front window looked out on a wild valley and the view from the kitchen was of an outcropping of rocks and a shallow ravine canopied by graceful willows.

"It's perfect," she exulted to Marc.

He agreed. He immediately laid claim to a rustic, much neglected cottage on the edge of the property. The walls could be knocked down and large windows installed.

"It's like an *isba*, my Russian studio," he enthused. "I will work there."

He met with the estate agent and arranged to buy the house that very day. The acquisition of a new house always energized him. Overjoyed, brimming with plans, he told Ida of the purchase as soon as they returned to New York. He had not anticipated the ferocity of her rage.

"You should have consulted me before making such a decision. You entered into a contract never thinking of the consequences, as you did when you bought the Gordes house," she said. She had not forgotten the purchase that had wiped out their savings and left them dependent on others for their visas and passage to New York.

"I do not need your approval. You do not control my life," he retorted.

"But I still manage your affairs," she reminded him. "Who makes deposits in the bank? Who pays the bills? Do you even know how much money you have or how much you will need to renovate this house? Of course, such mundane matters do not concern you."

"You will like the house, Ida," Virginia said softly.

Their confrontations frightened Virginia, but she had learned how to defuse the tension. She and Ida were uneasily balanced on the dangerous seesaw of Marc's affections.

And Ida did like the house. She saw at once how it might be improved. Always authoritative, she contracted with carpenters, plumbers, and painters. She strode across the property, wearing slacks and a white men's shirt, her bright hair tucked beneath a workman's cap, holding a clipboard, twirling a pencil. She was in her element, in charge of a project, issuing directives, organizing a schedule. The local contractors laughed at her accent, spoke to each other of her beauty, agreed to the reductions in estimates she demanded, and accepted the deadlines she set.

Virginia gratefully conceded control to her. She understood that Marc and Ida were forever bound to each other even as Bella lived on in his mind and heart and in his work, materializing still on his canvases. In a new painting he called *Lovers on a Bridge*, two figures stood together. One was clearly Marc himself, embraced by a dark-haired, dark-eyed Bella as he worked on a portrait of Virginia, who stood apart, the third lover, excluded from their closeness.

Virginia recognized the fierce ambition that consumed Ida and Marc. It was born, she thought forgivingly, of the deprivation and uncertainty they had endured for so many years in so many countries.

The gala Museum of Modern Art opening was attended by curators, artists, and writers, millionaire collectors and celebrities who anticipated becoming collectors. They flocked to East Fifty-Third Street to view the works of the artist whose life and work was vested with legendary drama. He was a hero who had not only eluded the Nazis, but had also triumphed over them by painting the Jewish world they had thought to destroy.

Marc made a triumphant entrance with Ida on his arm. It was thought best that Virginia not attend. The presence of his pregnant mistress would expose him to malicious gossip, and he was in search of respectability.

Expert costumiers, father and daughter had dressed for the cultural stage on which they would perform that evening. Ida was radiant in a gown of russet taffeta, the exact color of her hair, which she had sculpted into a coronet of braids, interwoven with narrow ribbons of gold. Marc wore a forest-green velvet jacket and the high-necked white shirt of a Russian troubadour. Virginia had combed his hair, taming the wild gray curls into smoother tufts that framed his elfin face. Their entrance was noted, their names whispered reverently.

"*Brilliant Marc Chagall.*" "*Beautiful Ida Chagall.*"

Ida radiated happiness. She smiled and answered questions. She spoke now in French, now in Russian, now in German, granting the editor of *Art News* a brief interview in her charmingly accented English. Marc circled the room, staring at his own paintings as though seeing them for the first time. Many of them were works painted in Russia and during his early years in Paris when he was very young. He paused in front of a portrait titled *Pregnant Woman*. Fela Cendrars, he remembered, the wife of a friend, had posed for it.

He wondered sadly why he had never painted Bella when she was pregnant with Ida. He would not paint Virginia either, he decided. It would be bad luck.

Virginia went to the retrospective alone some days later. She too studied the portrait of Fela Cendrars as she stroked the gentle rise of her pregnancy.

"Your father is a genius, David," she whispered to her unborn child.

The exhibition received extravagant reviews, and then, as Ida had arranged, it moved on to the Art Institute of Chicago, where crowds lined South Michigan Avenue, waiting to be admitted to the gallery. Ida engaged in intricate negotiations with the Institute for the sale of *The White Crucifixion* and emerged triumphant. She had arranged for a price that far exceeded her own expectations.

Flushed with success, she returned to New York. She showed the contract to Marc and playfully fanned his face with the check.

"We are rich," she exclaimed. "No more worries about money. Finally, finally."

She was liberated from the role of the supplicant. Never again would she have to write letters pleading for help; never again would she or her father be in need.

"Yes. We are rich. Finally," he echoed in delight.

He kissed her on both cheeks and danced her around the room in a rollicking musicless polka, their humming voices punctuated with laughter, step matching step. Virginia watched them in wonderment. Marc never danced with her as he danced with Ida. Their music was alien to her. Sighing, she rose from her seat and filled their glasses with the vodka she detested but that they downed with ease and pleasure.

They clinked the glasses.

"*L'chaim*," Marc said. "To life."

"To our good fortune," Ida added.

Within the week, Ida prepared to leave for France. Marc's success in New York and Chicago guaranteed a retrospective at the Musée d'Art Moderne in Paris. She would lobby for it. She would arrange it.

On her last day in New York, she wandered through the Riverside Drive apartment and recalled all that had occurred during their time there. She felt her mother's presence, Michel's tenderness. She lingered in her father's studio, inhaled the scent of linseed oil and turpentine, and studied the finished canvases and the works still in progress, some turned to the wall, some facing her. As always, Marc was involved in many projects, his working days divided between High Falls and New York. She glanced at his sketches of Virginia, his skillful charcoal drawings of her long, melancholy face, her high aristocratic cheekbones.

She realized that although she still missed her mother desperately, she was grateful for Virginia's presence in her father's life. It absolved her of responsibility and worry. She was grateful too that she would not be in America when Virginia's child was born. She did not want to witness the beginning of her father's second family.

She stood in the doorway of the bedroom that she and Michel had intermittently shared, sleeping beneath the painting of *The Bridal Chair*. She remembered how the light from the window had fallen across his avian face and how she had watched him as he slept. There had been other times when she had awakened to find his eyes upon her. They had been compassionate bedfellows, *amis* in the end, rather than the *amoureux* they had been in the beginning.

But then, of course, she told herself, to all things there are beginnings and endings, seasons for all of life. She sighed and removed the painting from the wall. It would have to be carefully crated for its return journey to Paris. Her smile was bittersweet. Her marriage was over, but her father's wedding gift endured.

"*Adieu,*" she whispered to the silent rooms. "*Adieu,*" she repeated silently to herself.

Her life in New York had ended. She would carry her memories home, home to Paris, to a new beginning. She slammed the door behind her, hugged the heavy painting, and hurried away.

Chapter Thirty-Three

That transatlantic crossing was the first vacation of Ida's life. Alone in her stateroom, she gazed for hours through the porthole at the endless ocean.

She walked the promenade deck each morning, her bright hair tied back with a gossamer, rainbow-colored scarf, the salt-tinged wind ruddying her face. Afterward, she sat on a deck chair, a plaid woolen blanket draped over her knees, and reviewed the correspondence from the curator of the Musée d'Art Moderne and Pierre Matisse's memo listing his own preferences.

"Perhaps *Homage to Apollinaire*, perhaps *Praying Jew*. But, of course, the decision rests with you," Pierre had written. His words, Ida realized, were a testimony to her knowledge and her ability to gauge the mood of the complex and competitive art world. Even Marc had grudgingly granted her a new respect for her acumen. He acknowledged, however reluctantly, that she was as insightful a critic of his work as Bella had been and a much shrewder manager. Virginia McNeil was carrying his child, but Ida knew that her role in her father's life was secure.

Seated at the captain's table, wearing one or another of her stylish new gem-colored gowns, she was known only as Mademoiselle Ida, a gay and intriguing young woman who told amusing stories about the art worlds of New York and Paris. All conversations with other passengers were casual. There was talk of the new Broadway musicals, amiable arguments about whether *Brigadoon* was superior to *Annie Get Your Gun*. The postwar world was intent on replacing the sad songs and dark tragedies of the war years with the lighthearted music and gentle stories of the new peace. An enduring peace. They assured themselves that the new United Nations would solve all future international conflicts. They had entered an age of reason.

She slept easily, dreamlessly, throughout the voyage, cradled in the gently rocking womb of the huge ship, her porthole open so that the ocean breeze brushed her face. But on the last night at sea, she was lost in a dream in which she walked slowly down a lavender-scented path, ribboned with vividly colored flowers that bent their heads toward her in friendly greeting. She paused beside a rose bush heavy with full-petaled white blossoms that matched those of the bouquet that rested on the bridal chair in her father's painting. A single flower fluttered to the ground, and she plucked it up and held it to her face, inhaling its rich fragrance. Smiling, she felt herself soar, not in flight, but in rapture. She was still smiling when the ship's strident horn invaded her reverie and thrust her into sudden wakefulness.

Disoriented, she looked around her stateroom, glancing in puzzlement at the steamer trunk and mystified by the crate that contained *The Bridal Chair* in place against the wall of her oak-paneled stateroom. She lifted her eyes to the porthole and saw a low-flying gull winging its way daringly across the upper deck.

Her confusion lifted. She realized at once where she was and how very close she was to her beloved France.

She sprang up and, still barefoot, she stared out at the brightness of the new dawn, her heart pounding with excitement. The ship was approaching the shore, sailing smoothly through French waters. They would reach Le Havre before noon. Soon, very soon, she would be in Paris, walking down the boulevards of her girlhood and through the gardens of her dreams.

———

It was late evening when she reached her small *pensione* in the Montmartre section of Paris. Overcome with exhaustion, she went to bed at once, leaving her window open to the scent of the early lilacs in the small garden. It was the aroma of her childhood, of the bouquets her mother carried home so tenderly throughout the early days of spring.

"I am in Paris," she thought sleepily. "I am home."

She did not draw the curtains and awakened the next morning to a room bathed in brilliant sunlight. She dressed quickly, eager to walk down the streets she knew so well. Her mother had once said that those who loved the City of Light had its scenes and scents engraved upon their memories. Bella had been right. Ida instinctively made the correct turns and walked down the boulevards she had once known so well, veering now and again into the charming side streets in search of a shop where she had bought fabric, a florist she had favored, the art supply store where she had purchased her own pastel chalks and her father's sable brushes. Some were still there; others had been destroyed in the war.

The carcasses of rusting tanks marred the beauty of the flowering chestnut trees that lined the curbs and the wisteria studded with shy blue blossoms. The facades of elegant buildings were pockmarked by bullets. Graceful balconies had been shattered and splintered. The war had left her beloved city wounded and hollow, its beauty strangely lifeless.

She stepped aside as a group of schoolchildren, their book bags strapped to their backs, hurried past her. They were pale and thin, their uniforms faded. She noticed a boy limping by, wearing unmatched shoes, one brown, one black. Two small sisters held hands and carefully crossed the broad street with their shaven heads lowered. Dispirited, she wandered aimlessly, her early exhilaration now a darkening melancholy.

On the rue des Grands Augustins, she entered a small café and realized that she had, serendipitously, stepped into her own past. She recognized the small smoke-filled Le Catalan, which she had often visited with her father, perhaps because it was the favored haunt of Picasso, the painter Marc both envied and admired.

She stared at the tattered posters tacked to the dingy walls, the same posters that had intrigued her as a child. Toulouse-Lautrec's dancers of the Folies Bergère, Daumier's bonneted women, Gauguin's naked South Sea beauties looked down at her, artifacts of a vanished world, another Paris.

She sat down at a small rectangular table at the rear of the café, ordered a coffee and a croissant, and looked across the room, stunned to see Picasso seated at his usual table with a very young woman whom Ida did not recognize.

The Spanish artist had not changed. His oversized bald head sat on a neck whose tendons were stretched to a dangerous tautness; his body was squat but muscular, the features of his weathered, bronzed face boldly sculpted. His lips were full and sensual, the nose bulbous and prominent.

Ida thought to cross the room and greet him but hesitated. He might not recognize her. She had been a young girl when he last saw her, a shy adolescent who moved obediently in her father's shadow. And unlike Henri Matisse who had treated her to éclairs and sketched her, Picasso had ignored her. It was rumored that while women intrigued him, children bored him.

She was startled when he strode over to her table.

"It is Mademoiselle Chagall, is it not?" he said, taking both her hands in his own. "Welcome to Paris. Are you in the vanguard of our returning expatriate colleagues?" His gimlet-bright eyes studied her face, her figure. He kissed both her cheeks. "You are what I always knew you would become," he said. "A beautiful woman."

"*Merci, Maître,*" she said and smiled, relieved to have her anonymity shattered, to be remembered and even admired on her first day in Paris.

He invited her to his table and introduced her to his companion.

"*Ma amie, ma belle amie,*" he said proudly. "Françoise Gilot."

Ida smiled at the beautiful, large-eyed young woman who nodded indifferently. It occurred to her that she and Françoise Gilot were of an age and she wondered why that should surprise her. Virginia McNeil, her father's mistress, was also her contemporary, and she herself had had an affair with Itzik Feffer, a man as old as her father. Perhaps, like King David and the Shulamite woman, aging artists needed young women to warm their chilled and weakened bodies. She smiled at the absurdity of her own thought. There was nothing chilled or weakened about either Pablo Picasso or Marc Chagall or, for that matter, Itzik Feffer.

They sat in the dimly lit café drinking bitter coffee and shredding dry croissants into crumbs. Picasso spoke softly and sadly of the years of war and darkness. He had remained in occupied Paris, cursing Pétain and the Nazis and painting works so dark that he himself was frightened by their ominous imagery.

"But that is how an artist protests," he said. "Our brushes, our palettes, and our canvases are our weapons. I painted my sadness, my despair. Your father would understand."

Ida nodded in agreement. Pablo Picasso had his *Guernica* and Marc Chagall had his suffering Jews, his tortured Christ wrapped in a tattered prayer shawl.

"Yes," she agreed. "He would understand."

There were others, he told her, who had submitted to the Nazi regime, artists and intellectuals who had collaborated with the Vichy government. His face was dark with fury. He spoke of the museums and galleries that the Nazis had looted, of the works of art that were publicly destroyed outside the Jeu de Paume.

"My paintings and those of Miró and Max Ernst and yes, one or more Chagalls," he said. "Your father was fortunate to have escaped to America," he added. "I hope he and your mother are well."

"My mother is dead." Ida's voice was barely audible.

Picasso sighed. "She was a beautiful woman, Bella Chagall," he said. "Your father must be devastated."

"Devastated," she agreed. "He plans to return to Paris very soon," she added and fell silent. She would not tell Picasso about the retrospective planned for the Musée d'Art Moderne. Artists were fiercely competitive, and Picasso might campaign for an exhibition of his own. She was once again navigating the tempestuous waters of the Paris art world, wary of betrayal and sabotage.

She rose to leave. Picasso again kissed her on both her cheeks.

Françoise Gilot smiled coldly. Ida hurried down the rue des Grand Augustins, propelled by new urgency, an acute awareness of all that she had to do, of all the people she had to see. Her meeting with Picasso had intimated all that had transpired in her absence and all that she would have to learn. Her work in Paris was at a beginning.

She was in a frenzy of activity. She found a pleasant apartment on the north side of place Saint-Germain and hung *The Bridal Chair* above her bed. The painting was her anchor, the constant sentinel of her slumber. She smiled at the whimsical thought that her dream persona might one night float upward and, seated in that white-shrouded chair, lay claim to the bridal bouquet that rested there.

She placed her easel in front of the large front window, situating it at an angle as her father had taught her so that it caught the earliest light of the morning and the last rays of a lingering sunset, the hours she might scavenge for her own painting.

She began an earnest search for Marc's engravings, illustrating Gogol's *Dead Souls* and La Fontaine's *Fables*, which had vanished, as had so many works of art during the years of the war. Marc had resigned himself to their loss, but Ida remained tenacious, following clue after clue until she discovered them in the hands of the heirs to the estate of Ambroise Vollard, Marc's representative. She reclaimed them and was stunned by the enormity of their valuation. Offers were made for their purchase, but she decided against making a sale until she consulted with Marc. She wrote him tantalizing letters, naming the sums at stake, urging him to come to Paris. His presence at the retrospective was important. Collectors would flock to the Musée, eager to meet the artist, and the fees for his work would skyrocket.

"Your friends are eager to see you. You will be the prince of Paris," she added, aware that such an inducement would weigh heavily. It would confirm his image of himself as the reigning royal in the kingdom of art. "And of course, your presence will impact the prices we can ask for your work." Marc might claim an indifference to material things, but she knew that money was always a magnet for him. "Virginia, who is so capable, will manage without you," she added.

Still, his responses remained cautious. Excuses mounted. It would be too sad to be in Paris without Bella. He was working well, his time divided between New York and High Falls. Virginia took wonderful care of him. But of course, he missed Ida, missed his old friends.

"Have you told them about Virginia and that I am to become a father again?" he asked.

He was, Ida knew, still a son of Vitebsk, overly concerned with the approval of others.

It did not surprise her that he asked nothing about her own life, nor did he ask about Isaac Rosenfeld, Bella's brother, and his family, who had survived the war. With Bella's death, her extended family no longer existed for Marc Chagall. It was ironic, Ida thought, that her father mourned the Jewish people as an abstract entity, but individual Jews did not engage his sympathies. That recognition pained her, but then so many things about her father pained her.

"His genius does not excuse everything," Michel had once said. His bitter words lingered in memory.

"I will not be like him," she promised herself.

She met with Tériade, the distinguished Greek publisher, and was immediately enchanted by him. Over smoky glasses of Pernod at Les Deux Magots, they discussed the Gogol and La Fontaine engravings and the substantial sum his publishing house was prepared to offer for exclusive rights to their publication in a limited edition volume. Their conversation drifted to revelations about their own lives, his troubled marriage, her sad divorce, their shared loneliness. They left the café at an hour when the boulevard Saint-Michel was bathed in the gentle pastel hues of sunset. Young men holding wilting bouquets of flowers walked by them. Girls glanced at themselves in plate glass windows and smiled at their reflections. Couples, young and old, arms entwined, fingers interlaced, bottles of wine and baguettes tucked into dangling cloth bags, hurried through the gentle twilight toward lamp-lit rooms soon to be curtained in welcome darkness. The dark war years were over; the season of light and hope had arrived.

They walked slowly. At the rue des Saints-Pères, he took her hand. At the place Saint-Germain, they entered her apartment building together and, in her dimly lit flat, still in silence, she melted into his arms. They offered each other the tenderness of tone and touch, an end to the painful solitude of the soft spring evening.

Late in the night, he looked up at the painting of *The Bridal Chair*. "Your father's work," he said. "I have never before slept beneath the work of a master."

"And have you ever before slept with the daughter of a master?" she asked teasingly.

His answer was irrelevant. She knew that their relationship would be an interlude, a prequel to her new world, her new independence.

"This Tériade is an exciting man," she wrote to Elsa in New York. "We have much in common. He is an honest critic of my drawings and paintings, but I know that I am not the only woman in his life, nor is he the only man in mine. It is a refreshing change for me, *n'est-ce pas*? And you must not worry, I am being careful," she assured her friend, slyly repeating the monitory advice that Elsa had offered her again and again through the years.

And she was being careful, careful to control her feelings, to avoid being swept into an emotional maelstrom. She was a latecomer to the transient world of teasing flirtations and love affairs, but she learned the rules quickly. Tériade, without resentment, understood that he occupied only a defined place in her bifurcated life.

One afternoon, as she lunched with a curator of the Musée d'Art Moderne in the dining room of the Hôtel Plaza Athénée, she glanced across the room and saw a couple seated at a red velvet banquette. The diminutive man, his thinning sandy hair combed skillfully to cover his incipient baldness, wore the newly fashionable morning coat with a diamond stick pin glittering in his striped silk cravat. The woman seemed more mannequin than human, her fine-boned face powdered and rouged, her dark hair swept upward into a waxen sculpture, her pale gray dress clinging to her very slender body. A triple strand of pearls shimmered at her neck, and nacreous droplets dangled from her ears and braceleted her wrists. She smoked a cigarette through a lacquer holder. The couple did not speak to each other. They did not lift their eyes to the waiters who served them and hovered nearby. A cairn terrier crouched at their feet.

The curator followed her gaze.

"They look familiar," Ida said apologetically, aware that she had been staring.

"Of course they look familiar. You have seen their pictures often enough in the newspapers. They are the Duke and Duchess of Windsor, once welcome guests of Herr Hitler himself." His lip curled in contempt.

Ida remembered how she had watched them dance at the Silver Jubilee cotillion in London. How young and naive she had been to sympathize with them then.

She turned away and did not look up as they left, walking with robotic stiffness, their small dog trailing after them, its leather collar studded with jewels.

She was glad that she was to be at Le Bar Vert on the rue Jacob in Saint-Germain that evening where the sybaritic Duke and Duchess of Windsor would not be welcome. Not that they would want to be among the poets, artists, and students of postwar Paris who gathered there to drink cheap wine and munch on stale sandwiches.

The young women of Saint-Germain wore black, high-necked, body-hugging tops and short skirts; their hair was long and fringed their foreheads, and their legs were bare. Ida ignored the requisite uniform of *la vie bohème*. She was her mother's daughter, a lover of color and costume. Radiant in her royal blue dress, her luxuriant bright hair capping her shoulders, she was pleasantly aware that men turned to look at her as she entered. She slid into a seat at a narrow triangular table scarred with cigarette burns and littered with the cheap overflowing ashtrays that advertised Byrrh and Dubonnet.

"I'll have an absinthe," she told the waiter.

"So that remains your favorite drink."

Michel stood beside her table, holding the hand of a slender young woman.

"Oh Michel. How wonderful to see you." She stood, flushed with pleasure, overwhelmed with affection.

He introduced her to his companion.

"Marina," he said, and she noted the softness in his eyes when he spoke the name. Once he had spoken her name in that same loving tone. She was happy for him even as she was brushed by a wisp of regret.

They exchanged news of each other's families. Ida had written to the Rapaports and she assured Michel that she intended to visit them as soon as she could to thank them for all that they had done. He, in turn, asked about Marc and Virginia. They were sincere in their concern, bonded as they were by the tempestuous times they had shared.

Eventually there was nothing left to say. They wished each other well and Ida watched as they crossed the room and joined a group of young people. She saw how Michel smiled with ease, spoke with confidence, how his friends deferred to him. How they had changed, she and the youth she had married. History had mischievously tricked them both. She sipped her absinthe, a drink that always soothed her.

It did not surprise her when Marc wrote that he would leave New York at the end of May when Virginia entered the last trimester of her pregnancy. "Virginia encourages me to leave," he wrote to Ida. It was a claim she neither believed nor disputed. He was a master of self-deception. He had escaped Ida's birth in Petrograd and he would escape the birth of his second child in France. Childbirth had always frightened him.

He arrived in early June, almost five years to the day that he and Bella had fled their Paris home. Greeting him at Le Havre, Ida saw with surprise that he seemed to have grown younger during her brief absence. He was infused with a new strength. His elfin face was radiant, his blue eyes sapphire-bright. He had survived exile and loss and was the rejuvenated lover of a very young woman, awaiting the birth of his child. His creative life had exploded, his horizons expanded. He was intent on experimenting in new and demanding genres, his sights fixed on murals, on triptychs, on stained glass windows. His return to France, to Paris, was a validation of both his suffering and his success. He had left, stripped of his French citizenship, and he returned as a celebrated artist, a favorite son of the City of Light.

"We are home, Idotchka," he said excitedly. "You and I will be together again in our beautiful Paris."

"You will find the city much changed, *Papochka*," she warned him.

"Nothing can change my feelings for Paris or my love for her," he protested.

Still, he was shocked by the devastation he found, shocked by the Nazi desecration of the city's beauty, the buildings destroyed, the gardens uprooted, the fallen trees and the shattered windows. Graffiti had been scraped away, the streets somewhat cleared of the detritus of war, but a necrotic aridity remained. He mourned for all that had been lost, but within days, Paris seduced him yet again.

He and Ida walked together through the Bois de Boulogne, both of them thinking of Bella, who had so often hurried across the green, her arms laden with flowers, her face lifted to the sun that stole its way in ribbons of light through the flowering chestnut trees. She would forever be their ghostly companion although they dared not speak of her. They stood before the Trocadéro building, their last address in Paris, and stared up at the windows of the flat that had once been their home. They imagined Bella's gamine face pressed to the pane, her graceful hands beckoning them to climb the long stairway and join her in the flower-filled salon.

"We were happy once, weren't we, Idotchka?" Marc asked.

She did not reply. The past, with all its sadness, with its brief moments of joy, was done with. It was the present that claimed her. She willed herself to a sustaining optimism. She turned away from the window and took her father's arm. They walked on in a complicit silence.

They visited the once-elegant Hôtel Lutetia, commandeered by the Germans during the Occupation and now a center for returning refugees in search of vanished friends and relatives. The grimy walls were papered with notes written in faltering hands. Tattered lists of names, addresses, and phone numbers fluttered in the weak breeze of the ceiling fan. They studied the notes and names in silence.

Greta Weissman seeks her sons Chaim and Moshe, now eight and ten. They both wear glasses. Last seen in Block 44 Auschwitz.

Yakov Altman searches for his wife Chana, last seen in the Lodz ghetto 1943.

Ida imagined two small bespectacled boys reading that note and hugging each other joyfully. They would find their mother. They would have a home. The image broke her heart. She knew that their glasses had been shattered years ago and that Greta Weissman would seek her small myopic sons in vain all the days of her life, just as Yakov Altman would forever search for his Chana. She turned to her father and saw that he was crying.

"Did you find the name of someone you knew?" she asked.

He shook his head. "No. But, Ida, our own names might have been on one of these lists. Marc Chagall searches for his daughter Ida. Ida Chagall seeks her father, Marc. Bella Chagall…" His voice broke as he finally recognized the reality of how close they had been to death.

"But that did not happen. We were spared." Her voice grew louder. "We are safe."

She put her arm through his, and like invalids supporting each other, they left the Lutetia, weaving their way through the sad-eyed men and women who continued to stare so wistfully, so hopefully, at the names and notes. Together they crossed the boulevard Raspail. The light was fading; it was the hour Parisians called *l'heure bleue*. They entered a small bistro and ordered anisette.

"*L'chaim*," Marc said and touched her glass with his.

"To life," she repeated.

The toast was a celebration of their survival. They were alive and in Paris, the taste of licorice tingling pleasantly upon their tongues.

Chapter Thirty-Four

heir nostalgic wanderings ended. Marc settled into the apartment Ida had rented for him on the avenue d'Iéna and they addressed the business at hand.

Arrangements with Tériade for the publication of the engravings were successfully concluded. It did not surprise Ida that when the final contract was signed, he abruptly left for Athens, sending her an apologetic note, citing the urgency of business, family problems.

Like all the intimacies of her life—her marriage to Michel, her affair with Itzik Feffer—their brief relationship was episodic. *Perhaps*, she thought cynically, *Marc was right*. It was only art that endured. Lives and loves were sadly impermanent. Immediately, she rejected the thought. An enduring love would come to her. She was young; her heart was open. She had only to wait, and she was accustomed to waiting.

Marc was caught up in a whirlwind of invitations. He had dinner with Henri Matisse, lunch with Picasso, and began a project with his old friend, the poet Paul Éluard. They were partners in sorrow. Marc had lost his Bella and Éluard his own longtime lover, the beautiful Nusch. Marc committed to illustrating Paul's poems.

"We will call it *Le dur désir de durer, The Lasting Wish to Last*," Marc told Ida.

"A wonderful title," she agreed. She too had a lasting wish to last. But that thought fluttered away, replaced by speculation as to how such a volume could be marketed. She discussed her ideas with Marc. He smiled.

"Ah, my Idotchka," he said. "You have an artist's heart and a businesswoman's head."

At the end of June, a cable arrived informing them that Virginia had delivered a healthy baby boy on the Jewish Sabbath.

Marc was jubilant. His hair tousled, his face aglow, he gripped Ida's wrists and spun her around the room.

"I have a son!" he shouted in Yiddish, in Russian, and in French. "A son named David."

"And a daughter named Ida," she murmured, but he did not hear her.

"A namesake for my brother." He swayed as though in prayer.

And I have a brother, Ida thought. *How absurd. I am thirty years old and sister to a newborn baby.* She struggled against a wild laughter, and subdued an invasive thought. *If Virginia is not my father's wife, is this baby actually my brother?* But it was a legal conundrum of no importance, she decided. The infant David was her father's son, blood of her blood, bone of her bone. That was sufficient.

Letters arrived, fat envelopes crammed with Virginia's exuberant descriptions of the baby, declarations of her love for Marc and the family they would build together, snapshots of the child, her own drawings. Marc tossed them carelessly onto his desk and Ida plucked them up and read them although they were not intended for her eyes. She was merely being vigilant, she assured herself. She wanted to protect her father. She wanted to understand Virginia better. Ida admired her strength, her ability to resist Marc when he demanded that she terminate her pregnancy. She had the cleverness of a survivor. Did she realize, Ida wondered, that David's birth gave her new and significant power? As the mother of Marc's son, she could demand marriage; she could demand money, their hard-earned wealth.

She shivered, chilled by her own cynical speculations, and stared down at the photograph of Virginia holding the infant. A fuzz of dark hair fringed David's head, which seemed too large for his very thin body; his narrow eyes were barely open. Virginia, seated on the shaded porch of the High Falls house, studying his upturned face tenderly, resembled a contented Madonna. But how contented could she be, Ida wondered. Virginia was a new mother, but her child's father had been absent at his birth. Was she still chained to an unhappy marriage? No legal provision had been made for her or for her baby. And yet her expression was radiant, and in her letter, she pledged her affection for Marc and for their son.

Virginia was an emotional chameleon, Ida decided, and chameleons were notoriously unpredictable. She wondered if they were dangerous as well. Did they bite? Were they perhaps poisonous? She smiled bitterly and arranged for the snapshot of Virginia and David to be placed in a frame of red Moroccan leather that she put on Marc's bedside table as an apology of a sort for the unkindness of her thought.

The glass that covered the photograph was soon oily with Marc's fingerprints as he lifted it and set it down then lifted it once more, brushing it with his lips.

"Does my David look Jewish?" he asked Ida one evening as he studied the photo.

"He is a baby," Ida replied drily. "He looks like a baby."

"But his hair is dark. Like Bella's hair." He passed his paint-encrusted finger across the photograph.

"He has nothing to do with Bella. Virginia is his mother." Irritation rimmed her voice.

"This child has everything to do with my Bella," he insisted, his voice rising in protest. "Bella sent Virginia to me."

"No," she retorted angrily. "It was I who brought Virginia to you, to darn your socks, to be our housekeeper."

Joseph Opatoshu sent the news that David had been circumcised eight days after his birth, in accordance with Jewish tradition.

"Your son has been entered into the covenant," the Yiddish writer wrote his friend, and Marc smiled proudly as he showed the letter to Ida.

"My son is now Jewish," he said proudly.

Ida told her uncle Isaac that the infant David had been circumcised and her father now claimed that he was Jewish. Bella's orthodox brother murmured his protest.

"The child is not Jewish," he said. "The absence of a foreskin does not make a child Jewish. He was born to a non-Jewish woman, and unless he is taken to the *mikveh*, the ritual bath, he has not been entered into the covenant."

He sighed and turned the brittle pages of a Talmudic text, his gnarled finger tracing its way down the column, searching out a text for corroboration.

"It is as I thought," he said at last. "This child cannot be considered to be Jewish. Marc Chagall can create worlds in his paintings. He can make fiddlers dance on rooftops and cows fly, but he cannot rewrite Jewish law. Tell him that his son is not yet a Jewish child."

"I will," she promised, but she knew she would say nothing. Her father lived by his own law. He had willed the son born to Virginia Haggard McNeil to be Jewish and that was how he would think of him, the rabbis be damned.

Virginia urged Marc to return to New York. "You missed David's first smile. You are losing precious moments," she wrote.

Marc apologized. He responded that he longed to see Virginia, longed to meet their son, but he had to remain in Paris until he completed a series of pastel sketches that reflected the postwar mood of the city. And of course there were still preparations for the retrospective. But his thoughts were never far from her. He described his new painting of a mother and an infant guarded by an artist holding his palette.

"It is my pledge of protection. I will always take care of you and our son," he promised.

Ida occasionally added an affectionate note to his letters, and finally, in August, it was she, their various projects completed, who booked the ticket for his return to America.

"Virginia needs you," she said as she packed his bags.

She felt a guilty relief at his departure. His presence overwhelmed. His demands were endless.

"It was draining to be with him constantly," she wrote ruefully to Elsa. "He left me no time to think of myself, of what I want."

She was aware of the disloyalty of her own words, but Elsa would understand. Her friend was, as always, a safe confidante.

And what, in fact, do I want? Ida wondered as she posted the letter. The time had come, she knew, to confront that question.

Chapter Thirty-Five

*I*da began a search for answers. Concentrating on her own work, spending long hours at the studio and in front of her own easel, she was intent on an honest exploration of the parameters of her own talent. She explored the city, keenly aware that it was permeated by a new volatility. She darted out of Le Bar Vert one evening when communists and Gaullists came to blows, knocking over fragile tables and dueling with wicker bar stools.

On another evening, as she sat with Picasso and his acolytes in Le Catalan, she listened to a variety of rumors. It was variously reported that the Soviet Union was planning to invade Paris, that communist cells planned a new regime, that the Duke and Duchess of Windsor were weighing their options and perhaps planning to leave France and return to Bermuda.

"Who cares what those parasites do?" Picasso asked. He smiled slyly at Ida. "Perhaps your father was wise to retreat once more to America. It is said that your people can sense danger and know how to avoid it. Is that not so?"

Ida stared him down. "Indeed, if our sense of danger is so acute, how is it that six million of our people were killed?" she snapped, pushing her chair back and stalking away from his table. She sailed across the room, her head held high, regal in her fury, and took a seat at the far end of the smoke-filled room. Admiring glances followed her. It was agreed that Chagall's daughter was brave as well as beautiful. It took courage to defy Pablo Picasso.

She looked up in annoyance as a fair-haired young man slid into the seat opposite her. She did not know his name, but she had seen him more than once in cafés and at the galleries she frequented, his sketchbook in hand, studying the paintings with the critical eye of an artist.

"May I join you, mademoiselle?" he asked. His voice was soft, his French oddly accented.

"It seems that you already have," she answered coldly.

"I presume," he acknowledged. "But I thought you might welcome a sympathetic companion. My name is Géa Augsbourg, and I promise not to discuss politics or the Duke and Duchess of Windsor. You see, I am Swiss and we are notoriously apolitical."

"It was very wise of you to be born in a neutral nation," she said teasingly.

"Indeed." He smiled. "After all, decades of peace have resulted in my country's perfecting the cuckoo clock."

His smile was contagious and irresistible to Ida. She marveled at his tone, so light and untroubled, and how his long body coiled gracefully into the narrow, wrought iron chair. Perhaps it was because he was the citizen of a country that had never known the ravages of war that lightness and grace came so easily to him.

They spoke easily as they sipped their drinks and nibbled at bits of cheese. He was a painter, but he was interested in ceramics and had visited Picasso's workshop in Vallauris. Like Ida, he loved the city and spent hours wandering its streets and boulevards.

"Paris is wonderful," he said. "Although I must confess that it is really the onion soup that keeps me here."

He grinned and she smiled. They left Le Catalan together, had dinner at a small bistro, and decided to go to a film.

"An American comedy," he insisted. "I want to laugh."

She nodded. She too wanted to laugh, inspired by his optimistic presence. Perhaps there would soon be gaiety. Hope was reawakened. The Soviet Union would not invade France. The fruit and vegetable bins in the Paris markets overflowed with newly harvested produce. Children wore new shoes. The privations of wartime were receding.

They smiled over dinner, laughed companionably at the cinema, wandered through Les Halles in search of a stall that Géa claimed offered the very best onion soup in all of Paris, and then walked back to Saint-Germain hand in hand through the lilac-scented darkness. They made no declarations but slipped easily into a new and relaxed togetherness.

The months passed swiftly. Ida worked on the retrospective and painted during the long, golden summer afternoons. Géa studied her work and suggested that she work principally with pastel chalk and watercolors, that she use thinner brushes because her touch was so light. He ordered a set of such brushes from Zurich and left them with a rose on her bed. He set up an easel beside her own and they often painted together. He worked in heavy oils, a vivid impasto of colors, while she experimented with gentler hues.

Mischievously, they undressed one afternoon and painted side by side, both of them naked. Playfully she daubed his shoulders blue. He scowled in mock annoyance and slashed streaks of madder red across her breasts. They showered together and soaped away the paint, his hands gentle, hers insistent. Their skin shimmered, his body pale, hers rose-gold.

She thought it magical to be with a lover who radiated good humor and amusement, who made love to her with exuberance, unburdened by either sadness or obligation. He knew and admired Marc's work, but he was indifferent to the fact that Ida was her father's daughter, the first person she had met who saw her as her own person. He was not a man who thought in terms of opportunity and connections.

Spring drifted into summer and the date of the autumn retrospective approached. It was important that Marc come to Paris for the opening. Ida wrote insistent letters emphasizing that his presence was vital to the success of the exhibition. Patrons and critics, curators and gallery owners eagerly awaited him.

Again he resisted. He was working well in the High Falls studio where Virginia saw to his every need. He did not want to leave his small son. He wanted only to paint.

"Do not pressure me, Idotchka," he pleaded plaintively.

She sighed and responded with cajoling letters, telling him that receptions in his honor were being planned, that interviews were sought by journals and magazines. He would be crowned the cultural king of all of France.

Géa frowned when she read such a letter to him.

"You write to him as though he is a small child to be coaxed with promises of sweets and parties," Géa said. "My mother would write me such letters when I was away at school. 'Study hard and I will buy you a pony. Eat your vegetables and when I visit I will give you a pastry. Go to mass and I will take you on a boat ride.' Mothers write such letters. But, Ida, surely you are not your father's mother?"

He laughed at the absurdity of his own question, but she looked at him gravely and framed her answer carefully.

"Yes. Sometimes I do feel that I play the part of a mother. I care for him, I advise him, I make him feel safe and secure. Is that so wrong, Géa?"

"It is neither wrong nor right. It is simply not what a daughter should be doing."

"But that is what this daughter does. You have not met my father. When you meet him, perhaps you will understand," she replied.

"Perhaps," he said, but the word was laced with doubt.

Marc finally agreed to return to France in the fall. He wrote that he would not abandon High Falls during the beautiful days of summer.

"It is wonderful here. Why do you expel me from such happiness?" he wrote petulantly. "I return to Paris only to please you."

Ida was not deceived. She knew he returned because he had been persuaded by her descriptions of the triumph that awaited him.

"He is coming to reclaim his throne," she told Géa. "I hope that you and he will like each other," she added worriedly.

"And what will happen if we don't?" he asked. "Is what he thinks really so important?"

She did not answer, ashamed to tell him exactly how important it was.

But there was no need to worry. Marc and Géa did like each other. Because Géa was indifferent to fame and recognition, Marc felt no tension, no need to impress. He saw that Géa made Ida happy and it pleased him to hear her laugh, to see the new softness in her eyes. Géa was admiring of Marc's work, and when he visited Géa's studio, he saw, with relief, that while the Swiss artist had talent, he would never achieve greatness.

"You see, *Papochka*," Ida said shrewdly, "Géa will never compete with you."

"Ah, but he already does," Marc said. "I think you love him more than you love your little father."

Ida laughed. "Do you think I could ever love anyone as much as I love you?" she asked. Her tone was light, but the gravity of her words hung heavily between them.

The exhibition succeeded even beyond their expectations. Paris fell in love with the brilliant and dramatic world of Marc Chagall. Crowds flocked to view his works and lines formed in front of the Musée d'Art from early morning until evening closing. The Jewish essence of the paintings, his daring vivid colors, were a redemptive triumph offering hope for a brighter future. Marc Chagall, the Jewish refugee artist, had returned, reclaimed, and celebrated. Such a reception was reparation of a kind to the many Jewish victims of Nazi-occupied Paris.

Ida encountered Picasso one evening as he left the exhibition.

"Your father is the only artist who understands colors," he said and kissed her on both cheeks.

She understood that his words and the touch of his lips constituted an apology. She smiled, her much-practiced brilliant smile, and then carefully wiped her face with her handkerchief when he turned away.

The success of the retrospective resulted in a flurry of new invitations, but Marc was determined to return to New York and Ida did not dissuade him. She knew he would come back to Paris. She bought gifts for Virginia, a crocodile purse, a luxurious cloak of beige velvet, lined with ecru-colored satin.

She showed her purchases to Marc, who frowned.

"You have been too extravagant, Ida," he said reprovingly.

"Not at all. Virginia deserves such gifts. She makes you happy. She has given you our little David," she replied. "And she has had so little luxury in her life."

Her feelings for her father's lover were ambivalent. She both liked Virginia and resented her. She was grateful to her and she distrusted her. The soft-spoken Englishwoman remained an alien presence in their passionate, cacophonous world. Hired to darn Marc's socks, it was his life that she now stitched together. Was Virginia in love with her demanding father, Ida wondered, or was she anchored to him by his terrible neediness and her own? There were no answers.

She was absorbed in arrangements for serial exhibitions. The curators of the Stedelijk in Amsterdam and the Tate in London approached her. There were urgent requests from the Kunsthaus in Zurich and the Kunsthalle in Bern. How honored they would be to host her father's work!

She remembered the desperate, unanswered letters she had sent to some of those same curators during the war years. "The honor they offer is a decade late," she said bitterly to Géa.

"That was then and this is now," he replied calmly. "Forget and forgive."

"I cannot forget and I don't yet have the luxury of forgiveness," she retorted angrily.

He could not understand; she could not expect him to understand. He was at a remove from all that they had endured.

She sent polite replies to London and Amsterdam, to Zurich and Bern, thanking them for their invitations that she would consider carefully. She explained that her father was returning to America, but she herself would soon visit and make arrangements for exhibitions. Hopefully, Marc himself would once again make his home in France and he would be pleased to visit their museums.

She and Géa saw Marc off on his return voyage to America.

"You will return to Paris soon, *Papochka*," she said. "You and

Virginia and David. Paris is the heart of the art world, your world, and you must live and work here. You owe it to your work, your reputation, to make this city your home. Isn't that so, Géa?"

He nodded laconically. "If you say so, Ida. You understand these things better than I do. You have a clever daughter, Marc. A very clever daughter."

Ida laughed, amused by the odd rapport between her father and her lover.

"You both know that I am right," she said. "Promise me that you will make plans to leave High Falls and return to your real home, to Paris, to France."

"Do I have a real home?" he asked. "Time and again, I have painted a man flying through air. It is myself whom I paint, Marc Chagall, a man without roots, without a home, without a place to rest."

"France is your home," she said. She thrust aside the thought that her father had painted her own sky-born dreams. "You have always said that. You have always claimed to be *un artiste français*, a French artist."

The ship's warning siren of departure sounded and she and Marc embraced. Ida felt the wild beat of his heart against her own and saw the mask of sadness darken his elfin face. She watched him walk onto the deck, his slender shoulders stooped, the sea mist pearling his gray curls. She saw him for the first time as an old man, fragile and vulnerable.

Lying beside Géa that night, she dreamed of Marc soaring effortlessly above pastel-colored clouds while she herself tried desperately to wing her way toward him. She awakened only when Géa held her close, his lips against her mouth, silencing the scream that shrilled from her haunted sleep.

Chapter Thirty-Six

A new era dawned for Paris. The city was energized. Damaged buildings were reconstructed; neglected parks were fragrant and verdant with young plantings. Lovers lingered at the repaired balustrades of graceful bridges, and fresh flowers were placed on the outdoor tables of crowded cafés. The art treasures of the Louvre, the Jeu de Paume, and the Musée de l'Orangerie were retrieved from their wartime hiding places and proudly displayed on freshly painted walls.

Géa and Ida visited the museums and galleries. They attended welcoming parties for artists who had fled Paris during the occupation. Ida was embraced by Léger and Ernst, by Zadkine and Breton, all of them overjoyed to find themselves once again in their beloved city.

"When will your father return?" Each returning artist asked Ida the same question.

"Soon, very soon," she assured them.

But Marc continued to delay his return to Paris. He wrote that his work was going well. He described David's second birthday celebration at which he had danced a *chazatska* with the child in his arms. Ida tried to remember if he had ever danced holding her in his arms and immediately chastised herself for her foolish jealousy of the half brother she had yet to meet.

"Fame is no longer important to your father," Virginia wrote in a rare letter.

Ida sighed. Virginia saw herself as a purist and wanted to believe that Marc shared her values. Ida, however, knew that fame and recognition would always be important to her father. He had sent detailed instructions about his exhibition at the Tate and asked how she was planning to publicize it.

"The words of a man who is no longer interested in fame," Ida said wryly to Géa.

What he was not interested in, she knew, was her life. His needs took precedence; her aspirations were forfeit. She struggled against a nagging discontent, an unarticulated desire to break free of his demands.

She traveled to London to curate the exhibition there. The reviews in the English newspapers were enthusiastic and very different from the critiques of his prewar exhibition at the Leicester Gallery. There were repeated references to the Jewish content, to religious symbols, speculation about the Jewish dimension of the crucifixion paintings. Ida realized that the Holocaust had thrust the Jewish people into the consciousness and the conscience of the world. It had exposed the toxicity of anti-Semitism. Marc's work was viewed and discussed with a new honesty.

She sent her father clippings of the London reviews and repeated her insistence that he return to France. Her pleas became commands that would not be denied.

He conceded at last, but not without resentment. He was sad to leave America, deeply grieved that he was abandoning his Bella to her lonely grave, breaking his promise to take her back to Europe.

"You have forced me to leave, Ida. Will my Bella, your *mamochka*, forgive me?" he wrote. The words were blotted as though a tear had smudged the ink.

He impressed upon her that it was a sacrifice, a great sacrifice, to leave his life in rural New York. Interesting people visited the High Falls house. He wrote that Ida might recall the Belgian photographer, Charles Leirens, who had visited them on Riverside Drive. He was now their guest and he thought that it was madness to leave their sylvan paradise for France. However he, Marc Chagall, recognized his obligations to Ida and would, with a heavy heart, make his home once again in France.

"This is what I do for you," he wrote, underlining the words that were more accusatory than benevolent. "It is for you that I uproot myself and my little family and return to the continent that betrayed me."

Ida recognized the falsity of his words. She knew that it was not his concern for her that informed his decision. He knew that Paris was the fulcrum of the art world, and he needed the excitement and the dramatic turmoil of that world. Europe remained the source of his inspiration. America had never ignited his creative imagination.

"My father arrives in August," she told Géa and handed him Marc's letter.

He scanned it and then held her close.

"Then we have a few weeks at least until our lives are changed forever," he said.

"Our lives will not change," she replied although her hands trembled and her heart beat too rapidly because she knew that he spoke the truth.

Chapter Thirty-Seven

The passenger ship *De Grasse* docked in Le Havre as France simmered in the punishing heat of the last days of summer. Small Jean, overcome with exhaustion, shielded her eyes against the golden light and wept as they walked onto the pier. Virginia, holding David in her arms, bent to comfort her, but Marc stared straight ahead. His heart was weighted with the memory of how he and Bella had left Europe, full of sorrow at having left Ida and Michel behind. And now Bella was dead, Michel and Ida were divorced, and he was a disoriented traveler, returning to a new life in a city grown unfamiliar to him. He sighed heavily.

"What's wrong?" Virginia asked.

"Nothing," he replied irritably. "I am looking for Ida. Do you see my Ida?"

And then suddenly she was upon them, her bright hair in wild disarray, her face flushed with excitement, her arms laden with a bouquet of irises and roses.

"Oh, you are here! At last, you are here," she shouted exuberantly, thrusting the flowers at Virginia. She plucked David from her arms, held him close, and covered him with kisses. "He's so beautiful. Such eyes, such golden skin," she exulted. "And, Jean, how you've grown. You're such a big girl. But why is such a big girl crying? Don't you know that it is forbidden to cry in France?" She laughed, coaxing forth Jean's laughter. Ida's exuberance was contagious.

"No words of welcome for your father, Idotchka?" Marc asked, and she laughed again and, still holding David, she embraced him.

"Not only the warmest of welcomes but surprise after surprise for my *papochka*," she said. "But let us collect your luggage and get out of this heat."

She reclaimed her familiar role of managing her father's life, relieving him of all practical arrangements. Swiftly and efficiently, she arranged for the collection of their baggage and assembled their customs documents. She smiled engagingly at the immigration officials and informed them that it was France's greatest artist whose documents they were processing. They nodded and each document was duly stamped.

"Welcome home, Monsieur Chagall," the customs supervisor said deferentially, and Marc rewarded him with a regal wave as he stepped onto French soil.

Géa strode toward them. He shook hands with Marc and kissed Virginia's hand as Ida surveyed the trunks and cartons, the scarred cases and oddly shaped bags, and briskly dictated what should be placed in their car and what should be sent on to the house.

"What house?" Marc asked impatiently.

"You will see. I told you there would be surprise after surprise."

"In what arrondissement is this house?" Marc asked. "You should have consulted me. I know Paris as well as you do, better, in fact."

"But the house is not in Paris," Ida replied teasingly. "You could not find such a house in Paris. You will be happy there, I promise."

"I am sure you will like it, Marc," Virginia said soothingly.

"I am certain that you will," Géa added. He flashed a complicit smile at Virginia. They would be the arbiters for their lovers, she for the father, he for the daughter.

They arrived at the house in the village of Orgeval at the twilight hour. Marc stared at the chalet, bathed in the gentle light of the dying sun.

"You have done well, Ida," he acknowledged. "Yes. I am pleased."

She smiled, and arm in arm, they walked about the property. He was enchanted by its charm, its wild garden, and the mysterious woodlands that surrounded it.

"Ah Virginia, look at what Ida has done for us. I can always depend on my Ida. She knows exactly what I want."

Ida frowned. She was too quickly being thrust into a role she no longer wanted.

Virginia trailed after them as they explored the house. Marc marveled at the drawing room whose French windows opened onto a terrace and a garden. Ida had carefully arranged framed photographs of her parents in Russia, in Berlin, and in Paris on the mantel. A sepia-toned portrait of Ida as a child in Bella's arms had pride of place on an ornate table. Virginia stared at them. She had sent Ida prints of Charles Leirens's studies of Marc and herself with David. Why were they not on display? She would find a place for them in this house that was to be her home.

Marc's paintings on the newly whitewashed walls were a montage, a visual record of his life from his days in St. Petersburg to his years in Paris. A portrait of Bella dominated the room, and Virginia, holding Jean's hand with David in her arms, stared up at it and too swiftly averted her eyes.

"Who is that lady?" Jean asked.

"She was your Aunt Ida's mother," Virginia replied softly.

"Is she dead?"

Marc wheeled about, flushed with anger. "Put the children to sleep," he ordered harshly, looking up at Bella's portrait, his narrow face a mask of sadness.

It was Géa who led Virginia and the children to the bedroom Ida had transformed into a nursery. She had placed a doll on Jean's bed, a stuffed teddy bear in David's crib, and filled the shelves with toys and picture books.

"How good of Ida to do all this for us," Virginia murmured as she placed her sleeping son in the crib.

"Ida is very good and very generous," Géa replied gently. "She very much wants you to be happy here at L'Aulnette."

"Is that the name of this house?" Virginia asked as she undressed her exhausted daughter. "I am pleased to know where I will be living."

"Yes, your home is called L'Aulnette," Géa repeated.

"Yes. My home. I must find a place here for my photographs,

my paintings." She spoke calmly and without bitterness. Géa looked at her as she stood at the window and gazed down at the garden. In her simple white blouse and dark skirt, her dark hair falling to her shoulders, her finely featured face pale and sad, she reminded him of a graceful, willowy school girl. But, he decided, for all the simplicity of her appearance and demeanor, Virginia was infinitely more complex than either Ida or Marc realized. She was clearly a woman who knew her own mind. It would be well for Ida to consider that.

He left the room, closing the door softly behind him because Jean was already asleep.

Life at L'Aulnette began happily. The village of Orgeval, with its ancient church and narrow streets, charmed them. Marc delighted in the light and landscape of the Seine and Oise region. They explored its fruit orchards and picnicked beneath the canopies of elms whose leaves were slowly drifting into the golden and scarlet hues of autumn. There was a pond in the heart of the forest, and they stared down at their reflections in its mysterious waters.

"We are in fairy land," Jean pronounced, and Virginia smiled at the truth of her daughter's words. They had sailed a vast and threatening ocean and arrived on an enchanted coast.

The house itself, with its turret and graceful gables, was comfortable during the mild months of early autumn. Its wide-windowed bedrooms were flooded with light throughout the day, and Marc converted two of them into studios. Ida had already claimed one bedroom as her own. Her clothes were in the closet; her own paintings and Géa's were on the walls. The painting of *The Bridal Chair* hung above her bed.

She and Géa lived in Paris, but she arrived each weekend laden with bottles of vodka and wine and packages of food, crowding the kitchen counters with jams and jellies, jars of caviar and foie gras. Ida was a talented and generous giver of gifts. She distributed whimsical toys to the children, draped a beautiful purple stole about Virginia's shoulders, helped Marc shrug into a blue velvet jacket that she had bought because it so closely matched his eyes.

Her enthusiasm electrified the household. She rushed from room to room, filling the vases with the bright branches of fall foliage, tossing colorful cushions onto sofas and chairs. She raced through the garden playing hide-and-seek with Jean and David and fed them bowls of ice cream, ignoring Virginia's disapproving frown. She invited her friends, a joyous coterie of young artists and writers, moody poets and beautiful girls who smiled a great deal and said very little. They were vested with a lightness and gaiety defiantly reclaimed after the dark years of war. Michel, newly married to his Marina, visited. Ida embraced them both and introduced them as her *plus chers amis*, her dearest friends. They smiled, but they never came again.

Marc's friends, dealers and publishers, writers and critics, gathered around the large dining room table and vigorously discussed new trends in art and literature, the symbolism in Jean Anouilh's new play and the merits of Camus's novels. There were teasing and occasionally malicious references to Picasso because they were all aware of Marc's jealousy of the Spanish artist.

Virginia wandered uneasily from group to group, neither hostess nor guest, feeling herself a displaced person in the house that was supposedly her home. She knew Ida's reason for renting such a huge house. It offered Marc an appropriate and attractive locale in which to host the intellectual and influential elite of Paris. She had rightly predicted that such generous hospitality would ease his acceptance into the art world of Paris after his long absence in America. *Clever Ida*, Virginia thought. Clever, clever Ida who had not thought to ask Virginia where she might prefer to live.

On occasional evenings, Marc and Virginia joined Ida and her friends at fashionable Paris bistros. Always stylishly dressed, her bright hair swirling about her radiant face, Ida laughed and told amusing stories. Champagne corks were popped, and empty bottles of wine littered the table. On such evenings, Virginia ate very little and said even less. Ida ordered great bowls of strawberries and mounds of whipped cream, platters of gâteaux, brimming dishes of golden crème brûlée.

"My papa wants everyone to eat, drink, and be merry," she insisted.

She was the generous hostess and Marc, despite his ingrained frugality, settled the bill, laboriously counting out great wads of francs. It was, he acknowledged, the price he paid for the attention and affection of Ida and her friends. It was an investment, Ida insisted. Her friends were critics and journalists. They had connections.

Géa watched Ida with amusement, bemused by her kinetic energy, her unabashed flamboyance, which he occasionally found exhausting. He said nothing. The happiness he and Ida shared sufficed for the present. He was too young to concern himself unduly with the future. For the moment, he was content with their life in Paris, and he waited patiently for Ida to extricate herself from her father's orbit. He was reluctant to think beyond that.

The months rushed past. A brutally cold winter assaulted them. The house that had so charmed them now disappointed. It was difficult to heat. A fire burned in Marc's studio, and although he wore layers of sweaters, he complained bitterly of the chill. They learned that during the war, L'Aulnette had been commandeered by the Gestapo and used as an interrogation center. The stable where they garaged their Peugeot was rumored to have been the site of more than one execution. Virginia avoided the building.

"It smells of blood and death," she told Ida.

"What do you know of blood and death?" Ida asked dismissively.

"Do you think that Jews have a monopoly on suffering?" Virginia retorted. Her tone was even, but her eyes burned with anger. It was a new and uneasy exchange.

The inclement weather meant that the children were often indoors. Marc complained that David was restless and craved attention, that Jean was increasingly moody and given to tantrums. Even Virginia began to irritate him. He told Ida that she did not comprehend the complexity of his paintings, the Jewish symbolism that danced across his canvases.

"But think of how good she is. She takes wonderful care of you, wonderful care of our David," Ida said soothingly. "It is only that you are tired, *Papochka*. The cold distresses you. Try to rest more."

He closed his eyes as he listened to her. The cadence of her voice was so familiar that for a brief magic moment, he imagined that it was Bella who spoke to him. Ida was right. He was tired, so very tired. He could not blame Virginia for not sharing his lifetime of memories, for not understanding his Jewish world. She was so beautiful, so innocent. And she was David's mother, his precious, annoying Dovidl.

Ida spoke to Virginia and advised her to arrange for the children to spend time away from the house, to make certain that they did not interfere with Marc's work.

"You know how he is," she said, and Virginia nodded. They both knew how he was.

Relief came with the warmth of spring and the exciting news that Marc was invited to the Biennale in Venice to accept an award for his graphic work.

Virginia snapped out of her winter lethargy. Venice had long been the city of her dreams, the vortex of her fantasies. She imagined traversing its canals with Marc seated beside her in a gondola. They would visit museums, walking hand in hand. It would be a time for them to be alone, to reclaim the intimacy of their early days together. Venice would be a honeymoon of a kind. Surely even those who lived together without marriage vows deserved a honeymoon.

Ida too was ecstatic. The award, one of the art world's greatest honors, signified international recognition and would increase the value of Marc's work. She and Géa would also travel to Venice for the Biennale.

"It will be wonderful," she said excitedly. "How marvelous that we will be in Venice together, the four of us. It will be wonderful, wonderful."

She hugged Géa and danced about the room with him. "Venice. *Venezia*," she sang.

"Venice, *Venezia*," Géa echoed, and Marc sprang up and joined them.

Ida's eyes sparkled, her face aglow. She whirled about, linking arms now with her father, now with her lover.

"It will be so exciting, Virginia," Ida called to her from across the room.

"Yes. Wonderfully exciting," Virginia agreed, her voice barely audible.

There would be no intimate honeymoon. She had been foolish to imagine that Marc would journey to Venice without his daughter. Ida would forever choreograph every aspect of their lives. It was a dominance that Virginia could not yet fight, dependent as she was on Marc, but she was well schooled in patience; she would wait. Her turn would come.

The celebratory dance ended. Géa, perched on the arm of Ida's chair, played with her hair, lifting the shining copper coil and brushing his lips across the pale nape of her neck. Virginia tried to remember when Marc had last kissed her, when, in fact, he had last touched her. With David in her arms, she left the salon. Smiling bitterly, she pressed her cheek against her son's silken hair and closed the door behind her.

Chapter Thirty-Eight

enice, *Venezia*." Ida uttered the name of the city in awe as though to convince herself that the wonderland that surrounded her was real, that she was not lost in a dream.

Géa smiled, amused at how childlike she was in her astonishment at the explosion of beauty that was Venice.

"I told you that it was the most beautiful city in the world," he said. "And we have arrived at its most beautiful season."

Marc and Virginia nodded. They too were entranced by the city. Together, they strolled through its narrow *calli*. Ida and Géa rushed ahead of them and then paused and waited, the pace of their shared vacation established. They formed an odd yet amiable quartet, the Jewish father and his daughter, each with a gentile lover, each armed with an open sketchbook, passing soft pencils and stubs of graphite from hand to hand.

The bright autumn sun splayed dancing ribs of light across the dark waters of the canals and turned the city's spires and rooftops the color of molten honey. As day drifted into evening, the light of the nascent moon silvered their faces, and together, the two couples cruised the tranquil lagoons in gondolas and vaporettos.

They wandered across ancient bridges, drifted in and out of the shops along the Rialto, and spent hours in the small museums they all agreed were more interesting than the elaborate pavilions of the Biennale.

Marc was the guest of honor at receptions and dinners. Ida, as always proud and exuberant, stood beside him as he patiently answered questions posed by interviewers. He occasionally turned to her so that she might provide him with an elusive word or clarify a statement he had phrased too awkwardly. When he accepted the

Grand Prix, Ida, elegant in her gown of rust-colored taffeta, leaned forward and almost rose from her seat. For the briefest moment, it seemed that she might ascend the podium with her father, that his triumph was her own. Géa and Virginia remained at a distance.

"It's as though Marc is a performer and Ida is both his prompter and his director," Virginia observed, and Géa did not disagree.

Late one morning, they sat at on the terrace of a café on the Piazza San Marco. They sipped their bitter espressos in silence, as though fearful that a single word might shatter the enchantment of the beauty that surrounded them.

Ida tossed crumbs to the pigeons and laughed as they took wing and flew in formation to the center of the piazza. Géa stroked her cheek absently and looked eastward toward the Cathedral of St. Mark.

"I should like to see the interior of the cathedral," he said. "Will you join me?"

"It is of no interest to me," Marc replied curtly.

"Nor to me," Ida added.

The Chagalls might not attend synagogues, but they did not enter churches.

"I will go with you," Virginia interjected and rose from the table.

"We won't be long," Géa assured them, and he and Virginia walked too swiftly up the broad marble steps as the bells of the campanile tolled the noon hour.

"Do you think they went inside to pray, our two goyim?" Marc asked sardonically.

"Does it matter?" Ida replied irritably. "They are Christian and we are Jewish. I suppose it is just as well that we do not trespass into each other's worlds."

"Could you marry your Géa, your Christian lover?" Marc asked.

"Could you marry Virginia, your Christian mistress?" Ida countered.

"The years have passed and I have not yet done so, have I?" he replied as Géa and Virginia emerged from the cathedral.

"The interior is quite beautiful," Géa said. "Especially the nave."

"Is it?" Marc asked without interest, his eyes turned away from the cathedral. He stared across the piazza to the Grand Canal, awash in sunlight.

They followed his gaze and watched a solitary gondola glide across the tranquil waters. Its passengers, a young couple, leaned toward each other, their bodies pressed close as they swayed in rhythm to the oar strokes of the gondolier.

"The gondolas of Venice are made for lovers," Ida murmured.

"May I invite you to sail away with me to Lido?" Géa asked Ida. "We too, after all, are lovers."

"I accept," Ida said. "You will excuse us, Papa, Virginia?"

"Of course," they replied in unison.

Géa and Ida, arm in arm, strolled toward the canal, pausing briefly in a circlet of sunlight where Géa adjusted Ida's stole and kissed her, first on each cheek and then on her lips. Virginia and Marc watched them in silence and sipped their coffee, grown tepid and bitter.

Their remaining days in Venice sped by in a haze of pleasurable excitement.

On the very last day of their stay, Marc reluctantly agreed to go shopping with Virginia for gifts for the children. Géa and Ida reveled in the luxury of an uninterrupted stretch of hours to be spent alone, wandering through the city without program or purpose.

Walking hand in hand, they explored unfamiliar neighborhoods and crossed arched bridges to emerge onto colorful piazzas crowded with busy stalls. Géa bargained expertly with a gold-toothed woman for a stole of royal blue iridescent silk that he draped about Ida's shoulders.

"I once had a cape of that same blue and a beret to match," Ida recalled dreamily as she fingered the delicate fabric.

"It must have suited you wonderfully," Géa said.

"Yes. But that was in another country, and the girl who wore it is no more."

They strolled through the leather market and the straw market. Géa bought a bouquet of fall flowers from an urchin who scurried away, laughing aloud at his good fortune.

Ida looked down at the bouquet as though to memorize the

colors and scent of the fragile blossoms. She understood the futility of the effort. Flowers died, possessions were lost or abandoned; only the memory of a face, a gesture, a fleeting expression of love, endured. She had learned as much from Bella who, in her memoir, had written of the candlelight that flickered across her mother's face each Sabbath eve, of her father's grave expression as he bent over a Talmudic text. It was the softness of her mother's eyes, the wistfulness of her fleeting smile, that Ida herself remembered, just as it was Géa's smile she would recall when she thought of this golden day in Venice.

In the glass market, she purchased a child's tea set crafted of golden Murano glass.

"For Jean," she said.

She had a special fondness for Virginia's daughter, who often seemed as lonely as Ida herself had been throughout her sequestered childhood.

They walked on, crossing the Rio di San Girolamo and continuing on through the Rio del Battello, charmed by the frenetic vitality of the pedestrians who rushed past them. Mothers called to their scampering children. Men in business suits clutched briefcases and perused documents as they hurried by. The dwellings that lined the streets were built in such close proximity that they resembled an impenetrable fortress.

Géa and Ida walked slowly through an alleyway where clotheslines weighted down by colorful garments fluttered in the gentle breeze. She paused in front of a dilapidated building.

"Look, Géa," she said.

A Jewish star was carved into its cornerstone.

Géa stopped a woman who was hurrying by, laden with a basket of vegetables.

"Excuse me," he asked in his stilted Swiss Italian. "Can you tell me the name of this neighborhood?"

"You are in the Ghetto Nuovo, signor," she replied without pausing. "Giudecca. The home of the Jews."

Ida fingered her flowers. "It appears that without a compass, I have managed to come home," she said.

She looked up at the windows of the surrounding houses and then glanced at two dark-haired, dark-eyed small girls playing a game of skipping stones in the narrow passageway.

"*Dov'è la sinagoga*? Where is the synagogue?" she asked.

They looked at each other, hesitated, and then scrambled to their feet. *It was not so long ago*, Ida thought, *that such a question would have filled them with fear*. But they smiled and ran ahead. Ida and Géa followed them around corners and across streets until they stopped in front of an ancient, perfectly proportioned stone building, its architecture similar to that of the ancient churches of Venice.

"*La Scuola Spagnola*," they said proudly in unison. "*Sinagoga*."

They pushed open the heavy door, and Géa and Ida followed them into the dimly lit vestibule. A white-bearded man, bent with age, wearing a black skullcap, ritual fringes dangling from his worn dark jacket, came forward.

"*Ebrei*?" he asked.

"*Si*," Ida said very softly.

He nodded and led them into the beautiful sanctuary where tall white candles in ornate chandeliers kept ghostly vigil, waiting for long-absent congregants to arrive and take their seats on the faded red velvet cushions of the serried pews. The stained glass windows were aglow in the afternoon sunlight. Here and there, a prayer shawl hung across a railing as though the worshipper had been interrupted in the middle of a service and departed in great haste. The dark wooden ark that contained the Torah scrolls was beautifully carved, and above it, a hanging lamp flickered weakly.

"The eternal light," Ida whispered to Géa.

"I see," he said, although he did not.

The old man led them back to the vestibule and pointed to a brass plaque engraved in both Italian and English. The little girls enunciated the Italian inscription aloud, their high sweet voices echoing through the empty space. Ida read the English, her voice muted by sadness.

"1939 to 1945. Two hundred Jews of Venice, eight thousand Jews of Italy, six million Jews of Europe were barbarously massacred and died as martyrs."

"Two hundred," Ida said, her voice breaking. "Eight thousand. Six million. There but for the grace of God..." The words trailed off as memory overcame her. She thought of the streets of Marseilles crowded with refugees; she remembered the stench of fear and her fierce and frantic struggle for her parents' survival and her own.

Géa watched as she covered her bright hair with the blue silk scarf. She lifted her hands to her eyes and he saw the lucent tears that trickled between her fingers.

Her lips moved.

"*Yitgadal v'yitkadash*," she intoned, and he knew that it was a Hebrew prayer that she murmured. The Kaddish, he thought it was called.

The small girls and the old man moved forward to join her, their voices joining hers in quiet and mournful chorus. The prayer continued, beautiful and heartbreaking in its rhythmic brevity. It ended. They stood together, wrapped in their silent sorrow. Ida kissed each small girl on the cheek. She opened her purse and pressed whatever notes she had into the old man's hand despite his weary protest. She bent and gently placed the bouquet of autumn flowers beneath the plaque.

They left the ghetto, walking too swiftly. Géa took Ida's hand, but they did not speak. He understood that he had no words to offer her. He was an alien in the wilderness of her grief. He was in her world but not of it. It had not occurred to him that the Judaism that neither she nor her father practiced could create such an abyss between them. He was inexplicably relieved that they would soon be returning to France.

Chapter Thirty-Nine

*T*heir enchanted days in Venice swiftly receded into wistful memory. Ida was once again caught up in the maelstrom of her frenetic life. She raced through her days, struggling to scavenge time for her own painting and drawing as she dashed from meetings with gallery owners to formal dinners with collectors.

The new postwar millionaires now saw art as an investment. A Chagall masterpiece was not just a painting; it was a financial asset. Ida was contemptuous of such businessmen buyers, but she was too shrewd to disregard them. She bargained vigorously, turning away with feigned indifference if her demands were resisted.

"I speak for my father. You must understand that when Ida Chagall, the daughter of the artist, says five thousand dollars, she means five thousand dollars," she told a pompous American collector. "I am not selling herrings, monsieur."

Obediently, he wrote her a check for five thousand dollars. She knew that he would never guess that she was, in fact, the granddaughter of a man who had hauled herring barrels and a woman who had probably bargained as vigorously in her tiny grocery store for a few kopeks as she now bargained for thousands of dollars.

Her days were punctuated by Marc's peevish phone calls, which were an insistent litany of complaints. The house was too cold, drafts of wind drifted in through windows that were improperly sealed, his studios were so overcrowded with his canvases and supplies that he could not work properly.

"How can I work like this, Ida?" he whined.

"I will take care of everything," she promised, but Marc's annoyances compounded. A cabinet collapsed. The children bothered him when he was working. He called Ida at all hours, angrily spewing his discontent.

"Does he expect you to become a babysitter?" Géa asked angrily. "Let Virginia control her children. Let him call a carpenter. Why are you responsible for all the trivia of his life?"

"Because I have always been responsible," she replied wearily.

She breathed a disloyal sigh of relief. Marc and Virginia had decided to spend the spring months in Saint-Jean-Cap-Ferrat where Tériade's home would be open to them. There was a pleasant, modest *pensione* nearby.

"Can we afford to do that?" Marc asked Ida worriedly. "It will be expensive to spend so many weeks at a *pensione*."

"You can afford to do whatever you like, *Papochka*," she replied, smiling indulgently. "Haven't you heard? Marc Chagall is a wealthy man."

He shrugged. "What does wealth mean?" he asked with feigned indifference. "It comes. It goes."

Ida was not deceived. "Wealth means freedom," she replied carefully. "It means that you have the freedom to spend the spring in the south of France. Am I right, Virginia?"

Virginia shrugged. She considered any discussion of money vulgar.

"Virginia sees me as a coarse cosmopolitan, overly concerned with money and material things," Ida observed to Géa.

"Has it never occurred to you that Virginia may be jealous of you?" Géa asked.

"Why should she be jealous of me? I am my father's daughter, not his lover," Ida replied, but his words troubled her.

She was relieved when Marc, Virginia, and the children left for the south of France.

Marc's absence afforded her relief from the frantic journeys to Orgeval and the many errands he imposed upon her. She was free to enjoy the soft spring sunlight of Paris, to walk with Géa at the twilight hour, to sit with friends at sidewalk cafés where she smiled with pleasure at the touch of her lover's hand light upon her thick auburn hair. She chose to ignore the intermittent discomfort of abdominal pains. She would not allow them to spoil her pleasant days and pleasanter evenings.

Marc wrote regularly from Saint-Jean-Cap-Ferrat. He was so enraptured by the Mediterranean that he placed his easel on the shore to better capture the hues of the magical sea. He worked his gouaches on sheets of chiffon paper, an involved and exciting process that had been greatly admired by Aimé Maeght, the influential dealer who represented Miró, Giacometti, and Braque.

"There are wonderful flowers here and Virginia arranges them beautifully," he wrote.

Ida wondered if he remembered that Bella had woven garlands of wildflowers and filled copper bowls with golden daffodils. She banished the thought. It was foolish and disloyal.

Virginia wrote that she and Marc were searching for property to buy. They were considering a charming house with a large garden, shaded by citrus trees.

Ida read the letter to Géa.

"Apparently, your father's Paris days are over. The Riviera has claimed him," he said.

She thought of Marc's impulsive purchases of property in Gordes and in High Falls and decided that she would travel south and visit the house he was considering.

She swept into the *pensione* like a whirlwind. She lifted a laughing David into her arms and thrust herself into Marc's embrace. She was, as always, laden with gifts, a huge red ball for David, a doll and games for Jean, a green velvet jacket for Marc, and a silk scarf patterned with pansies for Virginia. Marc shrugged into the jacket, found an ascot that matched it, and studied himself with satisfaction in the mirror. Virginia thanked Ida politely for the scarf that she did not remove from the box.

"Now tell me about this house," Ida said, sitting back and gratefully sipping a glass of absinthe that soothed the stomach cramp that assaulted her. Stress from the journey, she decided, and, as always, she ignored it. The pain would pass. It always did.

They described the house with enthusiasm. The rooms were large, the garden charming.

"And it is exactly where we want to live," Marc added. "The Riviera is now the center of the art world. Picasso has a home and a studio in Vallauris and Matisse is in Cimiez. It is so peaceful here, and I work so well. My illustrations for *The Decameron* commission are almost completed. Virginia reads the tales to me, just as Bella read La Fontaine's *Fables*."

Virginia looked away. References to Bella, a constant spectral presence in her life with Marc, filled her with unease. She despaired of competing with a ghost.

"The house sounds wonderful," Ida said pleasantly. "Let's visit it tomorrow and see if it is really suitable, and then you can make an offer."

"But we have already made an offer." Marc smiled engagingly, the practiced smile of a small boy who has been mischievous but knows that he will be forgiven. "I signed a three-month option, and I have already paid for it."

"Indeed," Ida said coldly. "All right. Of course, an option is not a sale."

"But I really love the house," Virginia murmured. "I want Marc to buy it."

"I look forward to seeing it," Ida said.

"Of course," Marc agreed. "I am certain you will like it, Idotchka."

"Why does Ida have to like it? She's not going to be living in it," asked Jean, who had been dressing and undressing her new doll in a corner of the room.

The child's unanswered question lingered in the uncomfortable silence. They went into the dining room and sat down to dinner. Ida, pleading fatigue, left the table before dessert. Her usual abdominal pains recurred with a new severity.

She felt better the next morning, and they drove to the house. It was, as Virginia and Marc had claimed, absolutely charming, but she saw at once that it was also absolutely unsuitable for her father. There were formidable flights of steps at every landing, and the antiquated plumbing was in disrepair. Little light penetrated the narrow windows.

"There is no light, *Papochka*," Ida said. "Can you paint in a studio that has no light?"

Virginia swiftly lit a lamp. "It casts a beautiful glow," she said. "I love to draw in lamp light."

"You are not Marc Chagall," Ida retorted. "My father needs natural light for his work."

"Yes. Yes, I do," Marc agreed sadly.

Ida shook her head and turned to her father. "This house is impossible. How could you think of buying it?" she asked.

It was Virginia who replied.

"I love it. The children love it. Repairs can be made."

"And it has a dignity," Marc added. "At this time in my life, I must have a house that reflects my status. Matisse and Picasso have wonderful homes. Chagall must have a home that compares to theirs."

"I am certain that Matisse and Picasso have toilets that flush. I am certain that they paint in light-filled studios. There are other houses on the Côte d'Azur that would surely be more suitable and perhaps even more elegant than those of Picasso and Matisse," Ida replied.

She sank into an overstuffed chair, and a cloud of dust from the neglected upholstery filled the room.

"You see that I am right, don't you, *Papochka*?"

Her tone turned coaxing, conciliatory, and Marc nodded.

"You are right. Of course you are right. Don't you see that Ida is right, Virginia? She understands such things."

"Of course. Ida is always right," Virginia replied, turning away, her eyes dulled with disappointment.

Ida went to the estate agent that afternoon. Ever the skillful negotiator, she informed him that although the house was dilapidated, although he had failed to point out the disrepair as was his obligation, she would take no legal action.

"But, mademoiselle," he protested. "I have your father's signature on a contract."

"And I have an excellent *avocat*," she retorted. "But I do not wish to have a lawsuit. My father contracted for a three-month option. You may keep his deposit and repair and clean the house so that he and his family can live in it for the next three months. Are we in agreement?"

"I cannot afford to disagree," he replied bitterly.

Satisfied, Ida reported the compromise to Marc, who smiled gratefully.

"I can always depend on you to work things out," he said. "We can always depend on Ida, isn't that true, Virginia?"

"Yes. You can always depend on Ida," she agreed and turned away.

Ida returned to Paris the next day. Unpacking her bag, she found the scarf she had given Virginia concealed in the folds of a nightdress.

"Surely an error," Géa said when she told him about it.

"Surely a statement of a kind," she replied and, still holding the scarf, she reclined on the divan. The abdominal pain had returned with a new intensity and she wondered for how much longer she could safely ignore it.

Chapter Forty

*P*ain, fierce and unremitting, invaded her dream. Still half asleep, Ida clutched her abdomen as though to smother the small gnawing animal that assaulted her body, sawing away with devilishly sharp incisors. She would conquer it, outrace it, as for so many years she had outraced the demons that haunted her sleep. She tossed and turned, her fingers biting into her flesh as the invader gathered strength and intensified its grip. The pain became unbearable, and her agonized scream pierced the nocturnal silence.

"Ida, Ida, what is it?" Géa cried.

As she opened her mouth to answer, she gagged and clots of bright red blood spurted out. Her face was blanched of all color. Her eyes fluttered closed, and she lost consciousness.

He dashed to the telephone and summoned an ambulance.

At the hospital, the weary, gray-eyed, gray-haired attending physician emerged from the examining room and stared at him gravely.

"Your wife is very ill, monsieur. Dangerously ill. She is bleeding internally and has already lost a great deal of blood. Every minute, every hour counts. We must operate at once or she will die. We must have your permission as her husband, her next of kin, to proceed."

Géa stared at the physician in bewilderment and struggled to comprehend his words. *Die.* His Ida, his vibrant, beautiful Ida. She could not die. *Next of kin?* They were not kin, only loving lovers.

"But she is not my wife," he managed to blurt out.

"Who then is her next of kin? Does she have parents, siblings? Perhaps a husband?" he added mischievously.

"A father. Yes, a father," Géa said. "But he lives in Orgeval."

"We require his permission," the doctor repeated. "Sister

Ursula will give you a form for him to sign. But hurry. Time is of the essence."

Géa nodded. He took the form from the nurse and hurried as the hesitant light of a breaking dawn streaked across the sky. The household in Orgeval would still be wrapped in sleep, but he knew that he could not delay. He found a pay phone and dialed the number.

The phone rang repeatedly, and it was Virginia who answered.

"I must speak to Marc," Géa said.

"Impossible. He is still sleeping."

"Wake him. This is an emergency. Ida is very ill."

She gasped, hesitated. She was frightened, Géa knew: not frightened for Ida but frightened of Marc's anger at being awakened.

He heard her murmur to Marc, heard his angry rebuke and then his voice, harsh with annoyance. But he did not interrupt as Géa explained the danger and how it was imperative that he sign the permission form.

"All right. Bring that form to me," he said. "I will sign it."

"But that will take too long," Géa protested. "I will have to travel to Orgeval and then return to Paris. The doctor said there is no time to waste. You must come to Paris."

"Impossible. I cannot do that. I will not do that," Marc replied defiantly and slammed the receiver down.

Géa stared at the newly silent phone in disbelief. He would not call again.

In despair, he returned home and called Michel. There was little that Ida's ex-husband did not know about Marc. Swiftly, Géa explained the situation.

"Could you prevail upon Marc to come to Paris?" he asked.

"He would not listen to me just as he did not listen to you," Michel replied. "He is Marc Chagall, king of his own universe. Nothing can persuade him to do anything that he is disinclined to do, damn him."

"Then what can I do?" Géa asked in desperation.

"Sign the form yourself," Michel advised. "Sign his name. The hospital will not question the signature, I can assure you of that." He spoke with the authoritative cynicism of the experienced journalist. "I will meet you at the hospital, Géa."

"All right. I will sign it," Géa agreed reluctantly. He was grateful that Michel would be with him. Michel was happy in his new marriage to Marina, but Ida's imprint was engraved indelibly upon on his heart.

He looked at the form, read it once and then again, then looked up at the painting of *The Bridal Chair* that hung above Ida's bed and studied Marc's signature, scrawled in a corner of the canvas. He copied it again and again onto a piece of scrap paper and then, his hand steady, he signed *Marc Chagall, Père* on the line indicated and rushed back to the hospital where he handed it to the doctor, who glanced at it and raised his eyebrows.

"Did you fly to Orgeval?" he asked wryly. He did not wait for an answer but instructed diligent Sister Ursula to arrange for an operating room. Michel rushed in. He handed Géa a steaming cup of coffee and a croissant and placed a reassuring arm on his shoulder. The two men sat side by side on a narrow bench and waited anxiously for news of the woman who meant so much to them.

Hours later, Sister Ursula emerged and informed them that the surgery was successful, adding that it was fortunate that they had been able to operate when they did. Ida had lost so much blood because of a bleeding ulcer that the slightest delay might have resulted in death.

"You were very fortunate, mademoiselle," the gray-eyed doctor told Ida when he visited her days after the surgery. "But ulcers are often caused by stress. You must live a calmer life, avoid tension."

"Ah, but my life is calm and I feel no tension, *cher professeur*," she assured him gaily and presented him with a pencil sketch of his face in profile she had dashed off as he spoke.

Was she lying to herself or to the doctor? Géa wondered as he thought of her exhausting journeys to London, Switzerland, and Berlin to curate exhibitions of Marc's work. And then there were her endless negotiations with galleries and collectors, her all-too-frequent journeys to Orgeval to deal with his discontents. She was her father's buffer, his human sponge, charged with the absorption of any irritations that might interfere with his work. Her denial was foolish. There was both stress and tension in her frenetic life. He stared at her but said nothing.

The doctor smiled. Ida had charmed him. She was once again irrepressible, lively, and laughing, aglow with her triumph over pain and death.

She rouged her cheeks and lips, fashioned her hair into a French braid that she flipped playfully at Marc when he at last visited her.

"Ah, my Ida. How good to see you healthy. You must convalesce at L'Aulnette. I will take care of you. I would do anything for my Ida," he said. He did not look at Géa, who turned away, his face frozen in anger. Marc, who refused to be inconvenienced even to save his daughter's life, had not uttered a single word of gratitude. Géa's efforts were simply his due.

The Orgeval house was serene during Ida's recuperation. The children no longer troubled Marc. David was cared for in the village and Jean had been sent to live with Virginia's parents in England.

"I want her to know her grandparents," Virginia explained, but Ida understood that Jean had been banished to placate Marc. Throughout her own childhood, her mother had cautioned her not to disturb him when he was painting. Bella too had feared his dark moods, his irritation, but nothing would have persuaded her to send Ida away. But Virginia had submitted to his tyranny and sacrificed her daughter on the altar of his discontent. If she had betrayed her daughter, she was surely capable of other betrayals. Ida filed that knowledge away.

Marc was a casual caregiver. Each morning, he asked Ida if she needed anything and hurried to his studio without waiting for an answer. He was absorbed in a painting that he considered to be an artistic breakthrough.

"I call it *The Red Sun*," he told Ida. "It will be my masterpiece. Aimé Maeght, the art dealer, said as much when he visited last week."

Ida went to his studio. *The Red Sun* was, she recognized at once, a stunning effort; the canvas was electric with shimmering primary colors. In daring strokes, Marc had painted a willowy woman in blue flying toward a youth in yellow who scissored his way through a brilliant and blinding red sun. There was great attention to detail— flowers sprouted on the canvas, and roosters and donkeys lurked in corners, enveloped in streams of radiance.

"It is wonderful, *Papochka*," she said. "More than wonderful."

"Yes," he agreed, lifting a brush to add a dab of cadmium yellow to the flying youth's robe. "That is what Maeght said. Did I tell you that I have agreed to allow him to represent me?"

She stared at him in disbelief, unable for the moment to speak, struggling against a commingling of grief and anger.

"But it is I who represent you," she said at last. Her voice broke as she grappled for words. "I have always represented you. I have devoted myself to you and your work. Surely you understand that, *Papochka*."

He did not turn to look at her but continued to study his canvas, centering it on the easel, adding the merest hint of burnt carmine to his exploding sun.

"Papa."

The desperate plea in her voice arrested him. He sighed and wiped his brush clean.

"I have not given Maeght exclusive rights, *ma chérie*," he said. "He will be helpful to both of us. He has contacts that you cannot match. Curators and wealthy collectors seek him out. Matisse himself is his client. And you will simply work with him, learn from him. Your fortunes will not suffer, if that is what concerns you. I believe that I have already made you a very rich young woman."

"Do you really think that that is all that concerns me?" she asked bitterly. "I have never thought of my fortunes as separate from your own."

Overcome with weakness, she clutched the back of a chair so that she would not fall. He took her arm, led her to a chaise in the garden. She fell into a deep sleep and awakened, recalling her dream in which a painting that Marc had titled *Double Portrait with Wine-Glass* had come to life. He had depicted Ida as a small girl, flying desperately above him. She realized with sudden clarity that her role in her father's life was as amorphous as the wind on whose wings she sailed in both the painting and the dream. Her fury and her grief dissipated. The new insight calmed her. She loved her father and he loved her, but she understood the limitations of that love.

The summer ended. Ida was restored to health and Marc completed his work on *The Red Sun*. As always, when a large project ended, he was seized by a restlessness, a need to absorb a new landscape or perhaps revisit half-remembered scenes of his past.

"Let us take a small vacation together," he suggested to Ida. "The four of us, Virginia and myself, you and Géa."

Ida was agreeable. Her energy was restored and she too wanted a change of scenery. They discussed destinations.

"Gordes," Marc decided. "We still own the house there. We should go there and decide whether to rent it or sell it. Virginia and I could never live there. It is too far from Paris, but a visit will be pleasant. Our garden there was so beautiful at this time of the year. Don't you remember how lovely it was, Ida?"

"I remember it well," she replied.

Her father, she knew, with his talent for selective memory, recalled only that he and Bella had been together there, their garden beautiful, their home a pleasant refuge. He did not remember the dangers and tension that had haunted them in that former convent school.

She had her own cameos of memory. She would never forget how Michel, returned from the war, had stood in a pool of silver moonlight in the doorway. And Michel had actually laid claim to the name of the village and reinvented himself as Michel Gordey. She sighed. It was time to deal with the landscapes of their past.

The house had been long vacant, but Ida had engaged a caretaker who had seen to its maintenance through the years, and it was still furnished. It would easily accommodate the four of them. She smiled at her father.

"What a good idea, Papa," she said. "Of course we will all go to Gordes together."

"I'm sure it will suit us well," Virginia said.

"Are you?" Ida asked.

"If my father suggested going to hell, Virginia would agree that it would surely suit us," she muttered to Géa later.

"Be kind, Ida," Géa said. "Virginia is not having an easy time."

"None of us are having an easy time," she retorted.

But Virginia was right. Gordes did suit them well. The house retained its charm; its stone walls were bleached and baked dry by the sun, and rhomboids of light danced off the large windows that Bella had so loved.

Once again, two couples ate their meals at the polished refectory table. Ida wandered restlessly from room to room as though touring a theater where the cast of characters had been altered although the set was unchanged. She paused at one window and stared out at the wild garden where she and her mother had created a whimsical rock garden. Yes, she had once called the Gordes house home, but then she had called so many places home. Too many places.

She and Géa slept in the bed where once Michel had wept as he spoke of the sadness of his war. The picture hook above the bed that had held *The Bridal Chair* in place dangled loosely, a sad and rusting reminder of those restless, fear-swept nights. She lay awake in the fragrant darkness, drifting through the presleep wilderness of memories and yearnings, recalling the many places she had stayed through the long years of her wandering. There were three rooms in New York and Paris, in the Loire valley, and on the Long Island shore. How often she had awakened struggling to remember where she was and how she had arrived there.

"*Assez*," she whispered. "Enough."

She wanted to be done with crates and trunks, with packing and unpacking, with carting the debris of her past into an all-too-temporary present. She wished away all the impermanence of her episodic life. She was a mature woman, in the fourth decade of her life. She needed gravity, grounding, a home of her own.

"Why should I not have it?" she asked herself and fell into a dreamless sleep.

She went into the village the next day and wandered through the narrow streets, avoiding the stares of the housewives who looked down at her from the narrow windows of their pale pink stone houses. She nodded to shopkeepers who looked at her as though they were seeing a ghost. She had not been forgotten in the years that had passed. She made her way to the post office.

Yvette looked at her from behind the counter and gasped.

"Madame Ida, it is you? Can it be you?" Her voice broke and tears streaked her cheeks.

"Yes, It's really me, Yvette," Ida said and wiped her own eyes.

They looked hard at each other, assessing the changes that the years had wrought. Fine wrinkles creased Yvette's plump and pleasant face, and her light brown hair was streaked with silver. She had gained weight—no, she was pregnant. Her simple gray smock draped the rise of her abdomen. She smiled shyly at Ida's surprise.

"Yes. My baby will be born in two months' time. And I have a son, two years old. Pierre. I named him for my first husband. I remarried a year after the war ended. Eduard owns a small welding shop in Avignon. He is a good man, a gentle man. We have built a good life together. I have not forgotten my Pierre. I mourn him still, but life goes on, Madame Ida. And we ourselves must go on."

Ida nodded. "I too have learned that," she said.

"And is your Monsieur Michel well?"

"He is well. But he is no longer my Monsieur Michel. Does it shock you to learn that we are divorced?"

"After the war, nothing shocks me," Yvette replied.

She closed the post office, and arm in arm, the two friends strolled down the narrow sun-spangled lane, bonded by their shared memories of the months of raging war, the weeks and days of troubled uncertainty. Their lives had changed, but they had forged new beginnings. There was joy in their reunion. They wished each other well in their very different lives.

"You must come back to Gordes, Madame Ida," Yvette said as they parted.

"Yes. Of course," Ida agreed, but even as she and Yvette exchanged kisses, she knew that she would not return. She was done with revisiting the scenes of her past. It was time for her to build a future.

Chapter Forty-One

Ida returned to Paris imbued with a new certainty, a new determination. Her reflection in the mirror told her that her very expression had altered. Her once-soft girlish features were finely chiseled. Her eyes were grave beneath the perfect arches of her russet brows. There was a new seriousness in her demeanor. She emanated the quiet maturity of a confident and prosperous woman, in control of her life, in control of her future.

She examined her impeccably maintained accounts and ledgers and calculated how much she could comfortably spend on a house. It would not be a careless purchase. She was not a careless woman. She wandered through the city day after day, crossing the Seine, strolling down the Right Bank and veering back to the Left Bank. She explored broad boulevards and narrow lanes, looked up at turreted mansions, and glanced into the gardens of graceful town houses. She rejected neighborhoods that were too isolated and neighborhoods that were too busy. She knew exactly what she wanted.

She envisioned a stately home set amid flower beds and conifers, large enough to accommodate her father during his stays in Paris. Its spacious rooms would have high ceilings and wide windows that flooded them with light. There were such homes in postwar Paris. The fifties promised to be a decade of plenty.

She imagined herself a hostess in a well-appointed salon, its wood floor gleaming gold, its vases overflowing with fresh flowers from her own garden.

She sketched her imagined home. She told Géa that she wanted to live in the heart of Paris.

"Why?" he asked, toying with a tendril of her hair.

"Because that is the most beautiful part of our beautiful city," she replied.

"And my beautiful Ida should live in the most beautiful part of her beautiful city," he agreed and laughed. He thought her aspirations childish. And he thought them charming. To please her—and he was always anxious to please her—he accompanied her now and again as she visited properties on offer.

On a wintry afternoon, they went together to view a house that a hopeful agent was certain would interest her. They climbed the high marble steps of the beautiful seventeenth-century town house, and Ida paused at the entry and stared down at the view below. Couples strolled along the Pont Neuf and stopped to look down at the sun-streaked Seine. Two small boys stood at a fretted iron railing and tossed stones into the bright water. Ida imagined herself crossing the bridge at the twilight hour, imagined the river breeze cooling her cheeks. The very street address of the house, the Quai de l'Horloge—the Wharf of the Clock—intrigued her. She thought it prescient, symbolic. The year was ending; the minutes and hours completed their cycle. Her years of wandering had ended. The clock, the *horloge*, would be rewound and there would be a new beginning.

Even before she entered the house, she knew instinctively that it was her safe haven. Its rooms would be spacious, its windows wide, its walls impenetrable. Exhilarated, she followed the estate agent into the imposing mansion, and although she listened carefully to the recitation of advantages, no inducements were necessary. She stood in front of the magnificent fireplace and decided that she would hang *The Bridal Chair* just above it. She loved the sound of her stiletto heels as they tapped across the polished parquet floors. Mentally, she furnished each room, imagined the swathes of silken draperies on the wide windows. Quiet colors. Periwinkle blue and silver gray. She would rescue her mother's heavy furniture from storage where it had miraculously survived the war. The love seat would be set beneath the bow window, the credenza against the far wall. This was the house that she would buy, the house that would be her home.

Still, Ida, as always a shrewd businesswoman, argued about the price and gained concessions. Renovations were required. The electrical system would have to be updated. Adjustments were offered, thousands of francs deducted. At last, agreement was reached. Holding the precious deed in her hand, Ida and Géa walked to the rear of the property that abutted the tranquil Place Dauphine.

"My father will love this view, this location," she exulted.

"He does not have to love it. This will be your home, not Marc's," Géa reminded her.

"But this will be his home in Paris. He will have his very own apartment here. Perhaps on the second floor," she replied. She looked up at the darkened windows as though envisioning Marc standing there, brush in hand, easel in place, studying the quiet street.

Géa said nothing. He understood wherever Ida lived, Marc would be a presence, just as she had a room in the Orgeval house and would surely have a room in any residence he might purchase on the Riviera. Always their separate homes would accommodate each other. They were too emotionally entwined to live totally apart.

"But you do like the house, don't you, Géa?" she asked.

"It is a beautiful house," he agreed. "But it is a bit too elegant for me."

She looked up at him and knew then that they would never live together on the Quai de l'Horloge. They had reached a crossroads in their lives. Impulsively, she stood on tiptoe and kissed him. He held her close and loosened the scarf of royal blue silk that bound her bright hair so that it cascaded in silken sheaves about her shoulders. It was, he realized, the scarf that he had bought for her in Venice all those months ago. He draped it around her neck and touched her cheek. He noted, for the first time, the new sharpness of her features; her high cheekbones, burnished to a rose-gold hue by the wintry sun, were more defined, and her full lips formed a cupid's bow. He held her hand as they walked to the Pont Neuf and looked down at their reflections in the clear water of the Seine, both of them sadly aware that they were parting ways forever.

Even before she decorated her own bedroom, Ida created an apartment for Marc in her new home, but his visits to the Quai de l'Horloge were infrequent. He disliked Orgeval, but he complained that Paris in the winter was grim and gray, and Paris in the spring was too crowded with tourists. He yearned for the Côte d'Azur, the warmth of its sun-bright days and the wondrous blue of the sea and sky that eased his eyes and animated his brush. He would visit Ida in Paris, but he wanted his own home in the south. He had been a wanderer for too many years.

"I am tired of being a gypsy," he told Virginia. "This wandering Jew is ready to settle down."

She nodded. It did not surprise her that Marc and Ida shared the same yearning. Ida had purchased a home. Marc would do the same.

Marc and Virginia left the Orgeval house without regret and rented a furnished house in Vence. Little David was happiest when he was at the seashore. Ida arrived for a visit and watched the small boy laugh as he darted excitedly into the sea and rushed back to Marc, pulling him into the surf.

Marc briefly submitted to his son's demands. But after some minutes, he trudged wearily back to the beach, exhausted by his race along the surf. Seawater pearled the white tufts of the ear locks that framed his narrow face, and his glinting eyes matched the hue of the surging waves. He collapsed onto the striped canvas beach chair.

"I am too old to be a father to such an active child," he told Ida ruefully.

"Was I such an active child?" she asked.

"I don't remember," he replied abruptly. "What a foolish question, Idotchka. You were a girl, a quiet girl. It is natural for a boy to be strong and boisterous."

His gaze was riveted to David, who was tossing a gaily striped

beach ball into the waves and rushing in after it, laughing exuberantly as it bobbed up and down.

Ida turned away. No, she had not been an active child. She had
not chased rainbow-colored balls in the surf. She had been patient
and quiescent, obediently posing for her father, frozen into stillness as
his brush flew across his canvas. She shook her head. Foolish to think
back. She was a grown woman, and her brother was a small boy
whom she loved. They were siblings of different generations, she
and David. They had been born to different mothers, but they were
her father's children both, vulnerable to his moods and expectations.

David dived beneath foam-fringed wavelets to retrieve his ball,
held it triumphantly above his head, and beckoned to her. She
laughed, sprang to her feet, and ran toward him.

"Throw the ball to me, David," she cried and they raced through
the sea, the small golden-haired boy and the graceful auburn-haired
woman, their laughter mounting as their game grew wilder.

Marc and Virginia continued to search for a permanent home.
Marc compared every property on offer with the homes that
belonged to Picasso and Matisse. He would not settle for less. It was
Ida who solved their problem.

"I've had a letter from my friend Claude Bourdet," she said one
afternoon. "He is selling Les Collines, the house he inherited from
his mother. I am told that it is an elegant home and the grounds
are majestic."

She had chosen her words well. *Elegant. Majestic.* They triggered
Marc's interest.

"Where is it?" he asked.

"It's on the Baou des Blancs, just off the road that goes from
Vence into Saint-Jeannet."

"But I don't like Saint-Jeannet," Virginia protested. "It's so isolated, so rocky, and its poor fountain gives forth only a trickle, as
though it can only manage to emit a few tears."

Ida ignored her and turned to Marc. "I think we should see it. I
am certain that we can get it for a very good price," she said.

"Let's have a look at it," Marc agreed. "You don't object to driving out there, do you, Virginia?"

"Would it matter if I did?" Her tone was light, but she did not smile. "As always, any suggestion from Ida is law."

Ida shrugged. She and Virginia no longer pretended to friendship. They had become wary rivals, competing for Marc's attention and approval. Ida inevitably held sway.

They did visit Les Collines the next day, driving up a cypress-lined driveway and circling past a clutch of eucalyptus trees toward the house. It was, as Ida had said, an elegant villa, dating back to the optimistic Belle Époque, but, Virginia noted with perverse satisfaction, it was in serious disrepair. It reeked of abandonment, its iron railing rusted and its yellow walls discolored by the moisture that leaked through the cracked roof of the terrace. Gleaming shards littered the shattered glass porch. The interior of the house disappointed. Every room required painting, and every window would have to be replaced. Water stains scarred and buckled the floors.

"This is a haunted house," David shouted, darting from room to room. "I don't want to live in a haunted house." But his voice throbbed with excitement rather than fear.

The state of the house did not trouble Ida. It meant, she told them, that the price would be greatly reduced. Despite their new prosperity, she was always in search of a bargain and she delighted in organizing renovations. It had occurred to her that in another era, she might have studied architecture.

"The house has a history," she told them.

Claude's mother, Catherine Pozzi, had lived there with her lover Paul Valéry before the war. Claude, who had been active in the French resistance, had hidden in an outbuilding.

"That is where I shall stay," Ida said as they examined his small self-contained unit.

Virginia stared at her. "Do you plan to live here with us should your father decide to buy Les Collines?" she asked.

Ida laughed. "Of course not. Don't I have my house on the Quai de l'Horloge? But just as my father has an apartment there, I will have rooms here. I will visit, perhaps on weekends, perhaps on holidays. Do you object to that, Virginia?"

"Of course she doesn't." It was Marc who replied.

Virginia turned and went into the garden.

Marc roamed the house and lingered for more than an hour in the large room that Ida suggested could be converted into an ideal studio. Its huge window overlooked the swaying fronds of stately date palms. The fragrance of orange blossoms from the grove below permeated the air. Through the branches of the trees, the Mediterranean and the ancient walls of Vence were visible.

"I could paint wonderful landscapes, never moving from this window," he murmured.

Ida smiled triumphantly.

They went outside and walked around, pausing at the rear of the property where the two majestic crags, Baou des Blancs and Baou des Noirs, stood vigil. Marc paced the property.

"I think that it is as large as Matisse's home in Cimiez and perhaps even larger than the Spaniard's house in Vallauris," he said and smiled complacently at the thought that he would live on a grander scale than his fellow artists.

"And is that important?" Virginia asked irritably.

"Of course it is important that Chagall live as well Matisse and Picasso," he replied. "It is decided. Chagall will buy this house."

"Do you like this haunted house, Mama?" David asked Virginia as they left.

"What I like is of no importance," she replied. "It has been ordained that we live here."

Ida returned to Paris and arranged for the sale, bargaining good-naturedly with Claude Bourdet until her price was agreed upon. Within months, the decrepit house was beautifully renovated. Its facade was painted a gleaming white, and bright green shutters framed the windows. She divided Bella's tables and sofas, her desks and tables rescued from storage, between her house on Quai de l'Horloge and Les Collines.

"You see, *Mamochka* lives on in both our homes," she told Marc as she arranged Bella's bibelots on a small end table, sweeping aside the framed photograph of David that Virginia had placed there.

Virginia smiled grimly. She waited until Ida left and then replaced the photograph.

Ida occasionally drove to Cimiez to visit Matisse. Matisse had sketched her when she was a small girl; he sketched her again during those lazy afternoons in Cimiez.

"I want to capture you as the woman you have become. I knew when you were a child that you would be beautiful," he told her, "but I never realized how beautiful."

"Do you know that everyone speaks the name of Henri Matisse with awe?" she said.

The artist's companion, Lydia Delectorskaya, listened with amusement.

Ida visited Picasso's home in Vallauris, where he showed her his most recent work and accepted her effusive praise. All previous tension between them had evaporated.

"My father says that you are the preeminent artist of our time," she enthused.

"And I am a great admirer of your father," he countered.

Later that week, Françoise Gilot, the artist's mistress, smiled sardonically at the polite exchange of lies.

Françoise Gilot and Lydia Delectorskaya met for coffee in Nice.

"Has the daughter of Chagall paid Henri a visit?" Lydia asked.

"Of course. Quite a seductive visit. I think she is in urgent need of a lover," Françoise said.

"No," Lydia disagreed and smiled benignly. "She is in urgent need of a husband."

The two women, who had no desire to marry their own elderly lovers, laughed, and arm in arm, they made their way down the sunswept rue d'Angleterre.

Chapter Forty-Two

ummer came to an end and the Riviera was draped in an autumnal melancholy. Marc, always unsettled by a change of seasons, decided to master the art of printmaking. He arranged to work at Fernand Mourlot's Paris studio.

"Why should I not have the same skills as the Spaniard?" he asked Virginia.

"Fine. Develop those skills," she said without interest.

They were increasingly reticent with each other, their discussions etched with irritation. He complained that Jean, who had returned from England, was sullen, David was undisciplined. She complained that he gave her too little money for household expenses. They ate their meals in silence.

"Ida will be delighted to have her Papa all to herself in Paris," Virginia added slyly.

"And I am sure your friends at Roquefort will be delighted to see you more frequently during my absence," he countered. He did not like Virginia's new friends at Roquefort-les-Pins who shared her nascent interest in holistic medicine.

Ida was delighted to welcome him to his own apartment in her home. He arrived just as she was planning a retrospective at the Kunsthaus in Zurich and an exhibition of his work in Israel. They worked together each evening, deciding on the disposition of his paintings.

"We must be careful," he cautioned her. "Israel is not Switzerland."

"Don't worry," she assured him. "I will curate both exhibitions."

Ida cooked the Russian foods that he loved and occasionally hosted parties where Marc was lionized by her coterie of friends, artists, and writers. Yet more and more often, she and her father preferred to be alone, wrapped in the cocoon of their shared memories and their mutual commitment to his work. Ida was once again the wise daughter nurturing her needy father.

Virginia did not join them in the city, claiming that a change of scene would be too disruptive for David and Jean. She insisted that she was not lonely without Marc. She and the children were always welcomed by her friends in Roquefort-les-Pins. It was said that the community there was dangerously radical, and Ida was concerned about the influence on Jean and David. On a brief visit to Les Collines, Ida decided to accompany Virginia there.

Her concern was warranted, she decided, after a visit to the communal house where Virginia's friends lived. Ida was repulsed by their self-righteous edicts and their strange domestic arrangements. The sink overflowed with unwashed dishes, the toilets were clogged, and naked children ran through the house. Nude couples wandered about and swam in a murky pond.

"How can you bring the children there, Virginia?" she asked as they drove back to Les Collines. "They're naïfs, pseudo-intellectuals who should have outgrown their foolish bohemianism years ago."

"As you did, Ida?" Virginia asked drily. "In one of your many past lives?"

Ida gripped the steering wheel, angered and startled. Virginia, she knew, was often quietly resentful but never confrontational. She had changed, and the change was profound. She doubted that her father had taken note of it. He reacted only if he was inconvenienced or if he was disturbed when he was working. Virginia, Ida imagined, was wise enough to observe the parameters. She understood that she was hostage to the Chagall largesse.

"Do you bring David and Jean there often?" Ida continued, struggling to keep her tone even. "Do you allow them to watch your friends swim naked?"

"How strange that you who posed naked for your father when you were still a girl should be ill at ease with nudity," Virginia retorted. "Why should David and Jean be shielded from the beauty of the human body? For your information, the children and I occasionally stay at the house when your father is with you in Paris. Which seems to happen more and more often."

"Let me assure you that I never posed nude in front of strangers. My father would not have allowed that then, nor would he allow it now. And he is in Paris because he is concentrating on printmaking and on arrangements for the exhibitions," Ida replied coldly.

"And you, of course, are concentrating on your papa," Virginia retorted daringly. "It must be wonderful to have him all to yourself. That's what you want, isn't it?"

Ida stared straight ahead and remained silent. She returned to Paris carrying a string bag of citrons and the last pale yellow roses of summer from the garden of Les Collines.

"Gifts from Virginia," she told Marc, although David and Jean had gathered the fragrant citrus and she herself had plucked the roses. She did not mention her visit to the commune to him, assuring him only that Virginia was managing well, that the children were in good health, nor did he press her for details. He was totally absorbed in working with her on the catalogs for both the Swiss and the Israeli exhibitions.

On the evening when the catalogs were at last completed, Ida and Marc sat opposite each other in her salon, bonded by their shared fatigue and the satisfaction of their accomplishment. She switched on the radio and they sipped small glasses of cognac as the strains of Mussorgsky's *Pictures at an Exhibition* swirled through the room. It was his favorite piece, Ida knew, igniting as it did memories of his vanished Russia. She herself would have preferred Debussy, but if he was content, she was content. His long, paint-stained fingers strummed the arm of his chair, and his eyes were closed. He was the willing prisoner of the passionate, resonant music that transported him back to the land of his birth.

She stared up at *The Bridal Chair* hanging above her fireplace. It occurred to her for the first time that the empty chair was a promise of a kind; she might yet occupy such a seat one day, as a more knowing and certain bride, and the bouquet she would hold then would be bursting with color. Her father would paint her a new and happier picture, a fitting gift for her new and happy life.

She smiled sadly at the absurdity of the thought and went to the window. The first snowflakes of winter danced in the glow of the street lamps that lined the Quai de l'Horloge and fell gently into the wind-tossed waters of the Seine. She drew the green velvet drapes and returned to her chair.

The Mussorgsky drifted into a new movement and Marc opened his eyes and looked at her. "Don't you ever grow lonely, living alone in this large house, Idotchka?" he asked softly.

"But you are here with me," she replied.

"But I am not always here."

"I don't have time to be lonely, *Papochka*. I have my work, my friends. And I travel so much. Soon I will leave to organize the exhibitions in Switzerland and in Israel. I live in a whirlwind. You must not worry about me."

But even as she reassured him, she was overtaken by a strange and inexplicable conviction that something momentous was about to occur, something that would sweep her into the dangerous vortex of that wild whirlwind she spoke of so casually.

Marc stared at her, aware of the sudden shift of her mood. He crossed the room, knelt beside her, and lifted her hand to his lips.

"I do not worry about you. I know how strong you are. But you must take very good care of yourself, my Ida. I need you more than I can say."

His words both surprised and unsettled her. He was, more often than not, an emotional miser, a hoarder of sentiment. He reserved his passion for his work, portioning out only scattered remnants to those who loved him.

"I know. We need each other," she said softly. She stroked his cheek, passed a finger across the arch of his eyebrow, so thick and gray in odd contrast to the glinting brightness of his blue eyes.

He stood abruptly, gripping his upper thigh, his face contorted with pain, his breath coming in small gasps.

"What is it, *Papochka*? Are you all right?" Her heart pounded with fear.

"A twinge. Just a twinge. It happens now and again. It is nothing, I am sure. But just to be certain, I asked Virginia to arrange for me to see Dr. Le Strange in Nice. There is nothing to worry about. I'm sure I'm all right."

"Of course you are," she said, but she gripped his hand and held it tightly as the Mussorgsky soared to its finale in a cacophonous crescendo.

He was not all right.

"Cancer," Virginia told Ida. Her voice, impeded by the static of the phone line, was eerily calm.

Ida clutched the back of her chair for support, dizzied and faint. Cancer. A word always whispered as though to pronounce it in full voice would be an invitation to the Angel of Death. Cancer, the crab of the zodiac, squeezing life to an end between cruel claws. Its very utterance filled her with terror.

"But I am not worried," Virginia continued. "It is prostate cancer, which is usually contained. My friends in Roquefort tell me that it can be cured by a healthy diet."

"Are your friends at Roquefort qualified physicians?" Ida asked contemptuously. Virginia's casualness, her ridiculous reference to her ridiculous friends, infuriated her. "I do not want to hear their opinions," she continued. "What does Dr. Le Strange say?"

"He advocates an operation. But it is not necessary, I assure you. My friends know a great deal about holistic medicine. They recommend natural cures. I am brewing herbal teas for your father."

"I am not interested in your assurances or your herbal teas," Ida retorted. "I will come to Les Collines and we will decide on a course of action."

"But I have already decided on a course of action," Virginia said defiantly.

"You have no authority to make any decision on my father's behalf. You are not his *wife*," Ida retorted. She slammed the phone down. She had no time to reason with Virginia. She called Elsa in New York. She would rely on her friend's advice.

Elsa listened carefully. "I will consult with our oncologist colleagues," she said.

She called back the next day. "It is true that prostate cancer is often contained, but there is always the danger of metastasis. The oncologists here agree that surgery is definitely the best option. I am sure you can persuade Virginia to agree," she said.

"I don't need her agreement," Ida retorted impatiently.

"But you do need her. At least your father needs her. Tread carefully, Ida."

Ida smiled. "You have advised me to be careful since the day we met," she reminded her friend.

"Advice you never took," Elsa rejoined. "All right, with or without Virginia's agreement, see that surgery is scheduled."

"I will," Ida promised. "When will I see you again, Elsa? You must come and stay at Les Collines with André and little Daniel."

"André is very resistant to returning to Europe. The war is still very much with him. But I promise you this, Ida. When you marry again, we will come to your wedding."

Ida laughed. "Are you so certain that I will marry again, Elsa?"

"Absolutely certain. Just look in the mirror, my dear friend. You are made for love. You will be a wife. You will be a mother," she replied. "You will make your father a proud grandfather. But for now, see to his health. Arrange for the operation."

"I will," she promised.

She immediately called Dr. Le Strange and scheduled the surgery.

"Time is of the essence, of course," he advised her gravely. "We must proceed as soon as possible."

"I understand," she assured him.

There would be no delay. She would travel south as soon all arrangements for the exhibitions in Israel and Switzerland were completed. Seized by a new sense of immediacy, she turned at once to the mountain of documents on her desk, intent on completing the remaining paperwork as swiftly as possible. Elsa had spoken of the danger of metastasis, and she understood what that meant. That would not happen. Her father could not die. She would not allow him to die.

That night, she was awakened by the same invasive dream in which she was, as always, racing hard, clutching her father's hand, in desperate flight from a dark hooded figure. As the menacing pursuer drew closer, she opened her arms and enfolded Marc in a protective embrace, and they soared skyward together, his heart beating against her own. The whistling wind carried them into the clouds, beyond the grasp of the predator she knew to be the *Malach HaMavet*, the Angel of Death, the ruler over the nocturnal kingdom of nightmare and terror.

"He will not win," she shouted into the darkness.

At last her work for the exhibitions was completed and she rushed to Marc's favorite patisserie where she purchased an assortment of éclairs, gâteaux, and strawberries dipped in chocolate. At a market in Les Halles, she bought a basket of black truffles and the wild sorrel for the schav soup he so often craved. She held the delicacies on her lap throughout the journey, and when she reached Les Collines, she spread the delicacies across the dining room table.

"I have brought your favorite sweets, Papa," she proclaimed, ripping open the stiff white boxes and displaying her treasures. "And tonight I shall make you a pasta with truffles in a wine sauce. And schav with sour cream."

Marc's face brightened, but Virginia glared at her.

"Your father must not have rich foods. He is on a strict diet that my friends designed especially for him," she said icily even as he lunged toward the pastries and seized an éclair.

"Am I to be denied all sweetness in my life?" he asked plaintively.

"*Non, mon père. Non.*" Ida assured him. "You shall have sweetness." She took the éclair he had selected, placed it on a plate, and handed him a fork. He ate greedily, the cream dripping down his chin, the chocolate staining his lips.

Ida wiped his mouth gently with her handkerchief, added an apple tart, and smiled as he ate. She and Virginia did not look at each other, nor did Virginia protest when small David popped a chocolate-covered strawberry into his mouth. The battle was over. Ida had prevailed yet again.

The next day, she accompanied Marc to the clinic in Nice and arrangements were made for the surgery.

"There will be two separate procedures," Dr. Le Strange told them. "I am afraid it will consume two months of your life, *cher maître*, but after that, you will be fully recovered." He smiled benignly. Artists were his favorite patients. "They are like children," he had told Madame Le Strange more than once. He reflected that Marc Chagall, whose work he so admired, behaved like a vulnerable child. The great artist's lip trembled, and his fingers curled into fists.

"Will it hurt?" he asked plaintively.

It was Ida who answered. "You won't feel a thing, Papa. You will be asleep," she said in the tone used by reassuring mothers. "Isn't that right, Doctor?"

"You may have some discomfort afterward," he acknowledged, "but that is to be expected."

Marc shrugged, but his face was ashen and drops of perspiration beaded his brow. Ida gently patted it dry with her embroidered white handkerchief.

"It will be all right, *Papochka*," Ida said softly when they were alone.

"I hate hospitals. Your mother died in a hospital." In his mind's eye, he saw Bella's slender lifeless body on the narrow white bed beneath the outline of the crucifix that the nursing sister had so sensitively removed.

"This is a clinic, not a hospital. Virginia will be able to stay in your room. And I too will be here," she assured him.

"But you must be in Zurich for the retrospective," he protested.

"Planes fly from Zurich to Nice. I can be back and forth within hours. It will be no problem." She smiled and rubbed his hands, which were as cold as ice, although the room was overheated. "I promise."

She sat beside Virginia in the hospital waiting room on the morning of the surgery. It would be a swift procedure, Dr. Le Strange assured them. No longer than two hours. But two hours passed and then three. Pale nurses hurried in and out of the operating theater. Virginia clutched her hand, sharp nails digging into the softness of her palm.

"Will he be all right, Ida?"

"He must be."

She thought to pray, but she knew only one prayer, and it was not a prayer for the living.

At last, Dr. Le Strange emerged. There had been complications, an unpredictable sudden loss of blood. But he was stabilized. He was fine. All was well.

Ida stood and held out her hand.

"Thank you," she said faintly. "Thank you so much."

She was with Virginia at Marc's bedside as he awakened from the anesthesia. She kissed him on the forehead and waited for his sleepy smile.

"You see, Papa. All is well. And now I am off to Zurich. I will see you in a few days' time."

"My Idotchka," he murmured and closed his eyes.

She turned to Virginia, mindful of Elsa's advice. "I am grateful to you," she said. "I will be at ease in Zurich knowing that you are here."

"I do not need your gratitude. Whatever I do, I do for Marc," Virginia replied. "I understand my duty. My duty to him. My debt to him."

Odd words, Ida thought. *Duty. Debt.* The single word *love* would have sufficed. She stared at Virginia, who busied herself with straightening the items on Marc's bedside table, lining up pill bottles and carafe, moving the bud vase with its single yellow rose to the windowsill.

Ida left, closing the door softly behind her. She sighed and glanced at her watch. She would have to hurry if she was to catch her plane.

Chapter Forty-Three

*Z*urich was gray and cold. Ida's hotel room was austere and spotless. Her bed faced the crescent-shaped Lake Zurich. White drapes, grayed by an excess of inferior laundering, covered the small-paned, frost-encrusted windows. She welcomed the monochromatic calm and the silence that was broken only by the tolling of the bells of the Grossmünster. She scanned the sheaf of messages the concierge had handed her. She was expected at a cocktail party in her honor that evening at six, hosted by patrons of the Kunsthaus. It was to be followed by a dinner in the grand ballroom of L'Hôtel Royale. The arts editor of *La Gazette* requested an interview. A commentator for Radio Suisse asked if she would consent to be a guest on his program.

"All of Switzerland is honored by your presence," the commentator wrote fawningly and she smiled bitterly, recalling the unanswered letters she had addressed to relief agencies in Switzerland in her desperate wartime struggle for refuge. A Chagall presence had been singularly unwelcome then. "All right," she told herself severely, recalling Géa's words. "That was then and this is now." She would not allow bitterness to hobble her forever.

The church bell tolled yet again. She counted.

"One. Two. Three. Good. I have time for a nap," she said aloud. An afternoon nap would be a luxury and a welcome one.

She unpacked swiftly and collapsed onto the bed, submitting to the exhaustion that had weighed her down for so many weeks. She closed her eyes, breathed deeply, and fell into a deep and blissfully dreamless sleep. The persistent ringing of the phone jarred her into wakefulness.

"Mademoiselle Chagall? Mademoiselle Ida Chagall?" The man's voice was deep and sonorous.

"Yes. I am Ida Chagall," she murmured drowsily.

The sky was dark and the church bells tolled the evening hour. It was seven o'clock. Her heart sank. She had missed the reception in her honor hosted by the patrons of the Kunsthaus.

"I am Franz Meyer," her caller continued. "We grew concerned when you did not come to the reception and I was asked to make certain that you are well."

"I must apologize, Monsieur Meyer."

She struggled to think of an excuse to offer this man whose voice was heavy with concern. She decided on the truth. This was Switzerland, the land of peace, honesty, and neutrality.

"I confess that I fell asleep. I hope you can forgive me."

"Of course. Of course. So foolish of us not to give you time to recover from the journey. Are you rested enough to join us for dinner?"

"I am. Thank you for being so understanding."

"I am in the lobby of the hotel. I shall wait for you there. May I presume to remind you that the dinner is formal?"

"Yes. Of course," she said, although she had not remembered that. What a kind and considerate man he was, this Franz Meyer, whose name was oddly familiar. "I will be with you shortly."

"Please do not hurry unnecessarily. L'Hôtel Royale is nearby."

"Thank you," she said gratefully.

She selected a russet-colored, full-skirted taffeta gown, the bodice artfully cut into a jeweled neckline that exposed her shoulders. It was perhaps too daring for the conventional patrons of the Kunsthaus, but she decided that she did not care. The daughter of Marc Chagall was allowed extravagancies of dress. She looped an amber necklace around her neck, twisted her hair into a loose chignon, shrugged into a hooded, fur-lined cape, and smiled at her reflection in the mirror. Her long nap had been wonderfully restorative. Her soft-skinned, full-featured face was no longer tight with tension, and her gold-flecked eyes were newly bright. She reached for her evening bag, left her room, and descended into the dimly lit lobby.

He stood at the concierge's desk, a slender dark-haired man in well-tailored evening dress, who, with great care, was wiping his spectacles clean. She watched him, amused by his absorption, recognizing him at once as a man who would focus his complete attention on the smallest of tasks. A careful man. She approached him.

"Monsieur Meyer?" She smiled her well-practiced engaging smile.

He stared at her as though taken by surprise, the color rising to his cheeks.

"I am Ida Chagall. Were you not expecting me?" she asked, amused by his confusion.

"Yes. Yes, of course I was expecting you. I was just not expecting you to be so beautiful." The words tumbled from his mouth unbidden, startling him because he was not given to such openness, and startling Ida because he spoke with such spontaneity.

"And I was not expecting you to be so young," she countered.

Franz Meyer, she remembered belatedly, was the distinguished art historian and the director of the Bern Kunsthalle, Switzerland's foremost museum. She had written to him regarding the transfer of the exhibition from Zurich to Bern and his replies had been cordial, his concern for detail matching her own. Her first impression had been correct. He was indeed a careful man.

She placed her hand on his arm and together they went out into the piercing cold of the wintry evening.

The dinner was pleasant and she played her role well. Her worries about her father fell away as she stepped back into her element. She was Marc Chagall's daughter, charming his admirers, cultivating critics and collectors. Across the table, seated beneath the glittering chandelier, Franz Meyer watched her and smiled. Aware of his attention, she nodded at him. He lifted his glass of wine and she lifted hers, a silent toast of companionable complicity.

They left together and walked through the silent streets.

"Will you be warm enough?" he asked.

"Of course," she replied and lifted the hood of her cape.

"It is wonderful to walk and talk in the silence of the night," he said.

"It is a luxury," she agreed, "and one I seldom have time to enjoy."

"I don't think of it as a luxury," he protested. "It is when I walk that I assimilate my ideas. I do my research in museums and libraries, but that knowledge becomes cohesive only when I walk. Sometimes when I return to my desk, I do not even take off my overcoat before I begin to write because I am afraid that I will lose the thought that came to me on the wings of the wind. Does that sound strange to you?"

"No," she replied. "My father has often said that the themes of his work came to him walking through a forest or staring out at the sea. That is how words must float toward you."

She had read several of his monographs in scholarly art journals and marveled at the depth of his knowledge and the insights of his perception.

"Are you yourself an artist, Ida?" he asked. He uttered her given name hesitantly as though he had too prematurely crossed the border into intimacy.

"I have a small gift, Franz." His name fell easily from her lips. "I do paint and sketch when time permits, but the pressures of being my father's representative make it difficult for me to concentrate on my own work."

"Your father is fortunate to have such a devoted daughter," he said.

"And I am fortunate to have such a father," she replied.

"Yes. It seems that you are both blessed."

His words surprised her. Franz Meyer, vested as he was with his insight into the artistic personality, understood her commitment. Unlike Géa and Michel, he did not challenge her devotion or question her willingness to prioritize her father's needs above her own. But then he was neither husband nor lover. They barely knew each other. Of course, his judgment was not compromised nor was it relevant to her. He would return to Bern before the week was out, and after the Chagall exhibition at his own museum, he would be gone from her life.

But when they reached her hotel, he impulsively removed her hood. "How beautiful your hair is," he said.

Wordlessly, she loosened the pins that held the chignon in place and allowed it to cascade about her shoulders.

He lifted a single swath and held it to his cheek. "*À demain*," he said softly. "May I see you then and show you our wonderful Zurich?"

"*À demain*," she agreed, suffused with delight at his invitation.

They met the next day and strolled slowly along the banks of the Limmat waterway and ate lunch at a quaint quayside café in the shadow of the twin towers of the Grossmünster. Franz ordered a cheese fondue, a dish that was new to her, and taught her how to dip the thinly sliced toast into the swirling pool of melted Gruyère. When she fumbled, he fed her from his own long fork, a gesture that delighted her and made her feel cared for. That, she realized, was a rare experience.

"Fondue was the food of my childhood," he said and spoke with ease and amusement of his family. "My mother thinks of us as Swiss aristocracy," he said, smiling wryly. "She is foolishly proud of our wealth and holdings. Foolish because they are inherited and came to us by accident of birth. I myself have always found that kind of wealth to be something of an embarrassment."

"Neither my father nor I have ever considered money to be an embarrassment," Ida said frankly. "Perhaps because we lived in fear for so many years, racing away from hatred and knowing that we would have to buy our way to freedom. I confess to being careful about money. I think of it as the key to independence. My father thinks of it as protection against the violent threats of a dangerous world."

"Yes. I have seen the terror in many of his paintings," Franz observed quietly. "The fierceness of his colors, his fleeing figures, his frightened creatures struggling for balance in an unbalanced landscape."

She stared at him in surprise. Few critics had recognized that dimension in Marc's work.

Although he had planned to leave after the opening of the retrospective, Franz remained in Zurich. He escorted her to the museum each day and drove her to the airport for her weekly flights to Nice.

She explained that she had promised Marc that she would visit him at the clinic as often as possible and she would not disappoint him.

"You are a remarkable and caring daughter," he said, taking her hand. "But then you are a remarkable and caring woman."

His words touched her heart. He valued her for who she was. She turned to him, her eyes soft with gratitude.

Elsa phoned from New York to inquire about Marc's recovery and was upset when Ida told her of her frequent visits to Nice.

"It is too exhausting. It will make you ill," she warned.

"My father needs me," Ida insisted.

"Or do you perhaps need him to need you?" Elsa asked.

Ida did not reply. She understood that with that question, Elsa was once again issuing a warning.

And Marc did need her. Virginia was solicitous, but he relied on Ida's presence and her assertiveness. It was Ida who persuaded the cook to prepare the tasty dishes and the sweet desserts that he preferred and Ida who arranged a room that looked out on the sea. He was painting again, but he was impatient to explore new dimensions, obsessed as he was by an irrational urgency. His ambitions soared and he feared that too few years were left for him to accomplish all that he envisioned.

"I want to work on a mural, on many murals. And in stained glass. And I have never done ceramics. If the Spaniard can work with clay, so can I," he said. "But to do all that, I must outrun the *Malach HaMavet*, the Angel of Death." He laughed bitterly.

"But you have already defeated him, *Papochka*," Ida said soothingly. His intensity frightened her.

"No one defeats him," he replied.

He complained that the household was badly run, that Virginia spent too much money.

"You must speak to her, Ida," he insisted.

With great hesitancy, she asked Virginia to try to practice some domestic economies. "You know how my father is about money," she said apologetically.

"I know that all too well," Virginia replied coldly. "I assure you that I do my best. The baker expects to be paid. As does the wine merchant and the butcher. And when guests come to stay, good meals must be prepared. And that costs money."

"Of course," Ida agreed. "And are guests expected?"

"Possibly. We've had a letter from Charles Leirens, the Belgian photographer who stayed with us at High Falls. He took those magnificent portraits of your father and David."

"They are quite wonderful," Ida agreed. "When he visited us in New York, he took beautiful photographs of my mother. I wonder what became of them."

"I don't know. I've never seen them," Virginia said too quickly. "Now he wants to come to Les Collines and shoot a film about Marc at work. What do you think?"

"If my father consents, I suppose it's all right."

"I did not think I needed your permission." Virginia's voice was edged with annoyance.

Virginia might resent Ida, but Jean and David delighted in her visits. "When are you coming again? Come soon," they shouted as she left.

That arduous commute between Nice and Zurich was repeated for two months. Franz drove her to the aerodrome each Friday and was waiting when she returned. They embraced at each parting and embraced again at each reunion. Their intimacy grew slowly. They were not yet lovers. Ida was at last being careful. Elsa, she thought, would be pleased.

The retrospective moved to the Kunsthalle in Bern, Franz's precinct. He and Ida acted as joint curators, working in tandem, anticipating each other's decisions, sharing ideas. Once again, the exhibition was a critical success. Reassuring reviews appeared in every newspaper and they read them together, their gratification mutual, their pleasure shared.

"We deserve a vacation," he said as she carefully clipped the most recent review of the exhibition. "Why not join me on a visit to my parents' estate?"

She sighed. "I'm afraid I can't. I must see my father in Nice and then I leave for Israel to arrange for his exhibitions there."

His eyes were dark with disappointment, but he did not pressure her. "I understand," he said quietly. "I think it is wonderful that you are so loyal to your father. To his work. But please write to me. I will need your letters. You have not yet left and I already miss you."

At the Bern aerodrome, he touched her cheek very gently and handed her a framed photograph of the two of them together, standing in a circlet of sunlight outside the Kunsthalle.

"I thought you beautiful when I first saw you," he murmured. "But now that I have come to know you, you are even more beautiful to me."

"Dear Franz. My dear good Franz." Her words, so softly spoken, were lost in the insistent revving of the small plane's motor.

He cupped his face in his large hands and, for the very first time, his lips brushed hers, lightly, tenderly. Her heart turned. Holding the photograph close, she walked very slowly up the tarmac and boarded the waiting aircraft.

Chapter Forty-Four

I srael is ablaze with sunlight and my heart is ablaze with joy at being here," Ida wrote in her first letter to Franz. "I feel as though I have come home."

She was certain that he would understand her passionate reaction to Israel just as he understood the impact Judaism had on her father's work. She had told him once, as they sat in their favorite café on the banks of the Limmat, sipping the hot chocolate they both favored, that it seemed to her that he had a Jewish heart.

It would not surprise him that from the moment of her arrival, from her first inhalation of the air so sweetly scented by orange blossoms, from the first touch of her foot on the friable earth, she had felt an intimate connection to the country. She was invigorated by the optimism and excitement of the people she encountered. They soared on the wings of history. Their war for independence and survival had been fought and won; they were in a new era of creativity and nation building. Their spirit, their hope for the future, their determination to seize each day, was contagious. Enthused by their enthusiasm, energized by their energy, she plunged into her own work, leaving from her bed each day at first light. She was in Israel on a mission. There was much that had to be accomplished in a very short time.

The Tel Aviv Museum, small and poorly lit, was the venue for her father's exhibition. Her heart sank when she first wandered through its narrow and badly lit galleries, but she struggled to hide her dismay and set to work.

"I know that the museum is not up to standard," the curator said apologetically.

"Do not worry," she said reassuringly. "We will manage."

Swiftly and decisively, she arranged for new lighting to be installed and for furnishings to be moved to accommodate the larger canvases. She charmed workmen and electricians alike, hoisting paintings herself, infusing those around her with her own energy.

"My father's work is very much at home on these walls," she said when the exhibition was in place.

In Jerusalem, she worked with the curators of the Israel Museum.

"We look forward to welcoming your father to Jerusalem," Moshe Sharett, the foreign minister, said. "Our president, Chaim Weizmann, will open the exhibition."

"And my father looks forward to being here," she replied, although she knew that Marc's presence was unlikely.

She traveled north to Kibbutz Ein Harod in the foothills of the lower Galilee where several paintings would be exhibited. She was entranced by the beauty of the sylvan glades and the soaring mountains that surrounded the settlement. It was the landscape that had so intrigued her father when he visited Palestine all those years ago, informing the biblical themes that he turned to again and again.

Hillel, the kibbutz secretary, a tall, sun-bronzed young man, welcomed her and proudly guided her through the orchards and the fields, the row of neat bungalows, and the airy dining hall. Her heart soared when she watched the kibbutz children, the sturdy boys and girls who raced among the flowers in the garden of the children's house. Toddlers tumbled about in the playground and plump infants crawled beneath a canopy of eucalyptus trees, smiled up at her. A little girl tugged at her skirt and Ida lifted her and briefly held her close, the child's breath warm and sweet against her face.

Kibbutz members returning from the fields nodded and whispered her name to each other. *Ida Chagall. The famous artist's daughter. Ida Chagall. How beautiful she is.*

She smiled at them, her color high, her eyes bright with a pleasure that matched their own.

"We are all excited by your visit. It is a great honor for us to exhibit your father's paintings here," Hillel said.

"My father and I feel that the honor is ours," she replied. "The very existence of Israel gives us comfort."

She looked up at the Jewish flag on the rough-hewn wooden pole outside the communal library that fluttered in the gentle mountain breeze and was briefly overcome with sorrow for all that might have been, for the tragic vagaries of history. Had there been a Jewish state before the war, her family would have had a place of sanctuary. If Israel had existed then, countless lives would have been saved. Small Shayna, whose hair was the color of the lemons that grew on the trees of Ein Harod, would not have been buried in the icy waters of the Atlantic. Bella Chagall would not have died among strangers.

"Comfort?" Hillel repeated. The word puzzled him.

"Yes. It comforts me to know that you are here, in this land, because there is an Israel. It comforts me to know that no child of mine will ever be a stateless person."

"How many children do you have?" he asked.

"None. I have not yet been blessed with children," she replied.

Her own words startled her. *Not yet*, she had said. A question invaded. *Then when?* It was not a question she had ever asked herself before, nor was it a question that she could answer.

Then when? That strange mental query lingered and teased as she read the letter from Franz Meyer that the concierge handed her on her return to Tel Aviv.

He wrote in his elegant script that he missed her, missed her laughter, missed the sound of her voice. It was very cold in Bern. How he envied her the sunlight and warmth of Israel and how he longed for the warmth and light she exuded wherever she went. "Are my words too daring?" he wrote. "Will you come to Bern when you return from Israel or shall I come to the Riviera?"

She understood that his question was not a question. It was a statement, a declaration.

She read and reread his letter, then stared at the photograph on her bedside table. How grave was his narrow face, how gentle his eyes behind those large rimless spectacles. How calm she felt when she was with him. How loved she felt when she read his letters, when she remembered the softness of his voice. *Franz*. She spoke his name softly and took up her pen.

"Franz, dear Franz. Come to the Riviera," she wrote. "Come to Les Collines, my father's home. We will meet there."

She would welcome this serious and careful man, her Franz, her dear Franz, into her father's home and into her life. She read his letter again. She had asked herself a question and mysteriously, an answer had come.

She opened the window and looked out at the sea, at the waves brushed silver by the newborn moon. Her sleep that night was deep and dreamless, suffused as she was with a new contentment, a new certainty.

Chapter Forty-Five

She returned to France and to her surprise, Franz awaited her at the Orly Airport, holding a bouquet of yellow roses. She melted into his arms, scattering fragrant petals at their feet.

"I know we were to have met in Nice, but there you would have been surrounded by your family," he explained. "I wanted to have you all to myself for a few days first. I hope you don't mind."

"I'm delighted," she said honestly and rested her head on his shoulder.

He had made the right decision. There would be too many claims on her at Les Collines. Her father would insist on a full report of the exhibitions in Israel, the children would clamor for her attention, and Virginia would pelt her with complaints. In Paris, she and Franz had the luxury of privacy, a respite from invasive demands and obligations.

At her home on the Quai de l'Horloge, they toasted each other with the champagne he had brought, both of them flushed with the simple pleasure of being together. Their words collided, their laughter melded. They spoke of the past and planned their future. His voice, as always, was very soft and hers throbbed with excitement. She could scarcely believe her good fortune.

It occurred to them that they were hungry. Her housekeeper had left meager provisions and she bustled about in her kitchen, still in her traveling clothes, tossing together a mushroom omelet and a salad, moving with her usual swift efficiency, aware of his admiring gaze. Her every gesture seemed wondrous to him. Growing up in a household staffed by servants, he found this new domestic intimacy endearing. But then he found everything about Ida endearing.

"Your father and I met briefly in Bern, when he visited the exhibition," he told her as they ate, occasionally replenishing their flutes of champagne. "We had much in common."

"And now you have even more in common," she said teasingly. *"Moi. Moi même."*

"You are certain that he will accept me into his family?" he asked apprehensively.

"It will not matter to me if he does not," she replied, matching his seriousness with her own. "I am a grown woman in charge of my own life, my own future. But you must not worry. He will accept you without reservation. He will recognize your goodness, your talent, your love of art, and the happiness you have given me. You will see that when you come to Les Collines."

"I will be there soon," he promised and caressed her face, tracing each feature with his long fingers, lightly touching her full lips and stroking her thick eyebrows.

"Very soon," she commanded sternly, removing his spectacles, twirling them playfully as she leaned forward and kissed him.

"Very soon," he agreed, retrieving the spectacles and holding her close.

Her beauty stopped his heart. Her gaiety intrigued; her vivacity delighted. She had penetrated the walls of a somber seriousness that had so long encircled him. He felt himself liberated. His scholarship, his dedication to art, would be enhanced by her talent and insight. He reached into his pocket and removed a small velvet box that contained an antique ring, an emerald set in filigreed gold. He slipped it onto her finger.

"My grandmother's," he said. "And my great-grandmother's before her. An emerald to match your eyes."

She looked at him, joyous and amazed. She understood what the ring meant. It was his formal commitment to the shared destiny they had already embraced. They were engaged. They would marry. Tears stood in her eyes. Tears of ecstasy, tears of hope and tenderness. She touched the verdant stone, amazed by its smoothness.

"An emerald," she said and recalled the tales her mother had told her of her grandparents' jewelry store in Vitebsk.

"I played with emeralds," Bella had said. "I wore a crown of real sapphires, real emeralds on Purim. Where are those emeralds and sapphires now, Idotchka? Where?"

Her mother's plaintive question lingered in memory. She marveled that she was marrying a man whose legacy was intact, whose inheritance had not been forfeit to war and hatred. She had entered a safe harbor.

She left for Nice and Franz accompanied her to the Gare de Lyon. They had agreed that it would be best for her to have some time alone with her family. She and Marc had a great deal to talk about. She wanted to tell him that Franz, who was so very important to her, would be coming to Les Collines. Marc did not enjoy surprises.

"I will be with you very soon," Franz promised as she boarded the train.

She waved to him from her carriage window and continued to wave until the train gathered speed and she could no longer see him. She held her hand up to the light. The emerald ring turned sea green at the touch of a vagrant sunbeam. Her father would delight in its protean hue, she knew, and he would surely delight in her new happiness. Of course he would accept Franz. He wanted her to have children. He would welcome grandchildren. She smiled at the extravagance of her own imaginings.

She swept into Les Collines, radiant and effervescent. She had bought a brightly colored high Bukharan skullcap for Marc. She planted it on his tangle of gray curls.

"You must wear it when you go to Israel for the Jerusalem opening," she said. "They are waiting for you, *Papochka*. They plan a grand reception. For you and for Virginia."

"For me?" Virginia asked sardonically. "They are waiting for Virginia McNeil in Israel? Are the rabbis of Jerusalem eager to greet Marc Chagall's *shiksa*?" She smiled wanly and opened and closed the elegant purse Ida had bought for her. It was not a gift that pleased her.

"You speak foolishly, Virginia," Marc said harshly.

"Do I?" The purse slid to the floor as she sprang to her feet and stared down at him, her cheeks mottled with anger. "Have you thought about the children? Who will care for them if I am trailing after you through synagogues and ruins? What about my own work, my friends?"

"Your work? Your friends?" he asked contemptuously, his voice rising dangerously. "Your work? Is the world waiting for your drawings, your poems? Did your friends at Roquefort rescue you from poverty as I did? It is your duty to accompany me."

Virginia glared at him and stalked out of the room.

He sank back into his chair, depleted by his own fury. The colorful Bukharan hat was askew, his cheeks rouged by a dangerous rise of blood pressure. Ida thought that he looked like a pathetic, aged clown. The disloyalty of the thought shamed her.

"How can I go to Israel alone?" he asked.

"Virginia will go with you," Ida assured him. "She needs time to think things through."

She understood that Virginia was an expert player in the game of survival. She might defy Marc by acting like a resentful and petulant schoolgirl, but she was actually biding her time. In the end, she would accompany Marc to Israel because she was not prepared for a final breach. She had not left John McNeil until she had found refuge with Marc. She would not leave Marc until another man offered her comfort and sanctuary. But such an offer had not presented itself. Not yet.

Ida was not wrong. In the end, Virginia agreed to go to Israel with Marc. The children would be cared for by her friends at Roquefort.

"A sensible decision," Ida said as they drove home from the spice market in Nice one afternoon. "The children will be fine."

"I see that you have abandoned your objections to my Bohemian friends now that it is convenient," Virginia replied coldly.

Ida hesitated. The time for honesty had come. She chose her words carefully.

"My opinion of your friends is unimportant. You do not need my approval. But what I do ask of you is that you care for my father, that you try once again to offer him some measure of contentment. He deserves that after all that he has done for you," she said at last.

Virginia swerved off the road and parked the car in the shade of an olive grove. She was very pale; her hands trembled.

"I do care for Marc," she said quietly. "He is David's father, and our son was born out of our love. Or what I thought was our love. But our relationship is greatly changed. He seems to feel no tenderness for me. I must ask him for the smallest amounts of money, and even that he seems to begrudge me. He turns to you to check the household accounts. I think he considers me a servant. He sees me as David's nursemaid, not his mother. I am his housekeeper, his chauffeur. I drive him to visit Matisse, to visit Picasso, but he often forgets to invite me to enter their homes with him. He summons me to be his model. I pose for him. He paints my body, but he no longer touches it. And I am young, Ida. I have needs. I want even a fraction of the passion he reserves for his paintings." Her voice broke. "Do you understand what I am saying?"

"I do," Ida replied.

How could she not understand? She and Virginia were almost the same age, their feelings similar, their needs and impulses shared. She thought of her own yearning for Franz's tenderness, the surge of joy that caused her to tremble at his touch. Virginia surely had similar yearnings; she too sought tenderness and joy. She sympathized with Virginia, but her loyalty to Marc was inviolate.

"My father is not a young man," she said. "You have always known that."

"It is not his age that has driven us apart. It is his attitude, his lack of sensitivity to me, to what I need," Virginia protested. "You know how distant we have become to each other. He does not talk to me. He issues instructions, reprimands."

"Perhaps you both need a vacation, a time to rebuild your closeness. Your time in Israel will give you that," Ida said, but she recognized the futility of her own words. Marc would treat Virginia no differently in Israel than he treated her at Les Collines.

"Perhaps," Virginia said, her voice heavy with doubt. She looked down at the ring on Ida's finger. "It's beautiful," she said, touching the smooth stone. "I haven't seen it before."

"Yes. It's a gift. A wonderful gift."

"I would guess that it is from Franz Meyer. We met him when we visited the exhibition in Bern there. He spoke endlessly about you. And with great admiration. More than admiration. I told Marc that we would soon see Franz Meyer again." Virginia smiled knowingly.

"Yes. The ring is a gift from Franz Meyer. It is a wonderful gift and he is a wonderful man. And you are right. You will see him again very soon. He will soon arrive at Les Collines."

"In all the years we have been together, Marc has never given me a ring," Virginia said wistfully.

"But he has given you a great deal, has he not?" Ida asked.

"Has he?" Virginia turned the key in the ignition, pressed down on the accelerator, and drove too swiftly back to Les Collines.

Franz, having arrived a day earlier than he was expected, ran toward them.

He embraced Ida and then turned to Virginia and kissed her on both cheeks.

"It is good to see you again," he said. "Our meeting in Bern was so enjoyable."

"We are glad you are here. And Ida, I think, is very glad." Virginia nodded and left them.

Ida smiled. She was glad that she and Virginia had spoken so openly. At the very least, there was finally peace of a kind between them.

She looked up at Franz. "Have you seen my father?" she asked.

"I have," he replied. "He welcomed me warmly. I told him of our feelings for each other and our plans for a future together. He was pleased. All he has ever wanted, he said, was your happiness. You were right. We do not have to fear his disapproval."

"You see," Ida said. "Of course I was right. I am always right. Remember that, Monsieur Meyer."

She kissed him on the lips, snatched the white silk scarf from his neck, and dashed away, laughing as he raced after her down the long driveway lined with eucalyptus trees. They did not look up at the terrace where Virginia stood staring down at them, sadness in her eyes and a wistful smile on her lips.

———

Marc's approval of Franz was enthusiastic. Ida, he proclaimed to Matisse as the two artists sat together on the balcony in Cimiez, could not have chosen better.

"He is a calm man. A serious man. And my Ida, you know, she is like a shooting star. This Franz Meyer will make certain that she remains anchored to earth. He earned his doctorate in art history and there is little that he does not know. Of course he was born into the art world. He comes from a family of collectors."

"Then he must be quite wealthy," Henri Matisse observed.

"Very wealthy," Marc agreed.

Franz's familial wealth pleased and reassured him. Ida's marriage would catapult her into a world of advantage and prestige that would extend to Marc himself.

"My hope is that he will make your daughter happy," Matisse said softly.

The renowned artist had always been fond of Ida. He had, through the years, sketched her as an enchanting child, then as a shy young girl, and most recently as a sensuous woman, aware of the power of her beauty. It saddened him that he would probably not live long enough to sketch her in the fullness of motherhood, perhaps holding an infant to her breast.

———

During Franz's frequent visits to Les Collines, he and Marc spent long hours in earnest discussions.

"I think you prefer my father's company to mine," Ida said teasingly, but the rapport between her father and her fiancé pleased her. For the first time since her mother's death, her family felt whole again.

Franz spoke easily of Picasso and Matisse, offered effortless insights on the impact of the Fauvists on the impressionists, of the ways in which religion influenced the nuances of artists of every generation. Marc, who was considering the decoration of the baptistery of a church in Haute-Savoie, asked him if he thought it necessary that an artist be of the religion of those who commissioned the work.

"But hasn't Jacques Lipchitz, a believing Jew, sculpted a bronze Virgin Mary?" Franz said in reply. "He is no less a Jew for creating a work of art for a church and the church is not compromised by offering a venue to the work of a Jew. We all worship one God."

Marc nodded. Franz's answer pleased and reassured him. Franz himself pleased and reassured him.

Ida and Franz saw Marc and Virginia off as they left for Israel.

"You are visiting the country when it is at its most beautiful," Ida effused to Virginia. "Everything is in blossom in June. It will be a wonderful trip."

Her words were sincere. Her own happiness allowed for generosity.

"You and my father will share so much," she added.

"I hope so," Virginia said dubiously. "I want us to be happy with each other again."

"You will be. You will be," Ida promised. "Israel will restore you to each other."

Chapter Forty-Six

*I*srael did not restore them to each other. It seemed to Ida that they were even more at odds when they returned. Marc was in high spirits, his blue eyes gimlet-sharp in his sun-bronzed face. In contrast, Virginia was pale and painfully thin. She had found the heat difficult to cope with and she could barely eat the food.

"All that herring, olives, salt cheese," she complained.

"What is wrong with herring?" Marc retorted jovially. "My father made his living carting herring barrels."

"Yes, I know. You've told me that often enough," she responded drily.

Marc ignored her and enthused about Israel. Its beauty and history engaged him and filled him with pride.

"Ah, how I love our country," he told Ida.

"It is hardly your country," Virginia murmured.

"I carried my sketchpad everywhere," Marc said, ignoring her yet again.

He flipped it open, showing Ida and Franz his depictions of the streets of Nazareth, the valleys and hills of the Galilee, the stately cypresses and ancient buildings of Jerusalem.

"They will guide me when I work on my illustrations for the Torah," he said.

Virginia sat in morose silence as he boasted of the reception he had been given. He described the state dinners with Chaim Weizmann, the president, and David Ben-Gurion, the prime minister. He had visited the army headquarters of General Moshe Dayan.

"Moshe Dayan asked me why Marc does not settle in Israel," Virginia said drily.

"And what did you tell him?" Ida asked.

"I told him it was because Israel is too hot," she replied and laughed harshly.

Marc shrugged, indifferent to the irony of her words. He described the crowds of Israelis who had flocked to the opening of his exhibition at the museum in Tel Aviv.

"You see, *Papochka*," Ida said. "I told you that the people of Israel would love Marc Chagall."

"Of course. Everyone loved Marc Chagall," he said merrily. "Even Golda Myerson, that ugly American woman who was born in Russia and is now a member of Ben-Gurion's cabinet. She is said to love no one, but she loved Marc Chagall. We went with her to the Habima Theater and saw *The Dybbuk*. Wasn't it a wonderful show, Virginia?"

"How could I tell? The performance was in Yiddish. I might have asked you to translate, but you and your ugly Golda were too engrossed in your own Yiddish conversation," Virginia replied.

Her tone was indifferent rather than accusatory. It occurred to Ida that Virginia no longer resented Marc's usage of Russian and Yiddish, languages that she did not understand. Conditioned to exclusion, she no longer cared.

"It was a beautiful production," Marc continued. "The klezmer musicians played the tunes that your mother loved, Idotchka. You must remember them." He hummed the joyous music, seized Ida's hands, and danced her around the room. Franz clapped appreciatively, but Virginia frowned and led Jean and David into the garden.

⸻

Summer drifted into autumn. Marc worked in ceramics and insisted that Virginia drive him each day to a pottery in Vence. She complained that the journeys intruded on her own work.

"Your little drawings?" he responded dismissively. "That is what you call your work? Can you compare it with what I am now doing? Ceramics opens a new world for me."

"Yes. Picasso's world," she retorted.

"Do not mention the Spaniard to me!" he shouted angrily.

His work progressed. The potters of Vence were intrigued by his designs and gathered to admire the newly fired works he removed from the kiln, his face aglow with the heat, his long fingers coated with clay. The Jewish artist, they marveled, was becoming a master ceramist.

"I have created this especially for you," he told Ida one afternoon and presented her with a package wrapped in coarse brown paper.

It was a white enamel tile on which he had painted a shy, seminude young woman, a yellow necklace encircling her slender neck, leaning into the embrace of her lover. He, in turn, was a beautiful young man, wearing a crown of delicate blue flowers. She turned it over and read the inscription. *"Les Fiancés,"* it read.

"An engagement gift," Marc said, beaming proudly.

"It's wonderful. Thank you, Papa," she said and studied it closely.

How different it was, she thought, from *The Bridal Chair*, that scheme of interior desolation, the seat draped in a shroud, the flowers starkly white. This new gift, in celebration of her new marriage, was crafted with love. It throbbed with color and life. She slid her hand across it, pleased by its cool smoothness. It was the first gift she had received for her new home.

"Do you like it?" she asked Virginia, who bent to look at it.

"I do," Virginia replied. "But does my opinion really matter?"

It was not a question that required an answer.

———

Arriving home from Vence one afternoon, Virginia looked up to see Jean running toward her, holding an envelope in her outstretched hand.

"A letter for you, Mama," the child called. "From Belgium. With such pretty stamps. May I have them?"

"Such excitement over a letter," Virginia said wearily. "Of course you may have the stamps."

The letter was from Charles Leirens, who had written some weeks earlier. He wrote that he had the time to shoot a sixteen-millimeter film of Marc at work. In his previous letter, he had described his interest in the emerging art of cinema verité, and he wanted to produce what he called a "fantasy a la Chagall."

"I want the world to see how a great artist works," he wrote. "I hope that I can obtain Monsieur Chagall's permission and your own to film at Les Collines."

She smiled. Her permission was gladly granted. She had enjoyed Charles Leirens's visit to their High Falls home. The portraits he had taken then were treasured reminders of happier days. In one photograph, Leirens had captured her looking straight ahead, her large hands resting protectively on Marc's shoulder while he leaned toward her, his cheek brushed by her hair, smiling whimsically. It was a bittersweet reminder of a time when Marc had smiled easily and she herself had been suffused with calm and optimism. That photograph of her and Marc was on her dressing table.

She shared Leirens's letter with Marc that evening.

"It is an interesting proposal," he agreed. "I like the title. 'Fantasy a la Chagall.' I should not mind being the subject of a fantasy. In fact, I prefer fantasy to reality. My paintings say as much. It will be amusing to see if Leirens can do with his camera what I can do with my paint brush. Tell him that he is welcome."

Virginia wrote at once, urging the photographer to come as soon as possible. She was haunted by a dark fear that Marc, always unpredictable, might regret his decision and withdraw the invitation. For reasons that she did not quite understand, she felt it important that she see Charles Leirens again.

Within a week, on an autumn day when the leaves of the olive trees in the Les Collines orchard were newly silvered and a sea breeze stirred the sere fronds of the palm trees, Charles Leirens made his way up the pathway to Les Collines. He proceeded slowly, clutching his heavy pigskin case, his cameras slung over his shoulders. It was Jean who saw him first.

"Mama, Mama," she shouted excitedly. "The man who takes pictures is here."

Virginia hurried out to the terrace and watched as Ida, who had been gathering flowers, glided toward him, a bouquet of russet asters in her arms.

"Welcome to Les Collines, Monsieur Leirens," she said, smiling. "It has been too many years since we last met. Do you remember me?"

"No one forgets the beautiful Ida Chagall," he replied and returned her smile, his eyes trained on her face. It was a photographer's gaze, anticipating planes and angles, shadows and light. He would ask her to pose for him in the olive grove, he decided, and he would use only natural light. Her own radiance would be sufficient.

Virginia joined them with Jean trailing after her, carrying a tall glass of water.

"Monsieur Leirens, I am happy to see you. But you should have told us when you were arriving. We would have arranged to meet you. You must be very thirsty." She motioned to Jean, who offered him the glass, which he took with trembling hands.

"I did not want to disturb you," he said. "And I quite enjoyed the walk. Thank you for the water, *ma petite*," he said to Jean, handing her the empty glass.

She curtsied. "My name is Jean," she said. "Will you take my picture?"

"We shall see," he said kindly.

Virginia smiled at him, struggling to mask the distress she felt at seeing how he had changed since she had last seen him at High Falls. He was handsome still, but his fine-featured face was thin, his complexion waxen. His well-tailored suit hung too loosely on his much-diminished body. She had forgotten that his eyes were of disparate colors, the left one green, the right one brown. How odd that she should forget such an endearing and unique feature.

"And I am very happy to be here with three beautiful young

women, *les demoiselles* Jean and Virginia and the lovely Ida Chagall," he added.

"Soon to be Ida Meyer," she corrected him. "I will be married in January. I have an idea. Wouldn't it be wonderful if you would photograph my wedding?"

"If I am still in France, I should be happy to be of service," he said.

"Then you must remain in France until January." Ida spoke with the flirtatious assurance unique to beautiful women who have absolute faith that their slightest wish will be fulfilled.

Virginia frowned and reached for the photographer's bag. "You must be very tired," she said.

"No. I'm fine," he protested even as he allowed her to take it. He smiled gratefully as Jean relieved him of his heavy camera, holding it as carefully as she had held the glass of water.

At dinner that night, he told them that he had, in fact, been very ill.

"Something to do with my heart. It was, I am told, very serious, particularly because I am, after all, not a young man. But to everyone's surprise, including my own, I recovered."

"I think we are of an age, Leirens," Marc said. "And I do not consider myself an old man. Nor should you. We are artists, Leirens, and artists never grow old."

"I should like to believe that you are right, *cher maître*." He smiled, a self-deprecating smile.

Marc shrugged. He opened a bottle of brandy, filled his glass, and passed it to Charles.

"Did I ever tell you, *mon ami*, of my unhappy and very brief apprenticeship to a prosperous photographer in Vitebsk? It was arranged by my mother who worried, as all good Jewish mothers do, about my future. He was a large and ugly man, this photographer, with a large and ugly wife, and they lived in a large and ugly house. I was afraid that if I became a photographer, I too would become fat and ugly, but fortunately I was a terrible apprentice. I spilled chemicals and ruined every print he asked me to retouch. So I never became a village photographer doomed to photograph large and ugly families all the days of my life."

He turned to his guest and laughed.

"But I meant no offense. You, of course, are a different kind of photographer. I recognize that," he added hastily.

"And Charles is far from fat and ugly. In fact, he is too thin and quite handsome," Virginia said daringly.

"And, of course, if Charles had a wife, she too would be thin and quite beautiful. She might perhaps look like you, Virginia," Ida added mischievously.

An awkward silence followed. Too swiftly, they left the table. Marc returned to his studio and Charles and Virginia walked through the citrus orchard. Ida watched them from the terrace. Virginia's expression, the softness in her eyes when she looked at Charles Leirens, reminded Ida of how she had looked at Marc when they first met. He had been vulnerable and weak then, depleted by Bella's death, even as Charles was now vulnerable and weak, depleted by the long months of his illness.

"A stupid parallel," she told herself. "I should return to Paris."

But she had agreed to stay at Les Collines and continue to pose for her portrait that Marc wanted to present to Franz as a wedding gift. The sittings were not going well. After each session, they studied the canvas together and inevitably, he scraped it clean.

"I cannot capture your spirit, your vitality," he complained. "Your energy, your strength, eludes my brush."

Ida repeated his words to Virginia. "I cannot remember him ever before having such difficulty with a portrait," she said.

"Perhaps he does not want to share his image of you with Franz," Virginia suggested.

Ida glared at her, but lying awake that night, she reflected that Virginia had touched upon a kernel of truth. Her father had painted her throughout her life, but he jealously guarded those paintings, retaining them in his own collection, never offering them for sale, rarely lending them to exhibitions. He claimed her for his own. He did not want another man to own her visage, not even if that man was her husband.

She spoke to him the very next morning.

"I think it would be best if we abandoned the idea of a portrait. It interferes with your other work and you will have to devote a good deal of time to Leirens's film. Let us forget it for now."

"Perhaps you are right," he agreed, and she heard the relief in his voice.

Charles Leirens's cinematography soon dominated life at Les Collines. Marc reveled in his role as the star performer, prancing through his daily routine as the photographer trailed after him camera in hand, followed by Virginia, laden with ancillary equipment. Photography was now her passion. She learned how to focus a camera, how to use a light meter, and spoke knowingly of angles and exposures. She handed film and equipment to Charles, responding swiftly to his directives.

"It is as though he is a surgeon and she his nurse in an operating room," Ida observed wryly to Franz.

"What is the harm in her helping Leirens if it gives her pleasure and if your father does not object?" Franz said mildly.

And Marc did not object. He was concerned only with his own role. The camera followed him as he sketched the bantams that Jean and David kept as pets. He played with the children in the olive grove, always careful to turn his face to a flattering angle, pausing to run his fingers through his gray hair. He practiced smiles and asked whether a half smile was more photogenic than openmouthed laughter. At the Madoura pottery works, Leirens photographed him as he spun a vase about on a potter's wheel, dancing about it and waving a brush that dripped droplets of glaze. He was crafting a complete dinner service as a wedding gift for Ida and Franz.

"I will make sixty, perhaps seventy pieces," he announced.

"My daughter and her husband will do a great deal of entertaining. Collectors, art critics, even those of royal blood may well be guests in their home." He smiled at the thought that European nobility would be hosted by his Ida. Together, he and his beautiful, vibrant daughter had triumphed over history.

Leirens trained his camera on Ida herself as she stood before the kiln and studied one plate after another. Marc was using only two colors, a fiery vermilion and a gentle blue to create charming and fanciful vignettes, images of nurturing mothers and loving couples, graceful dancers and airborne animals. Each piece was different. Each place setting told a story. She laughed at the circus scenes and puzzled over his hybrid creatures, human and animal magically melded. She imagined setting a table with those plates and platters, using a linen cloth of a deep rich blue. She would place a tall crystal vase containing long-stemmed red and white roses at its center. She was Bella's daughter, and her mother's loving conceits were now her own.

Tears clouded her eyes. The memory of her mother surfaced unbidden and ambushed her happiness. She hurried out of the pottery. She did not want Charles Leirens to film her sorrow.

They screened the first reels of film. Marc was an enthusiastic viewer, applauding his own antics. He congratulated Charles Leirens on his work and then followed Ida onto the terrace.

"I hope that this cinematography is over and done with. It has taken far too much of my time, and Leirens has been at Les Collines long enough. Virginia is so often with him that David is neglected," he complained.

"David is hardly a neglected child," Ida protested. Still, she suggested to Virginia that she concentrate more on David and spend less time with Charles Leirens. Virginia stared her down.

"It is hardly your concern as to how I spend my time," she said.

"It becomes my concern when I must take care of the children while you learn how to photograph roosters and discuss cameras with our guest," Ida retorted.

"Your worries about that will soon be over," Virginia said. "Charles is going to Belgium for Christmas."

"I see." Ida was at once relieved that Marc's annoyance would be abated and disappointed that Leirens, renowned for his portraiture, would not photograph her as a bride.

"Do not worry. He will return for your wedding," Virginia added, as though intuiting her thought. "As always, Ida, your wish is a command."

"Will my wedding be his only reason for his return to Les Collines?"

Ida's question was loaded with sarcasm. Virginia blushed but said nothing. Their verbal duel was over, but boundaries had been drawn. Too much had been said and yet nothing had been revealed.

Days later, Ida stood on the terrace and watched Charles Leirens's leave-taking. He shook hands with Marc and kissed Virginia on both cheeks, handing her his photograph of Jean and David, their heads bent close. She in turn gave him a sealed envelope that he tucked into the pocket of his brown velvet jacket. Ida was certain that he would open the envelope as soon as the car pulled away.

"Did you write him an affectionate billet-doux?" she asked Virginia that evening as she sat at her desk, glancing over the household accounts.

"I wrote him a note of appreciation," Virginia replied coldly. "I told him how pleased we were with the film and how much his friendship means to us."

"To us?"

"Yes. To us. To myself, to Marc and the children. And I assume to you as well, Ida."

"You assume a great deal, Virginia," Ida said.

She turned back to her work. It occurred to her that she might write to Charles Leirens and tell him that she had made other arrangements for her wedding photographs and there was no need for him

to return to Les Collines, but almost immediately, she dismissed the
thought. The photographer presented no danger. Virginia's enthu-
siasms were transient. Her only constants were her children. David
was Marc's son. Virginia would not endanger his role, or her own, in
Marc's life. She was Marc's buffer against a terrifying solitude, Ida's
guarantor that he would not feel himself forlorn and abandoned. No,
she told herself. Her fears were foolish.

She resolved to make peace with Virginia. They had had a friendship of a kind. It could be re-created. It was in her father's interest, and her own, that Virginia should feel herself loved and valued
enough to remain with Marc at Les Collines.

Their own Christmas visitors at Les Collines were Virginia's parents, Godfrey and Georgianna Haggard. It was a happy visit. Ida
welcomed them with great exuberance and told them how fond she
was of Virginia.

"Ida is so gracious," Georgianna Haggard told her daughter. "It is
rare that a stepdaughter is so welcoming."

"Stepdaughter?" Virginia repeated, as though the word was foreign to her. But of course, if she and Marc married, she would be
Ida's stepmother, and Marc, in turn, would be Jean's stepfather. She
struggled to contain the hilarity that overcame her at the thought of
such an odd configuration.

"Your mother and I assume that you will become Chagall's wife
once your divorce from John McNeil is final," Godfrey said sternly.
"This charade has gone on long enough. Do you plan to marry here
or in England?"

It did not occur to either of her parents until weeks later that
Virginia had not answered his question.

Their leave-taking was affectionate. The Haggards congratulated
Ida on her forthcoming marriage. Georgianna asked where she and
Franz would make their home.

"We will spend much of our time in Switzerland and in Paris.
Virginia will be the chatelaine of Les Collines."

"And what have I been until now?" Virginia asked sharply.

Ida shrugged. It was a question that did not require an answer.

Smiling vaguely, she kissed Georgianna and Godfrey good-bye. After all, she thought to herself with much amusement, they might soon be her step-grandparents.

Virginia and Ida stood together on the terrace and waved as the car sped away. They turned then and went their separate ways, Ida to enter her father's studio and Virginia to stroll listlessly through the garden.

Chapter Forty-Seven

*V*ence was electric with energy and excitement as Ida's wedding day grew closer. *Pensiones* prepared for the arrival of important guests from Paris and London, from Zurich and Bern, and even from the United States. The lorries of linen suppliers navigated the narrow lanes, and housewives chattered in the outdoor spice market about the bride's apparel. The postmistress revealed that boxes had arrived from a Paris couturier, but the mayor's wife, who frequented a boutique in Nice, told them that Ida Chagall had purchased a plum-colored satin and velvet suit. She had learned as much from the seamstress who had been summoned to Les Collines to make some small alterations on the velvet jacket.

"She won't wear a white dress?" someone asked.

"It is not her first marriage," the mayor's wife said knowingly. She went to a hairdresser in Nice frequented by Françoise Gilot, who was not averse to sharing her knowledge of Ida's past. There had been a husband; there had been lovers. She was hardly a virgin bride. Besides, she was Jewish. There was some uncertainty as to whether Jewish brides wore white.

They argued about whether or not she would wear a hat, agreeing that it would be a shame to cover her glorious hair.

Ida herself sped through the town day after day, rushing from one shop to another, beaming happily as she made her purchases and issued orders. She conferred with Madame Fevre, the greengrocer, about the menus for the wedding breakfast, and she planned an exciting buffet.

"A *salade Niçoise*," she decided. "The freshest greens."

She lifted sprays of arugula, examined heads of romaine lettuce, and frowned.

"Not fresh enough," she declared.

"But it is January," Madame Fevre protested. "The harvest is not yet in."

"Then you must send to the greenhouses in Nice for their produce, madame. Do not worry about the expense. It is for my wedding day, after all."

Madame Fevre nodded. Nothing could be denied this whirling dervish of a bride who knew exactly what she wanted.

"Ah, but your little red potatoes are beautiful," she enthused. She lifted three of the miniature spuds and laughingly juggled them, delighting the children who were even more delighted as she dove into her pockets and tossed them chocolates.

The baker promised freshly baked croissants and baguettes as well as a wedding cake that would rival the finest patisseries of Paris.

Rented trestle tables and chairs were arranged in a horseshoe in Marc's studio.

"You have taken all my space. Where am I to do my work?" he grumbled.

"Your work can wait, *Papochka*," she retorted. "My wedding breakfast cannot."

She hugged him, ran her fingers through his tangled curls, kissed his cheeks, the happy bride, the playful cajoling daughter.

Virginia and the children were caught up in the frenzy. Virginia arranged the flowers. Jean, a serious child, designed the menus, laboring over each with great care.

Ida lavished praise on her.

"You are a wonderful little artist, Jean," she said, studying one gaily decorated menu card. "Where did you learn so much about colors?"

"My father is an artist," Jean reminded her gravely.

Ida nodded. John McNeil was a shadowy presence in their lives. David carried his name by virtue of a legal quirk that stipulated that any child born to a married woman was given her husband's name regardless of biological paternity. Only when Virginia and Marc married would he become David Chagall. Until then, Marc had no legal claim to his own son. John McNeil had at last agreed to a divorce, but it had not yet been granted. Jean, however, would always be Jean McNeil, her name a reminder of Virginia's past.

Virginia filled bowls with flowers and then worked on a garland of laurel leaves that would be Marc's crown at the wedding breakfast. When Charles Leirens arrived, she busied herself arranging his photographic equipment, playfully draping his cameras with chains of flowers, a gesture that at once annoyed and amused Ida. Virginia once again trailed after Leirens, carrying his equipment, studying his techniques.

In a prewedding photograph, Charles posed Ida standing beneath Marc's painting *Bride and Groom with Eiffel Tower*. Marc had painted the graceful, silvery Eiffel Tower standing sentinel in the background while he and Bella embraced beneath a canopy of falling leaves. A young girl, her features clearly those of Ida, flew toward them offering a bouquet of flowers. It occurred to Ida that the painting reflected the dream in which she herself was flying, but suddenly it became clear to her that it was her dream that had been plucked from the painting.

Guests began arriving. Marc welcomed them, proudly escorting each arrival through the house and the grounds. They were witness to his achievements, his hard-earned prosperity. He changed his velvet jackets several times a day, first choosing one of peacock blue and then another of burgundy red. He knotted silk ascots around his neck with a dramatic flair and posed for numerous photographs.

Franz and his family arrived, and he moved among the guests with a shy dignity.

Claude Bourdet, the former owner of Les Collines, introduced him to his wife who was also named Ida. "Idas make wonderful wives," he said, and both Idas clapped and laughed.

The day before the wedding, Elsa, André, and their son, Daniel, arrived from New York. Ida was overjoyed to see them.

"It is wonderful that you are here. I never thought you would come," she said excitedly.

"When André came home after the war, he swore that he would never go back to Europe," Elsa said. "But I promised to be here for your marriage and so he agreed. Your marriage has given us a new beginning, Ida."

Ida embraced her friend.

"And you have not yet advised me to be careful," she said laughingly.

"Ah, this time I think you know exactly what you are doing," Elsa replied.

Writers and artists, curators and collectors, invaded the town, their irreverent laughter and their lively conversations echoing in bistros and cafés.

"You are marrying into artistic royalty," Arnold Rüdlinger, the Swiss art historian who was Franz's best man, told his friend.

"And Ida Chagall is marrying into Swiss aristocracy," Franz's sister observed drily.

Franz glared at her.

"We do not think in those terms. We are marrying because we love each other. Our backgrounds are irrelevant. Ida feels a great allegiance to her Jewish heritage, and I respect her for it. It will not come between us."

"Of course not," Arnold Rüdlinger said. He had worked with Ida in Bern and Zurich and admired her knowledge and exuberant energy. She would add laughter and excitement to the life of his too-serious scholarly friend. He thought of how he would describe her when he made his toast at the wedding breakfast. Adjectives flooded his mind. *Exuberant. Energetic. Charming. Warm. Generous. Devoted.* He shuffled them about and watched Ida cross the lawn, hand in hand with Marc. Yes, *devoted.* He hoped that her devotion to her father would be matched by her devotion to Franz.

The sky was wondrously bright on the morning of the wedding. Ida went to the window, inhaled deeply, and glanced at her bedside clock. She had awakened early and there was no need to rush. Slowly, languidly, she drew her bath, filling the tub with lavender bath salts. Her mother would approve, she thought as she lowered herself into the fragrant water and passed a soft cloth across her legs, her torso, gently caressing first one breast and then the other. She reflected that Franz would touch them carefully, tenderly, and she smiled in sensual anticipation.

Eighteen years had passed since her marriage to Michel. Then she had been a terrified child bride, but on this, her second wedding day, she was a woman, a woman who had experienced tenderness and passion, anguish and delight, and now embraced her future joyfully, zestfully.

She toweled herself dry in front of the long bathroom mirror and studied her full-figured body, her skin rosy and firm, her waist still slender, her auburn hair thick and luxurious. She swept it up and arranged it in two curling silken swaths across her high forehead, allowing teasing tendrils to curl about her ears.

She dressed with ease and swiftness, pleased with the plum-colored velvet suit she had chosen so carefully. She applied makeup sparingly, barely rouging her high soft cheeks and lightly brushing her long eyelashes.

"You look beautiful," Franz said when she greeted him at the door. "But then you always look beautiful."

She blushed and looked up at him.

"And you yourself look very handsome," she said.

His fine-featured face was narrow and pale, but his eyes glinted behind his black-framed glasses. His shirt was starched and sparkling white against the well-cut jacket of his gray suit, and he wore a perfectly knotted silk tie that, oddly enough, was the same plum color as her jacket. She smoothed the lock of thick dark hair that fell so boyishly across his forehead.

Marc had abandoned his usual quasi-Bohemian garb in favor of a dark suit and a conventional shirt and tie. Virginia, as usual, wore a simple white blouse and dark skirt, but she had taken care to dress the children in their best clothes. Jean had been given a small bouquet that she clutched tightly. They drove to the Vence town hall, where Franz's father and sister and Arnold Rüdlinger awaited them.

The civil service, performed by the mayor of Vence, was swift and simple. The portly mayor beamed as he pronounced them *mari et femme*, husband and wife. Franz kissed Ida's cheek and shook hands with Marc. Their eyes locked in a silent acknowledgment that Ida was now, for each of them, the focus of their shared lives.

A small crowd had gathered outside the town hall. *"Bonne chance!"* *"Heureuse! Toujours heureuse!"* the excited villagers shouted. Children tossed flowers at them and laughing women pelted them with rice. They waved and hurried to the waiting cars. Ida took the bouquet from Jean, turned, and tossed it into the crowd. It was caught by a pigtailed schoolgirl, prompting a new round of laughter and gaiety.

At Les Collines, their exuberant guests awaited them in the flower-filled studio. A violinist played a triumphant and happy medley as they burst into the room. Several magnums of champagne had already been emptied and new rounds were poured. Laughter and excited chatter filled the room. Trays of food were consumed and refilled in an orgy of appetite and contentment. The children scurried about, Jean and David happily including Elsa's son Daniel in the merriment. Virginia crowned Marc with the garland of laurel leaves she had fashioned.

"Je suis le roi," he shouted. "I am the king!" He stood on his chair, his crown askew, and waved his champagne flute as though it were his scepter.

"Et je suis la princesse," Ida retorted. "And I am the princess!"

The violinist struck up a lively tune. Ida pulled Marc onto the floor and they danced a rollicking jig. His face flushed, his blue eyes sparkling, he turned to his friend, Jacques Prévert, and the two men whirled about in a wild hora, and then Marc crouched and, to the wild applause of the guests, he danced a Russian *kazatzka*. His crown of leaves tumbled onto the floor and small David plucked it up and placed it on his own head.

Charles Leirens darted between guests, his camera at the ready, feverishly finishing one roll of film and inserting yet another, Virginia holding his equipment. He photographed Franz and Ida as they glided across the floor in a stately waltz. Their dance ended abruptly as Marc tried to dunk Ida's nose into a glass of champagne.

"Papochka," she chastised him laughingly as she pulled away. "You must behave."

"No. I must misbehave," he countered, smiling impishly. He was once again the mischievous Vitebsk schoolboy who had so often provoked and amused. The toasts began. Cries of *"L'chaim!"* rang out. Franz, with his usual shy dignity, spoke of the happiness and levity Ida had brought into his life. Arnold Rüdlinger lifted his glass to the bridal couple.

"They are bound by their love of art, their love of life, their love for each other," he said. "They provide each other with perfect balance. I drink to beautiful, generous Ida and to my dear friend, Franz."

And Marc too rose, his garland once more in place, his tie whipped off and his blue eyes aglitter. He smiled broadly, lifted his glass high, and turned to Ida.

"I wish *l'chaim*, a long and happy life, to the best daughter in the world. Our daughter, mine and my beloved Bella's. *Mazel tov*." His eyes filled with tears, but the smile never left his lips.

Virginia turned away.

The dancing resumed. Elsa and André joined other couples in a dabke, André oddly agile despite his limp. Elsa turned to Ida, who briefly danced beside her.

"André is dancing. André is smiling," she said. "He has not danced since the war. He seldom smiles. Your happiness is contagious, Ida."

Ida smiled and kissed her friend's cheek lightly as Franz swept her away into another couples formation. There were impromptu bursts of song, chansons and lieder. They sang the songs of the war they had wanted to forget in all the languages of their lives.

Claude and Ida Bourdet offered a melancholy rendition of "La Vie en Rose."

The room fell quiet as Marc sang a Yiddish lullaby.

"*Rozhinkes mit mandlen*, raisins and almonds," he sang and Ida closed her eyes. It was the song Bella had sung to her throughout her childhood, the words and melody that had soothed her into sleep. She would remember the words.

I will one day sing them to our children, she thought, suffused with happy certainty.

She smiled up at Franz. What a wonderful father he would be, this gentle serious man who was now her husband.

The wedding cake was carried in to cries of admiration. The Vence baker had fulfilled his promise, producing a masterpiece of sweet marzipan and varicolored icings adorned with chocolate hearts and flowers formed by blueberries and pecans. It was placed in front of Ida who took one last sip of champagne, laughed merrily, and seized the cake knife. Deftly, she sliced off the creamy top layer, transferred it to a plate, and laughing wildly, she crowned Franz with it as the crowd exploded with laughter. He looked at her in astonishment, matched her laughter with his own, and mischievously placed a hand on his head, covered it with cream, and fed it to his bride.

His sister turned to Arnold Rüdlinger. "It seems that Ida has turned our Franz into a new man," she said disapprovingly.

"It seems that Ida has brought laughter and joy into his life," Arnold countered.

Charles Leirens glided into a seat beside Ida. "I hope you and Franz like my photographs," he said.

"I am sure we will. It seems that you were everywhere. I don't think your camera missed anything. Thank you so much."

"I leave for Italy tomorrow," he said. "I will develop the prints when I return and we will arrange a time to study them. It was a privilege for me to photograph your wedding celebration. Of course you know that I wish you and your husband every happiness. *Au revoir*, Madame Meyer."

He kissed her hand and she smiled. He was, after all, a very charming man, she thought, and he had been the first to call her Madame Meyer.

"Madame Meyer." She uttered her new name softly, smiled, and shook her head. In her heart of hearts, she knew, she was and always would be Ida Chagall. But on this, her wedding day, she was happy to add an equally important name. Yes, it was sheer happiness to be Ida Chagall *Meyer*.

Chapter Forty-Eight

*F*ranz and Ida, arms linked, stood on the deck of the ferry that carried them to Corsica and lifted their faces to the soft Mediterranean breeze. Ida relaxed into an unfamiliar serenity. *This is what it means to be content*, she thought. They leaned against the rail, their companionable silence occasionally broken by sudden bursts of shared laughter as they recalled the more comical moments of their wedding celebration.

They were complicit confederates, mutually aware that they were making the first deposits in the memory bank of their marriage.

When they disembarked at Ajaccio, she knew at once that Corsica, with its untamed rustic landscape, had been a perfect choice for their brief honeymoon. Here, on this wild island, there were no museums or galleries, no libraries or sculpture gardens, no one who might recognize their names. They were reliant solely, and wonderfully, on each other.

They wandered along the wharf of Ajaccio and created fanciful stories about the fishermen whose graceful sailboats lined the harbor. They decided that young sailor was a prospective bridegroom, saving for his wedding. Two small boys nearby were planning to stow away on a passenger ship. Franz claimed that the rotund bearded man with the broken nose hauling in a net of silver-gilled small fish had surely been a resistance fighter during the island's occupation by German and Italian troops.

"How many Nazis do you think he killed?" he asked, inviting Ida into his fantasy.

"You know, Franz, I cannot joke about the Nazis. I still fear them," she replied. "You must remember that you have married a Jew who might have ended her life in a Nazi death camp."

"I'm sorry." He held her close. "You have no need to be afraid. I will protect you."

Her mood lifted.

"Of course, I am safe," she said. "I am married to a gallant citizen of Switzerland." She spoke with a forced gaiety, but there was an underlying seriousness to her words. "Our children must be born in Switzerland," she added.

"Yes. All dozen of them will be born in Zurich," he assured her, smiling fondly. It was the first time they had spoken of children.

They followed a trail up Monte Cinto and leaned against an escarpment that overlooked a small torrential stream that rocketed below them.

"Amazing how nature changes from one moment to another," Franz murmured.

"Like life itself," Ida said.

She felt the chill of an inexplicable sadness, an odd presentiment of lurking danger. When they returned to the hotel, she called her father. He was fine, he assured her, working very hard on the ceramics he would display at the Riviera and Paris exhibitions.

"I need your help, Idotchka," he said. "There are so many arrangements to be made, and Virginia is going to London for her divorce proceedings."

The familiar whine in his voice irritated her.

"I can't worry about your exhibitions. I'm on my honeymoon," she replied firmly.

"I know. Enjoy. Enjoy," he muttered.

She hung up, struggling to contain her annoyance. She did not mention the conversation to Franz.

In Corte, a charming hilltop town, they rented a spacious villa and slept each night on a high white bed, the windows open so that the cool mountain wind wafted across their entwined bodies. They took long walks and paused one afternoon to stare into a meadow where a nanny goat suckled her newborn kid. They watched as the white, long-haired animal tenderly licked the residue of her milk from her spindly offspring's lip. The rush of emotion Ida felt as she watched the two animals surprised her.

"How beautiful," Ida said. "Motherhood is a miracle, isn't it, Franz?"

"I think so," he replied and kissed her forehead. "You will make a beautiful mother, Ida."

She smiled. "All in good time," she said. "For now I want to be a good wife."

"And you are my good wife, my wonderful wife," he assured her, and they walked on.

The days passed too swiftly and they treasured every hour, every sunrise, every velvet dark night. As they sat on their balcony at the twilight hour of their very last day in Corsica, she turned to Franz.

"Will we always be this happy?" she asked.

"Even happier," he assured her and pressed his cheek to hers as the sun turned a fiery red and drifted into the sea.

Franz had pressing business in Bern and Ida returned to Les Collines, oddly grateful for the rare opportunity to be alone with her father, although she knew she would have to deal with his petulance, his feelings of neglect and abandonment.

Virginia was still in London although she had phoned with the welcome news that her divorce had been granted and she would soon return.

"What good news, *Papochka*," Ida said. "Now you are free to marry and give David your name."

"We will see," he said noncommittally and tried on the rough woven smock Ida had bought for him. She had chosen it because the blue fabric matched his eyes, something she knew he was sure to notice. He was a man who never passed a mirror without glancing at his own reflection.

Jean and David seized upon their gifts with delight and danced about the garden in their oversized Corsican shirts, the fisherman caps perched jauntily on their heads.

"Ida, you're the most wonderful sister," David proclaimed, hugging her knees. "You always know exactly what to buy for us." He had grown into a handsome, smiling child, his small, sculpted features similar to Marc's, his hair dark and silken, his eyebrows thick and jet-colored.

"My David looks like my brother, Dovidl. He has a real Jewish face," Marc often told Ida, although never in Virginia's hearing.

On the morning of Virginia's return from London, he and Ida stood on the doorstep to welcome her, but there was an odd formality, an absence of sensual intimacy, to their exchanged greetings. He did not embrace her but kissed her on both cheeks, and she in turn simply touched his face with her gloved hand as though shielding his flesh from her own.

Ida embraced Virginia, peppered her with questions about London, asked after her parents, and carried her portmanteau into the house where she presented her with the handsome leather suitcase she had bought for her in Corsica. Virginia opened it, examined the cream-colored satin lining, and passed her hand across the soft pigskin.

"Thank you, Ida," she said at last. "It's very beautiful. But when am I to use it?"

"Surely you and my father will take a holiday after you marry," Ida replied.

"Yes. After we marry," Virginia repeated wearily. "If we marry," she added.

"Of course you'll marry. It is possible now that you have your divorce."

"Has your father said as much?" Virginia asked. She knew that there was nothing that Marc kept from Ida.

"There has been no time to talk. This is such a busy time for us," Ida equivocated.

It was a busy time. There were frenetic preparations for the vernissage at the Galerie des Ponchettes in Nice. In Paris, the completed etchings for La Fontaine's *Fables* as well as Marc's new ceramics had to be arranged. Virginia was soon dashing from the house to the studio, obeying Marc's instructions as to the handling and crating of his work as Ida prepared to travel to Paris to deal with the logistics there.

"Managing the Nice exhibition will be very difficult for Virginia," Ida said worriedly before she left.

"It will be all right," Marc said dismissively. "Leirens wrote to me. He is back in France. I asked him to return to Les Collines so that he can photograph the pictures at the Nice gallery. He will help Virginia."

"Is that wise, *Papochka*?" Ida asked.

"Why is it not wise?" he asked irritably.

She said no more. Her concern was irrational and without substance, she told herself.

Charles Leirens was pleased to be back at Les Collines. He had been lonely in Italy, he told Virginia.

"It is difficult to be always on my own," he said sadly. "You live in the heart of a family. I suppose you cannot understand the desolation of constant loneliness."

"One can live with others and still feel a terrible loneliness," she replied, her eyes downcast.

They stared at each other and fell silent. But as they drove to Nice later that morning, he reached for her hand. She did not pull away. Day after day, he photographed Marc's work, and during each journey, she drew closer to him, their thighs touching, his breath warm upon her cheek, her leg pressed against his. They did not speak. At the gallery, they worked together, their movements synchronized, their silence eloquent.

With the completion of the photographs, he was ready to return to Paris. Marc was lavish in his praise of the montages.

"Wonderful of you to give so much time to my work, Leirens," he said and presented him with a small drawing of the Les Collines orchard. "Take good care of that. It will be worth a great deal one day," he advised. "And of course Ida and I are looking forward to seeing the wedding photographs. Can we meet at her home at the Quai de l'Horloge?" He consulted his pocket calendar. "Let us say on the fifteenth of the month. Is that convenient for you?"

Charles nodded and jotted the date down in his notebook.

"Are you all packed, my friend?" Marc asked.

"Almost," Charles said.

"But Virginia must help you. She is wonderful at packing. I must go to the studio now so I will bid you *au revoir, mon ami.*"

Virginia and Charles stared after him and then went together to Charles's bedroom. His suitcase lay open on the bed, and standing on either side of it, they leaned toward each other and kissed for the first time. Within moments, she was in his arms.

"What will we do?" she asked. "What can we do?"

"You must leave Chagall and come away with me," he replied.

"How can I leave him? He is part of me. And there is David, our son. What of David?"

"I don't know," he replied. "I only know that we must be together. Somehow we will manage. I promise."

She said nothing. It was a promise that could not be kept. She rested her head against his chest, her eyes closed, her heart pounding.

He left the next morning. Within hours of his departure, Ida phoned, insisting that Marc come to Paris immediately.

He protested that it was impossible. His new ceramics, the center-pieces of the Paris exhibition, had not yet been fired.

"It is important that you come now. We must decide on asking prices for the major pieces and I cannot make the decision alone. It is too much for me to manage. Franz is growing impatient and wants me to come to Bern as soon as possible. We have not been together since we returned from our honeymoon. My husband deserves some consideration." She reminded him, not for the first time, of the shift in her priorities.

"Very well," he agreed reluctantly. "I will take the train to Paris today. Virginia will wait until the new ceramics are completed and then drive with them to Paris."

"Is that all right with you?" he asked Virginia belatedly.

She shrugged.

"Does it matter?" she asked. "Do you really care?"

She drove him to the train station and he turned to her as they waited on the platform.

"You see that I rely on you more and more, Virginia," he said. "Ida has a new life, new responsibilities. But I am hopeful that you have learned from her, that you can perhaps take on her role, her responsibilities."

"I see. You are hoping that I will become more like Ida and perhaps more like your Bella," Virginia said daringly. It was the first time that she had ever spoken to him of Bella, although her spectral presence had hovered over them.

"Perhaps." He did not meet her eyes as he answered.

"But I do not want to become like your charismatic Ida. I do not want to become more like your elegant Bella. I want you to accept me for who I am, for who I will always be, Virginia Haggard McNeil, the mother of your son."

The roar of the approaching train muffled his reply, but she saw that his eyes had darkened in anger and his brow was creased in a frown. Briefly, his hand rested heavily on her shoulder, and he boarded without kissing her. Although she remained on the platform and saw him take his window seat in the first-class compartment, he did not turn to look at her. He did not wave but stared straight ahead.

Virginia was heavyhearted when she returned to Les Collines, but before she could remove her coat, Charles phoned from Paris, his voice desperate.

"I must see you," he pleaded. "Let us have at least one night together."

She trembled. Jean and David were playing in the garden. David's lilting laughter drifted into the room. He saw her at the window and waved to her, her lovely, loving son. She could not risk losing him. But then Charles was not asking her to abandon her children. He spoke of one night. One night that would assuage her loneliness, affirm their love. Surely she deserved that. She would manage it.

"All right," she agreed. "One last night."

"I will fly to Nice," he said.

She smiled. Their clandestine assignation had become a romantic adventure.

She called Marc at Ida's Paris apartment.

"My friend Yvonne in Menton is ill, and she asked if I could stay with her for a day or so," she said. "It is important that she not be alone. Jean and David will be with the housekeeper."

"Do as you please," he said harshly.

Ida's voice came over the wire.

"Is there a number where you can be reached?" she asked.

"There will be no need to call me, but Marc does have Yvonne's phone number," she said curtly and slammed the receiver down.

She met Charles's plane in Nice, and they spent a day and night at a small *pensione* in a hillside village, plunged into a whirlpool of wild intimacy. His desire ignited her own. He whispered her name, spoke of how he valued her gentleness, her loveliness, and her inner beauty.

"I love you because you are Virginia," he said, the very words she yearned to hear.

They parted tearfully, agreeing that Charles could not miss his appointment to show Marc the photos he had taken at Ida's wedding. Their relationship would have to remain a secret until they came to a decision about their future.

Chapter Forty-Nine

$\mathcal{V}$irginia returned to Les Collines. She was surprised when Marc called and asked with false solicitude about her friend's health and about the weather in Menton. His questions unnerved her. It occurred to her that he might have discovered her deception, but she immediately dismissed the thought. When Marc was with Ida, he thought of no one else, least of all Virginia.

"When will you come to Paris?" he asked more urgently.

"As soon as the ceramics are ready," she replied. "The kiln has promised them for the late afternoon of next Monday, and I will leave as soon as they crate them and put them in the car. But of course, I cannot drive through the night. It will be too exhausting. I will stay over somewhere, perhaps in Dijon."

"If you must," he agreed sullenly.

"I must."

She hung up elated. She and Charles would have yet another night together.

She called him, and his excitement matched her own. They met in Auxerre, and once again, their night together commingled passion and tenderness. As dawn broke, they spoke with great sadness of what they had to do. They could not and would not be illicit lovers forever.

She wept at the thought of hurting Marc. She trembled at the thought of Ida's fierce anger. And the possibility of losing David loosed a torrent of wild grief.

"And what of David, my David?" she asked.

"David is still David McNeil. Marc has no legal claim to him," Charles said firmly. "You are not married. His biological paternity is irrelevant. You will not lose your son."

He explained that he had consulted a lawyer friend who had given him that assurance. Virginia stared at him. *A lawyer.* That he had taken such a step gave their situation a new and frightening reality.

She wept again. Charles wiped away her tears and held her close.

"We cannot part," he said. "We must not part. Not ever."

He held her close and gave her a sealed envelope.

"My letter to you," he said. "My pledge. Do not open it until you are in Paris."

She nodded her agreement.

The letter was still in her purse when she reached Ida's home on the Quai de l'Horloge.

Neither Marc nor Ida embraced her. They did not even rise from their seats to greet her.

"We are exhausted," Marc claimed. "We have been working hard, very hard. There have been many meetings with collectors and dealers. Endless negotiations. Marc Chagall, it seems, has become an industry."

"But that is your choice," Virginia responded. "No one forces you to sell your work, to negotiate for the best venues, the best prices. You are an artist, not a business."

Ida wheeled about, her face frozen in anger.

"But those very negotiations you hold in such contempt pay for your life at Les Collines, for your children's tuitions, for your automobile. My father's work, and my own, subsidize your freedom," she retorted.

"What freedom?" Virginia asked bitterly. "The freedom to be at his beck and call—and yours? The freedom to account to you for my every move?" She stood defiantly before Ida, her hands on her hips, her eyes ablaze with anger.

Ida was seized by a sudden fear. It was a new Virginia who confronted her, a woman whose passive acquiescence had dissipated, a woman who was drawing from a new source of strength.

She knew, with a sinking heart, that her suspicions had become a certainty. Virginia had not been caring for a friend in Menton. Clearly, there was another man in Virginia's life. Despite her previous fears, she did not believe that it was Charles Leirens. After all, he had come to Quai de l'Horloge during Virginia's absence from Les Collines, exuding avuncular good will as he showed them the wedding photographs. He was, Ida thought, incapable of such artful deception.

She thought of what she might say to Virginia, of the questions she might ask, and decided at once that she would say nothing, ask nothing. Virginia's fidelity was irrelevant. It was selfish, perhaps, but it was important to her that Virginia and her father remain together. Virginia and the children guaranteed him companionship. Marc was incapable of living alone. He would sink back into the quagmire of depression that had engulfed him after Bella's death, a depression that had swallowed up Ida's own life until Virginia's arrival. If Virginia left him, he would once again be dependent on Ida. That inevitable dependency would impact on her own life and on her new and as yet untested marriage.

She turned to Virginia.

"I misspoke," she said apologetically. "Certainly I recognize and appreciate all that you do for my father. As does he. Isn't that true, *Papochka*?"

He shrugged and did not reply. Their exchange had unnerved and angered him. How dared Virginia complain about her life with him? He had rescued her from poverty, given her a home, a son. Her ingratitude astonished. Who knew what else she was capable of?

He continued to unpack the ceramics, his back to her. Virginia recognized his punishment by silence. He and Ida ignored her as they studied the pieces, discussed their placement at the vernissage and speculated about the prices they might command. Ida had visited the galleries that had Picasso's ceramics on offer and had been startled to see the large sums that were demanded for the smallest works.

"And I think the work of Marc Chagall is as good as the work of the Spaniard," he said, once again in the mode of referring to himself in the third person.

"Of course it is," Ida agreed.

At last, the ceramics were safely stored, and Marc and Virginia left for their hotel. Ida had made it clear that the separate apartment in her home was for her father's use only. Virginia was not welcome, an arrangement that suited Virginia, who preferred the privacy of the small hotel. They entered their room in silence and Marc immediately drew the blinds, blocking out the invasive lights of the Quai Voltaire. They sat briefly in the darkness and then Virginia lit the bedside lamp, opened her case, and removed her floral-patterned dressing gown.

"I am exhausted," she said. "I am just going to shower and go to bed."

He watched as she draped the dressing gown over her arm, picked up her purse, and walked toward the bathroom. Suddenly he sprang from the bed, leapt across the room, and wrenched the purse from her hand.

"Why would you take your purse into the bathroom?" he asked harshly.

He opened it and dumped the contents on the floor. Her wallet, the photos of the children, a battered compact, a comb missing several teeth, lozenges wrapped in cellophane, fell into a pathetic heap, topped by a sealed white envelope. She rushed to seize it, tears streaking her cheeks, but he grabbed it and waved it triumphantly.

"Now we shall know the truth," he shouted.

"Give that to me. It's mine," she pleaded.

"Nothing is yours. You have nothing but what I've given you. The clothes you wear, the shoes you stand in—it is I who paid for them." He kicked at the contents of her purse, lifted her wallet, and shook out the franc notes. "Did you earn these?" he shouted. He waved the envelope, ripped it open, and removed the letter.

"You have no right." She lunged toward him, but he thrust her away.

"I have every right. But do not fear. I will read it to you," he said. "My darling." His voice quivered, but he continued. "How wonderful our nights together have been. You are part of my life. We cannot ever part. We are both free. We must marry and live together for the rest of our lives. No matter what it takes. *Je t'aime. Votre* Charles." Marc's voice escalated to a shriek. "*Votre* Charles," he repeated, his face mottled with fury. "This Charles of yours, this miserable Leirens, he is a monster. A liar and a deceiver. And you are a whore, worse than a whore, a mother who abandons her children to be with her lover, a woman who lies to me, her protector, a woman who lies to my Ida who has been a friend to you."

He shredded the letter and tossed the scraps of paper at Virginia, who crouched on the floor. They fell onto her hair, covered her shoulders. He thrust her onto her back and struck her across one cheek and then the other. He pounded her mouth with his clenched fist. She moaned softly, too weak to scream. He gripped her wrists and held her prisoner.

"Tell me. Tell me everything. For how long has this been going on? For how long have you been deceiving me?" he hissed.

She struggled to find her voice, aware of the strength of his body, of the closeness of his face to her own. His blue eyes blazed, and his breath was soured by fury.

She spoke. She told him of how she and Charles had been drawn to each other, that they had shared two wonderful nights together.

"You were lovers?" He thrust her away as though the sight and touch of her were repulsive.

"We are lovers," she replied. "We will remain lovers."

"You dare to tell me, after all our years together, after all that I have done for you and your children, that you have been with this liar, this hypocrite. He came to Ida's house and pretended to be an innocent friend of the family. He had the nerve to sit with me, I who am the father of your child. He spoke, that charlatan, as though nothing had happened, although he must have come to us only hours after being with you. How could you have deceived me so cruelly?

When did you intend to tell me about him? Did you intend to ever tell me about him?"

"Yes. I intended to tell you. I needed to find the right time, the right place. I did not want it to be like this," she replied.

Her mouth tasted of blood. She patted it with her handkerchief and she saw that he was staring down at the scarlet stains on the white linen square. It occurred to her that he was memorizing the color, that he was already translating their confrontation into a painting.

"I am going to Ida," he said. "I must speak with her."

He turned then and left the room, slamming the door behind him. She remembered his quarrel with Ida, all those years ago, when infuriated by her demand for money, he had lifted a chair then and would have bludgeoned her with it had not Virginia intervened.

There had been no one in this hotel room at the Hôtel du Quai Voltaire to intervene for her. She wept then because her life with Marc, a life that for so many years had been infused with beauty and adventure, had come to such a bitter end. She wept for her small son who might lose his father, and for her daughter who would surely lose her home. She hugged herself and swayed back and forth, her bruised body racked with sobs, and then she reached for the phone and called Charles Leirens. In a trembling voice, she told him that Marc knew they were lovers. She did not tell him of the violence of his reaction. She did not want Charles to hate Marc. She herself did not want to hate him.

Charles rushed to meet her, and they walked at a funereal pace along the Seine. It had snowed earlier in the day and the silvered frost that carpeted the river path crackled beneath their feet. Icicles, like frozen tears, dangled from the low branches of trees. Charles wore a heavy jacket, but in his haste to meet her, he had forgotten his scarf. She removed her own and tied it around his neck.

"I don't want you to be cold," he said.

"But I'm not cold," she assured him. "In fact, I am too warm."

She felt as though she were in the grip of a fever, so soaked with sweat that her clothing adhered to her skin. And then suddenly a chill ambushed her. She shivered and pressed her body against his for warmth. They reached the Champ-de-Mars and went into a café.

"All will be well, Virginia," Charles assured her softly. "We love each other and we will be married. Your children will be my children. I have savings. I have work. You have nothing to fear. Marc will soon realize that he must accept what has happened between us."

"Strangely enough," she said, stirring her café au lait, "it is not Marc whom I fear. It is Ida."

He nodded.

"I understand," he said.

He knew Ida to be a formidable woman, as ferocious when she was angered as she was passionately generous when she was pleased. He had photographed her often enough to understand the complexity of her moods, the depths of her affection.

"I must go back to the hotel," Virginia said. "I must find out how the children are. They were to have called this evening."

"Will Marc return?" he asked.

"I imagine so. But it will be all right. He will be calmer."

He had, after all, been quiescent after his fierce quarrel with Ida. His violence, even unrealized, had drained his fury. So it would be with her now, she told herself.

She was not wrong. He returned, his face still frozen in anger, but he was restrained. He paced the room, now spewing bitter words, now weeping, now accusatory, now pleading.

"How could you have betrayed me? Don't you recall all I did for you? I rescued you from poverty. I educated your daughter and gave her a home. Ah, you are cruel. You are a cruel and ungrateful woman. A harlot."

He muttered in Yiddish, went to the window, pulled the shades up and down. Minutes later, he wept, fell to his knees.

"What am I to do? Am I to be alone? Will you leave me?"

His bright blue eyes were red-rimmed, his shoulders bowed, his hair a tangle of uncombed, steel gray curls. She sat very still. She could not comfort him. Such comfort demanded words she could not say, promises she could not make.

"You must go to Ida with me tomorrow," he commanded. "Will you do that?" The command became a plea.

They went together the next day to Ida's home. Ida, regal in a black velvet dress offset by a heavy silver necklace, her hair in a severe bun, directed them into her living room. Seated in a large chair upholstered in a gold fabric, she motioned Virginia to the low seat opposite her. Her living room was a court room. She was the judge and Virginia was the defendant. Virginia shrugged and sat down. She stared up at the painting of *The Bridal Chair*, surprised that Ida had not yet moved it to her home in Switzerland. But then perhaps she did not want her home with Franz to be haunted by this relic of her first marriage.

Marc roamed the room, barely glancing at either woman. Ida would do battle for him. He relied on her. She was his protector, his advocate.

Ida fixed her gaze on Virginia.

"We trusted you, my father and I. And we trusted Charles Leirens. He came to my house to show us the wedding photos. His behavior was cruel, duplicitous. For how long has this affair between you been going on while you accepted my father's largesse and he accepted my father's hospitality?" Her tone was frigid, prosecutorial.

Marc broke in before Virginia could reply. He shook his fist at her and spat out his words, trembling with anger.

"Perhaps you and he were lovers back in America when he stayed with us at High Falls? Perhaps you were lovers even while he took those photographs of both of us together, those portraits of David? David, our son. Did you even think of our David, our Dovidl, when you lay in your lover's arms?" he shouted.

"Our feelings for each other, Charles and mine, became clear only weeks ago. We were together for only two nights. And yes, of course, I thought of David. David is never far from my thoughts. He is always in my heart," Virginia replied.

She willed herself to be calm, although she trembled in the face of Marc's fury. He moved threateningly toward her, but Ida lifted a monitory hand.

"Shhh, *Papochka*," she said softly, and he, like an obedient child, fell silent. She turned to Virginia.

"What happened over a few weeks can perhaps vanish over a few more weeks," she suggested, her tone more conciliatory. "My father loves you in spite of what you have done. He can be reconciled to your error. He loves you and he needs you. And you know that I have always had great affection for you."

"And you also need me," Virginia said drily.

"And there is my brother, David, to be considered," she continued.

"Your half brother. My son," Virginia corrected her.

The phone rang. Ida left the room to answer it. Virginia went to the window and stared out at the Seine. She did not turn when Ida rejoined them.

"I am sorry, but I must leave," Ida said. "I am needed at the gallery to cope with an urgent problem. Nothing that I can't correct," she assured Marc, who looked at her worriedly.

"Of course. My Ida can correct anything, cope with anything," he said.

Virginia smiled grimly. She knew that he had expected Ida to solve their dilemma as efficiently as she solved curatorial problems. Perhaps he assumed that a solution was in place.

Ida held her hand out to Virginia. Virginia took it, surprised that Ida's fingers were so warm when her own were as cold as ice.

"We will talk more, Virginia," Ida said. "I will see you at the vernissage."

"I don't think there is much more to talk about," Virginia said. "And considering all that has happened, I do not think that I can go to the vernissage."

"But of course you will go," Ida insisted. "How would we explain your absence?"

"You might tell the truth," Virginia said.

In the end, she did go to the vernissage. She owed that much to Marc. The gallery was crowded. Marc's sculptures and ceramics and the etchings for La Fontaine's *Fables* were much admired. He himself exuded charm, delighting the viewers with anecdotes, delivering explanations of the more complicated pieces. He had created fanciful and complex creatures, cows that symbolized fecundity, goats wearing garlands of flowers, airborne lovers flying across platters or clinging to the handle of a cup.

An earnest young woman, her notebook open, asked breathlessly how his ideas came to him.

"I do not know," he replied. "Marc Chagall is a wanderer in the wilderness of his own imagination."

Ida was never far from his side. Radiant in a new gown of shimmering blue silk, her color high, her hair swept up and held in place by sparkling sapphire butterflies, she smiled happily, waved to new arrivals, urged him to join one group and then another. She occasionally motioned Virginia over and introduced her.

"My father's very dear friend and companion," she said, her voice warm and affectionate.

Virginia stared at her in wonderment. The Ida who had spoken to her so coldly and judged her so harshly now masqueraded as an affectionate friend. She was a chameleon, Virginia decided, a charismatic chameleon capable of magical transformations. Father and daughter alike were accomplished thespians on the stage of public opinion. They betrayed no hint of the personal upheaval that confronted them.

Virginia was relieved that Charles had not come to the vernissage. It had been agreed that she would retrieve her suitcase after the exhibition and then meet him.

Virginia and Marc returned to the Hôtel du Quai Voltaire together. Exhilarated by the success of the vernissage, Marc tossed his cloak onto the sofa in the salon, opened a bottle of brandy, and poured a tumbler for each of them, even as Virginia methodically packed her bag.

"To our future," he said.

"What future?" she asked wearily.

"Our future together. Ah, Virginitchka, we have been through a difficult time, you and I. I made mistakes. You made mistakes, but that is in the past. I speak of all the years to come. Surely you will not turn away from the life I offer you and the children. I am among the most famous artists in France, equal to Picasso, equal to Matisse. Think of what that means to us, Virginia. The world is ours."

"It means nothing to me," she replied. "All that was important to me was your love. But that vanished. For a long time, I thought of myself as a widow, but how could I be your widow if I never became your wife? And always it was Ida who ruled our home and managed our household."

"But now Ida has a new life with Franz. She will live in Switzerland and you and I and the children will be together at Les Collines. Won't it please you to be in charge of our home?" He trained his beneficent engaging smile on her.

"It will make no difference to me," she said, her voice firm, impervious to argument. "Les Collines is no longer my home. I am taking the children and leaving you. Our life together is over. I belong to Charles. I belong with Charles."

He stared at her, his face a mask of disbelief.

"You do not know what you are saying."

"I know exactly what I am saying."

"But what of my son?" he cried. "I cannot live without my David."

"You will see David as often as you like," she replied calmly.

"You cannot take him. You will not take him."

Tears streamed down his cheeks. The glass of brandy slipped from his trembling hand and fell to the floor.

"I can and I will."

She turned then, valise in hand, and left the room that stank of liquor and misery.

Ida arranged to meet Virginia at the hotel the next day. They sat together in the drab lobby. Ida had changed from judge to supplicant.

"Please, please, stay with my father. He will break down if you leave. You know how dependent he is," she said.

"Dependent on you. Never on me," Virginia insisted. "I was simply a presence, a caretaker."

"You were more than that. Think of what you will give up, Virginia. You were not his wife. He is not required to offer you any financial support. He has no legal obligation to support David. The law of France does not consider David his son. Do you want to return to a life of poverty? Have you forgotten how you lived before you met us? Think of your children if not of yourself." She gripped Virginia's wrists, stared hard at her, and then turned away.

Virginia was unmoved.

"Money is not important to me. I will take care of David. Charles will provide for us. Marc will see David as often as he wishes," she said and wrested herself free from Ida's grasp.

"We will see," Ida said.

She too consulted a lawyer. She listened to his advice, made copious notes, and she and Virginia met again.

They sat side by side on a bench in the Tuileries gardens on a cold and gray afternoon. Ida's cheeks were rouged by the thrust of the wind. Virginia was pale, her head bare, her hands ungloved. She lifted her eyes to the crescent of a pale sun that offered no warmth.

"Perhaps you will agree to a trial separation from my father," Ida suggested. "I would be prepared to rent an apartment for you."

Virginia shook her head.

"I will never live with Marc again. I must begin a new life, a life with Charles Leirens."

"I see," Ida said wearily.

She was resigned to defeat. She understood that Virginia's decision was firm. She would have to create a new scenario for this new chapter in her father's life and her own.

She spoke to Marc that night, her heart heavy, her voice solemn.

"It is over, *Papochka*. She is resolved and nothing we can do will dissuade her," she said.

"But David, what will happen to David?" he asked, his voice quivering, his blue eyes awash with tears.

"The lawyer told me that you have no legal right to David. He is David McNeil, not David Chagall."

Marc sank into a chair. "But he is my son. My Dovidl. Named for my brother," he said plaintively.

Ida knelt before him, wrapped her arms about his trembling body, patted his head. She was, once more, the comforting mother to her newly bereft father.

"It will be all right, *Papochka*," she said softly. "David will remain in your life. Virginia will allow you to be with him whenever it pleases you."

He shook his head, beat his breast with clenched fists.

"Tell her to return to me," he pleaded. "I cannot live alone."

"She will not come back, *Papochka*, but you will not be alone," Ida promised.

He would not be comforted. Despair weighted his limbs. He moved with difficulty.

Days later he returned to Les Collines unaccompanied. He wandered through the large house, sitting for long hours on David's empty bed, barefoot and unshaven, a mourner draped in a dangerous and melancholy silence.

Chapter Fifty

*I*da understood that her father was incapable of living alone. Solitude oppressed him.

"He needs a woman," she told Franz. "A companion, a house-keeper, someone who will care for him, see to his needs."

"A consort," Franz said drily. "I have never seen such a position advertised. How do you intend to find such a person?"

"I found Virginia, didn't I?" she retorted.

He laughed. His Ida could do anything.

With studied casualness, she mentioned that her father might be interested in meeting an appropriate woman. Meanwhile, she found an apartment in Paris where he could live for part of the year. That, she decided, would lessen his sense of isolation. And it was important too, she thought, that both he and she have an ongoing relationship with David. To that end, she called Virginia and invited her to lunch.

They met in a small restaurant in the Place Dauphine, known for its very excellent and very expensive food. A vase of forsythia stood on the table. A solicitous waiter hovered. Ida found a stain on her spoon and sent it back. He bowed obsequiously and handed them the menus. He was accustomed to demanding women who ordered expensive lunches and even more expensive wines.

Ida and Virginia were oddly relaxed. Their war was over and all that remained was to establish the terms of their peace treaty.

Ida lifted her wineglass and proposed a toast. "To David," she said.

"To David," Virginia echoed.

It was clear that it was because of David that they were sharing a meal.

They sipped the wine slowly.

"I have bought my father an apartment near my own home where he can live for part of the year. It will make it easier for him to see David fairly often, that is, if you do not object."

Ida chose her words carefully. She wanted Virginia to understand that she was making a request rather than issuing a demand.

"David is Marc's son. He can see him as often as he wishes," Virginia said.

She was relieved that Ida had finally accepted her departure from Marc's life and was moving ahead. Established in his own apartment, Marc would no longer need his rooms at the Quai de l'Horloge. Ida and Franz would have complete privacy when they visited Paris. How swiftly and with what efficiency Ida had adjusted to this change in their lives. How clever Ida was. She would have her husband, her home, her generous commissions as Marc's agent, and an even greater dominance over his life. Eventually, Virginia supposed, just as Ida had brought her into Marc's New York home, she would bring another woman into his Paris apartment. Clever, resourceful Ida.

"Shall we share a parfait?" Ida asked.

"Of course," Virginia agreed.

The waiter watched as the two very different women dipped their long spoons into the creamy desserts and ate with great concentration. They did not speak. He supposed that whatever had brought them together had been accomplished.

It did not surprise him that it was the auburn-haired woman in the tasteful black Chanel suit who paid the check. He watched as they shook hands at the door and went their separate ways down the windswept Place Dauphine. It amused him that they both walked briskly, their heads held high, and that neither of them turned back.

It was only a week later that Ida met her good friend Ida Bourdet at the very same restaurant. As the two Idas sipped their wine, Ida Bourdet smiled slyly.

"I have a surprise for you, but you will have to pay me a

commission or, at the very least, offer me one of your father's sketches," she said.

"First reveal your surprise," Ida replied. "It will have to be worthwhile. My father's sketches do not come cheap."

"Oh, it is very worthwhile," her friend assured her. "I am certain that I have found exactly the right companion for your father. She is a very accomplished and sophisticated woman, quite beautiful, a Russian Jew. She lives in London, but I think she would not be averse to coming to France."

Ida leaned forward, her interest piqued. She knew that the Bourdets' connections stretched across continents and included an eclectic community of artists and intellectuals, businessmen, and government officials.

"And who is she?" Ida asked as she carefully buttered her croissant.

"Her name is Valentina Brodsky, but she prefers to be called Vava. She runs a millinery shop in Hampstead, a rather chic shop," Ida Bourdet replied. "I met her when I went in to buy a hat. She is a divorcée, but her marriage was very brief and she has no contact with her former husband. Thus no complications," Ida Bourdet said.

"So you bought a hat and acquired a friend. How like you. Was it a nice hat?" Ida asked mischievously.

"Actually I never wore it. It was a plum-colored cloche that suited me not at all. Claude hated it, but yes, Vava and I did become friends. Buying a hat takes time and invites conversation. After I had tried on ten different creations, I knew her life story and I must admit she knew mine. We liked each other. An instant friendship, if you will. I admired her courage and found her story moving."

"Why do you admire her courage? And what is her story?"

"She was born in Kiev into the very wealthy and supposedly well-known Brodsky family. They were, she claims, considered to be Jewish aristocracy in imperial Russia. She was only thirteen when the Revolution decimated her family and their fortune. She and her brother Michel fled Russia. Somehow they reached Berlin. They were two penniless adolescents, entirely on their own, forced to scavenge for survival. And somehow she went to school in Germany and even completed her matriculation exam. It appears she and her brother became a cult of two, supporting each other both emotionally and financially. They had a talent for improvising and managed to live on very little. Vava might find a remaindered bolt of very good fabric, buy it for a song, and create an elegant and fashionable gown that she then sold at an impressive price. They haunted vintage shops where they bartered their tailoring skills for decent clothing. They were attractive and well-dressed, fluent in several languages, and so amusing that they were invited to fashionable parties and receptions and probably attended others uninvited."

"Where I suppose the hors d'oeuvres became dinner and enough tarts and tea sandwiches could be thrust into their pockets for breakfast and lunch the next day," Ida said knowingly.

She had seen such scavengers at gallery openings and cocktail parties, their once-expensive clothing frayed but mended, their worn shoes too highly polished. They edged stealthily toward the buffet, snatched drinks from the trays of passing waiters, and sipped them in the corner of the room. She often wished that she could fill a basket and simply offer it to them.

"Probably," Ida Bourdet agreed. She herself had scrounged for food during the years of the German occupation, and she appreciated and applauded the survival skills of others.

"In any case," she continued, "they finally left Berlin and came to Paris. Vava told me that her brother, who is homosexual, very sensibly took a lover who was a successful fashion designer. That gave them access to more expensive clothing, more invitations, more entrées into society, more steps up the ladder to a kind of respectability."

"And she married for that respectability," Ida surmised. She was intrigued. There was a pattern to the life of this unknown woman that curiously paralleled her own familial history. The flight from Russia, the exile to Berlin, the life in Paris—her story was not unlike that of the Chagalls. They too had lived on the fringes of established society, as strangers in strange new lands. Her father and this mysterious Vava might find much in common.

"Yes, she married," Ida Bourdet continued. "But it was a marriage in name only. Her husband refused to consummate it and she remained a virgin. I believe they call that a *mariage blanc*. Of course they divorced and Vava went to London, which is where I met her. She told me that she is interested in returning to France if she could find a suitable position."

"And you think she might be an appropriate companion for my father?"

"I have an intuition that it would work out. And as Claude can tell you, my intuitions are usually correct."

Ida was silent. She refilled her glass and considered all that her friend had said. Valentina Brodsky was indeed interesting. Like Marc, she spoke Russian, German, and French. She wondered if she spoke Yiddish. Probably not, she decided, but that would not matter. She would, of course, be familiar with the customs and cuisine of Russia, the mores of France, which was more important. And having lived in London, her English might be good enough to translate the correspondence from England, a task that Ida had begun to find onerous.

She nodded and smiled at Ida Bourdet.

"Yes. It may well work out. My father is partial to women from prestigious families. He may even recognize the Brodsky name. All right. Let us offer her that suitable position. Write to her and suggest that she come to Les Collines as the manager of the estate."

She knew that such phrasing would be acceptable to a Russian émigré with pretensions to respectability. The word *housekeeper* would, of course, be anathema.

Vava Brodsky's response was swift. She would assume the position for a trial period, perhaps of two or three months. It was a sacrifice for her to leave her thriving millinery shop, but she had always admired the work of Monsieur Chagall, especially his crucifixion paintings. She was making a personal sacrifice so that she might assist the great artist.

Ida frowned as she read the letter. Valentina Brodsky had transformed the acceptance of an offer of employment into an act of personal generosity. She was surely a shrewd woman, an agile manipulator and probably not without ambition. The lessons of her admittedly difficult life had been well learned. She showed the letter to Franz and asked if he did not think it odd that she mentioned only the crucifixion paintings out of all Marc's work.

"But the crucifixions are wonderfully realized works," Franz replied. "I myself study them again and again. Each of his Christs tells a different story, offers a different perspective. I think she sounds very suitable."

He admitted to himself that he wanted Valentina Brodsky to take up residence at Les Collines so that Ida would curtail her journeys to France, cease obsessing about her father, and spend more time in Switzerland. He yearned to start a family. He also wanted to begin work on what he hoped would be his magnum opus—a comprehensive study of Marc's work. Given his obligations as director of the Bern Kunsthalle, he needed Ida to assist him with the research. If this Russian woman could assume the management of Les Collines and, hopefully, of Marc's life, Ida could concentrate on her life in Switzerland, her life with him.

Ida hesitated. She read the letter yet again. Valentina Brodsky's stationery was embossed with her raised monogram. Her penmanship was graceful, strangely reminiscent of Bella's. Ida supposed that she, like Bella, had been instructed by the tutors employed by their wealthy Jewish parents to master such elegant script. It was an essential mark of their status.

"All right," Ida said at last. "I will ask her to come very soon. It is important that he have company. His doctor says that his heart is being affected by his depression. Let us hope that this Vava, as she prefers to be called, will be helpful to him."

"A wise decision, *ma chérie*," Franz said and drew her close. How beautiful she was, his Ida. How wonderful it was that the long winter was over and springtime had come. Soon Ida would be free to concentrate on their life together, on his work, and on her own future.

Ida wrote a detailed letter to Valentina Brodsky, assuring her of a warm welcome and generous compensation, choosing her words carefully. But that night, for the first time in months, the familiar dream recurred. Once again, she raced down a country road, but now it was her father who outpaced her, and as she struggled to keep up with him, a veiled woman appeared and took his hand. Together they soared skyward while Ida stared after them, alone and abandoned.

"*Papochka*," she shouted, her throat tight with terror.

She awakened to find Franz's arms about her trembling body.

"It was only a dream," he said softly.

"Of course. Only a dream," she agreed and shivered although the room was very warm.

Valentina Brodsky arrived on the specified date and Ida met her at the Bourdet home. She was a petite woman. Her features were delicate and her dark hair, pulled sleekly back from her high pale forehead, gave her face an oriental cast. She wore an austerely cut navy blue dress, offset by a soft wool patterned scarf that Ida immediately identified as Liberty of London. She was, Ida knew instinctively, a woman whose understated classic clothing would always be fashioned from the finest fabrics. There were probably blouses of iridescent silk in the hues of an early spring garden in her worn black leather trunk, a relic of another era, probably scavenged from a secondhand shop and painstakingly refurbished. Elegant Vava would, of course, scorn the pathetic luggage of the refugee.

She extended a gloved hand to Ida, smiled thinly, and spoke very softly in French.

"I am pleased to accommodate you and your father, Madame Meyer," she said.

"My father is looking forward to meeting you," Ida replied.

She noted the pearl button on Vava's white leather glove and wondered maliciously if the gloves concealed a roughness of skin caused by caustic cleaning soaps and the pricks of a milliner's needle. She herself had been raised by a mother who had stressed the importance of soft and well-manicured hands.

"It is important to have the hands of a rabbi's daughter who has never had to put a finger in cold water," Bella had often cautioned, rubbing fragrant creams across Ida's palms and her own. Ida was willing to wager that Valentina Brodsky did not have the hands of a rabbi's daughter.

As she drove southward, Ida described the charms of Les Collines, and Vava occasionally interrupted her with casually phrased but penetrating questions.

"Has it been many years since your dear mother passed away?" she asked.

Ida nodded. "Yes. Many years."

It occurred to her suddenly that this seemingly fragile woman with her dark hair and dark eyes bore an odd resemblance to Bella. But she dismissed the thought at once. No one could be compared to her mother.

"And you were your parents' only child?" Vava continued.

"Yes. But I do have a half brother," she added. "Much younger than myself. His name is David."

She realized, almost at once, that Ida Bourdet had surely mentioned David. Vava, it seemed, asked questions to which she already knew the answers. She would not tell Vava that her father refused to see David. He had irrationally projected his fury with Virginia onto his son.

"And you, I understand, have a brother. What are his future plans? What is his profession?" Ida asked, entering into Vava's interrogatory game.

"Michel," Vava replied stiffly. "My brother's name is Michel. I do not know his plans. Do you often travel from Switzerland to your father's home, Madame Meyer?"

Ida nodded. Skilled strategists both, thrust into an uneasy intimacy, they engaged in an intricate conversational chess match,
moving each carefully plotted revelation across an increasingly hazardous board as they traveled down the sun-spangled road that led
to Vence. Marc met them there, and Ida's heart turned with pity to
see how diminished he had become even in the short while since she
had last seen him. Loneliness had withered him. His pale face was
mottled, his blue eyes faded, and his creased, paint-stained clothing
hung too loosely on his gaunt body. He acknowledged Vava with a
dismissive wave of his hand.

"Mademoiselle Brodsky has come all the way from England to
help you at Les Collines," Ida said too brightly.

"Do I need help?" he asked disconsolately.

It was Vava Brodsky who replied.

"But of course, everyone needs help," she said gently in Russian.

He sat up straighter and turned to her. "You speak Russian?"

"I do. I was born in Kiev."

"Ah, Kiev. I know about Kiev," he said dreamily. "A city of
cafés, *n'est-ce pas*? They say that Kiev became a refuge for those who
left Petrograd after the revolution. Refugees have a great need of
cafés, of course. I heard that in Kiev, after the revolution, there was 'a
department of the arts' that launched a steamboat that floated down
the Dnieper flying the banner of the revolution. Did you ever see
that steamboat, Mademoiselle Brodsky?"

"I left Kiev in 1918. I was only thirteen years old. I never sat in a
café. I never saw such a steamboat," she said. "And I have, of course,
never returned. I am unwelcome in Russia."

"As I am," Marc said, and his eyes filled with tears. "I left Mother
Russia in 1922. Never to return. Never to return to the land of my
birth." His voice broke.

"But Russia has never left you," Vava responded. "You have captured our motherland in your wonderful work."

She took his hand in her own, a gesture of understanding and
reassurance. Ida looked at her in surprise, startled and unnerved

by the sudden intimacy between her father and this woman he barely knew.

"We really must go to Les Collines," she said. "It is getting late."

During the short ride, Ida worried that her father would once again collapse beneath the weight of his memories. She parked the car, took his arm, and slowly walked him up to the veranda, littered with fallen twigs and branches, the remnants of the winter's wrath. The staff had been negligent, she thought angrily. Vava trailed behind them. Ida turned the key in the lock, opened the heavy door, and breathed deeply before entering.

Les Collines had the desolate, musty ambience of an abandoned home. Marc stood hesitantly in his own doorway, his head bent forward, as though listening for voices that had been stilled for so many weeks, perhaps anticipating Virginia's too soft and placating tones or David's mischievous laughter.

Vava looked around and wandered into the rear of the house as Ida rushed about lighting lamps, thrusting open windows, settling her father into a comfortable chair in the salon. She sorted swiftly through the mail and parcels that had accumulated during their absence, angry that the staff had ignored her instruction to send them on to her.

Exhausted by her own efforts, she sank onto the sofa as Vava entered the room carrying a tray laden with three tall glasses set in silver holders, filled to the brim with steaming tea, a bowl of sugar cubes, and a small platter of golden brown apple strudel studded with walnuts. She had discovered the kitchen. There had been no need for her to ask how Marc liked his tea. She had known. She watched him place a cube of sugar beneath his tongue and lift the fragrant hot brew to his lips. She smiled as he bit into the cake.

"It is of my own baking," she said. "I brought it with me from London."

"It is delicious," he said. "My mother baked such a cake."

"I learned the recipe from our cook in Kiev," she said.

They spoke softly in Russian. He smiled. She smiled. They were cocooned for the moment in a mutuality of remembrance.

Ida sipped her own tea, but she did not eat the cake. Vava rose to retrieve a blanket from the sofa, and she placed it across Marc's knees.

"The house is a bit chilly," she said, and she closed a window that Ida had opened.

Ida rose. "I think I will start to drive to Paris," she said. "If I get tired, I can stop in Toulon."

"Of course," Marc agreed.

"Shall I show you through the rest of the house before I leave?" she asked Vava.

"There is no need. I think I can manage," Vava said.

"Yes. I am sure that you can," Ida replied drily.

She understood instinctively that Vava was a woman with impeccable survival skills. She had been conditioned to assess new and challenging situations and manipulate them to her advantage. It was a role that history had thrust upon her and one that she had carefully cultivated. In accepting the position at Les Collines, she surely had her own agenda. Ida supposed that she should consider herself fortunate that Vava's agenda matched her own.

She bent over her father and kissed him on both cheeks, pleased to see that his color had been restored, that his eyes had regained their luster.

"*Au revoir, Papochka,*" she said.

She held her hand out to Vava who had finally removed her leather gloves. She noted with satisfaction that she had not been wrong. Vava's palms were rough, her fingers punctured by the pricks of many needles. They were not the hands of a rabbi's daughter.

"*À bientôt,*" they said in unison.

Ida left and closed the door softly behind her. She heard Vava secure the bolt and, with that simple action, establish her dominion over Les Collines.

———

Spring burst onto the Riviera in all its glory. The flower beds of Les Collines exploded into a riot of color. Dark-hearted pansies nestled beside tender carpets of lavender; the air was heavy with the sweet scent of orange blossoms, and the silver branches of the olive trees were already laden with small ovoids of pale green fruit. Virginia had loved a wild garden, but Vava mandated that borders be trimmed, the bushes pruned, the fallen fruit removed from the ground before it could rot. She arranged flowers for the house in discreet bouquets. Girls from Vence were hired to scour the kitchen, to beat the carpets, to polish and wax the hardwood floors. They were instructed to arrive when Marc was already in his studio and to leave when he emerged.

"Nothing must disturb *le maître*," Vava told them sternly.

She moved through the rooms, rearranging furniture, altering the placement of paintings. The children's bedrooms became guest rooms. Their toys and books were placed in cartons and sent to the church as donations to the crèche. Within weeks of Vava's arrival, there was no hint that a small boy and girl had ever lived at Les Collines. Only Ida's suite remained untouched. Vava was too wise to intrude on Ida's precinct.

Ida, during a brief visit, appraised the changes, approval and disapproval commingled.

"I bought David a wonderful train set," she said. "It was in the nursery. Surely you did not give that away. He will want to play with it when he visits."

"I understand that he has been sent to a boarding school in England, and your father has said that even when he returns to France, he does not want to see him," Vava replied. "He finds all reminders of the boy to be painful, so of course I discarded the toys."

"Indeed." Ida's voice was laced with annoyance, but she said nothing more. She would not discuss her brother with Vava. Instead she went into Marc's studio, carrying an envelope of notes and drawings that David had sent to her, asking that she give them to their father.

"*Papochka*, these are from your son, David," she said, holding the envelope out to him.

"I do not have a son," he said angrily. "He is the son of the Englishwoman. She has taken him from me. His name is McNeil, not Chagall. That is what the law says, and I am a man who obeys the law. If the law says he is not my son, why should I answer his letters? Why should I support him?"

"Because you know that he is your son. You raised him. He is named for your brother. Of course he is your son, your Jewish son," Ida insisted.

Ida loved and cherished her half brother. She remembered the sweet scent of his little body as she wiped him dry after a bath, the games they had played together and the books she had read to him. There was no need to lose him. Virginia, to her credit, was willing to share David with both Marc and Ida.

"If he is my son, he must live only with me. Virginia McNeil must be gone from his life as she is gone from my life. If David lives in my house, I will not allow her to see him," Marc shouted.

"You cannot ask a mother to give up her son," Ida said quietly. She placed the envelope with David's letters and drawings on a table beside his easel and left the studio.

Later that week, she and Franz attended a performance of *Tosca* at the Paris Opera House. During the entr'acte, as they stood in the great hall sipping champagne, Pablo Picasso and Françoise Gilot approached them.

"Ah, the lovely daughter of Marc Chagall," the artist said, kissing her on both cheeks, his breath sour with the mingled odors of garlic and wine.

"And now the wife of Franz Meyer," Ida said. "May I introduce you?"

"Yes. Of course. The distinguished curator from Bern. I congratulate you both on your marriage." He shook Franz's hand and flashed them a wide smile, his teeth startlingly white against his earth-colored complexion. Françoise Gilot nodded an indifferent greeting. Ida, when she was single, had mildly amused her. Ida, as a married woman, interested her not at all.

"And how is your father bearing up since being deserted by the Englishwoman?" he asked and laughed harshly.

"He is fine," Ida answered coldly.

"I am told that the Englishwoman married her photographer lover this very afternoon," Picasso added.

"I had not heard that, and it is of little interest to us," Ida retorted with a calm she did not feel. "Any love affair may come to an end."

"Not mine," he replied arrogantly. "My Françoise would never leave her Pablo. Isn't that so, Françoise?"

She shrugged.

"Pablo thinks himself invincible," Françoise said coldly.

The warning bell sounded, and they hurried to take their seats for the second act.

"He is a very unpleasant man, this Picasso," Franz said.

"Unpleasantness is the prerogative of geniuses," Ida replied and studied her program.

So Virginia and Leirens are married, she thought. Another chapter closed. She sighed and turned her attention to the music.

She did not mention Virginia's marriage to Marc when she and Franz next visited Les Collines. They ate the Russian delicacies Vava prepared for their dinner. She was an excellent cook, and each dish that she offered arrived with a story. They praised the wild sorrel soup garnished with scallions that had been a staple of Marc's childhood, and Vava told them that she traveled to the farmers' market in Nice to find the freshest greens. Platters of blini and pirogen appeared. She explained that she foraged for the mushrooms herself, discovering them at the base of the eucalyptus trees, whose leaves she gathered for their curative properties. The chicken was stewed with root vegetables that she purchased from a farmer who set aside his best produce and poultry for her.

"No one can resist Vava," Marc said proudly.

"I carry everything home from the farm myself," she claimed.

"But isn't that difficult for you?" Franz asked.

"I am used to difficulty," she replied piously.

She ladled the stew onto their plates, selecting the choicest white meat for Marc.

"When I eat Vava's food, I imagine that I am sitting in my mother's kitchen," he said appreciatively.

The dining room table groaned beneath Vava's desserts, strudels and sponge cakes, tarts that sparkled with orange rind from the citrus that she plucked from their own trees, and pots of sweet plum jam, her own comfitures.

"I am partial to sugar," Vava confessed. "My family owned a sugar brokerage. My father was called the Sugar Baron of Russia. But of course, that was long ago." Her voice drifted into a soft sadness.

It occurred to Ida that Vava seemed to speak from a script. Her fluent words rang with a rehearsed theatricality. But then, she knew that Vava was an accomplished actress, aware of both her stage set and her costume. She wore an elegant black dress, covered with an impeccable starched white apron for the first act of her culinary tableau. She removed the apron as the meal progressed and she assumed different roles. She was at once chef and hostess, servant and mistress.

Ida also noted that while Marc helped himself to two slices of sponge cake and his lips were rimmed with the purple jam that he ate with a spoon, Vava, despite her proclaimed partiality for sugar, ate only an apple that she cut into elegant slices, playfully popping a sliver of fruit into Marc's mouth.

"*Spasibo*," he said, thanking her in Russian and she smiled.

"*Pozhaluysta*," she replied.

In deference to Franz, the conversation at the table was in French, but it was clear that when Marc and Vava were alone, they spoke in Russian.

Vava served tea in glasses encased in polished silver holders, careful to place a platter with sugar cubes next to Marc.

Later in the evening, Marc and Ida conferred in the living room over arrangements with dealers and offers for paintings that had been made by collectors. Jewish themes were sought after by wealthy American Jewish collectors, and Marc's works were much in demand.

They spoke of francs and dollars, of demanding sterling from one gallery, deutsche marks from another. Vava sat quietly, diligently darning socks. When her mending basket was empty, she sat back with her eyes closed as the talk of money hummed about her.

Franz and Ida left for Switzerland the next morning, but before they departed, Vava insisted that they sit down for a few minutes.

"Yes. You must do that," Marc agreed.

Ida smiled. "It is a Russian custom," she explained to Franz. "You sit before a journey so that you will have a safe return. Magical thinking of a kind. My mother sometimes insisted on it."

"Vava knows and understands the old customs," Marc said.

Obediently they sat.

"So what do you think of Valentina Brodsky?" Ida asked Franz as they drove back to Paris.

"It is important that she brings your father contentment," he said carefully.

"Contentment, yes," she agreed. "And dependence. She even spooned his egg out of the shell at breakfast. It would not surprise me if she offered to urinate for him."

Franz laughed. Words that he might consider vulgar when spoken by others had an amusing charm when Ida uttered them.

Ida was excited when she discovered an apartment on the Île Saint-Louis that she knew would be ideal for her father when he had to spend time in Paris. Reluctantly, he agreed to see it and at once decided to buy it. The large, wide-windowed rooms were flooded with light and overlooked the Seine. The master bedroom overlooked a garden where lilacs were already in bloom. Ida led him to a smaller bedroom.

"It is just the right size for David," she said daringly.

"Why do I need a room for David? Is he in my life? Do I want him in my life? He lives with the Englishwoman and her lying and deceitful husband, does he not?" he asked bitterly.

Ida did not answer. She understood that Marc was a prisoner of his own irrational hatred. She would wait for his anger to dissipate and for his longing for his son to emerge.

"You will do wonderful work here, *Papochka*," she said.

"Perhaps. But Vava does not think I should interrupt my work by traveling back and forth to Paris. She worries that I will lose the continuity of my vision."

"Vava is hardly an art critic," Ida retorted. "She is at Les Collines to manage your household, not to serve as your mentor. You will come to Paris whenever it pleases you. And Vava will have her room here. She will keep house for you in Paris as she does at Les Collines."

He was silent. After some minutes, he went over to the window and stared down at the Seine, where green waves, laced with froth, rippled downstream. He spoke without looking at Ida, his voice so soft she had to strain to hear him.

"Vava has told me that she wants to return to England. She has her business, her millinery shop that is suffering in her absence. She will remain in France, remain with me, only if we are married," he said. "And she wants that marriage to take place very soon. In early July."

"Married?" Ida repeated, her voice faint with shock and disbelief. "But, *Papochka*, you've known each other for only a few months. Surely it would be wise to wait until you are certain that such a marriage will be successful."

She gripped the edge of a chair to steady herself against a sudden dizziness. *Marriage? Could her father really contemplate marriage with a woman he had known for a scarce few months?* The thought sickened her, but she willed herself to be calm as Marc continued, his voice firm.

"We are not children. She is, of course, some years younger than me, but that is not a problem." His voice gathered strength. "She is a mature woman. She knows her own mind. She understands my feelings and I understand hers. This is the way many marriages were arranged in our Russia. A Jewish man and woman of the same background, each offering the other something important, agree to share their lives. Such marriages were successful more often than not." He did not turn from the window. He did not look at Ida.

"All right. You offer her a home. Financial security. Your famous name. What does she offer you?" Ida asked.

"Sanity. I will go mad if she leaves and I remain alone in that house, which has too many rooms, too many memories. Can I live alone in this wonderful apartment that you have found? What will I do on my own here—wander all night from bed to bed? Vava takes care of me. She sees that I can work without interruption, that there is a meal on the table when I leave the studio. Idotchka, there is peace and order in the house that she keeps for me. She is a companion. When I talk, she listens. We speak in Russian, the language of our homeland. When I want quiet, she is silent. And she is beautiful. Sometimes I look at her and I think I am seeing your mother, my Bella. She is pure, as Bella was when she came to me. She has told me that her previous marriage was a marriage in name only. She is from a Jewish family, like Bella's, a cultured family, a wealthy family. The Brodsky name was known throughout Russia. We are well matched. She has said so and I believe her. I cannot risk losing her. So I ask you, what do you think about my marrying Vava?"

Ida hesitated before answering. She knew he could not live alone. He might die of grief. His doctor had said as much. That was why she had brought Vava into his life after Virginia's desertion, just as she had brought Virginia into his life after Bella's death. How odd it was for a daughter to be her father's procurer, she thought bitterly.

But Vava, unlike Virginia, had taken control. She was at once housekeeper and companion, nurse and hostess. As Ida had surmised, she had arrived at Les Collines with her own agenda and her own ambition. Ida recalled the questions she had asked and the swiftness with which she had asserted her dominance over the household and indeed over Marc himself. She had been attentive to their discussions of money because she craved financial security. She wanted recognition and respectability. She was no longer a young woman whose charms were her passport to survival. She was middle-aged, her past suspect, her future uncertain. Marriage to Marc Chagall afforded her all that she was desperate to achieve. She did not want to spend her life selling hats to imperious English women, carrying huge boxes out to their cars and pricking her fingers as she sewed flowers and veils onto her clever creations. Her small millinery shop could not give her the income necessary for the life she wanted to live. An alternative had presented itself and, like the opportunist she was and had been forced to be, she had seized it.

Ida acknowledged that this Valentina Brodsky had played her cards well. She had recognized Marc's vulnerability, cultivated his dependence, and then issued her ultimatum. She was blackmailing him into marriage. That much was clear.

Ida paced the room, not looking at her father as she struggled to organize her thoughts. Wearily and with great reluctance, she recognized that such a marriage might actually be for the best. It would be good for Marc and good for Ida herself. She would be liberated from her constant concern for him. Vava had proven herself an accomplished caregiver, a talented companion. Her motives might be devious, but her performance was exemplary.

"So, Idotchka, what do you think of such a marriage?" he asked again.

She smiled. "What I think is of no importance. It is your life, your decision. If Vava makes you happy, then I too will be happy. If and when she becomes your wife, Franz and I will welcome her into our family."

His shoulders quivered. He turned to face her and she held her arms out. Wordlessly he moved into her embrace.

"Shhh, *Papochka*. Everything will be all right. All will be well," she murmured in Yiddish.

They stood in the empty room, locked in each other's arms, as the dying sun bled into the Seine. They left, walking arm in arm, father and daughter supporting each other as the pealing bells of Notre Dame tolled the twilight hour.

———

It was decided that Marc and Vava would marry at the home of Ida and Claude Bourdet in Rambouillet. The Bourdets, delighted with the success of their match, insisted on arranging every aspect of the nuptials.

"I myself have seen that the banns were published," Claude announced proudly.

"Banns? Why should banns be published when two Jews marry?" Ida asked.

"Vava asked me to see to publishing them and I obliged. Perhaps she thinks it is a French custom," he replied.

"Perhaps," Ida agreed, although the strangeness of the request troubled her. She wondered, yet again, if Vava, during the course of her wanderings, had shed her very inconvenient Jewishness. It was not a suspicion she would share with her father, who had written to his Yiddishist friends about his marriage.

"I am marrying a Jewish woman," he had assured them. "A Russian Jewish woman like my Bella from a good Jewish family who will make me happy."

Marc and Vava were married on the sun-drenched terrace of the Bourdets' home. Regal in a loose chemise of golden linen, Bella's pearls warm against her neck, Ida stood at her father's side during the quiet ceremony. It pleased her that he wore the blue velvet jacket that had been her gift to him, chosen because it matched his eyes. She glanced at Vava, solemn and confident in a black silk dress that hugged her slender form. She held a single white orchid, a gift from her brother Michel. He was a slender man, his angular face as pale as the flower he had chosen, his dark eyes watchful. Vava's jet-colored hair was brushed into a sleek and shining helmet and her lips were bared in a half smile. Her voice was barely audible as she uttered her vows. The officiant nodded, smiled, and pronounced Marc Chagall and Valentina Brodsky man and wife in accordance with the laws of France. Someone clapped very softly as a small girl tossed white rose petals into the air. Ida turned to her father.

"*Mazel tov*," she said, and he smiled.

"But my *mazel* is already *tov*," he replied. "My luck is very good indeed."

Ida kissed Vava on both cheeks. "Please make my father happy," she murmured.

"But I do," Vava rejoined and brushed a vagrant petal from Marc's shoulder.

At the reception, Ida lifted her glass and smiled as Franz offered a toast that welcomed Vava into *la famille Chagall*.

The wedding cake was carried in, and Vava cut it and placed the first slice on a plate. Smiling, she fed it to Marc. The elderly bridegroom opened his mouth like an obedient child. He ate it with great appreciation, and when he was done, his bride deftly wiped away the small mustache of cream that had formed on his upper lip.

Ida leaned against Franz's shoulder as they drove home.

"Don't you think that Vava looked like a cat?" she asked sleepily. "A sleek black cat."

"A very contented cat," Franz agreed.

"Perhaps my father will paint her as one. He is partial to cats, you know."

"Is he?" Franz asked. "Are you partial to cats? Perhaps we will keep one as a pet in our Basel house."

"No. I don't trust them. I think they are treacherous creatures. I have been told that they are jealous of infants," Ida replied.

She thought of the large empty room in their Basel home that she had envisioned as a nursery. She had hung gossamer curtains on its windows and had imagined placing a crib of pale wood against the whitewashed wall where an infant, as yet unconceived and unborn, would surely sleep. She smiled at the thought that came unbidden.

"Ida, you must not worry. I believe that Vava will make your father happy," Franz said. "As you make me happy."

"Then I must believe as you believe."

She closed her eyes and drifted into a light sleep, startled into wakefulness when they reached the Quai de l'Horloge.

Chapter Fifty-One

ranz appeared to be right. It appeared that Marc and Vava were happy. Assurances of that happiness were scrawled across the postcards that arrived regularly at the Meyer home in Basel.

Marc wrote that they were enjoying a long and leisurely honeymoon. He loved Rome, loved guiding Vava through the museums and gardens, delighted in her delight as he explained the paintings and sculptures, as they rested in the Borghese Gardens and visited the Colosseum at sunset. He sent Ida a photograph of Vava standing before the Trevi Fountain, a loose fringed shawl draped over her shoulders, her black hair swept back and held in place with gleaming amber combs.

"My mother had such combs," Ida recalled. "And she loved shawls. Oh they were beautiful, brightly colored, some of silk, some of wool." She stared hard at the photo. "I wonder if Vava is channeling herself into my mother's persona."

"I shouldn't think so," Franz replied, looking up from his newspaper. "I imagine she is simply dressing to please your father. Perhaps your mother did the same."

"No. My mother pleased my father simply by being Bella," Ida said. "Vava has to work at it."

She had noted Vava's tireless efforts to please Marc and had more than once seen her studying photographs of Bella. She tried to believe that her father's new wife was concerned only with his contentment, but she could not overcome her feeling that there was a patent contrived falsity in Vava's actions. It seemed to Ida that it was not enough for Vava that she had taken Bella's place as Madame Chagall—she wanted to *be* Bella. Ida wondered bitterly if she would model for him dressed in white, or perhaps he would paint her dancing toward him in a gown of green velvet. The bitterness of the thought shamed her. She would have to learn to like Vava and, perhaps, even to trust her.

Marc sent Ida a page ripped from his drawing tablet on which he had sketched the Colosseum. She and Franz studied it carefully.

"It has a classic element that is very different from his previous work," Franz, the scholarly art historian, observed.

She wondered if the shift in his technique would affect the sale of his work but immediately reassured herself. Her father's art had always been protean, often surprising. His audience was faithful. He would, of course, continue to sell and sell well. Her own commissions from the sales of his paintings and drawings were mounting. Ever the shrewd businesswoman, she kept careful accounts and invested wisely, buying a small villa in Toulon.

"I would prefer to stay in Toulon when I visit my father. It will be more comfortable for us in our own place, don't you think?" she asked Franz.

He agreed hesitantly, understanding that Ida did not want to be a guest in a home that would now be controlled by Vava. The parameters of her power were altered.

"It is an expensive undertaking," he said mildly. "There is the Paris house and our home in Basel. Can you really afford the Toulon house?"

"Property is an investment," she replied.

She did not add that because Franz's life had always been safely anchored, he did not understand that owning property gave her a sense of security. Many homes meant many places of refuge, many seats of comfort. She had not forgotten her uneasy years of wandering, seeking refuge in the houses of other people. That long-ago life continued to shadow her bright present that grew even brighter when she became pregnant. She and Franz were delighted, and she immediately traveled to Les Collines to share the happy news with her father.

"I am going to be a mother, *Papochka*," she said jubilantly. "You will have a grandchild."

She danced toward him, giddy with joy, her hands held out, inviting him to dance the polka remembered from her childhood, when good news signaled an exuberant whirl about the room.

He ignored her outstretched hands.

"A grandfather," Marc said.

He looked in the mirror, studied his face newly ruddied by the southern sun, thrust his fingers through his gray hair, still so thick and curly, as though to reassure himself that he looked too young to be a grandfather. She had always understood his ingrained vanity, his desire to appear younger than he was, intensified now because he was the husband of a much younger woman. But she had wanted him to set that vanity aside and to rejoice in the news she had brought him, for her sake as well as his own.

"That is good news," he said at last. "You must take good care of yourself."

"I will," she assured him, hiding her disappointment although he could not notice it. He had already turned away. Vava had called to him from the garden, and he rarely kept Vava waiting.

Ida did take good care of herself. She blossomed in pregnancy. Her hair, now the color of burnished bronze, grew thicker. Her skin was aglow and her eyes glittered. She moved with an easy grace, sailing through the streets of Basel and Paris, proud of the gentle rise of her abdomen beneath the loose, rainbow-colored garments she favored, proud of the fullness of her breasts, enchanted with the realization that a life dwelled within her body. Each movement from the baby enthralled her.

"Feel," she called to Franz, placing his hand on her body.

He touched her tenderly, smiled, and rested his head on the swell beneath which the unborn child stirred.

"Feel," she commanded her father, but Marc turned away.

Pregnancy and birth had always filled him with discomfort.

Vava frowned. She thought Ida's enthusiasm vulgar, her pregnancy

repellent. She herself had never wanted children. They did not interest her. There was no room in her life or in her home for a child.
She had no intention of ever welcoming David, Marc's son, born
to a woman who had not been his wife, into their home. She was
relieved that Marc rarely mentioned him.

"The boy is *un bâtard*," she told her brother Michel. "He is nothing to me. I do not want him here."

"You are right," Michel agreed. "For many reasons."

He and Vava smiled at each other, acknowledging the complicity
that had protected them for so many years.

Piet Meyer was born in Zurich early in July, his Swiss citizenship
guaranteed. He would never face the dangers that had confronted
his mother and his maternal grandparents. The lusty, golden-haired
baby boy met his famous grandfather when Ida took him to Vence
to celebrate Vava and Marc's first wedding anniversary. Only two
weeks old, he did not open his eyes as Marc stroked his cheek and
twisted a strand of the infant's fine hair about his paint-stained finger.

"*Azoi shein*, so beautiful," he said in Yiddish, and a tear fell from
his eye onto the sleeping child's petal-soft pink cheek. "If only your
mother could see her grandchild," he said mournfully. "*Ach*, my
Bella, my poor Bella."

Vava moved swiftly across the room, her face tight and unsmiling,
Bella's silver teapot in her hand, Bella's paisley scarf draped about her
narrow shoulders.

"You must have some tea, Marc," she said sternly. "You grow
too tired."

She did not look at Piet.

"Your father is working very hard," she told Ida. "He is busy
with his biblical etchings and the sketches of Paris."

"No longer sketches," Marc said, his attention diverted from the
baby. "But paintings. Major paintings. Do you think we should sell
them as a collection or each scene separately, Ida?"

"I will consult with the galleries and then we will decide what is
best," she replied.

She lifted Piet from his cot and pressed him to her breast, now engorged with her milk. She left swiftly, offering Marc a quick embrace. She and Vava nodded politely, but they did not kiss.

Months later, happily pregnant again, Ida returned to Paris, delighted with the knowledge that she carried twins. Piet was less than a year old and she thought it wonderful that her three children would grow up together, caring companions to each other, spared the loneliness of her own childhood.

She and Franz had planned their Paris stay as a vacation gift to themselves. He had research to complete and she wanted to see the gardens ablaze with spring flowers; she wanted to stare out of the window of the Quai de l'Horloge home at the shimmering white birch trees, their tender young leaves slowly unfurling. Marc had agreed to come to the city alone because Vava was overseeing renovations at Les Collines. She imagined strolling with her father across the sun-spangled bridges, free of what she perceived to be Vava's subtly intrusive presence.

She especially looked forward to seeing the new works by emergent surrealist artists. Braque had invited Franz and herself to an informal reception at his own studio.

Undeterred by the hugeness of her pregnancy, ignoring the slight discomfort of all-too-familiar cramps, with Piet in the care of a sweet mademoiselle from a reputable agency, Ida and Franz took a cab to Braque's address. The cluttered, smoke-filled studio was already crowded and abuzz with excited conversation. Beautiful Meret Oppenheim, a surrealist painter, approached Ida languidly and brushed her lips across her cheek. Picasso leapt forward to greet her, to study the enormous rise of her pregnancy and, with mischievous impudence, to press his paint-stained hand against her abdomen.

"But I must paint you just as you are," he said. "Where will I find a model as beautiful as the daughter of Chagall, her body swollen with life?"

She laughed. "I believe you have lost that opportunity, *cher maître*," she said teasingly, because even as he spoke, she felt the onset of what she recognized to be serious and painful contractions. She clutched Franz's hand, and within minutes, they were speeding to a maternity hospital.

"So much for their Swiss passports," she told Franz jokingly as she was wheeled into the delivery room.

He smiled. Ida's resilience never failed to amaze him.

Her labor was startlingly swift and she was overcome with joy when her dark-haired daughters, their features as delicate as those of their grandmother Bella, entered the world. She rested one on each breast, stroked the shining tendrils of their surprisingly thick hair, and murmured their names.

"You will be Bella," she told the child on her left breast. "You have my mother's name. Your grandmother. Your beautiful grandmother."

It was, she realized, almost exactly ten years since Bella's death, ten years crowded with loves and losses, season tumbling after season, deaths and births swirling in wild confluence. But now, at last, her mother had a namesake. Her soul could come to rest.

"And you," she said to the infant on her right breast, "you will be Meret."

She had always admired Meret Oppenheim, whose lips had been so soft upon her cheek only hours before her daughters were born. She had once asked her about her name, so singular and so mysterious.

"My parents named me for Meretlein, a free-spirited heroine in a German novel my mother had always loved. Somehow it became Meret," the painter had explained.

"Such a beautiful name," Ida had said, deciding at that moment that she would not allow her antipathy to Germany to mar her appreciation of a name so lyrical and lovely.

Meret. Bella. The names danced through her mind, a quartet of graceful syllables. These children, these newborn daughters, Ida decided, surely would be free spirits. Fanciful. Whimsical. Creative. Yes, all that. They and their brother would have the freedom that

Ida, forever burdened with worry about her parents, had rarely known. Yes, she pledged silently, her children would have all that she herself had been denied.

"Do you like the names?" she asked Franz, who moved across the room to stand beside her.

"I love the names," he said. "I love my daughters and I love their mother."

A nursing sister entered and took the infants from her, and Franz sat beside her bed and held her hand as she drifted into a dreamless sleep.

—

Ida was suffused with the contentment she had sought for so many years. Her children, toddler Piet and his infant sisters, constantly delighted her. The fresh air of Switzerland invigorated them, and the Alpine winds rouged their plump cheeks. She brought them to Paris on a visit and Marc came to see them. Vava sent her regrets. She was ill. A summer cold.

Smiling, Marc dandled them on his knee. That smile infused her with courage.

"David will be visiting us tomorrow," she told him.

"David?" he asked as though uttering the name of a vaguely remembered acquaintance.

"David," she repeated. "Your son. My brother. I want him to meet my children, his nieces, his nephew." She laughed. "How strange that our little David should be an uncle."

"They are babies," Marc said angrily. "They will not know him. And if they do not know him, they will never miss him."

"But I miss him," Ida said firmly. "He is part of me. I have kept him in my heart. As I believe you have."

"Your heart is too big, Idotchka," he replied.

Meret whimpered and she took the baby from him.

"As is yours," she said, cradling her daughter, stroking Piet's golden hair. "I know that David's mother hurt you and I do not defend her. But David is blood of our blood, bone of our bone. Have we so much family left that we dare to lose this precious boy who you named for your brother?"

He went to the window and stared down at the Seine. A lone barge moved slowly through the silken green waters, disappearing from view as it sailed beneath the next bridge. *How swiftly things disappeared, how swiftly people vanished*, Marc thought. His Bella was dead, but the small girl Ida had named for her chortled happily. Friends and relatives were no longer in his world, some killed by Hitler, some by Stalin. His brother David, the Dovidl of his Vitebsk childhood, lay in an untended grave. But Dovidl's namesake, his son David, was alive. Ida was not wrong. David had been only six when Virginia left, and Marc had not seen him for two years, during which so much had happened. Virginia had married, he himself had married, Ida had become a mother, and friends had drifted in and out of their lives. But David had been a constant in his memory. He acknowledged that he had kept his son in his heart, never forgetting the sound of his laughter, the sharpness of his imagination, the sweetness of his shy smile, his wondrous response to music. He hesitated, turned from the window, spoke very slowly.

"Vava fears that it would be harmful for me to see David," he said. "She worries that it will upset me."

"But Vava is at Les Collines. She has a summer cold," Ida reminded him. "Surely she would not object if you saw David purely by chance at my home."

She understood the danger of her suggestion. She was inviting Marc into a complicity of deception. She waited. He was silent. At last he smiled; his blue eyes twinkled. He had the look of a schoolboy contemplating a mischievous prank.

"Of course. If I saw him purely by chance," he said. "Why not?"

The next day, eight-year-old David, wearing the short pants of a child and the white shirt and tie of a man, perched nervously on a sofa beside Marc, dressed in a dark shirt and even darker tie, the uniform of a respectable and responsible father. Ida, her thick hair gathered into a bun, full-figured in a dress of forest green, sat across from them, her daughters on her lap, her own son beside her, and smiled benignly at her father and her brother. They were a family bonded in blood. Marc and David were restored to each other. It was natural, as the afternoon wore on, for Marc to open his sketchbook and show David the work that he was doing, explaining his choice of colors, the importance of perspective and texture. It was natural for him to take his son's hand in his own and to sit beside him, with Piet resting against his knees, three generations of Chagalls enjoying a peaceful summer afternoon in Paris.

Ida wondered if he would mention David to Vava when he returned to Vence, if he would tell her that he had seen his son and that the meeting had filled him with joy rather than with pain. She did not think so, but it did not matter. She had accomplished what she had set out to do.

Weeks later, Marc wrote to tell her that he had settled an allowance on David. He understood that Virginia's situation was difficult. Charles Leirens was ill and her resources were limited. He did not pity her, he said. She had been the architect of her own misfortune, but David was his son and he would provide for him. The boy would spend his holidays at Les Collines.

Ida wondered how Vava had reacted to such an arrangement, but Marc did not mention his wife except to report that she had recovered from her summer cold.

Chapter Fifty-Two

I da drifted into a time of contentment. She was a devoted wife and mother, a gracious hostess, and her father's diligent representative. There were frequent trips to Paris with Franz where they worked together on his study of Marc's work. Marc occasionally joined them there, but Vava was rarely with him. Vague excuses were offered. She was not well. She had obligations in Vence. Her brother was visiting. Ida dutifully expressed regret, but she acknowledged her relief at Vava's absence.

She was, however, infuriated when Vava reproved her for accepting what she considered to be an insufficient sum for the sale of a group of lithographs.

"My husband and I are disappointed. You underestimated the value of his work," Vava wrote.

"The milliner, the sales lady of hats, is now an authority on art," Ida fumed to Franz.

"Ignore her," Franz advised. "You are your father's representative."

She did not answer Vava's letter but instead sent her father photos of her children at play. He did not acknowledge receiving them, and she understood that Vava had not passed them on to him. She said nothing. There was, after all, nothing to say.

Ida's family spent the month of July on the Riviera so that they might jointly celebrate Piet's birthday and Vava and Marc's anniversary. As always, they stayed at their Toulon villa, but the celebration meal was to be held at Les Collines. Ida had purchased an intricately tatted white lace shawl for Vava and a leather portfolio for her father's lithographs. They arrived at the house laden with gifts and delicacies. Marc was still at work in his studio and Vava was resting. The children ran down to the orchard. They delighted in the citrus trees. Oranges and lemons did not grow in Switzerland's colder clime.

Ida and Franz wandered into the suite at Les Collines that she still considered her own. She had left her possessions in place there even after her marriage. They granted her provenance of a kind in her father's home.

She opened the door and gasped in disbelief. The room was bare; every trace of her presence was eradicated. The scent of tobacco smoke lingered in the air. She opened the closet where she stored the clothing she occasionally wore at Les Collines. Trousers, blazers, and a man's white linen suit had displaced her dresses and skirts. She opened the drawers and found that her nightclothes and undergarments, her scarves and sweaters, were gone. In their stead were men's singlets and shorts, striped pajamas, and an assortment of monogrammed linen handkerchiefs.

She gripped Franz's arm, tears streaking her cheeks, and together they hurried into the house where Vava, immaculate in a dress of pale green linen, her shining dark hair arranged in a smooth chignon, was arranging flowers for the table.

"I have just been to my apartment," Ida said angrily.

"Your apartment?" Vava raised her eyebrows. "But you no longer live at Les Collines. I cannot think of why you should think you have an apartment here."

"I have always had rooms in my father's house. You know that. My closets and drawers are full of the clothing of a strange man."

"Hardly a strange man. My brother Michel uses that room when he stays here. And of course he keeps his own things in the closet and drawers that are no longer your closets and drawers. You have a home of your own. Several homes, actually." Vava smiled her catlike smile. "It amazes me that one family should need so many homes," she added. "Nor can I understand why you, who have so many homes, would lay claim to rooms in my house."

"My father's house," Ida corrected her.

"I am your father's wife." Vava's tone was very calm, her intent clear. "So Les Collines is my house. As for your things, I have packed them carefully. Please take them with you when you leave."

She turned away and left the room as Ida, hot with fury, struggled to find the words that expressed her anger. Franz placed a restraining hand on her shoulder.

"Say nothing," he advised sadly. "What's done is done."

She nodded. She would not allow her confrontation with Vava to ruin her children's day. She smiled at her son and allowed him to pull her onto the terrace.

She watched as Marc, looking like a disheveled, aging elf, romped with her children. His white hair was askew, his blue eyes glittered, and his painter's smock flared behind him as he raced after them in the citrus orchard. He sparred with Piet in a mock duel, using olive tree branches as swords.

The day passed pleasantly. Guests arrived. The birthday cakes were brought out to applause and admiration. Everyone sang happy birthday to Piet.

"Four years old. Can you believe that he is four years old?" Ida asked Franz.

He nodded. The years of their happiness had flown by on wings of joy.

The adults lifted their glasses in a toast to Marc and Vava.

"Happy anniversary," they shouted.

"Five years. As long as that," Franz said softly.

"It feels even longer," Ida rejoined and looked swiftly around, relieved that her words had gone unheard. She would have to be careful, she reminded herself. Positions were altered. The rules had been changed.

She offered her own gifts, draping the white lace shawl over Vava's shoulders.

"I thought of you as soon as I saw it," she said. Her tone was even.

Vava fingered it tentatively and smiled her feline smile.

"It is quite lovely," she said. "Not quite my sort of thing, but lovely."

She slipped free of the shawl, which fell soundlessly to the ground. "Are you tired, Marc?" Vava asked.

The guests scrambled to their feet. They understood that her question and his slow nod of acquiescence was an invitation to leave.

Ida kissed her father good-bye. The children hugged him and they hurried to their car. The maid rushed after them.

"Madame Ida. Madame Ida, you must wait. Madame Chagall is sending your trunk to you," she called breathlessly.

The gardener trudged down the path, laboring under the weight of Vava's black trunk that contained the remnants of Ida's life at Les Collines. Ida looked back. The terrace was deserted and the white lace shawl she had selected so carefully lay across the red slate floor.

Chapter Fifty-Three

*A*t home in Basel, Ida carefully considered her position. She determined that she would continue to represent her father and that she would treat Vava with cautious courtesy. A cold peace was in place.

Vava now dealt with all correspondence that came to Les Collines. She wrote replies to requests that had once been referred to Ida, patently unapologetic about the role she had appropriated.

"I am the guardian of my husband's privacy," she told Ida Bourdet. "I will allow nothing to disturb him. He gets letters from vultures, carrions who will devour his talent. Letters come from the Jewish *shnorrers* in Israel and in Russia pleading for money. When mail arrives from Russia or Israel, I just toss it away unopened."

Ida Bourdet was shocked. She wondered if she had ever known the real Vava. The woman who so haughtily called herself Madame Chagall bore no resemblance to the self-effacing London milliner, the victimized refugee, who had sold her an unbecoming plum-colored cloche.

She and Claude curtailed their visits to Les Collines. Their absence was scarcely noted. Vava's acquaintances, her brother Michel and his friends, were frequent visitors. They wandered through the orchards, reclined on the terrace, ate at Marc's table, and profusely praised his new works. Their flattery pleased him. He offered them his choicest wines and beamed proudly as they toasted his talent and his generosity, Vava's very white hand resting on his shoulder.

He was painting with new vigor and verve. Entranced by the Mediterranean landscape, he captured the elusive translucence of its light, the brilliant fecundity of its soil ablaze with flowers on verges and hillsides. He feverishly refreshed his palette, and in a riot of colors, he painted gay bouquets in graceful vases, soaring waves, lovers walking beneath floral canopies.

Ida, in Switzerland, replied to queries from his friends in Israel and Russia who asked why their letters went unanswered. They worried that their friend Moshe was not well. She reassured them as to his health, but she did not tell them that he no longer answered to the name Moshe, because his wife intensely disliked it. Vava wondered what the name Moshe ben Yechezkel had to do with her husband, Marc Chagall, the internationally famous French artist.

"We live in Paris, not in a shtetl. Would you have collectors call your father Moshe Siegel?" she asked Ida. "You know that the name Chagall, written in Hebrew script, *sin, gimel, lamed,* could also be read as Siegel. Moshe Siegel. A fine name for an artist."

"An artist is judged by his work, not his name. Chaim is not a French name, but it does not seem to have prevented collectors like Mr. Barnes of Philadelphia and the Museum of Modern Art in New York from buying up the work of poor Chaim Soutine," Ida replied drily.

Vava did not answer her. She did not care about Chaim Soutine, who had died during the war. She did not care about any of the artists of the École de Paris, a much diminished group. The only artist who concerned her was her husband, Marc Chagall. She was the conservator of his time, the protector of his sensibilities. She intercepted Yiddish journals and communications from Israel.

"He grows too upset when there is bad news from Israel. He cares too much. I do not know why he worries so much about events happening so far away. He lives in Vence, not in Jerusalem," she told Ida.

She rejected a proposal that Marc illustrate a Haggadah for a prestigious publishing house. "My husband does not wish to be known as a Jewish painter," she wrote. "He prefers universal, ecumenical themes such as his mural in the baptistery of the church in Plateau d'Assy."

There was no need for her to disclose that she often visited that church, sometimes with her brother, sometimes alone, her face veiled, a white mantilla covering her smooth black hair.

Ida was angered when she learned that the commission for a Haggadah had been rejected.

"A Haggadah would be an excellent vehicle for my father and it would sell well. You should have consulted me," she told Vava.

"Why? I understand my husband's inclinations. I alone am responsible for his welfare, and I make certain that nothing interferes with the work that is most important to him, work that fully engages him," she said dismissively.

"There is nothing you can tell me about his work. My life has been dedicated to his work," Ida replied coldly.

She knew that Marc's pace was formidable, every hour of his day crammed with discrete projects. He created stained glass panels and crafted fanciful ceramics. He painted tapestries that magically trapped light and color in the folds of fabric. But always he prioritized his paintings. He completed *Red Roofs*, a painting that spoke to his Russian past and his French present, with Vitebsk and Notre Dame oddly neighbored in a single composition.

Ida in turn raced from one European city to another to exhibit, curate, and promote his work. A major exhibition in Paris forced her to leave her family for a protracted period.

"You know that I must help your *grandpère*," she told her children when they protested. She sent them extravagant gifts, beautiful dolls for Bella and Meret, an electric train set for Piet, but she was heavyhearted because she knew that her gifts were no compensation for her absence. She called her children each evening.

"Are you coming home soon, *Maman*?"

The little girls' voices were plaintive, Piet's angry. Arguments about her duty to his *grandpère* did not sway him.

"Do you love him more than you love us?" he asked and hung up before she could reply.

It was just as well. She had no adequate answer to offer him.

The Paris exhibition closed, and she returned to Switzerland, knowing that her stay at home would be brief. An English retrospective loomed and she had given her word that she would be in

London when it opened. She had no choice. Her presence was specifically mentioned in the contract.

"But after this trip, I will concentrate on the children," she told Franz.

"Be careful not to make promises that you cannot keep," he said.

She understood that he was becoming increasingly frustrated by her devotion to her father's work.

The afternoon she was to leave for London, at an hour when she was already packed and dressed for the journey, Piet was sent home from his nursery school. He was very ill, the school nurse said severely. His face was flushed and his small body shook uncontrollably. Ida took his temperature and her heart sank. The thermometer reading was dangerously high. She called the doctor, who advised her to apply cold compresses, administer half an aspirin, and see that he rested.

She put him to bed in her dressing room, and he stared with glazed eyes up at the painting of *The Bridal Chair* that hung there.

"Why is there no one sitting on that chair, *Maman*?" he asked fretfully. "If it is a chair for a bride, why doesn't she sit in it? Did she die before her wedding? Are the flowers for her funeral?"

His words pierced Ida to the core. He had seen that picture many times, had been told its title, but never before had he asked such a question. He was a fanciful child, prone to dark imaginings. The Angel of Death often flew through his dreams and he awakened in the night shouting that evil spirits lurked beneath his bed. Ida, so familiar with night terrors, had always known how to comfort him, but this feverish fantasy, fueled as it was by delirium, was different. She understood how the empty chair, shrouded in white, might frighten him. She had always loved the painting although it had frightened her often enough. She had no answer to offer him. Piet sat upright, his sweat-streaked body writhing, then sank back, closed his eyes, and fell into a frighteningly heavy sleep.

"Piet," she said, but he did not stir. "Piet!" she shouted, but he remained immobile.

She rushed to the phone and called the doctor again. "My son is unconscious," she shouted. "He will not wake up."

The doctor arrived swiftly. He examined Piet without even removing his overcoat and sighed.

"It is influenza. It has been going around, Madame Meyer," he said. "Many children have been infected."

"But it's not dangerous, is it?" Ida asked, glancing at her watch, her hand resting on her son's brow, so hot to her touch that she thought her fingers might burn.

"Such an illness in a young child is always dangerous," he replied gravely. "But I would not consider it life-threatening. He must be closely watched, of course. He must have plenty to drink, the medicine I prescribe administered regularly, sponge baths to lower the fever."

"Of course," she agreed. "Our au pair is extremely diligent, extremely capable."

"You will not be here?" he asked, his voice laced with disapproval.

"I am expected in London," she explained. "I have business obligations that cannot be canceled. His father will be at home this evening and our housekeeper will also be here. He will be well cared for."

She did not tell him that there was a reception that very evening at the Leicester Gallery to which royalty had been invited, that she was scheduled to give an interview on the BBC the next morning, and a journalist for the *Times* in London had asked her to sit for a photograph for an article titled "The Artist's Daughter and the Artist's Work." Such longstanding arrangements, involving so many people, could not be canceled. Her father's reputation and her own were at stake. But none of that, she knew, would make any difference to this stern, very caring physician. It was a matter of indifference to him that the mother of his young, dangerously ill patient was the daughter of Marc Chagall.

"I would suggest you engage a nurse," he said icily. "I will arrange it."

"I should appreciate that."

He shrugged. He did not need the appreciation of this fashionably

dressed, beautifully coiffed woman who placed professional consid-
erations above the comfort of her child. He slammed his black bag
shut and left.

The nurse arrived within the hour. "I am Sister Marie Grace,"
she announced.

She was stern-faced, a fringed white cap crowning her cropped
gray hair, her uniform startlingly white. Ida took her up to Piet's
room. The small boy, newly awake, sat up in bed and stared at his
mother and Sister Marie Grace. His eyes widened in fear, and his
small hands were clenched into fists. Perspiration darkened his pale
blue night shirt, and fever rouged his cheeks.

"A ghost. She is a ghost. She fell out of the painting. *Maman*, tell
the horrible ghost to go away," he shrieked.

"No, no, Piet. Don't be foolish. This is a lovely nurse who has
come to take care of you. Sister Marie Grace is here to help you get
better," Ida said soothingly. She knelt beside him, stroked his hair,
the golden ringlets damp between her fingers. "You must calm yourself. You must get better. I want to see a healthy boy when I return
from London."

He clung to her, pressed his face against her bosom, his tears
soaking her white silk blouse. "Don't go, *Maman*. Don't leave me.
Don't leave your Piet. I will be good. I will be excellent. Don't go,
Maman," he wailed.

Her heart turned. Sister Marie Grace examined the medicine the
pharmacy had delivered, set a pitcher of water on the bedside table,
and lowered the window shades. She moved silently on her rubber-
soled white shoes, a competent spectral presence.

"The child will be all right, madame," she said softly to Ida. "I
believe a car has arrived for you."

Again Ida looked at her watch. Of course she had to leave. She
could not miss her plane. "Be a brave boy," she said to Piet, but he
tightened his grasp, his hands tight about her neck.

"*Maman. Maman. Maman.*" The wail drifted into a moan, a
mournful plea.

Gently, gently, she pried his fingers loose. Gently, gently, she kissed his burning cheeks, and too swiftly she left, closing the door softly behind her. There were instructions to be given to the housekeeper and to the au pair, a call to be placed to Franz at the Kunsthalle. He was not in the gallery, but she left a message with his secretary. Their son was ill, but a nurse had been engaged. Everything was organized. She would call Professor Meyer from London.

All swiftly accomplished, she handed her bag to the waiting driver, checked her briefcase, tossed a cape over her shoulders, and hurried into the car, her heart pounding. She looked up at the window as the car pulled away. Sister Marie Grace lifted her hand in a gentle wave meant to reassure. Ida was not reassured. Her abdomen contorted in the grip of a sudden cramp that did not subside until she reached her London hotel room.

Even before removing her cape, she called Franz. Piet was much better, he told her. His fever was down and Sister Marie Grace was remarkably competent. She was careful to keep Meret and Bella away from their brother.

"I should not have left them," Ida said.

He hesitated. "Perhaps not," he agreed.

His words fell like stones upon her heart. There was nothing more to be said. She hung up and shrugged out of her cape. Almost immediately, the phone rang. It was Marc, calling from Vence to remind her to buy the sable brushes that were sold only at an art supply shop in Soho. And Vava needed the herbal supplements from a health food store in Hampstead.

"She gets too many colds," he said worriedly.

"I will take care of everything," she assured him wearily and added, "I am concerned about Piet. He was running a high fever when I left."

"Children recover very quickly," Marc said. Piet's illness did not interest him. "You won't forget Vava's vitamins," he said again.

"I will remember," she promised reluctantly. She hung up, seething at his indifference to Piet, his absurd concern for Vava.

She dressed carefully in a blue velvet gown for the reception at the Leicester Gallery where she would greet the royals who had come to pay homage to the daughter of Marc Chagall. Hanging her traveling clothes in the closet, she saw that Piet's tears were imprinted on the burgundy silk of her blouse. She pressed it to her lips as if to taste her small son's sorrow.

At the Leicester Gallery, she forced herself to smile as, with her usual grace, she swept into the crowded room, her head held high, aware of the murmurs of admiration and the whispered utterances of her name.

"Ida Chagall. The daughter of the artist." "Isn't she beautiful?" "Isn't she lovely?"

She was introduced to the Princess Royal and curtsied, wondering all the while when she could next call home, whether Piet would forgive her for her absence at the hour of his terror, and worried that Franz's understated anger would endure.

The week in London passed swiftly. The critiques of the exhibition were laudatory. Ida was, as always, an authoritative presence in the gallery. She smiled and granted interviews.

The art editor of the *Sunday Times* asked about Picasso, whose work was being exhibited in Paris, Hamburg, and Munich.

"Your father and Pablo Picasso are now the most famous living artists in Europe," he said. "Are they competitive with each other?"

"Marc Chagall and Pablo Picasso have long been close friends. They live near each other on the Riviera and they enjoy each other's success," she said smoothly.

She smiled at the audacity of her own dissimulation. The two artists haunted each other's exhibitions, read critiques of each other's works, always searching for the stray negative observation intimating that Chagall's work was too kitschy, Picasso's too obscure. Picasso's pleasure in Virginia's betrayal had been matched by Marc's own unconcealed satisfaction when Françoise Gilot in turn abandoned Picasso. The *Sunday Times* would manage without that information.

She posed for photographs, always arranging to stand beneath *The Red Roofs* because a photographer who worked with color film had told her that her auburn hair provided a subdued contrast to her father's brilliant carmine impasto.

Each evening, she called home and began to be reassured. Piet was almost fully recovered. The girls had not been infected. Franz was conciliatory. He was pleased that she was enjoying success in London. Her father would also be pleased. They agreed that it would be best if she went to Vence before returning to Switzerland. There were contracts for Marc to sign, checks that had to be deposited.

On her last night in London, Piet himself spoke to her on the phone.

"I am much better, *Maman*," he said cheerfully. "Sister Marie Grace has left, but she was a very nice woman, after all. She took good care of me. What have you bought for us in London?"

She laughed aloud. He was fine. She was forgiven. No harm had been done after all.

"I have many presents for you and your sisters," she said. She looked across the room where gift-wrapped parcels from Selfridges and Harrods formed a colorful hillock and wondered how she would manage to get all the toys and clothing she had purchased back to Switzerland.

"You will not be disappointed," she promised him. "I will be home soon. I must spend one or two days in Vence with your *grandpère* and then we will be together."

"You are going to France before you come home?" he asked, the disappointment clear in his voice.

"But I must, Piet," she said. "Your father will explain. It is only a day or two. And then we will be together for months and months."

"Promise?" he asked petulantly.

"Don't be a silly boy," she chided.

She was wary of promises. In the Jewish tradition, a promise was a covenant. A promise broken was an oath betrayed. She marveled that she was still hostage to the superstitions of her childhood, but she was relieved when Piet offered no argument.

"All right, *Maman*," he said. "I won't be silly. Come home soon and don't forget our presents."

Franz came to the phone then.

"Be careful, Ida," he said.

"No need to worry," she protested. "I am only going to my father's home."

"Do not let Vava upset you," he warned.

"She will not upset me," she assured him, but already she felt the all-too-familiar cramp always triggered by the very mention of Vava's name.

It was late afternoon when her plane landed in Nice. Although she had sent her father a telegram with her flight information, he was not at the airport nor had he sent a driver. She shrugged and arranged for a cab to take her to Vence. She kept the window open and welcomed the touch of the soft sea-scented breeze on her face. The familiar aroma of Riviera roses mingled with the sweetness of orange blossoms drifted into the car. She fell into a light sleep and awakened only when the driver ascended the incline that led to Les Collines and braked a bit too suddenly. Eager to see her father and report on the London success, she hurtled out of the cab and dashed up the slate steps to the terrace.

"*Papochka*," she called excitedly.

Marc was seated opposite Vava at the small wrought iron table. He turned and looked at Ida, his expression puzzled as though mystified by her arrival.

Ida stared at them, startled by their appearance. Marc wore the elegant blue velvet jacket he reserved for special occasions, a paisley ascot knotted around his neck. Vava was elegant in a white silk dress, the white lace shawl, Ida's gift once dismissed as "not her sort of thing," draped around her shoulders. Her smooth black hair was pulled back into a chignon threaded with sprigs of baby's breath. She was surprised to see that they were drinking champagne, using the flutes of amber glass that Bella had discovered in a Paris flea market. Her father rarely drank; since his illness, he had never had a drink in the middle of the afternoon. Vava, she knew, considered herself an oenophile, but she was too frugal to indulge in champagne.

Ida hesitated for a moment and then hurried to her father and kissed him on both cheeks.

"Didn't you remember that I was coming today?" she asked.

"But how would I have known that?"

"I did send a telegram from London," she said and turned to Vava who shrugged.

"Telegrams are often misdirected," she murmured.

"Are they?" Her question was tinged with ironic disbelief. But this was no time to launch a quarrel. "How splendid you look, Vava, absolutely bridal."

The slightest of blushes tinged Vava's pale cheeks.

"Yes. Bridal," she murmured as Marc rose and paid the driver who deposited Ida's luggage and stood awkwardly twirling his cap, awaiting further instructions.

"Please wait in the kitchen," Ida said.

"Of course, madame." He hurried away as though anxious to distance himself from the odd trio clustered on the terrace.

They were silent until he vanished into the house.

"Your daughter is so clever, Marc," Vava said then. "She has said that I look bridal."

"Of course Vava looks bridal." Marc spoke too loudly, injecting a forced gaiety into his voice. "She became a bride today. We have just returned from the office of the mairie of Vence where we took our marriage vows. Here, Ida, drink to our happiness, to our good fortune."

He held a flute of champagne out to her, his hands trembling.

She took it from him and set it down on the table.

"Marriage vows? But you have been married for years now. I don't understand," she protested.

"It's very simple," Vava said, enunciating each word carefully as though explaining a difficult concept to a student who might be slow to understand. "We were divorced some weeks ago on the advice of my attorney. The agreement we entered into when we first married at the Bourdet home did not offer me sufficient protection. My brother felt that I needed more security, greater legal assurances. He was right, of course, and your father agreed. So a new settlement was drawn up that is fairer to me, and we remarried this very day under the new agreement." She smiled. "How fortunate that you should be here to celebrate with us."

Dizzy and light-headed, Ida clutched the arms of her chair. She bit her lips, fearful of uttering words that she would regret. She turned Vava's words over and over in her mind as her father looked at her nervously. At last she lifted the glass of champagne and took a sip. The amber flute was warm in her hand and she remembered suddenly how proud Bella had been of that purchase. She had discovered them in a stall as she wandered through the *marché aux puces* and bought them because their color matched Ida's hair.

Ida sighed. Her hair was no longer a match for the amber shade of those fragile glasses. It had darkened and was lightly threaded with tendrils of silver. But then everything had changed. Her mother's tender treasures now belonged to Vava. Her father's house, the house she had discovered for him, was closed against her, and his allegiance was vested in the woman he had married not once but twice. The wine was sour on her tongue, but she took yet another sip.

"I take it that this new arrangement is legal?" she asked.

"Why should it not be legal?" Vava moved closer to Marc, covered his trembling hand with her own as though to calm him.

It was obvious, Ida realized, that Vava had not shown him her telegram because she wanted the new marriage to be accomplished before Ida reached Vence. Vava had anticipated her objections, had anticipated Marc's fear of her reaction. How swiftly and cleverly she had moved, this woman, but then her entire life had depended on swiftness and cleverness.

"It is my understanding that relations who may be affected by a revised settlement must be informed of it," Ida said.

Franz had said as much six years earlier on the very day that Marc and Vava were first married. She had been concerned that her father's marriage might impact on her eventual inheritance although he had assured her then that she would be adequately protected. *Protected.* The very word that Vava had used to explain the settlement. Vava's new protection surely meant that Ida's own was forfeit.

"And if you were so informed, would you go against your dear father's wishes?" Vava asked.

"Of course she wouldn't. Not my Ida. Now drink to our happiness, Idotchka."

She recognized the plea in his voice, saw the terror in his eyes. She knew that Vava had threatened to leave him if he had not consented to the new settlement, the absurd divorce and the even more absurd remarriage. She had, after all, issued that threat after knowing him for only three months. Now, after all these years, with his dependence on her so reinforced, his life with her so calm and comfortable, he would surely have accepted such an ultimatum. Ida understood his self-protective rationales. He had, she supposed, told himself that Ida was strong; she would survive and forgive, but he could not survive Vava's desertion.

She stared at him. His face crumbled. He pulled the ascot from his neck and toyed with it nervously. He dared not look at her. She raised her glass again.

"To your happiness, *Papochka*," she said quietly.

"And to Vava's, of course," he insisted.

She said nothing but drank deeply, setting the empty flute on the table.

Suddenly eager to leave Les Collines, she opened her briefcase and removed the contracts that he had to sign, the checks that he had to endorse.

"As you will see, the London exhibition was a very successful undertaking for us," she said. "It was exhausting but well worth it."

It was Vava who reached for the sheaf of papers. She set the contracts aside and studied the checks.

"You look tired. It pains me to see you work so hard, Ida," Marc said.

"I do it for you, Papa," she replied.

"And for yourself," Vava added. "But of course you will not be troubled with so much work on your father's behalf again. Please tell her what we have decided, Marc."

"Vava and I think it best if you no longer act at all on my behalf."

He spoke so softly that Ida had to lean forward to catch his meaning, and even then, she could not believe that she had heard him correctly.

"Not act at all on your behalf?" she repeated.

He nodded, his expression pained.

"Are you saying that you no longer want me to represent you in any negotiation?" she asked in bewilderment.

"It is no longer necessary. You know of course that Vava is very capable. She has made more convenient arrangements." He stumbled over his words, and his hands shook anew as he refilled his glass.

"Yes. I am sure she has."

Ida stared at him in disbelief. Was this really her father, Marc Chagall, this trembling old man who sat before her looking like a frightened child? When had he morphed into a white-haired, blue-eyed marionette who spoke the words mandated by his wife, that pale, dark-haired puppeteer who would forever control his strings? But then she had always known that his life was bifurcated. In his art, he was suffused with power, the magnitude of his talent, his genius, unmatched. But in his life, even in his beliefs, he was weak and vulnerable, a man so insecure that he could not be alone, a Jew who plundered the symbols of his people but never entered a synagogue. He was a father who had, for a time, rejected his son out of anger. He was a father who now betrayed his daughter. She pitied him. She pitied herself. She had been blind. Blind and foolish.

She stood abruptly and called to her driver. He trudged out of the kitchen. She pointed to her bags. "Put them in the car," she ordered. "I want you to drive me to Toulon."

"But why are you leaving?" Marc gripped her hands. "You must stay. We will have dinner. We will celebrate."

"I cannot celebrate with you, Papa. Not today. Perhaps not ever again."

"Idotchka. Idotchka," he moaned.

She held his face, his aged elfin face, in her hands and kissed him on both cheeks. "We will talk soon," she promised. "Soon."

She did not look at Vava but hurried into the car, grateful to the driver who drove speedily away from Les Collines, the house she would never again think of as her home.

Her tears came when she reached Toulon. She stretched out on her bed and submitted to the sobs that racked her body. They subsided at last, leaving her suffused with a new calm, an unexpected and incomprehensible lightness of heart. She was, she realized, disappointed and wounded, yet strangely relieved. Never again would she be compelled to leave a weeping child in favor of her father's interests. She could reclaim her own life, return to her own neglected talent. She phoned Franz, heard her children laughing in the background. Briefly she told him that she would no longer be representing her father.

"All to the good," he responded. "It was time."

Time for what? she wondered, but she knew that she would have to puzzle out that answer on her own.

"*À bientôt, ma chérie,*" Franz said very softly.

"*À bientôt, mon cher,*" she repeated.

Her sleep that night was deep and dreamless.

Chapter Fifty-Four

*H*er children swarmed about her, Meret and Bella clutching her knees, Piet burying his bright and shining face in her lap. Her arrival meant a cacophony of joy, a chorus of gladness.

"*Maman, Maman,* you're home," the little girls shouted in unison.

"I missed you the most of all," Piet proclaimed.

"No, no, we missed you the most," the little girls protested. She laughed, kissed them one by one, their skin, smelling sweetly of soap, soft upon her lips.

"And I missed you all equally," she said. "But maybe your father most of all."

Franz smiled, and together they carried the brightly wrapped packages from Harrods and Selfridges into her dressing room. The three children scampered after them and watched impatiently as the boxes were piled onto the floor.

"Oh, you didn't forget our presents. You are the best mother in the world," Piet shouted.

Ida sat beside Franz on the couch, beneath the painting of *The Bridal Chair*. She smiled.

"Of course I am," she said contentedly.

She watched as the gay paper was pulled off box after box and the shouts of excitement grew louder and louder. Every hour of her evening belonged to her children. There was no need to rush to her desk to deal with correspondence, with bills of lading, to answer calls from galleries and collectors. There was no need to place conciliatory calls to Vence, to soothe Marc, to reassure him, to advise him. That chapter of her life was over. She would always be her father's daughter, she would always love him, but now, at last, she had only her own children to mother. How oddly ironic, she thought, that it was Vava who had released her into this new and precious peace.

She flicked off the light in Piet's room, stood for a moment and listened to the rhythmic hum of his sleep-bound breath.

She returned to her dressing room and removed the painting of *The Bridal Chair* from the wall. Piet's feverish fears had not been unfounded. A ghost hovered over that empty chair, shrouded in white and flanked by roses of a cold alabaster. It was the ghost of the girl she had been, the reluctant bride, the submissive daughter, a ghost now banished by the daughter become a mother, the girl become a woman, a happy and fortunate wife. She would find a place for her father's bitter gift in another room, perhaps in another house. She placed it in a corner as Franz came up behind her, touched her shoulder lightly.

"What is it?" he asked.

She shook her head. She could not tell him that she felt a quiet happiness, a new and unfamiliar freedom, a certainty that her desperate nocturnal flights through flower-strewn heavens to an elusive safety had ended. Instead she took his hand and together they walked into their garden where a cherry tree had suddenly burst into new and brilliant blossom.

About the Author

Gloria Goldreich is the critically acclaimed author of several novels, including the bestselling *Leah's Journey*. Her stories have appeared in numerous magazines, such as *McCalls*, *Redbook*, *Ms. Magazine*, and *Ladies' Home Journal*. She lives in Tuckahoe, New York.